Clare Dowling is an *Irish Times* number one bestselling novelist. She was born in Kilkenny in 1968 and trained as an actress before working in theatre, film and radio. She has had drama and children's fiction published and she writes scripts for Ireland's top soap, *Fair City*. She lives in Dublin and is married with one son and one daughter.

Clare Dowling's previous novels are also available from Headline Review and have been highly praised:

'For Sheila O'Flanagan and Cathy Kelly fans, a warm, Irish, poignant read'   *Bookseller*

'Very funny, very warm, witty and honest'   *Irish World*

'One for Marian Keyes fans. ★★★★'   *Cosmopolitan*

'What sets this apart is the quality of the writing. It is great fun, a great read'   *RTE*

'A refreshingly funny read, full of telling insight, which is what we expect from this accomplished author'
Irish Independent

'A great laugh'   *Wiltshire Times*

'An amusing tale filled with quirky humour'
Ireland on Sunday

Just the Three of Us

Clare Dowling

headline
review

First published in 2009 by HEADLINE REVIEW
An imprint of HEADLINE PUBLISHING GROUP

First published in paperback in 2009 by HEADLINE REVIEW
An imprint of HEADLINE PUBLISHING GROUP

6

Cataloguing in Publication Data is available from the British Library

ISBN 978 0 7553 4153 5 (B Format)
ISBN 978 0 7553 5655 3 (A Format)

Typeset in Bembo by Palimpsest Book Production Limited,
Grangemouth, Stirlingshire

Printed and bound in Great Britain by
CPI Mackays, Chatham ME5 8TD

Headline's policy is to use papers that are natural, renewable and recyclable
products and made from wood grown in sustainable forests. The logging
and manufacturing processes are expected to conform to the environmental
regulations of the country of origin.

HEADLINE PUBLISHING GROUP
An Hachette UK Company
338 Euston Road
London NW1 3BH

www.headline.co.uk
www.hachette.co.uk

For Sean and Ella

ACKNOWLEDGEMENTS

Many, many thanks to my editor Clare Foss for her patience and support during the writing of this book – it must have seemed as though it was never going to arrive on her desk. Thanks also to Leah Woodburn for her brilliant efficiency and good-humoured emails. Thanks to Breda Purdue and all in Hachette Book Group Ireland for doing a great job. A big thanks, too, to my agent Darley Anderson, and everybody at the agency, who all seem to work much harder than me. And a very special thanks to my son Sean, my daughter Ella, and my husband Stewart for just being great.

Chapter One

It all started so innocently. Over a ham and salad sand-wich, in fact. That's what Debs usually had for her lunch at the little takeaway sandwich shop run by two Polish guys, which was round the corner from the office.

'Would you like crisps with that?'

That was their daily joke, the little pups. Goading her. Enjoying the look of naked temptation on her face. Then the ensuing internal battle, which, to her credit, she usually won. Well, if she didn't, her backside would be a foot wider than it was. Mind you, sometimes she did give in – on Mondays, usually, to cheer herself up. Or else if Alex came in looking even more gorgeous and waiflike than usual in some designer garb, leaving Debs feeling like a heifer in comparison. It was straight for the crisps after that, so long as they were Walkers cheese and onion. Oh, who was she kidding? She'd rob a packet of Monster Munch from a child if she could get away with it.

'Not today,' she said, feeling strong and virtuous. She had

read a motivational book last night, which had required her to lie on the floor and close her eyes whilst visualising her greatest dream – being a size ten – and then saying special inspirational words, which went something like, 'I believe in myself unconditionally . . . must open my heart to enlightenment . . . I am strong and beautiful . . . or would be if I could stop eating Walkers crisps . . .'

She'd kept her voice down low in case Fiona, her flatmate, and Fiona's boyfriend, Stevo, could hear her through the walls and might fall around laughing: 'Poor old Debs. As if she'll ever see a size ten.'

Then, to crown it all, she had dropped off in the middle of her enlightenment, only to wake on the hard floor at two a.m., frozen and stiff, and with her mouth bone dry from snoring. She'd had to tiptoe past Fiona's room to go to the bathroom to brush her teeth. Then, foolishly optimistic, she had eased out the weighing scales as quietly as she could. Maybe the inspirational words had mysteriously knocked five pounds off her while she'd slept. But the scales were depressingly the same. She had looked at herself in the mirror, her hair askew and her big boobs droopy under her pyjamas, and she had never felt less strong and beautiful.

But today was a new day. Also, there was another, more powerful, motivational tool coming up: the office Christmas party, in five months' time. And she couldn't even take cover under a slimming black dress. Because they spent the entire Christmas season organising other people's Christmas parties, Fitz Communications had theirs early, usually in the middle of September. Nobody ever felt a bit Christmassy, especially with Marty, the boss, flipping steaks on the barbecue if it was in any way sunny at all. It had been suggested last year that they scrap the whole Christmas thing and just call it the summer party instead. But then didn't a whole other faction get outraged – 'What, no Christmas party? It's a disgrace!' – and so the tradition remained. Debs would be forced to brave it in something summery. So, crisps were out the window. And her nightly glass of white wine. All right, her *two* nightly glasses of white wine; three if it was the weekend. She was even toying with the idea of buying a set of electronic scales to give herself a necessary fright. A friend of hers in America had a *talking* set of scales, which might even be better. Although Debs didn't know if she could cope with a weighing device that shouted at her, 'For fuck's sake, get off, you're killing me.'

So far she had got away with her rusting old scales from college. By now she had developed a close personal relationship with it. Sometimes she even spoke to it, usually when she was just about to step up on it. 'Come on now, don't let me down. You can't hold that piece of cake last night against me.'

The scales weighed in two-pound increments, which was fine if your weight was in even numbers but unsettling if not. Was the dial closer to the four or the six? If you squinted, could it reasonably be assumed to be the four? Or were you just delusional? Also, you could knock a pound, or even two, off Debs's scales by stepping on it very, very slowly. It clearly wasn't a scales that liked frights. You had to humour it, coax it; approach it stealthily from

3

behind, before gently easing one foot onto it. Some mornings, when Debs had had a blow-out the night before, she stepped on that scales so slowly that she'd miss her bus.

Her stomach rumbled now as she watched Dodek, one of the Polish guys, make up her sandwich. Thinking of the scales she murmured, 'Just a scraping of butter.'

Oh, for heaven's sake, she hadn't meant *that* little.

The queue in the sandwich shop was long today. Because she was such a regular – the Polish guys did the best sandwiches and were the cheapest, which was important when you were on a crap salary – Debs vaguely recognised most of the other regulars. They shifted from foot to foot, desperately avoiding eye contact with each other, while the man Debs had mentally christened Mr Bean held up the whole queue by faffing about with the napkin dispenser, and helping himself to sachets of mustard and mayonnaise. For feck's sake, hurry up, she urged him on silently. Her lunch hour would be up at this rate and she would have to bolt down her sandwich and then go for a meeting with Alex with bits of ham stuck between her teeth.

Alex never had anything stuck between her teeth. There wasn't room, not with the mouthful of white, scarily even gnashers she had. Oh, I'm such a bitch, Debs thought guiltily. But that was only because she actually wanted to *be* Alex. She had finally admitted this to herself several months ago, after a bottle of wine. She might also have admitted it to Fiona, who was kind enough not to say anything about it the following morning.

Alex was a size eight. Debs knew this because she had

found one of her skirts hanging up in the women's toilets. Alex often jogged home from work, which was probably why she was a size eight, and changed into a serious-looking tracksuit before she left. Debs remembered holding the skirt up, her breath catching enviously in her throat. So that was what a size eight looked like. She had never had a proper look before, because in shops she lacked the nerve to stray too far from the size four-teens in case the sales staff burst out laughing.

To her eternal shame, and after checking that nobody else was in the loos, Debs had locked herself into one of the cubicles and tried the skirt on. She didn't even know why – maybe she just wanted to see what it would be like to wear a skinny girl's clothes. Maybe she just wanted to judge how wide of the mark she was, in the hope that it might spur her on to greater dieting efforts. It certainly wasn't because she entertained any hope of actually fitting into it.

She was right not to. The skirt waistband lodged some-where above her knees and no amount of pulling or tugging would ease it an inch further up her pudgy thighs. Then, in some horrible moment of self-flagellation, she tried putting it on over her head. It got stuck around her boobs like a vice, with her arms trapped skywards, and for a panic-stricken moment she thought she might have to call the fire brigade. Imagine Alex's face – all of their faces – when they found out that she'd had to be cut out of Alex's skirt.

Afterwards she thought the skirt looked a bit loose around the backside on Alex, no doubt from all the stretching it had endured.

She did at that point wonder fleetingly whether there might be something wrong with her. Surely, at her age, she should be fretting about her starter mortgage or the tax on her car rather than obsessing about other women's skirts. But that would involve actually owning an apartment and a car, neither of which she did. Acquiring such things would have meant getting her act together in her twenties. Saving. Planning. Being dedicated to her job to the extent that she had risen spectacularly through the ranks, bagging pay rises upon the way – all that kind of grown-up stuff that she never really seemed very good at. Somehow she had always thought, One day. One day when she found a job she actually liked, and when she finally lost that stone and a half. Boyfriends would follow naturally once she was thin and successful, and then suddenly her whole life would come together in a wonderful, happy cohesion, instead of the rather chaotic mess it was right now.

'Debra Manning! Apply yourself!' her English teacher used to bellow at her every now and again when she would drift off in the middle of writing some essay on how she would change the world if she got elected Prime Minister (as if).

And that seemed to be the main problem: application. It certainly wasn't because she didn't know what she wanted. She did. In fact there was nothing she liked doing more than drawing up a list of *Things To Do To Change My Life*. It usually went something like this:

1. Join Weight Watchers. (But, hang on; imagine the horror of stepping on a scales in front of a load of other fat people. A set of talking scales. So she crossed that out,

and wrote, 'Go on the Slim Fast diet'. Their chocolate bars were quite moreish. Which, actually, had been her downfall the last time she had gone on their diet. Scratch that. In the end she just wrote, 'Get Thin Immediately'.)

2. Start saving for a house. (By her own grim calculations, if she started saving half of her weekly salary now, she'd be able to afford a one-bedroom flat when she was forty-nine.)

3. Find a boyfriend. (She had better impose as few conditions as possible on that one. Just so long as he was male.)

4. Stop drinking. (Not that she was a problem drinker. It was simply that her level of consumption tended to sabotage efforts at achieving numbers 1 and 2. Also number 3 as, whilst men loved drunken girls on a Friday night, they generally didn't marry them.)

Debs always felt great after she made a plan. It was like grabbing back a tiny bit of control in a life that seemed to be otherwise ruled by sleep, alcohol and lunch breaks. ('So?' Fiona would say. 'What's wrong with that?' But that was before Stevo.) She would go to bed and sleep like a baby, knowing that the blueprint for a better life was right there under her pillow.

But then came the tricky bit: the application. She usually sailed through Monday on sheer willpower alone, and her horror of yet more failure. Tuesday saw her will-power waning, and her fear of failure had diminished rather worryingly. Nobody's perfect, a little voice in her head would start up. By Wednesday the bartering had started: if she ate a packet of crisps at lunchtime, she would go without dinner, that kind of thing. By Wednesday night she would have cracked completely and eaten a whole sliced pan with Nutella and washed it down with a bottle of white wine that had cost her an extortionate amount in the local Spar.

She might as well face it: she was weak, pathetic and desperate. Not to mention fat and poor. Men didn't even warrant a mention. Or apartments.

'You're just a late developer,' Fiona had attempted to console her. 'Anyway, I'm thirty-two as well. And I don't own an apartment either.'

Debs had looked at her darkly. She needn't imply they were in this mess together. Or, at least, not any more. Fiona had a boyfriend. A partner. All right, so he may be a little on the short side but he owned his own house, and had a car. He was a man with *prospects*. All Fiona had to do was not feck it up.

She didn't. She must have seen her thirty-third birthday coming at her like a steam train, because she fell spectacularly, hopelessly in love with little Stevo, and he with her.

Of course, they tried to be considerate about it. They went out as much as possible and kindly refrained from humping each other on the sofa. And there was his place, a three-bed terraced, where they spent more and more time, probably to avoid upsetting Debs. She didn't know which was worse: watching him surreptitiously stroke Fiona's inner thigh during *Who Wants to Be a Millionaire?* ('Me! Me!' Debs always wanted to howl pitifully), or being abandoned to her own devices, which usually involved eating lots of bad food, before hopping up and down on the scales. Slowly, naturally.

Then came the final insult.

'I wonder if Stevo's got any single friends?' Fiona pondered one day.

'You think I can't find a man by myself?' Debs cut in defensively. Well, of course she couldn't. Which was why she was sitting in on a Friday night yet again.

'I didn't mean that,' Fiona protested, who did.

'Anyway, I'm still not over Jacob.'

Fiona was immediately contrite. 'Of course.'

Jacob was this American student studying in Trinity College, whom Debs had briefly dated a year back. He was sweet, if a little boring, and when he'd gone back home Debs had been quite relievĕd. But every so often when she got drunk and lonely, she would imagine that things had been much better than they were, and she would go ringing him up at four in the morning, or send him an embarrassing home-made poem by email. This would elicit a nice, if rather puzzled reply from him, which, mortified, she would totally ignore. Also – and she was ashamed about this – she used him as a handy scapegoat for her lack of success in the dating department since he'd gone. She could plausibly blame everything on the fact that her heart was still broken by his departure. She hoped to God he never took it into his head to come back for a visit, because she would be hard-pressed even to recognise him.

At least she still had food, her best friend and bitterest enemy; offering enormous amounts of comfort on the one hand, and mortifying run-ins with the scales on the other.

When she resisted it she felt great; but not as good as when she was stuffing down a sixteen-inch pizza with all the pineapple they could fit on it. But only for about ten minutes. Then the familiar feelings of self-loathing would creep over her, the internal recriminations.

'Honestly! You can't keep your snout out of it for two minutes! Look at Joan Collins – over twice your age and still with a figure like Twiggy. Fat bitch. Me, I mean. Not Twiggy. Or Joan. I'm so weak and . . . and *pathetic*. Right, that's it. I am not eating until next Friday! Or at least only fruit. That will teach me. Oh, shag it, seeing as I've already blown it for today I might as well have that Snickers bar belonging to Fiona.'

And right now she was going to have a bag of Walkers crisps with her ham sandwich. For all her talk. It was the Polish guys' fault. Why didn't they have a selection of fresh fruit for people to augment their lunch with? A nice apple or a banana or something. It wouldn't kill them, instead of piling high all those crisps and peanuts and pre-packed slices of cake, right at nose height. What did they expect – that people had a never-ending supply of willpower? They were morally bankrupt, she decided viciously, and for two pins she would report them to the obese watchdog, whatever building they were in.

She had one last stab at resistance. Be strong, girl. Open your heart to enlightenment, for God's sake. Think about Joan Collins.

She also thought about Gavin and Liam in the office, with whom she usually ate lunch. They were boys, and so didn't experience any of the feelings about food that women did. To them, a bag of crisps was simply a bag of crisps, not a little sack of calories, saturated fat, deep-fried guilt and flavoured with recriminations that were on time release. She hadn't liked eating her crisps in front of them in the beginning, in case they thought she was a hog, but they always ate crisps as well, and big greasy breakfast rolls, and drank litres of Coke, so Debs's bag of crisps always seemed demure in comparison. And she always ate them daintily in front of them, as though that somehow made a difference.

But yesterday she thought she had seen Gavin give her a little look. She had been eating crisps at the time, her cheeks working away like a hamster's. Had he been thinking, God, that girl should really do something about herself?

It was only Gavin, but still Debs felt herself go a bit red now.

Dodek said, 'Are you sure you don't want a packet of—'

'All right! I'll have one! The things I do to keep you two in business.' She snatched a pack and tossed it down on the counter. Might as well be hung for a sheep as a lamb. She had no idea what that meant, but any snippet of self-justification at all was welcome.

Bob must have been right behind her in the queue that day, only she was so absorbed in the crisps dilemma that she didn't register him. He came in later than she did usually, and would join the back of the queue just as she was leaving. A lot of days he wouldn't be there at all. Well, there were dozens of sandwich shops to choose from up and down Baggot Street, and he might even go for lunch regularly with clients. Judging from his dark suits and shiny shoes, Debs idly wondered sometimes whether he was a solicitor or an accountant, or something like that. Not that she gave it much thought. To be honest, she hardly noticed him at all, and certainly not that day.

All that was about to change. Her sandwich was ready. She grabbed it, paid, and said, unnecessarily, 'See you tomorrow.'

She was halfway down the road when she felt a hand on her shoulder. Her first instinct was that she was being mugged. After all, she was a country girl, even if she had been in the city for over ten years, and her mother still had her on high alert for chance assaults, thefts and general attacks by persons unknown.

Mum would read the newspapers and then go ringing Debs up breathlessly. 'I see here that there was some poor girl in west Dublin who was attacked and beaten up and all her stuff robbed. *In her own apartment.*' Not down some seedy dark alley then, which she was forever warning Debs against walking down.

'It wasn't me,' Debs had told her helpfully. 'I haven't been back to my apartment in weeks anyway, because I've been sleeping around.'

'So have I,' her mother came right back with. That was the only way to deal with these smart-aleck missies who went off to Dublin and tried to shock you with their talk of drugs and sex and threesomes. They needn't think that they could treat their parents like country hicks who knew nothing. No matter what shocker Debs came out with, her mother was ready with a response.

'Anyway,' she had gone on, 'it'd do you the world of

good if you *did* sleep with someone. It might put you in a better mood.'

'There's nothing wrong with my mood.'

Debs's mother hadn't pursued it. Instead she'd said, rather worriedly, 'We haven't seen you in two months.'

Every phone call was the same: when was Debs coming home? What was keeping her in Dublin, that den of iniquity (because it certainly wasn't a man)? Why didn't she hop on the next bus, and bring her dirty washing down while she was at it, and Dad would collect her at the bus stop? And there would be steak and kidney pie waiting for her on the table, and chips, and her favourite sticky toffee pudding for afters, with custard and a big mound of whipped cream.

Honestly, was it any wonder that Debs was the way she was, after being reared on that kind of fare? You couldn't do it now without social services becoming involved.

'I'll come down soon,' Debs had said limply.

It wasn't that she didn't want to go home. It was just somehow rather depressing to get a CIE bus home, like she was still a student, and have her father pick her up, and spend the weekend at home like nothing had changed. Like her life in Dublin didn't count. Like she wasn't a proper adult yet.

Her sister, Edel, was married with two kids, and when they came over from Galway to visit they stayed in the hotel at the top of the town. 'We'd be too much for you now, Mum. Especially with the boys. We'll just call over for tea,' Edel would say maturely.

You see, that was the proper way to do things. Stay in

a hotel, like responsible grown-ups, with your family, and make an appointment to walk down for tea. Not like Debs, back in her old bedroom and even her old clothes, sometimes, being fed like a pig by Mum, before straggling back to Dublin on a bus to her rented flat, and her rented life. Meanwhile, Edel drove back to her lovely house in Galway in her Land Rover with her businessman husband beside her and her two children fighting in the back seat.

Debs didn't really want to be Edel. She'd quite like the Land Rover, though.

One day, she thought.

But not today, because right now she was being attacked from behind by a person or persons unknown. In broad daylight, on a busy street. It was so audacious that it may well be the apartment-maniac that Mum had warned her about.

And so Debs swung round, hand fiercely clamped to her handbag – he could take her down, but he wouldn't make off with her fake Gucci – and let out a strangled, 'Help!'

It was Bob. Not that she knew his name then. It took her a moment to even recognise him, which she did after the fog of paranoia lifted.

He looked a bit startled at her reaction and took a careful step back, dropping his hand immediately.

'I called out, but you didn't hear,' he explained.

He sounded eminently sane and reasonable, in contrast to her near-hysteria.

'Sorry,' she said, trying to sound equally brisk and together, even though her heart was still thumping with fright. Her blooming mother.

He looked down at her brown paper bag, and held up his own. 'You picked up the wrong sandwich.'

'What?'

'I think this one is yours. There seems to be a packet of cheese and onion crisps in there.'

He handed the bag over. Her face flamed. He was probably thinking to himself, The last thing *she* needs is crisps.

But he just said, 'And you must have my salt and vinegar ones.'

And he smiled.

Debs smiled back. It was the first time in a long while that nobody had made her feel bad about eating something.

'I only have them occasionally,' she added hurriedly, just in case he thought she was out of control.

'Me too,' he assured her. 'I have to watch my cholesterol.' And his eyes twinkled.

Debs wasn't used to being twinkled at. It was an older man thing, wasn't it? Granddads twinkled, and favourite uncles. But then again Bob *was* a little older. Plus, he was poking fun at his cholesterol levels.

But he wasn't ancient. Not like those harassed men with receding hairlines and big bellies that she would see lumbering up office steps. Bob was scarcely into his forties, Debs reckoned. In his expensive grey suit he looked solid and suave, and, well, successful.

Debs, unused to a surplus of success in her own life, was suddenly shy. She felt a bit inadequate in the presence of someone who clearly had a more salubrious career than she did.

'Anyway,' she said, certain that he had to go off and clinch a big deal and that she was keeping him, 'I'd better go.'

He sighed. 'Me too.'

There was something in his voice that she recognised; a certain frustration. A dissatisfaction. She could sing it in her sleep.

'Mondays, eh?' she said to him impulsively. 'Even though it's Thursday.'

He laughed, and his eyes did their twinkling thing again. This time she felt a jolt in her stomach.

'Well, I'll probably see you tomorrow,' he said.

'You probably will,' she said back.

Chapter Two

The truth was that Geri never noticed that her husband had begun an affair. Her friends consoled her afterwards that it was common to go into denial: the idea of your husband cheating was naturally so painful, so devastating, that women often blocked out the warning signs for months, or even years. He could be going around stinking of Poison and with a pair of black lace knickers stashed in the glove compartment of the family car, and his wife would merrily continue on with the washing-up. So Geri wasn't strange, or odd, or uncaring. She had simply engaged in a form of self-protection until her subconscious mind felt ready to deal with the blow.

But Geri knew that none of that was true. She hadn't noticed because she was too blinking busy.

'If you could sit up there, Mr O'Reilly . . . I'll just slip this bedpan under you . . . lovely. I'll pull the curtain over now and you give me a shout when you're ready, OK?'

She checked her watch as she waited. Her shift wasn't

17

over for another hour, and Susan had to be picked up from hockey practice in forty-five minutes. Rebecca's mum usually brought them both home, but Rebecca was sick that week and so wasn't at hockey, and Bob was working late again. She could ring Davey, she supposed, and bribe him to walk down to meet Susan, but Susan would be furious at being met by her brother (she was so moody recently that Geri wondered whether she was on drugs. And if she wasn't, she might suggest it) and, oh, it just wasn't worth it. She would try and get off half an hour early.

'Are you nearly done, Mr O'Reilly?' She didn't want to put pressure on him, but he could take an age. Sometimes he even wanted a magazine.

There was a big long pause. 'I don't think I can,' he said eventually.

Geri sighed. But inwardly.

'Try for another minute and if you have no luck I'll get you something.'

'OK.'

He liked Geri. Or at least she was the only one he would accept a bedpan from. He would call plaintively for her ten times a day, his chin only lifting from his chest when he heard her approaching efficiently in her Scholl sandals and tan tights. ('Go on, leave them on,' Bob would joke to her sometimes during sex.)

Geri seemed to have the knack of dealing with the older patients. She was cheerful yet firm, and they seemed to like that. In fact, the firmer she was the more they seemed to enjoy it. Some days she felt like she was in a *Carry On* movie.

'Mr Murphy!' she would say mock-sternly. 'I just hope you're not sneaking out in your pyjamas for a crafty puff!'

And he would scuttle back to bed, ashamed yet delighted that he had been noticed at all.

Sometimes, especially after a night shift when everything was a bit surreal anyway, she went on speaking that way when she got home.

'Right, everybody! Let's all come sit up at the table and have our breakfast, will we?'

Susan would roll her thickly mascaraed eyes – Clinique, no less – and mutter, '*God.*' And, actually, Geri couldn't blame her.

Davey would just pat her affectionately on the shoulder, knowing that it would wear off as the day went on, until she ended up glued to the sofa as usual with a cup of tea and communicating only in growls.

Sometimes Geri wasn't sure where the nurse in her ended and her real personality began. There were often days when she went around in a semi-schizophrenic state, pushing a trolley around the supermarket with a mad smile pinned to her face whilst simultaneously bitching and cursing under her breath because they were out of baguettes.

One of these days she would crack. It was bound to happen. It'd probably be in the supermarket too, right by the cooked chickens going round on spits. Some days Geri could really empathise with those chickens.

Andrea stopped by her briefly now, a syringe cocked and aimed in her hand.

'Are you coming to the pub?' she said out of the side of her mouth. There was no sense in alarming the patients.

Geri had a brief image of a tall, frosted glass with a huge gin and tonic in it, and she nearly drooled.

'It's Sharon's leaving do,' Andrea added persuasively.

Sharon was going to America for a year to take up a job in a private hospital in Texas, where allegedly she would earn five times more than she did now. They were all sick of hearing about the perks and the benefits, and the blooming sun, which apparently shone twenty-four hours a day.

'But it's *Texas*,' they would say, just to make themselves feel better.

'Yes, and full of rich oil barons, and I'll probably end up marrying one of them,' Sharon had returned triumphantly. 'They love fat Irish girls with red hair.'

'They'd want to,' Andrea had said under her breath.

Sharon was having her leaving do in O'Shea's pub, which was down the road from the hospital. It was always full of medical personnel, day or night, and you couldn't go to the loo without tripping over a tipsy radiographer. She was having baskets of chips and sausages on sticks, and she had vowed to get off her face and, she hoped, snog a house doctor, if any of them showed up.

It would be worth going along just for the spectacle.

'I have to pick up Susan in an hour,' Geri told Andrea regretfully. Less than an hour. Forty minutes now. And how was she going to slip off early if everybody else was legging it to the pub?

'You could always drop her at home and come back.'

Andrea was dangerous that way; she was always entreating Geri to come out drinking when she should have been at home doing the dishes or putting on five loads of washing.

'It'll still be there when you get home,' Andrea would say – and she was always right, damn her. The kids would never dream of putting on a load of washing. They seemed to think that their dirty clothes magically found their way to the washing basket, then into the machine, then into the dryer, only to reappear days later in their closets, freshly pressed and smelling of lavender.

'Hanging is too good for them,' Bob would console her, even though he never put on a wash either. Or at least only when he was down to his very last shirt for work – that nasty lemon-coloured one that made him look like he was suffering from a bout of jaundice.

'I can't,' Geri insisted.

Andrea, of course, didn't understand. She had never found Mr Right, and it showed – she had lovely glossy dark hair, an unlined face, and was always plucked, waxed and made up. Geri was careful never to stand too close to her for fear of comparison. Andrea complained that people thought she had BO, the way Geri kept leaping away from her.

'Of course you can. A nice gin and tonic. With ice,' she murmured persuasively. Then, the clincher. 'Rumour has it that Dr Foley is going to be there.'

Every nurse in the place broke out in a sweat when his name was mentioned, including the males ones. He had turned thirty-six in February (someone had hacked into his personal details on the computer system), had crinkly dark hair and a smile that would put the heart crossways in you. He had arrived only a month ago, fresh from a stint somewhere in Saudi Arabia, and with the tan to show for it, and so, in hospital parlance, was fresh meat. He seemed endearingly unaware of the dozens of pairs of eyes that followed his progress closely as he strode boyishly up and down the hospital corridors, leaving a trail of aftershave behind. It was only a matter of time before he was bedded, whether he liked it or not.

But not by Andrea. She had a strict policy: she would look, but there was no touching. Like, ever, even when she was on the floor of O'Shea's pub after eleven gin and tonics and that guy from Admissions with the beard was looking good.

But a deep-seated fear of The Morning After kept her 'clean'. After fifteen years in the medical profession, she had seen too many horror stories: otherwise sane and skilled people who lost the run of themselves after two glasses of wine and publicly straddled Dr Hartigan, who could sometimes look a bit like Brad Pitt in the dim lights of O'Shea's pub. But only at two a.m. And only in a *very* dim light. Certainly not five hours later in his dirty apartment as you hunted frantically for your bra, hungover to hell and riddled with mortification, and legged it out to make the eight a.m. shift.

Awaiting you was the walk of shame. Andrea's voice always lowered when she mentioned this. Before you even passed through those double glass doors, the whispering campaign would have begun. Actually, it was mostly by email, using something euphemistic like, 'Jane and Dr Jones went to the races last night,' just in case they got caught. The wards would be unbearable; the locker room a no-go zone. You could be the butt of gossip for a whole week, until the following Saturday night when somebody else would drink too much and make complete and utter eejits of themselves.

Mortifying.

'I'm sticking to random strangers I pick up in bars,' was Andrea's motto, and generally she was true to her word. But just on the off-chance that she might ever be tempted by a hospital romance, she went out of her way to be extremely rude to any male co-workers who were even slightly attractive. 'That way they all think I'm a total cow and wouldn't give me a second glance anyway.'

Dr Foley was presenting a new challenge, though, by virtue of his fabulous good looks. He was also very, very nice, and said things like 'please' and 'thank you', and remembered people's birthdays. The first time he had seen Andrea, with her aforementioned long dark glossy hair and perfect skin, his breath had caught in his throat. Geri had actually seen it.

'I think he has an eye for you.'

'Jesus Christ.' Andrea looked around quickly in case anybody had overheard. 'Don't even start a rumour like that, otherwise everybody will have me in bed with him by the end of the week.'

And she was acting like this was a *bad* thing?

But Andrea was holding firm. She was so rude to him – 'Don't touch that file! Don't even *look* at that file' – that he took quite a fright and now hung around the ward entrance fearfully.

'Is she . . . ?'

'No, no, you're quite safe.'

Tonight Andrea would have to practise her look-don't-touch campaign on her own.

'Look, I said I'd bake forty-eight chocolate chip

muffins for a cake sale in Davey's school tomorrow,' Geri confessed.

Andrea's reaction was predictable.

'Only forty-eight?'

Andrea was always trying to teach Geri how to say no. Sometimes she even took her into the toilets and made her look herself in the eye in the grainy mirror and repeat after her, 'I am not a dogsbody.'

But what else was she supposed to say? No, I don't give a shite about the school's need for new gym equipment, or the orphans in Africa, or the cake sale in aid of dogs being neutered? Actually, she really *didn't* give a shite about that last one, but Davey had been only ten at the time, and had been on the organisation committee, and she didn't want him to have to admit to everyone that his mummy was refusing to take part and had used bad language to boot.

So she baked. And drove gangs of kids to sporting events. And took in a foreign student on a language exchange programme. Enric had lounged in front of the telly for two whole weeks, ignoring all their stilted attempts to communicate with him: 'I am going to the corner shop to buy some bread! Would you like to come?' Bob had lost his rag eventually. 'Turn off that crap,' he'd said bluntly. Enric had understood that perfectly.

Geri had been resentful about that: how come Bob got to be all authoritative and bossy, while she was the one who was left to ring Enric's mother in Florence to find out what Enric actually ate? Because it certainly wasn't anything that Geri cooked. Or indeed baked.

'It's because I'm the strong, silent type,' Bob had explained, delighted with himself, even though he later confessed that, for a moment, he had been terrified that Enric would leap off the couch in a rage and beat him to a pulp.

So where did that leave Geri? The soft, caring type? The one who baked and dispensed bedpans?

The irony was that she hadn't started out caring at all. Back then nursing hadn't been about saving lives so much as the relatively decent pay and the great stories she had heard about flat-sharing with seventeen other trainee nurses. Apparently she would be getting langered every weekend, and riding loads of gorgeous junior doctors. There was even the possibility of marrying one of them in the distant future, and moving out to Foxrock to live in a detached house, and giving up that working lark altogether. Fantastic!

Except, of course, that hardly any of it was true, especially the bit about marrying a doctor and becoming a lady of leisure. But – and this was probably the important bit – somewhere along the way she had become a good nurse. She had started to care. Really care. There had even been a brief period where she had cared too much.

'Mr Magee is going to DIE,' she had hiccuped hysterically into Bob's shoulder in the early days. He was always great, stroking and soothing her, and murmuring comforting things like, 'We all have to die sometime. Some of us even on your shift.' He would pause delicately. 'Could you give him a little something to speed him on his way?'

'Bob!'

Of course she had calmed down since then. You couldn't keep that up or you'd end up in a ward yourself. No, now she had a developed a certain dissociation from her patients, a healthy distance.

Or so she told herself. Then the blooming phone would ring at seven a.m. on a Saturday morning: two staff members were down with the flu and was there any chance at all that Geri could cover?

'Tell them no,' Bob would implore her. 'Tell them you have a husband and two needy children at home.'

She would go in. She felt awful leaving the kids, of course, especially when they had been very small, and didn't want to be left with Bob at all. And vice versa. But she didn't want to leave those at work in the lurch, either. Anyway, she got great overtime and nobody complained when she took them all out for a pizza.

Except Susan, of course. Apparently she didn't eat pizza any more. If Geri's memory served her right, she possibly hadn't eaten anything at all since Tuesday.

'Do drugs decrease your appetite?' Geri asked Andrea. Andrea was youngish and happening – she would know these things, surely.

'I'd try the gym first if I were you,' Andrea advised.

'I mean Susan.'

Andrea clicked her tongue sympathetically. She had been following the saga for the last couple of months: Susan's defiance, the inexplicable absences (she was probably off shooting up, now that Geri thought about it), the way she'd started dressing like a hooker. A hooker who didn't charge too much either, which was even worse.

'Have you tried giving her a good slap?' Andrea wondered.

Geri was briefly tempted. 'I don't know if I should go around hitting her if she's on drugs.'

Andrea was blunt. 'Read her diary and then you'll know.'

'I can't believe you suggested that!' Geri spluttered. Honestly, what kind of a person was Andrea? 'That's an invasion of her privacy!'

Andrea looked at her. 'You already have, haven't you?'

'Yes.'

'What did it say?'

Geri's guilt had let her have only the briefest peek. Also, she was worried that she would find something rather unflattering to herself: a kind of *Mommie Dearest* character assassination, where Susan would list all of Geri's failings as a mother and a human being, beginning with that time she had stuffed Susan into that awful pink scratchy dress to impress some relatives over from Boston, and the frills had left deep marks all around her fat little neck.

Geri didn't think she could bear being torn asunder on the cream scented pages of her daughter's diary. But then she thought about the way Susan looked at her these days, as though Geri were something she'd discovered on the bottom of her shoe, and she thought, Sod it, I'll read the little cow's diary.

'It was all quite innocent, actually,' she told Andrea with great relief. 'Just bits and pieces about school, and how she's planning on having hair extensions.'

It had been a bit of a let-down in the end. There Geri had been, almost too frightened to turn the page for fear of being hit with lurid passages about experimental sex.

But sex hadn't featured at all, or drugs, or anything mood-altering, no matter how hard she looked. There hadn't even been an innocent mention of getting completely bladdered on sherry from the family drinks cabinet. The bit about the hair extensions had gone on interminably. Oh, come on, Geri had found herself thinking irritably – where was all the experimental sex?

Then she'd pulled herself up. Susan was fine. Susan was getting *hair extensions*. See, Geri thought smugly, I really *am* a good mother.

But now Andrea had to go and ruin it by saying kindly, 'It's a plant.'

'What?'

'The diary you read. Trust me. The real diary she probably has nailed down under the floorboards.'

Damn her anyway. Just as Geri was starting to feel OK about herself. Now she'd have to go and find something sharp in Bob's toolbox and prise the floor up. Which wasn't as easy as it sounded. Finding something sharp in Bob's toolbox, that was. His toolbox was one of those massive fold-out jobs, with at least five different layers, some with miniature plastic drawers for screws and nails. There were compartments for nuts, bolts, screwdrivers, rolls of black Sellotape ('Duct tape, Geri,' he would correct her in a superior tone), and a great big handle in the middle of it for lifting the thing, which usually took two people.

Bob was proud of his toolbox. He spent a lot of time in the garden shed stroking it, or tenderly packing and repacking boxes of screws. His toolbox was, in Geri's opinion anyway, compensation for the fact that he spent all day in meetings with computer illiterates, trying to sell them Windows 2019, or whatever version they were on now. Other men kicked a football around to let off steam, or climbed steep hills in Wales with a lot of beardy friends. Bob came home and pulverised something with a hammer. If so much as a light bulb in the house blew, he went skipping off happily to the garden shed to retrieve the toolbox. He would spread it out on the kitchen floor, all manly grunts and testosterone, and command, 'Step back, ladies.' Luckily Davey never took offence.

Bob was a simple soul, Geri often thought fondly. A solid, reliable presence in the backyard, banging away methodically at something whilst Susan screamed in the kitchen, 'I'm moving out of this fucking house when I'm eighteen.'

'Go, go,' Geri had encouraged her. But then, as usual, she had spoiled it by saying, 'And mind your language.'

'Good for you,' Bob had said afterwards. He always waited until the shouting was over before he came back in, often to pick up any broken ornaments or smashed plates. After Geri's front-line battle, his job was search and rescue. They had it down pat. After half an hour cooling-down period he would go upstairs to Susan's bedroom – sometimes armed with a pliers if she wouldn't let him in – and try to have the requisite post-fight awkward conversation with her.

'Your mother and I love you very much . . .' embarrassed cough, '. . . but we can't tolerate this kind of behaviour . . .' He would discover something fascinating on the carpet. 'If there's anything troubling you at school . . . bullying . . .'

'Oh, leave me *alone*!' Susan would eventually howl in anguish.

'Certainly,' Bob would say with relief, and hurry back down to Geri, and they would crack open two bottles of beer to get over the excitement.

He wasn't with her on the drugs thing, though. Normally he didn't dispute anything she said. She was The Boss. Everybody had known this from the beginning, and there had rarely been a challenge to her authority, except over bread. She got brown for the roughage, but everybody else preferred white. They didn't care about their bowels the way she did. One day she wouldn't care, and let them stay constipated.

But Bob had bravely mounted a challenge against her drugs allegation. He had said, 'Do you not think you're reading a bit too much into things?'

Geri had smiled kindly at him. Bob was so terribly naïve. He had no idea what teenagers were really like. He hardly even ventured into their bedrooms any more, usually because the smell was so overwhelming – eau de sex in Susan's bedroom, and rancid socks in Davey's – never mind go through their drawers, like Geri did. He didn't overhear the contents of their telephone conversations from the kitchen and was an innocent when it came to the kind of filth children could access on the internet.

'Wow!' he had said happily when she had shown him.

It was up to Geri to be the worldly-wise one. No doubt it would be she who would find the kilo of hard stuff under the floorboards alongside the diary – the real diary. Bob would be in awe at her detective skills, and would get down on his knees in worship. Then, no doubt, once the initial shock had worn off, they would turn on each other viciously with cries of, 'It's all your fault my daughter is a strung-out junkie!'

'Me?' she would challenge. 'What about your family? Half of them are on antidepressants!'

Well, it was kind of true. Bob's mother was addicted to the codeine in painkillers. She wouldn't admit it, of course. But she was always driving around different pharmacies to stock up secretly. And she had got very antsy that time Geri had a headache when they were over for dinner, and had asked for a couple of Solpadeine. She had counted out two very reluctantly indeed.

'Are you sure it's that bad?' she had asked hopefully.

Still, that was the high-octane world of modelling for you. Bob's mother did a bit of modelling, mostly over-sixties stuff and a bit of hand modelling, which meant that she was always going around with her hands held out in front of her as though they were made of glass. According to Bob she had never cooked a dinner or done a bit of hoovering in her life in case she broke a nail. She was a bit cracked. It was no wonder that Bob had turned out so firmly on the other side of the spectrum.

But back to Susan. Supposing she *was* on drugs. Would it really be so bad? Geri didn't mean heroin or anything like that (please God). But maybe a bit of marijuana? That was fairly harmless, wasn't it? Some of Geri's patients smoked it at home on the sly to relieve pain, or so they said. Of course, most people took it to get off their heads. Geri herself had tried it in her day. Oh, yes. She wasn't some ancient hick who knew nothing. She had been at a party once in college where absolutely everybody had been high as kites and Geri had even skinned up her own joint – she knew the right jargon too – and smoked the whole lot.

'But didn't you have to ring for an ambulance then?' Bob wondered, spoiling things. 'Did your heart not start beating really fast, and you thought you were having a massive coronary, and you got someone to ring 999 and someone else to perform CPR on you until they arrived—'

'All right! I just hadn't eaten. That was all, OK? It was nothing to do with the *drugs*.'

Why had she even told Bob about the ambulance? Why hadn't she just left it at the glamorous bit where she had skinned up?

But of course they had told each other absolutely everything back in the beginning. The way you do. Within five minutes of meeting Bob, she was telling him all about her psychological problems growing up as the middle child – no identity, taken for granted – still was, come to think of it – whilst he was unburdening himself about his failed bid at sixteen to become a professional swimmer – dashed, he maintained, when his arms stopped growing. There was nothing they didn't tell each other, holed up in Geri's little room in the flat she shared with numerous other student nurses, and slugging back cheap red wine. Every conversation began excitedly with, 'Oh! I never told you about the time I . . .' and, 'This is *so* embarrassing that I've never told anybody before, but once I . . .'

Honestly, someone should have stopped them. Some mature soul should have confiscated the wine and explained to them firmly that it was a good idea to leave a bit of mystery. You know, a shred of suspense. Someone should have warned them that they had their whole lives to go yet, and that if they kept that up, they would quickly run out of things to say – which they did, of course, and promptly got married and had children. In their ignorance, they hadn't known back then that those stories about ambulances that had once sounded so funny and cute would only end up being used as ammunition nearly two decades later.

'Anyway, you didn't even *try* drugs,' she had said to Bob in retaliation. Sometimes, when he had that snooty expression on his face, she almost hated him.

'I just did the drink and sex thing,' Bob had agreed sagely.

The drink and sex thing! Geri had wanted to snigger viciously. At least she had stuck to her stories over the years, even if they were pathetic. Bob's memory seemed to vacillate, usually in his favour. Geri seemed to remember that when she'd first met him, his experience under the sheets had been strictly limited – to over the waist, actually.

'Let's not fight about it,' she had said automatically.

As if they would. Fighting required energy. Passion. *Dedication.* Who had any of that after a long day of swilling out bedpans and upgrading computers? No, it was with great relief that they had both reached a kind of unspoken agreement back around 2002 that they wouldn't fight any more. They could still grumble, of course, and bitch, and have occasional digs at each other, but outright fighting wasn't allowed. It was much more considerate all round.

Naturally, it wouldn't do to admit that they basically

couldn't be bothered to have a good old row any more. So they both pretended that they were too mature to fight.

'Would you listen to those Finnegans next door tearing strips off each other!' they would say, shaking their heads in sad bemusement. 'Why they can't just sit down and discuss things in a mature fashion . . .'

Also, it was a great example to the kids. *They* would never see their parents chucking pots and pans and calling each other useless feckers. Wouldn't you think they'd show some gratitude by not taking drugs?

'Nurse Murphy!'

Geri was jolted from her ramblings. It was Mr O'Reilly. He must have managed something, judging by the excited tone of his voice. It was funny how both the very early and very late years of life were dominated by poos, she sometimes observed. It was the bits in the middle that were tricky.

'My daughter is coming to visit tomorrow afternoon,' he told her.

He always made a point of telling the nurses when he had visitors. To show that he belonged to someone, she supposed. Because some of them in the ward didn't, or at least nobody ever came to visit them.

Sometimes Geri tried to imagine what it would be like to have no family – no Susan or Davey, no Bob – and she just couldn't. At some point she had melded with them, become part of them so completely that she, Geri, didn't really exist as a separate entity any more.

And now she really must go and collect Susan.

Chapter Three

Debs didn't start sleeping with Bob for ages. She didn't even see him for a whole fortnight after that first exchange, because there was a Massive Crisis in work. Personally Debs would have termed it a Storm in a Teacup, but nobody ever listened to her, mostly because she never spoke. Well, there was no need, not when the office was full of the kind of people who got off on the sound of their own voices.

'We're fucked,' ranted Marty, the main offender. At first Debs took no notice. He often did that several times a day for effect. Also, it gave the impression that what they all did was extremely important, if not life-saving, and everybody got all excited and tended to forget about the rubbish salaries he was paying them.

Besides, Debs was busy trying to write a press release. It was for a Christian youth organisation that was doing a national recruitment drive, and they had requested something with 'colloquial language and teen appeal'. Given that

Debs hadn't seen her teen years in well over a decade, this was more difficult than it seemed. She kept writing things like, 'Come and join our gang, we're really cool!' but only ended up embarrassing herself. What they really wanted was, 'Hang with us, motherfucker, or we'll blow your head off', but they couldn't think up something like that themselves. Hence they were paying Debs to. Or, rather, Fitz Communications, who then paid Debs a tiny, tiny amount of the original sum.

Still, it was only another hour and ten minutes to go to lunch. And crisps. Today was definitely a crisps day. Plus, it was Wednesday, and she had already blown her diet for the week on Monday night with a whole packet of Wagon Wheels, mostly because Fiona and Stevo were cooing to each other on the sofa in the living room and the kitchen had become her refuge. Pathetic, she sighed.

'I'll have to fucking do it myself!' Marty impinged upon her misery again. It was becoming difficult to ignore him, given that he was pacing up and down beside her desk, his plump little bottom quivering indignantly with each step. She had to restrain herself from reaching across and giving it a good slap.

But that would be the end of her career with Fitz Communications. If you could even call it a career. It wasn't as though she had advanced spectacularly through the ranks since joining the company three years ago. If her desk position was anything to go by, she had regressed: she had started off over in the corner by the draughty swing doors, but had somehow been demoted to a cubbyhole under the stairs, and found herself ducking every time someone thundered up and down them.

Her self-esteem issues weren't helped by the fact that Alex's desk was directly in her line of vision. Every time she looked up from her computer, there Alex was, like something out of *Cosmo*. (Debs would be more from the *Woman's Own* stable.)

Alex. Young. Gorgeous. Successful. Marty's right-hand woman. Size eight. *Eight*, for fuck's sake. It wasn't natural.

It didn't help matters that she and Debs had got off to a bad start. On Debs's very first morning at Fitz Communications, Alex had strode up at ten o'clock in all her perfection and introduced herself by saying, 'Do you want anything to eat from the shop?'

Debs had coloured. It was surely a dig at her weight. Alex must have already formed the impression that she wouldn't last until lunchtime without a constant drip-feed of Mars bars.

'No,' she had growled back.

Alex had given her a look as though to say, God, not another lunatic. It was only when she went round to everybody else's desk and asked the same question that Debs realised that Alex was, in fact, on shop duty that day and was only being polite. To add insult to injury, she had come back with a huge jam doughnut, which she proceeded to wolf down in front of Debs. She then washed it down with a can of Coke – full-fat Coke – and let out a little burp afterwards.

Dear God. Was there *any* justice in this world? Who the heck was upstairs making the decisions? Did they look down upon their flock, and say, 'Hmm, let me see. That one there. Let's make her thin and successful and able to eat unlimited junk food without putting on a single ounce. And that one lurking over there – let's try fat and miserable, and put her sitting *behind* Alex, just for the giggle.'

Debs and Alex had been rather wary of each other since. But Debs was probably flattering herself. It was unlikely Alex gave Debs much thought at all. She probably just thought of her as the weird chubby girl with the personality defect.

Little did she know that Debs spent a large part of the day at her desk staring obsessively at Alex's back. If she wore a sheer top, sometimes Debs could count her ribs (and, actually, she was missing one by Debs's calculations). Debs would surreptitiously eavesdrop on Alex's phone conversations and spy on her computer screen, torn between dark envy and an unseemly desire to lick her shoes.

It wasn't right that one person had so much, and other people had so little. Except for an enormous arse, that was.

The icing on Alex's cake was a boyfriend called Greg, who was desperately in love with her. Or his name might be Jed. Nobody had actually met him yet. But rumour had it that he had taken one look at Alex and had fallen to his knees in a semi-faint and tried to get her to marry him on the spot. She was apparently holding out, displaying a cruel streak that only added to her ratings.

'He's a banker,' maintained Jennifer, the rather aloof receptionist with the sing-song voice ('Hello, Fitz Communi-KAY-tions').

'No, he's not. He's a fitness instructor. They met at the gym. And his name is Jack,' Tanya said eagerly. But it turned out that she was only making all this up to garner favour, as usual, and was forced miserably to retract in the end, and was sent off to phone in the order for paperclips.

'Why don't we just ask her?' Janice said, cross that everybody was spending so much time on Alex's love life, and hardly any on hers. As if they wanted to. They had to put up with her rudeness and ambition all day long without straying into her private life.

But nobody had the bottle to ask Alex. She was the boss, after all.

'No, she's bloody not,' Janice said, even crosser.

Her denial was just cosmetic. Alex had a foot in the door of Marty's office and everybody knew it. If only she'd sleep with him it would be a done deal. But she wasn't putting out. This was perfectly understandable, given Marty's rock-bottom position in the attractiveness ratings. So it looked like Alex was going to have to win the promotion on sheer brilliance and hard work, a concept completely alien to most of the other staff, and so they disliked her even more.

Dislike was probably the wrong word. They didn't really know her that well, even though she'd been there years. There was something a bit aloof about her. She was perfectly pleasant, but you just knew she wasn't going to welcome any questions about her personal life. She never confided, 'We got absolutely smashed on Friday night,' like everybody else did on Monday mornings. When half-past five came she was gone from the office and you never knew whether she was meeting Greg or Jed or Jack, or indeed all three of them together. Lucky girl.

Of course this all added to her cachet. Nobody else

in the office could pull that kind of mysteriousness off. Janice was always trying to, but could never keep her mouth shut long enough, and everybody knew all the tedious details of her on-off relationship with Pete, another PR twit who wore pink shirts and buckets of hair gel.

But Greg was something else. Even though nobody had met him yet, Debs just knew he would be special. She spent an unseemly amount of time at her desk engaged in lurid imaginings of what he was like. Wide shoulders? Definitely. Cute, slightly ruffled hair? Yes, please. He would also have the kind of green eyes that nobody in real life had, only people in books. He would have a lopsided grin – God, it would launch a ship, that smile, or else sink one – and he would know that it is never, ever sexy to say, 'Your friend Chloe is quite cute, isn't she?' in bed.

He would be amazing, simply because he was Alex's boyfriend.

Lucky, lucky bitch.

Debs wasn't holding out for a boyfriend like Greg. She wasn't *totally* deluded. No, she would settle for someone to call her own. Well, so long as he didn't have too much hair on his back – she had a bit of a thing about that. She just wanted a guy who might one day call by the office on a Friday evening to take her off for dinner. That would show them all. Then she'd be more than just the girl under the stairs with the rented flat and the tent-like trousers.

No crisps at lunchtime, she resolved fiercely. It was time to get control of her life once and for all. How was she ever going to meet someone unless she made an effort to make it happen? The whinging and excuses had to stop right now, Debra Manning (her English teacher's voice again). She was thirty-two years of age. If she didn't start making some kind of headway on life's essentials, then she might as well give up.

'We're screwed!' Marty screamed again.

Ah, yes. Never mind about Debs's pathetic little life. Back to Marty and his Massive Crisis. Probably they had run out of coffee and he was in withdrawal.

But then Debs noticed that Alex was missing. And had been all morning. The reason for Marty's misery began to become clearer.

Marty was what people would call highly strung. This was probably because he was extremely creative. At any rate he drank a lot of black coffee and smoked forty Marlboro a day in his office and fuck the smoking regulations. He also ran up a mammoth monthly mobile phone bill and had a little black book that was bursting at the seams with contacts. And that was the secret of his success: his little black book basically ran the agency, and it was never, ever let out of his sight. Indeed, a large part of everybody's job was keeping track of the thing. At home, Marty's wife, Patricia, monitored it, and often there would be early morning frantic telephone conversations between home and the office that went along the lines of:

'I'm telling you, I put it into his briefcase before he left. With my own hands!'

'Well, it's not there now. Only his inhaler and a packet of Marlboro.'

'I wonder did he take it out in the car on the way in?'

A semi-hysterical pause. 'I wonder did he leave it on the *roof* of the car, like that time he stopped for coffee?'

'Dear God.'

'I know, I know . . .'

'If only we had a back-up . . .'

'Or could wean him onto a BlackBerry . . .'

But Marty was old-fashioned that way. He didn't trust technology. He liked to have things written down in black and white on a bit of paper. And he wouldn't allow anybody to make a copy of his contacts. What if it went missing and Tom Cruise's mobile number fell into the wrong hands? Knowing Irish petty thieves, they would probably just try to order a pizza from him for the laugh, but there was no talking to Marty. His contacts and sources must be 'protected' at all costs, even if most of them never rang him back, and Tom Cruise's mobile number had gone out of use five minutes after Marty got hold of it.

Alex understood his paranoia. After all these years she was keenly attuned to Marty's ups and downs, of which there were many more downs. She only had to look out the office window in the morning and see the way he parked to gauge his mood.

'Someone put a pot of coffee on, quick,' she would instruct with a sigh, and everybody knew that meant he was in a rotten, filthy humour, and the best thing to do was to keep out of his way. Only Alex would brave it into his office, and whatever magic she wrought in there – someone said once that she made him deep-breathe while she chopped his shoulders like an amateur masseuse – his mood would lighten, if only by a degree or two.

But Alex wasn't there today. Consternation. Nobody

else knew how to chop Marty's shoulders. Although Debs would quite like to try. Hard.

The other girls – Janice and Tanya, and Mia, the trainee who was a mini Janice – fluttered anxiously around Marty now in his moment of distress. The scenario often reminded Debs of Hugh Hefner and his playmates. And they were lovely girls, young and perky and horribly ambitious, just the kind he liked, but they weren't Alex, dammit. Who wasn't in today for some inexplicable reason.

Debs herself was ambivalent about the news. On the one hand, it was great not to have all that perfection shoved in her face every moment of the day. The downside was that they had to put up with Marty.

'Now she can't do Tom!'

Fitz Communications handled quite a lot of promotional work for famous personalities, or at least people who were allegedly famous. Alex usually dealt exclusively with these, because, well, she was Alex. From the murmurings going on around her, Debs was able to deduce that Alex had phoned in five minutes ago with a vomiting virus – oh, how delicious. A world-famous golfing personality was scheduled to fly into town this very week to flog his new autobiography, *The Iron Man*, and there was Alex with her lovely head stuck down the jacks.

'I'll do him instead,' Janice offered. She would too. She was as bold as brass, that one: bright red lipstick and heels that left violent holes in the wooden floor of the conference room, much to Marty's fury. Rumour had it that she would steal your desk if you were missing for more than two hours.

Everybody knew, of course, that the desk she *really* wanted was Alex's.

'Or me,' piped up Tanya eagerly.

But she was too late. Janice turned her gaze rather malevolently on her. She quivered. It was like watching one of those nature programmes where David Attenborough would murmur, 'The young lemur is the tiger's favourite food.'

'You can't,' Janice said to her triumphantly. 'You're doing Bogger.'

Bogger was the affectionate office nickname for a politician who hailed from deepest rural Ireland, and had, on his file at least, a 'strong regional accent'. Before they'd taken him on nobody knew with any degree of certainty what he was saying. But he had been going up in the world for a while now, with more TV appearances and various speeches to be made at government level. It would take a better PR firm than Fitz Communications to have him speaking the Queen's English, but Tanya was doing wonders with him by the use of flash cards. She would make him repeat everything after her, and clap enthusiastically when he got it right. After these sessions he would do really well for a couple of weeks, until someone heckled him during one of his speeches, and he would lose it and lapse into a volley of colloquial insults, such as, 'Go home and boil your head, yeh fuckin' hoor, yeh.'

'Looks like I'll have to do Tom myself then,' Marty shouted, in an idle threat.

Gavin and Liam kept their heads low. They had no intention of squiring some guy around town. As far as they were concerned, that was strictly a girl's job. They preferred to confine themselves to corporate affairs, where they could go off to long lunch meetings with heavy-set clients or else inveigle themselves on to the golf course with Marty whenever he was entertaining some big gun. They would be sure to play much worse than him – bettering his handicap risked instant dismissal – and then lounge about afterwards drinking bottled foreign beer in the bar.

Gavin winked at Debs dangerously now and she stiff-ened. She hoped he wasn't going to embarrass her. He was always playing practical jokes and tricks upon her. Some of them were funny. Some of them, like that time he had sent her an anonymous email from an 'admirer', and to which *she had replied*, were not.

'Don't even think about it,' she hissed at him now.

'You could do Tom,' he whispered back encouragingly. Of course he had to make it sound sexual.

Debs went pink. 'I don't want to do Tom!'

Gavin's hand hovered in the air, as though to attract Marty's attention. 'I hear he's a good-looking guy,' he whispered. 'Plus, isn't it ages since you had a bit?'

Because Debs didn't fit in with the playmates in Fitz Communications, who went on voracious shopping sprees at lunchtime instead of horsing down sandwiches and crisps, and who were altogether more stylish and together than Debs, she had got thrown in with the two lads in the office instead. They would all tuck into their sand-wiches and crisps back at their desks, and tell each other rude jokes they'd read on the internet, and gossip about Marty. She was no threat to them professionally, and neither of them fancied her. Which said a lot, really, as

Liam by his own admission would ride anything after three pints. Gavin, who was better-looking, was more circumspect, but only slightly.

'Anyway,' he would say stoically, 'I'm saving myself for Alex.'

Who wasn't? God love him, he was always ploughing a furrow to her desk with some useless report or other, or asking to borrow her four-hole punch. She, to her credit, pretended not to notice how pathetic he was.

'If it wasn't for Greg, I really feel I'd be in with a chance,' he would say earnestly to Debs, whilst she rolled around laughing hysterically.

They were great confidants, he and Debs, especially after a few pints. It all worked out grand, except that she often made the mistake of telling him things about her personal life that she sincerely wished she hadn't the following morning. Like she hadn't had a ride in months and months.

'Take your hand down!' she commanded him in a hiss, her mortification growing.

Marty turned round, cross at all the whispering going on behind his back, especially when there was a Massive Crisis going on.

'What is it?' he barked at Gavin.

Gavin put on his most helpful expression. 'I was just wondering whether Debs could do Tom.'

Debs looked at the back of Gavin's neatly cropped head and wished some vile disease upon him.

It took Marty a moment to recognise the name. Then he looked about the office fruitlessly, trying to locate her amongst the playmates. Trouble was, they were all blonde, dammit.

Finally Janice, her disbelief at this turn of events plain, murmured distastefully, 'Under the stairs.'

Marty finally found Debs. She was no Alex, that much was evident on his face. No doubt when he'd taken her on he had thought she would be the jolly fat girl, only to discover that she was just the fat girl.

Into the uncomfortable silence, Debs stuttered, 'I really don't think so . . .'

But Marty was obviously tiring of the whole drama, and also getting desperate for a fag, because he just said, 'Meet him off the plane at six,' and lumbered back into his office.

Gavin turned to Debs. 'See the things I do for you?'

She wanted to slap his face.

'I am never going drinking with you again,' was the best she could threaten. Hit him where it hurt – in the liver.

He managed to look wounded. 'What? It's a good opportunity for you.'

Some opportunity. Therein started a week of hell. It began at the airport that evening when Debs failed to recognise Tom. This was partly his fault, as the file photo he had forwarded was clearly of a younger man, a *much* younger man, who had a lot more hair and a lot less gut to boot. Debs had ended up cheerily alighting upon a rather bemused man with a set of golf clubs – bound to be Tom – and tried to ferry him towards the exit until he finally managed to explain that he was only coming home from a spot of golfing in Malaga. And that the angry-looking woman behind Debs was his wife.

When she finally located Tom by a sweets dispensing

machine, he wasn't all that endearing. 'What's the hotel like?' he asked immediately, his eyes barely skimming over her.

The hotel wasn't up to expectations. The bed was hard, there were no individual bottles of mineral water and, worse, the staff didn't recognise him either.

'Do you guys not have TV in Ireland or something?' he asked belligerently.

Debs was apologetic. 'There's generally only one per village, and the local people gather round it on a Saturday night, and afterwards there's music and craic. I had to pull massive strings to get one in your hotel room, you know.'

Tom looked uncertain. 'Thanks, honey.'

In five seconds he was back to himself and he made her run down the street in the pouring rain to get him six bottles of mineral water – 'Perrier if they have it, honey.'

The mornings usually kicked off with a round of early morning breakfast TV shows and radio slots.

'Tell us, Tom, when exactly did you find out you had a talent for golfing?'

'Well, Rita – and this is kind of funny, which is why I put it in my book – I was about nine at the time, and my father, who is also in my book, which is on sale now in all good bookshops, price fifteen euro . . .'

Debs would sit in reception swallowing back yawns and gagging for a cup of coffee. Not to mention four slices of buttered toast. Breakfast had become a distant memory since Tom had come to town. Lunch, too. Twice this week dinner had been trade events with booksellers, and it was Debs's job to talk to every one of them about

Tom's book, not to sit in the corner and stuff her face with three starters. Drink was out the window too, as it was a no-no to get pissed at work events, and she was too tired when she got home to hit the Chardonnay.

The weekend offered no respite. On Saturday they scheduled a book signing in one of the big bookshops in town. Embarrassingly, only eleven people turned up.

'Who do you have to be around here, Joan Collins?' Tom had snarled.

OK, Debs had been nice so far. She had endured his whinging and complaining. She had found him a cushion for his chair yesterday because he complained that his back was hurting when in reality she suspected he had piles.

But *this*? This was too much.

He didn't know of her admiration for Joan Collins. A woman who had the figure of a sixteen year old, and she must be pushing ninety by now. How dare he sit there and cast aspersions on her? He, whom people didn't even *recognise*?

'I'll buy one,' she said clearly.

'What? Don't be ridiculous . . .' He had grown more and more wary of her during the week, especially after that tale she told him about leprechauns living in the water system of the hotel and who accounted for the strange banging noise in the pipes that he had bitterly complained was disturbing his sleep.

'No, let me,' she insisted. 'That'll up the takings a bit.'

And she went and she bought a copy at the till, watched by the bemused staff, and Tom. Then she walked back to the table and she made him sign it.

He didn't like it. But what could he do? He duly applied his pen, simmering with resentment and loathing for her, and didn't speak to her for the rest of the day.

By the time Sunday evening came round, and she loaded him back onto the plane, they were delighted to see the back of each other.

On Monday morning Debs woke with an urgent desire to be sick. And she hadn't even gone on the rip the previous night; she had been too shattered. What could have brought this awful nausea upon her? Tom?

But as she kneeled over the none-too-clean toilet bowl, shaking and clammy, the truth dawned upon her: blooming Alex, and her vomiting bug. Not content with ruining Debs's life in every other way, she was now passing on her diseases.

Debs was off sick for the whole week. She huddled in bed under the duvet while her stomach lurched and growled and sent her running to the bathroom several times a day. She couldn't even keep a Snickers bar down, even though Fiona went to the corner shop and bought six of them.

'Are you sure you're all right in there?' she had called on Tuesday night through the bathroom door.

'Fine,' Debs had replied, with just enough of a croak in her voice to make Fiona feel guilty.

She had a date at the cinema with Stevo. But naturally she couldn't go if Debs was on the verge of death.

'Would you like a cup of tea or anything?' she called now in an attempt to assuage her guilt.

'Oh, just go!' Let them sit in the cinema and paw each

other in the back row. At least then Debs could vomit and pass wind in peace.

On Friday morning she felt well enough to get up. She staggered on shaky legs into the bathroom. The mirror told her she was a sight; straggly, dirty hair, face the colour of concrete, eyes pasty and puffy. They'd have to believe her in work now, even if Marty had hinted that he thought she was pulling a fast one.

Now for the weigh-in. She hadn't got on the scales the whole week, that was how sick she was.

She pulled them out. A thin layer of dust, and the beardy residue from Stevo's morning shaves, covered it.

'You poor thing,' Debs clucked, wiping it away tenderly with a piece of tissue. No doubt it would repay her negligence by informing her she had gained a pound from drinking all those gallons of Lucozade, the only thing she had been able to keep down all week.

She eased on to it. Slowly, slowly, that's the job . . . no sudden jerks, no threatening movements . . . there. She eased open her eyes and squinted down.

Damn. She had put on eight pounds. Eight fucking pounds! Unbelievable.

'Right,' she told the scales viciously. 'That's it. You and me are done.'

She would buy a new scales. No more Miss Nice Guy. *Eight pounds.* How did that happen? It was impossible.

Then she realised with a start that the dial on the scales was in fact correct. It was she, Debs, who was reading it incorrectly. She had been looking at the pounds, not the stones − which had jumped back by one whole stone. She had *lost* six pounds, not gained eight.

'Oh my God . . . oh my God . . .' She was trembling like a lunatic.

But wait. There was no sense in getting over-excited. She had better do it again. The scales might be having an identity crisis after being separated from her for so long. Or else Stevo had plonked himself on it that morning and it was stuck on his reading. Debs was heavier than Stevo. How sad was that?

She stepped off and back on. The same reading.

The third time she stepped on quite smartly, no inching on this time. The *same reading*.

The fourth time she leaped on the scales with all her might. The dial quivered horribly in shock for a moment, but settled down again. The same reading! Except that she was a pound heavier now, which just went to prove her theory that it paid to take things slowly.

But six pounds. Six whole pounds. She couldn't believe it. It had never happened in the history of her whole life. The most she had ever lost in a single week before, which had been on the F-Plan diet, was three pounds, which she had promptly put back on in a massive blow-out at Pasta Heaven.

'I love you,' she told the scales, tears coursing down her cheeks.

She even loved Tom. All those early starts and dashing down streets for bottles of water must have played their bit too. She would, she decided emotionally, actually read his book. At the moment it was being used as a doorstop for the creaky kitchen door, with the words, 'To Debra. Thanks for the memories, honey,' inscribed sarcastically on the inside flap.

It had all been worth it: the vomiting, the stress, every-thing.

When she hobbled back to the bedroom to get dressed she discovered that her jeans were too big.

'Hurrah!' she yelled happily. Thankfully Fiona was gone to work. In a frenzy now, even though she was still wobbly and weak, she tried on every single thing in her wardrobe. It all was gloriously too big. Except, of course, for the stash of clothes at the back that were actually too small; clothes that she had, ahem, grown out of over the years.

But one pair of jeans still fitted. They were a whole size smaller than what she usually wore. She slipped them on, feeling like a million dollars, even though her bum was still on the large side. It was only six pounds, after all, not a stone and a half, which was what she *really* needed to lose.

'You might put some of it back on too,' Fiona offered tentatively that evening when she got home from work.

'Oh, thanks a bunch!' But Debs had that worry too. Puking your guts up for a week wasn't the most recom-mended method of losing weight and keeping it off. And she had enough experience of crash diets to know that they often back-fired, leaving you fatter than ever.

Still, she would worry about that tomorrow. Right now she was feeling too good to be brought down.

But Fiona was going to have a good try anyway.

'Stevo and me have something to tell you,' she said. She sounded a bit worried.

Little Stevo materialised behind Fiona. So far he had sensibly kept out of any conversations about weight loss and size. He looked a bit off too.

Debs looked at the two of them, standing there like naughty children, and began shaking her head from side to side incredulously. 'Honestly,' she clucked. 'Have you two never heard of contraception?'

Fiona tossed her head impatiently. 'It's not that.'

Stevo looked indignant. Short he might be, but he took his responsibilities very seriously.

He looked at Fiona for a minute. When it became apparent that she was unable to meet Debs's eye, he took the bull by the horns.

'I've asked Fiona to move in with me, Debs.'

For a minute Debs thought they were joking. Fiona, moving out? Of the little flat they had shared for five years now? What about all the mad parties they'd thrown, mostly in an attempt to get off with the good-looking guys from the flat beneath? Didn't she remember the many nights they had sat in moaning about their jobs, and their weight, and the lack of decent men? And then there was the time they had discovered a mouse in Fiona's room. It was debatable who had been more terrified, the mouse or them. In the end it had been Debs who had mustered up the courage to trap it in a boot and throw it out the window while Fiona had run round in circles behind her, shrieking.

But Fiona had forgotten all that now. She was standing there shoulder to shoulder with little Stevo. It was true: she was going to waltz out with him.

Debs felt abandoned, betrayed.

'I'm sorry, Debs.' She looked the picture of misery. Like that was going to make Debs feel better.

'We're hoping to get married, you see,' Stevo explained

rather gruffly. 'It doesn't really make any sense for Fiona to still stay here, and pay rent. Not if we're saving for a wedding.'

Debs was proud of herself afterwards. She stood up tall, and put the biggest, sunniest smile on her face, and she threw open her arms wide and said, 'Congratulations!'

'He hasn't actually *asked* me yet,' Fiona grumbled, but she hugged Debs hard anyway, relief written all over her.

'What about you?' she said, pulling away.

Debs wasn't going to go there. Not in front of the two of them. 'Me? I'll be fine!'

Stevo said, 'Do you think you'll get someone else in to share?'

Debs waved a hand casually. 'Oh, probably. Who knows? I'll leave it a couple of weeks anyway. You never know – I might actually enjoy living on my own!'

And they all laughed, pretending that it might be a whole new chapter for her, an opportunity instead of another instalment in the sad mess of her life. Abandoned, alone, paying massive rent on her own . . . holy shit. This was serious.

'I hate leaving you,' Fiona blubbered, the eejit. Now that the nasty bit was out of the way she probably wanted to open a bottle of wine and reminisce about the good times they'd had.

'Well, don't,' said Debs. She couldn't bear any more of it. 'Because I'll be absolutely fine.'

Stevo wisely took Fiona off to start packing her stuff even though she promised she wouldn't be leaving until next month. But Debs knew that now that the decision had been made, Fiona would spend only an occasional night at the flat. To all intents and purposes she was already gone.

And Debs was more alone than ever.

'Hi again.'

It was the man in the nice suit. Only a different nice suit this time. He was standing behind her in the queue at the sandwich bar.

'Oh. Hi!' she twittered, thinking immediately, Thank Christ I didn't order crisps.

'Haven't seen you in a while.'

It was just a casual thing to have said, but Debs felt ridiculously pleased. It probably showed on her face, sad eejit that she was.

'Work,' she said, with a sigh.

'Another rubbish day?' he said sympathetically.

Suddenly it was a running joke between them, Debs's rubbish days at work.

And she laughed. 'Even worse than yesterday,' she said cheerfully.

It was true. Tom Brunt had phoned up Marty and had apparently said something about her that had him giving her very dark looks all morning.

Bob's eyes twinkled again. He found her funny. Not funny as in comical and ludicrous, the way she saw herself a lot of the time, but wittily funny. Attractively funny — even though she had, predictably, put back on four of the six pounds she had lost. She put the entire blame for that on little Stevo.

Standing there, she sucked her stomach in. Which was all very well until she had to speak again.

'Let me guess,' he said. 'You work in the bank.'

'How dare you?' she said, looking outraged.

He laughed again.

Suddenly she was Miss Witty. Someone had better stop her before she lost the run of herself altogether.

'Actually,' she said, lowering her voice, 'I work in PR.'

She made it sound seedy and nasty, just to make him laugh again.

But Bob was impressed, bless him. He must be in a totally shite job himself.

'Really?' he said.

'Don't get excited,' she warned him. 'It's not all it's cracked up to be.'

But he wasn't going to be put off. 'Who are your clients then?' he said, with such eagerness that she suspected he worked in the bank himself.

She was going to go on about the Christian youth organisation, just to give him a laugh, but then changed her mind. Might as well scrape the bottom of the barrel. 'Tom Brunt,' she said with a bit of a snicker.

She waited in great anticipation for his blank expression.

'The golfer?' he said immediately, even more impressed.

Oh feck, thought Debs. She felt she was leading him on now. Letting him think she had some big swing job, with a whole portfolio of rich and famous clients. Little did he know that her usual home was under the stairs.

'Strictly speaking he wasn't really mine,' she admitted. 'He was actually Alex's client.'

Surely he must have heard of Alex. Debs always had the feeling that she was famous up and down Baggot Street, and that men in office blocks everywhere kept a very close eye on the windows in case she happened to walk past in one of her fitted pairs of trousers: 'Hurry up, lads, quick! It's Alex! Cor, cop a load of that top she's wearing!'

The very thought of Alex made Debs immediately feel less funny, plumper, plainer.

But he didn't appear to have heard about Alex. He just kept looking at Debs with great interest, as though she alone had brightened up his lunch hour. And his eyes were twinkling so hard that she was nearly blinded.

She wondered if hers were twinkling back.

'One Cheddar cheese on brown!' Dodek called, putting a brown paper bag on the counter.

The man in the nice suit picked it up. 'See you tomorrow,' he said to Debs.

'Yes,' she said back. Far too eagerly, of course. But no matter how hard she tried, she couldn't keep the grin from her face.

Chapter Four

Bob was going away for the weekend. It was a work thing. Loads and loads of computer salespeople were gathering in a posh hotel in Paris for the annual international conference, entitled 'Computer Bytes!' which usually meant lots of drinking and playing golf and sucking up to each other.

Bob seemed to be in a bad mood about the whole thing.

'I don't know why,' Geri said. They were packing his underpants. 'You're great at sucking up to people.'

'You're so kind, Geri.'

Well. She had only been joking. She wished now she hadn't gone out and bought him a little travel pack of toothpaste and deodorant and everything, just so that he could get it past security at the airport and not have to wander out onto the Parisian streets on his own and try and buy the necessaries with his pathetic broken French.

'Do you have the map?' she asked rather brusquely.

Bob was short-sighted. He would never admit to this. Really he needed glasses, but for some reason he seemed to think that if he wore glasses his entire personality would be misrepresented, and that people would assume that he was bookish and intelligent, and that they would ask him at dinner parties difficult questions about the European Union and what he really thought of the situation in Ecuador.

'I'm not even that sure what continent it's on,' he would fret to Geri.

Geri assured him that nobody could possibly mistake him for an intellectual, but he still preferred to wander around bumping into doors and having people think he was as thick as a ditch.

And now he was off to Paris on his own. With a map he couldn't read, only by lifting it to the light and holding it two inches from his nose. He might as well put a sign on his back saying 'Mug me', for all the thugs and robbers who would undoubtedly follow him around in droves.

'I have the map,' he confirmed in a very confident tone.

'And your passport?'

'Now, Geri,' he said. 'Cool it.'

He always got a bit cocky when he got out on his own, which wasn't often. It wasn't for the want of trying on Geri's part. She was always exhorting him to go out with the lads and get blind drunk like other, normal men. But Bob didn't seem to have many friends any more, not like Geri, who had about eight hundred close friends, and several thousand acquaintances. Most of these had come about through her extensive involvement in cake baking. She had made ten new friends alone through one mammoth cake sale at the local church last year.

Bob didn't bake. His hobby – playing with his toolbox – didn't lead to many new friendships, although Geri bet there were hundreds of other sad men across the city who also had similar fetishes with toolboxes and who would love to meet up with Bob and form some kind of an underground club.

And there was Maurice, of course, from two doors down, and with whom Bob would have shouted conversations over the garden fence:

'Did you watch the match on Thursday?'

'They need to sack that fucking manager.'

'Don't talk to me.'

Much gloomy shaking of heads and tutting. Then: 'Are you going to watch the match on Sunday?'

'I don't know. Are you?'

'I might.'

Geri usually tuned out at that point.

Bob used to have friends. When she had first met him he used to hang around with a whole gang of people: Bomber Nolan and Philo and Jackser McCabe. Then, about five years after Geri and Bob got married, Bomber got a green card and went to America to set up a pizza restaurant. Philo married a woman from the North and settled up in Belfast, and they fell out of touch. Jackser was still around, but Bob met him only at weddings and funerals now. Geri would occasionally try to set up a dinner date or something, but Bob was never that enthusiastic.

'I'm too tired,' he would moan. 'I've been talking to

CLARE DOWLING

scourges the whole day long. Now I just want to sit down and watch *Top Gear*.'

In one way she couldn't blame him. Imagine having to chat about megabytes and hard disks all day long. It made emptying bedpans look like a walk in the park. He even managed to make his job sound fun, laughing and having a joke with customers. Not like George, the other salesman in the office, who was tall and stooped and had funny, sharp teeth that looked like fangs. George tended not to sell as much as Bob.

As Bob had got older he had become more of a home bird. He liked to mooch around the house at the weekends, fixing things and sparring with Susan – 'You're not going out dressed like that, young lady! Well, OK, if you insist' – and trying to get Davey to watch some football on the telly with him, to no avail. (Davey hated sports. At one point Bob had been quite worried about him.)

And it suited Geri, too, to have him around the place. He was like background noise, comforting and reliable, and always on hand to take out the rubbish or change a fuse. She had even stopped nagging him to go out as much. They were like two old boots, sitting on the couch night after night, flicking channels and letting the occasional grunt at each other. Sometimes it was hard to believe that they were only in their early forties, and not ninety-two.

But now Paris. He'd be away for the whole weekend. Geri would undoubtedly get up every two hours during the night to check that she hadn't left the kettle on and that the alarm was set. It would be just her in the big king-sized bed, driving herself mad with imaginary

62

creaking noises; no Bob beside her, with his solid broad back.

'It's a shame I can't go with you,' she told him in a rare burst of sentimentality.

Even Bob looked a bit surprised. 'But the kids . . .'

Well, yes. Susan would have a rave organised before they'd pulled out of the garage. But he could look a bit more enthusiastic, couldn't he? He could say, 'I know, I'll be lost without you, I won't be able to eat or sleep, and if it wasn't for those miserly feckers I work for, we could be doing the Champs-Elysées together!'

Wives and girlfriends weren't invited to Paris. This rudeness was normal. The company was famous for its tight-fistedness. At last year's sales conference they had tried to make everybody double up and share bedrooms, but there had been a revolt. Nobody wanted to share a twin room, unless it was with Amanda from accounts. Mind you, last year's sales conference had been in Bundoran. They were furious about Paris this year, apparently − all that expense − but had had no choice because the Spanish arm of the company was coming along too, and they had refused to go any further north.

'Anyway, you hate my company dos,' Bob pointed out, looking even less enthusiastic.

'I do not,' Geri insisted. Of course she did. She'd rather spend an evening with Bruce Forsyth than with George and his wife, Lisa, but that wasn't the point.

'You do,' said Bob doggedly. He was starting to annoy her now. 'Look how much you gave out after the one last Christmas.'

'That's because we had to bring our own food,' Geri

retaliated. She had ended up making a massive lemon meringue pie, having received a phone call from the office chirpily inviting her to bring a dessert. Lisa was on starters. The whole party had cost the firm about twelve euro. Mean, mean, mean. Why Bob insisted on defending them Geri never understood. Never mind staying on to work late, like he'd been doing for the past two months. She had questioned him closely about whether they were paying him overtime, but he had gone all squirmy and evasive, confirming her suspicions that they were not.

Innocent. That was Bob. Letting himself get taken advantage of. He would even sit through a wrong order in a restaurant rather than assert his rights.

'Don't complain, for God's sake,' he would hiss worriedly, 'or the kitchen staff will spit in the food.'

But he wasn't lacking in confidence today. 'Anyway, don't say you'd have come to Paris, when you'd have spent the entire time finding things to give out about,' he burst out suddenly.

Geri was taken aback. 'I would not!'

'Or trying to control everything. You've already nagged me about the map and my passport and whether I've packed flat shoes. As opposed to what – stilettos?'

What on earth was wrong with him today? He was normally so placid that unless you tripped over him, which Geri often did, he didn't utter a word of protest.

'I said comfortable shoes. Not stilettos. Wear thigh-high boots if you want!'

'Now that,' he said, 'would look stupid.'

'Anyway,' she said, feeling very hurt now, 'you were the

one who promised to take me to Paris for my birthday five years ago!'

That momentarily blind-sided him. 'What? I did not!'

'I can't believe you don't even remember!' Geri cried, looking shocked, even though she hardly remembered it herself. It had been more of a drunken, 'Oh, we really must go to Paris sometime. Maybe on your birthday,' kind of thing. The thoughts of romantic hikes up the Eiffel Tower had made them all lusty and silly and they had ended up leaping on each other on the couch.

But surely that must be more than five years ago. There had been no sex on the couch in a very long time, not since the kids could make their way downstairs by themselves. Geri couldn't imagine risking Davey, or worse, Susan, discovering her in her greyish knickers astride Bob on the sagging cushions.

'You didn't take *me* to Paris for my birthday either,' Bob retaliated. He looked a bit pinched or something.

Well, of course. She'd treated him at Pizza Hut — what more did he want?

'I'll have your sixteen-inch Meat Feast,' he had told the waitress, voice quivering with excitement.

And now he was moaning and groaning about not being taken anywhere special?

Geri wasn't even going to remind him of the smoothie maker he'd got her for her birthday once. It was as close to a kitchen appliance as you could get.

All the little hurts and insensitivities, seventeen years' worth, began to mount up in Geri now, and she changed her mind about missing him. She'd be delighted when that taxi finally drew up and took him away. Let him get on a flipping plane to Paris. Let him stay there! She would have a lovely weekend, just her and the kids, without him hanging around the place, annoying her, and making his smelly bacon sandwiches that stank the whole place out. And not even cleaning up after himself. Leaving it to her, like she was some kind of servant.

'Oh, go to Paris,' she told him coldly.

He sighed like she was being unreasonable. 'Geri . . .'

'And don't forget your athlete's foot cream,' she said sarcastically before walking into the en suite and slamming the door for good measure.

She hoped he did forget his blooming cream. She hoped he had a flare-up and was in agony. Maybe the conference would include one of those touchy-feely motivational sessions where everybody was required to take off their shoes and socks and play in a sandbox or something, and Bob's feet would cause revulsion and horror, and he'd be ostracised for the weekend. Then he would *wish* she had nagged and reminded him.

'Balls!' she shouted in frustration. Only in her head, though. She did it in work a lot too. If some of the patients could read her thoughts they would be revolted. 'And she looks so nice too,' they would say to each other.

She took a deep breath and looked at herself in the mirror over the sink: a forty-two-year-old woman with shoulder-length, crinkly blondish hair looked back. She had an upturned nose and lots of deep laughter lines running from her nose to her mouth. And – blast it – was that two *new* sets of crow's feet at either side of her eyes? Pretty soon she'd be able to open her own rookery.

She was sadly starting to be surprised when she saw

her reflection these days; to see a middle-aged woman slowly emerge when inside she still felt nineteen.

'It's all downhill from here,' Andrea often said, the harbinger of doom.

As if she would know anything about it, with her weekly beauty regime. And when the time came, no doubt she would pump herself full of Botox. Her lips were already looking suspiciously plump.

But Geri was inclined to think she was right about the downhill thing. Her boobs were certainly a good six inches lower than they had started out. And there were weird flaps of stray flesh beginning to develop on the undersides of her upper arms, even though she wasn't overweight. There was a home video of Bob's mother's birthday party last year, and there was Geri in a T-shirt, clapping energetically as the cake was brought out, unaware that the undersides of her arms were flapping merrily from side to side like little udders. ('Batwings,' Andrea said, unhelpfully.) Only for the home video, she'd never have noticed it. Which begged a more worrying question: what else was flapping that she hadn't yet noticed? Would new horrors be revealed on future family footage for all the world to see? Maybe she should cover up now and be done with it.

She was feeling a bit teary now. And unloved. When was the last time Bob had even given her a compliment? A simple 'You look nice today'? Years ago! Most of the time when he looked at her he didn't even see her any more. She knew this because when she was putting on a wash and finding things to put into it, she would wonder what Bob was wearing that day and she wouldn't know.

Wouldn't have a clue, even though she'd sat opposite him for an hour at the dinner table. So she didn't see him either.

But that was still no excuse for him not telling her at least once a week that she was stunningly beautiful.

There was a knock on the bathroom door.

'Go away,' she growled.

She felt *very* weepy now. Not only was she ancient and falling apart, but the change of life could well be upon her too. Not that Bob would understand. Or if he did he would just tell her she was fussing about nothing, as usual. Oh, he was a desperate, useless lump and she was sorry she'd ever married him.

And now here he was, crawling back to make it up to her. No doubt he would buy her a bottle of L'Eau D'Issey in the airport on the way back, even though she had three unopened bottles of it in the bathroom cabinet. He had given her all of them.

'Don't forget to close the front door on your way out!' she threw at him now, just for good measure.

There was an uncertain pause.

'Can I borrow your Clinique moisturiser?' came the reply.

OK, that was definitely not Bob.

'Give me a minute!' Geri blinked back her tears quickly and flushed the toilet as a cover. It was very dangerous to show any sign of weakness in front of Susan.

She opened the door briskly. Susan stood there in what seemed to be a pink cocktail dress, black biker boots, and enough make-up to replaster the garage.

'Susan?' she said, just to clarify. Often Susan would

have friends over who would wander about the house, all with the exact same iron-straight hair and elaborate make-up, and you couldn't be too sure. 'Sit down there this minute, young lady, and do your homework,' Bob had instructed one of them last week sternly, only realising afterwards that she wasn't his daughter at all. She did her homework, though.

'Don't you have hockey practice?' Geri asked carefully.

'Oh, I've given up hockey,' Susan announced with great relief.

Geri showed admirable lack of interest. 'Really?' she enquired. 'I thought you were aiming to get on the Irish team.'

It had been Susan's whole life since she'd been about nine. She was obsessed with hockey and would practise every minute she got. She would even take her hockey stick to bed with her at night, and Geri would have to prise it gently out of her hands once she'd fallen asleep. 'Bless,' she and Bob would say to each other, looking down at her tenderly. They'd had no idea back then, of course, that she had a split personality and that instead of cooing over her they should have been seeking psychiatric help.

Susan looked at Geri now as though she was speaking in strange tongues. 'No,' she said at last, with a toss of her head. Her hair hardly moved, which was an indication of how much product was in it. 'Me and Rebecca think they all look a bit butch.'

'Ah!' said Geri, nodding seriously as though she understood.

'Have you seen some of their thighs?' Susan enquired.

'Not recently.'

'Huge. Tree trunks. I don't want my thighs to look like that. It puts fellas right off.'

Geri was starting to feel faint at this point. Fellas? And her daughter's *thighs*?

'Anyway,' Susan went on, 'can I borrow some moisturiser? Karen and me are going down the town and I need to put on some make-up.'

Geri hadn't heard of Karen before. It seemed that every week there was a new friend.

'But you already have make-up on,' she said. Stupidly, as it turned out.

Susan gave her one of her most condescending looks. She had it down to a T: eyebrows up, mouth turned down cynically, arms folded across her chest (in a padded push-up bra that could walk across the room by itself).

She gave a little sigh that left Geri in no doubt that she was backward, Neanderthal, embarrassing and should probably be put down.

'This is my *day* make-up. I have to take it off and put on my *night* make-up.'

'Ah!' said Geri again enthusiastically, and was immediately raging with herself. A year ago she'd have said, 'Get up that stairs, you little pup, and take that muck off your face before I redden your backside for you.' Now here she was, pandering to her, terrified that she would go off the deep end.

Geri wasn't sure how she had allowed this to happen. How her authority had been diluted to such an extent that Susan seemed like the forty-two year old, and Geri the child? A witless child at that, with udders growing under her arms.

And they used to be so close, too. From the moment Susan had been born she had sensed a kindred spirit, another female presence in the house. 'Thank God,' she had whispered to her, 'now I can buy pink clothes.' And Susan had chortled up at her – a beautiful, beautiful baby, even if Geri said so herself.

They'd waltzed through Susan's early years together, always holding hands and wearing the occasional matching outfit. Whilst Davey was adorable but largely self-sufficient, Susan was needy and possessive, and didn't like to let Geri out of her sight for too long, to the extent that she had bawled the place down on her first day at school when Geri had gone home. Geri had been secretly flattered – Susan hadn't bawled for Bob, nor was she likely to. Nobody will ever love me like Susan does, she had thought mistily.

Fast forward ten years or so, and the picture was somewhat different. Her lovely, soft, adorable Susan was now a rampaging teen, who wanted body piercings in places that were never likely to see the light of day unless she took up porn acting – and nothing was outside the realms of possibility.

'It's nothing we've done,' Bob kept insisting. 'She's had the best of everything. When she goes to gaol, nobody will ever be able to say it's because she didn't get her three-in-one vaccine on time.'

He wasn't taking it as badly as Geri was. But then Susan treated him as though he was merely a buffoon, some laughable character to be squeezed for lifts and money.

It was Geri she reserved her derision and disgust for. Whatever Geri had done to deserve it she wasn't sure. But everything she did, or said, elicited a look of such contempt, such disappointment, that half the time Geri was afraid to open her mouth at all. In her own home!

It wasn't right. Determined to reassert herself, she opened the bathroom cabinet briskly.

'Here,' she said, handing over the moisturiser in the full knowledge that she would probably never see it again. She steeled herself. 'But you have to be back home by ten.'

Susan smiled at her as though she had cracked a great joke.

'I mean it, Susan.'

'Ten? Nobody goes home at ten. Not even Rebecca, and her mother is a total dinosaur.'

The implication being that Geri was beyond the pale. She felt herself redden. Blast it, now she would have to create a scene to try to win her daughter's respect, but the question was, how? What dire threat could she use? Insist that she would turn up and drag her home by the hair of her head? Tricky, given that she didn't know where Susan was going in the first place. Ground her? She had tried that one last month and Susan had just screeched with laughter. 'Good one, Mum,' she had said.

So Geri just stood there, opening her mouth and closing it again. Great. Highly effective.

Then Bob stepped up behind Susan. Geri forgot she hated him and was delighted at the reinforcements.

He gave Geri a don't-worry-I'll-sort-this-out look before puffing out his chest and telling Susan in his most threatening voice, 'Now listen here!'

Susan turned to look at him and let out a peal of laughter.

'What?' said Bob, deflating.

'Your hair!'

'What about my hair?' His hand went defensively to his head.

'You've had it cut.' She was laughing harder now. Her whole face transformed when she laughed, and she looked sixteen again, instead of a hardened thirty-five.

Geri looked at his hair too. To her shame, she hadn't noticed it until now. It put the whole not-noticing-what-each-other-was-wearing issue into the shade. He had indeed had his hair cut, and of his own volition, which was in itself a surprise. Normally it was black and wiry and tended to grow thickly down his neck, and Geri would have to start making gorilla noises behind him before he'd finally haul himself off to the barber's. One year he had gone so long between cuts that it had been like living with Leo Sayer.

But this wasn't his normal cut. Instead of the usual short back and sides, it seemed to be *sculpted*, and there was gel in it, and somebody had finger-styled the front so that it stuck up in what could only be described as spikes.

It was, undoubtedly, a younger man's cut.

'Was Fat Larry's closed?' Susan asked sympathetically.

Fat Larry was the barber who had done Bob's hair for the past twenty years.

'I just fancied a change,' Bob said defensively. 'I have an important sales conference to go to, you know.'

He hadn't bothered getting a haircut for the sales conference last year. But who would, for Bundoran? The prospect of Paris, and all those stylish gorgeous Frenchmen, must have put the frighteners on him, because not only had he had his hair shorn so that his ears stood out pink and naked–looking, but he had also packed his nice new shirt and those racy socks that she had picked up in Brown Thomas last year at half-price.

'It'll grow out,' Susan consoled him. 'What are you bringing me back?'

'What?'

'From Paris.'

Bob had obviously not thought this far ahead. 'I don't know . . .'

'You could get me some underwear,' Susan told him helpfully.

Bob looked at Geri for direction.

'Underwear!' said Geri, snorting wildly.

'Ridiculous!' Bob chorused on her heels.

Susan speared Geri with another disparaging look. 'Some of the girls in school have French underwear,' she explained patiently.

How she knew this was anybody's guess. Unless they were experimenting with each other in the bushes after school rather than with men. Which was OK in Geri's book – at least there'd be no chance of them getting pregnant.

'I'll bring you back a French maid's outfit, how about that?' Bob joked.

He thought he was hilarious. Geri glared at him. Imagine saying something like that to a teen with a drug habit and a diary full of filth hidden under the floorboards.

Allegedly, anyway.

Geri resolved to sort the whole thing out while Bob was away. In fact she had a whole list of things to do once she had him out from under her feet – including a clean-out of his wardrobe. There were jumpers in there from 1984, awful woolly things with turtlenecks and naff designs on the front that Bob refused to throw away because they were, he maintained, still 'in good condition'. It was doubtful the charity shops would even take them: things were bad enough for the poor people in Africa without making them go around in jumpers with kites on the front.

He was a hoarder, Bob. He still doggedly believed that some day he would get back up on his ancient skis, even though they would now be deemed a safety risk to other skiers. He had also maintained a deep, emotional attachment to several television sets that had been replaced over the years by newer models.

'There's nothing wrong with those tellies. You never know when they might come in handy,' he told her whenever she tried to throw them out.

Geri indulged him. She kind of liked it that he wanted to hold on to old things. It might come in useful when she turned eighty.

'OK, I'm going out now,' Susan announced ten minutes later, having put on the requisite 'night' make-up. Kohl, in other words, and lashings of it.

Bob looked at Geri automatically; she would do the nasty confrontation bit, like she always did, and he would then flap after Susan and do his good cop routine: 'Your mother has been under a lot of stress recently . . . all those muffins she has to bake . . . those old farts on her ward . . .

her mad, crying sister . . . we should really go easy on her.'
That kind of thing.

So it was a great surprise to him when she turned to
Susan and said, 'I think your father will have something
to say about that.'

Bob wasn't a bit happy. Still, he was off to Paris for
the weekend; he might as well experience a bit of pain
before he left.

He gave her a furious look before saying, 'Yes.' Then
there was a very long silence.

Susan folded her arms across her enormous padded
chest and waited. It was very unnerving. Then, thankfully,
he rallied.

'No,' he announced at last.

Yes? No? Now everybody was confused. Susan looked
at Geri, her eyebrows raised. At least when Geri was the
baddie everybody knew where they stood.

'I mean, not until you tell us where you're going,' Bob
clarified quickly.

OK, that was more like it, even if he sounded a bit
nervous.

'Why?' Susan enquired.

He clearly wasn't expecting that. He had braced himself
for an outright refusal, but as for these trick questions . . .
He looked at Geri imploringly. But she remained resolute
and silent. It would be character-building for him.

'Because you might get murdered,' he said at last.

'Murdered?' At least he had her interest now. 'How?'

'I don't know . . . strangled or something.'

Susan looked quite stimulated by this. Geri closed
her eyes in pain. No doubt Susan thought it would be

glamorous and exciting to be discovered strangled, and get her picture in the paper. Websites dedicated to her might follow, and possibly even a fan club.

But Bob misread it as fear and he warmed to the topic. 'I've read it in the papers. Young girls like you going out wearing . . .' he looked at Susan's cocktail dress, 'whatever it is you're wearing. Hanging out with the wrong crowd.' He put a strong emphasis on that last bit. 'Next thing you know, you're in a situation that you didn't intend to get into, and anything could happen.'

'Including me being strangled?'

'Possibly.'

'I wonder, would it hurt?' Susan mused.

'Stop!' Geri screeched at that point. She couldn't bear the conversation any more. She had a paralysing image of Susan lying under some bushes somewhere, her pink cocktail dress torn and dirty, one of her boots missing. Her baby. Dead.

Bob, meanwhile, was looking at her as though he hadn't a clue as to her upset. Not a breeze. He even seemed quite irked that she had interrupted him mid-spiel.

'It won't happen, Mum,' Susan consoled her. She, at least, understood. 'Me and Karen are only going to the cinema, so I'd say the chances of us getting murdered up there are fairly slim.'

And she went off in great good humour, leaving Geri and Bob looking at each other over his packed suitcase.

'My hero,' she said.

He winked. 'Hey, baby, you ain't seen nothing yet.'

Then there was the beep of the taxi outside and they scrambled downstairs.

Chapter Five

Debs fell in love with Bob in the park. They had taken to meeting there at lunchtime if it was dry, and would sit on a bench eating their sandwiches and being watched closely by the ducks.

'Talk about pressure,' Bob would complain. 'Oh, go on then.'

And he would tear off the crust of his sandwich and throw it to them. But usually they were too well fed to bother with crusts, and would intimidate him into giving them the juicy bit in the middle containing the tuna and mayonnaise.

Debs would giggle. But he was like that; a bit of a softie. And polite too. He always remained standing until Debs was seated comfortably on the park bench. She was so unused to being treated that way that the first time it happened, she had looked suspiciously at the bench, sure that he must have spotted bird poo on it.

While they ate their sandwiches Debs would fill him

in on all the office gossip. He always acted like he was looking forward to it. Naturally this made her ham it up to get a laugh out of him, especially bits like the day Marty lost his mobile phone in a shop in town, causing widespread panic – 'I had a text from Westlife on it!' – but had a mental block on what shop he'd been in, until someone from a hair restoration outlet phoned up the office to say that he'd left it behind.

Bob thought it was hilarious. Debs had been rather chuffed. The more self-deprecating and mean she was about the office, the more he laughed. He knew now, of course, that her job wasn't the high-octane rollercoaster that he'd believed at the beginning. Over the weeks she had filled him in – amusingly, of course – on her position under the stairs, and being stuck with the Christian youth organisation's recruitment campaign.

'I'm hoping to tackle Buddhism next,' she had quipped.

More pleasing laughter. See? She didn't have to be the sour, fat girl in the corner. And she wasn't even that fat either, or at least not as fat as she'd been last week. Ruthless self-control combined with many supermarket low-fat ready meals – so small that she had to eat two at a time – meant that she had lost another pound. It might even be two, depending on the scales. It seemed like an awful lot of work for such a meagre loss, but she was delighted all the same.

There was something about Bob that made her very aware of her body. Normally she was merely aware of how large it was. But when she was with Bob she was acutely conscious of the way she moved, and the feel of her office skirt brushing against her legs. She was always careful to sit nicely on the bench, rather than throw herself around the place had she been with Gavin and Liam.

'So, tell me about your career,' she invited one day.

She always seemed to be talking about herself. Which was great, but she didn't want to bore him all the same.

Bob looked rather startled. You would think that nobody had asked him a direct question in years. He almost cast a look over his shoulder to check that there was nobody behind him, nobody more interesting, to whom she might be directing her question.

'It's just a job,' he replied cautiously.

Because Debs herself had such a crap job, she recognised a well-paid one when she saw it. It was in his wool suits, and his shoes, which didn't come from Primark. He had car keys that belonged to a BMW and a nice black leather briefcase.

So he needn't do the whole 'it's just a job' routine with her. She knew about these things. 'You *do* work in the bank,' she cried, mock accusingly.

That had him laughing again. He seemed to think things were safer that way. He didn't want to get serious.

Not that she did either. Good God, no. The very idea. She was only asking him about himself to be polite.

Finally he admitted rather sheepishly, 'I sell computer software.'

'Do you?' she said.

'There's no need to try to sound interested.'

'But I am.' Well, she wasn't really.

'Honestly,' he assured her. 'Because I'm not.'

'But . . . but . . .' All right, so she didn't really want to get into the nuts and bolts of his job, and clearly he didn't either, but at the same time she didn't want to cheat him, seeing as they spent so much time talking about *her* job. 'There must be some good things about it,' she said brightly.

He considered this for a long moment. 'I can't think of any off the top of my head,' he said at last.

The way he was so accepting of his uninspiring lot made her suddenly cross. She conveniently forgot that she herself had been languishing in a total dead-end job for the past three years, and lectured him sternly, 'Well, then you should leave.'

Bob smiled, as though she didn't really understand the situation. 'And where would I go? To another computer software company?'

She should have left it at that, but she didn't, of course. 'If you're that miserable, then you should change careers altogether!'

She really was in pot-calling-kettle-black territory now.

'I never said I was miserable,' Bob corrected her. 'Anyway, what else would I do?'

He looked amused now, as though she was young and a bit naïve of the harsh ways of the world, and she was crosser still.

'I don't know! Become . . . an artist!'

He looked startled. So did she, a bit. She didn't even want to become an artist herself. No money in it, and they all looked a bit crusty and unwashed.

'Or retrain as a doctor or something.' That was better, even if it wasn't that realistic, given his age. He wouldn't be qualified until he was about sixty-eight. 'Or a solicitor maybe.' Dreadful. She should shut up now.

Bob was chuckling now, and twinkling, and she felt silly and out of her depth.

'Suit yourself,' she said, quickly scrunching up her empty brown paper bag. 'But none of us knows what we're capable of unless we try and . . . discover ourselves!'

OK, it really was time to leave. In another moment she would be offering to lend him her vast collection of self-help books, and they could lie down together on the damp grass and mutter hoary inspirational words to change their lives.

'You've done this before, haven't you?' Bob said suddenly.

Oh! It was like he had seen right into her head, and read her thoughts about the self-help books, and knew her miserable history of failed change in her own life. He must know that she was a right one to be telling other people how to improve their lives, when she couldn't even lose a lousy stone herself.

But instead he said, rather gratefully, 'You probably befriend sad eejits in sandwich shops all the time and try to turn us around.'

And Debs laughed. 'Hardly.'

'Am I a hopeless case?' he asked lightly.

He asked like she was the one with all the answers, the successful, accomplished one, and he was the one in dire need of help.

They locked gazes for a moment.

'Not at all,' she said.

They didn't meet every day. Of course not. After all, they were just acquaintances, really: two bored office workers making the most of the early summer sunshine, that was all. There was never any formal arrangement made, no phone numbers exchanged or anything like that. It was simply a question of 'if you're there, you're there'.

Bob was, after all, married. Debs knew this because he had a whacking great wedding ring on his finger, which he made no attempt to hide; no furtive stuffing of his left hand deep into his trousers pocket like some of the guys Debs and Fiona had encountered over the years in pubs. 'Itchy nuts,' Fiona used to christen them. They were always careful to avoid those kinds of men.

Bob also spoke occasionally about his children. She didn't know their names. He referred to them only as 'my son' or 'my daughter'. They were teenagers, and one of them was apparently a bit wild.

She knew his wife's name, though: Geri. He had mentioned it one day, quite deliberately, as if making sure that she knew he had one. Debs had flushed. Did he think she was thick, that she somehow hadn't noticed he was taken? Was he warning her off, in case she got notions about her station? As if! She was only meeting him in the bloody park to get away from Gavin and Liam, whose obsession with Liam's new car – sat nav, hydraulics, alloy wheels, the whole lot – was doing her head in. (Note to self: if she ever saw Bob again, which was unlikely, she must make sure to mention Gavin and Liam. As in, she was perfectly capable of having male friends without wanting to jump them.)

She felt he had cast aspersions upon the innocence of their friendship; worse, that he had implied that she was in some way unclear about the boundaries.

She recognised a boundary as well as the next person. She wasn't the one who had a wife and children in the first place.

She was so cross about the whole thing that she resolved to change sandwich shops immediately. That was the end of Bob, as far as she was concerned.

And so she began to frequent Krusty's at the other end of the street. It was all right, even if it was a longer walk from the office, and they were a bit mean with the ham.

Never mind. It would do her good to lose a few more pounds. The Christmas party wasn't far off, and already Janice and Mia and Tanya were setting off on military-style shopping trips down Grafton Street at lunchtimes in search of the perfect dresses.

'I haven't a stitch to wear,' Janice had sighed.

Lying bitch (Debs wasn't sparing anybody that week). Knowing Janice she had a wardrobe full of Barbie-like clothes that she could wear for any occasion.

Even worse, Debs found herself on the Christmas party organisation committee with Alex. This meant working closely with her to book venue, caterers and other assorted sundries. Possibly it was her punishment for the Tom Brunt fracas.

Anyhow, on Wednesday morning she shuffled reluctantly into the vast conference room to meet with Alex. Normally she was only let into the conference room at all when Marty had left his reading glasses behind and she was sent to fetch them.

But Alex had secured the room for the two of them, and she was waiting for Debs at the head of the table, looking as always like something off the telly in her cream trousers and fitted blouse.

Debs flopped down opposite her, feeling like a rhino.

There was an awkward moment. She didn't think she had ever been alone in a room with Alex, not even in the kitchenette. Talk about throwing two people together who didn't have a single thing in common

'I suppose we'd better get started,' said Alex, cool and in control as ever.

'Yes,' said Debs, scrabbling for her notebook, and hoping to God that it didn't fall open on her latest diet notes. Usually these consisted of, 'Try harder, fat bitch,' and variations thereon.

She cleared her throat and said sternly, 'I think the main concern at this year's event is drink.'

'You're absolutely right,' Alex concurred disapprovingly. 'Look what happened last year!'

This was nothing to do with people getting off their faces and singing 'Come On, Eileen', in their underwear, but rather a *deficiency* of hard liquor. There had been widespread pandemonium when it became apparent that there was only a six-pack of Heineken left and it wasn't yet eight o'clock. There had been unseemly scenes of people trying to persuade taxis to deliver kegs of beer and crates of vodka.

'We should double the volume this year,' Debs suggested.

'I'd even treble it,' Alex advised. 'Marty's wife is coming, after all.'

Debs's lips twitched. Everybody knew of Patricia's fondness for chilled white wine but nobody was ever foolhardy enough to mention it.

The ice broken slightly, Alex wondered aloud, 'What about the food?'

Last year they had gone for platters of miniature lamb koftas and meatballs. These had ended up being used by some of the more undesirable elements as missiles as the night had worn on.

'Nothing with cocktail sticks,' Debs suggested.

'Absolutely. And I think the main priority is soakage.'

'I'll mention it to the caterers,' Debs promised.

The meeting was going smoother than Debs had hoped. Alex wasn't bad, she decided. She might come across as the ice queen, but she really was OK once you got to know her.

'I'll do it if you like,' Alex offered, very pleasant now.

Maybe they could even become friends, Debs thought giddily. Imagine – her and Alex going for cosy lunches together, and gossiping about Marty's wife behind his back. They might even progress to drinking sessions and pyjama parties.

She got a bit carried away because she ended up blurting chummily, 'Who are you bringing with you to the party?'

She didn't want to say Greg in case his name wasn't actually Greg. But at least now the matter would be clarified.

Or not. Alex looked up sharply from her notebook. Debs saw immediately that there would be no girlish discussion on the size of Greg's biceps. She had, she saw, seriously overstepped the mark.

'I don't think I'd want to expose anybody to that lot,' Alex said thinly.

'Me neither,' Debs stuttered placatingly. She desperately wanted to get back into Alex's good books. 'That Janice!' she huffed for good measure, but really it masked a fawning desire to be pally with Alex again.

It was not to be. Alex briskly closed her notebook and said distantly, 'If that's everything then I suppose we'd better get back to work.'

Shit, Debs raged, as she trailed miserably out after Alex's shapely bottom. There would be no pyjama party in Alex's duplex now. She had squandered her chance to hang slavishly around the fringes of beauty and success. Some of it might actually have rubbed off on her.

Alex was just snobbish, she decided bitchily; too uppity to expose her boyfriend to the admittedly robust behaviour at the office Christmas party. Did she think she was somehow better than everybody else?

Well, of course she was. That was just a rhetorical question. But she didn't always have to *act* like she was.

The week only got worse. The new sandwich shop got her order wrong two days in a row. The weather was dull and grey. Work was shite. She didn't even bother storing up witty little tales of the office goings-on because there wasn't anybody to tell them to at lunchtimes any more.

'Are you coming to the pub?' Gavin and Liam enquired the Friday night of that long, long week.

Yes! Actually, no. She was still working on a report for the Christian youth people for some conference they were having the following week. She was tempted to sign off on the words, 'Go to hell.'

'No,' she snapped. The best she could hope for was to limp out of there before midnight and straight home for a weekend of food and misery.

Gavin and Liam were beginning to cop that things were not OK: it wasn't like Debs to let a deadline interfere with her drinking.

'I'll pay,' Gavin offered reluctantly.

'Oh, just leave me alone,' she said.

She heard some unsubtle whispering behind her – 'You stay and talk to her,' and, 'Don't make me. Anyway, you know her better than I do' – and then the office door opened and closed again. When she looked around, Gavin was still there, already wincing. Clearly he had drawn the short straw.

'Look, what's wrong with you?' he asked. Subtle as a chainsaw, God love him. 'We've been afraid to look at you all week.'

So they had noticed. Debs was mildly touched.

'And you hardly ever have lunch with us any more.' He looked a bit hurt.

Debs turned to look at him contemplatively. He was a man, wasn't he? Well, sort of. He might know the answer to her question.

'Do you think that men and women can really just be friends?' she said.

OK, so it was a hoary old question, asked zillions of times before, but Debs didn't think she'd ever come across a satisfactory answer.

Clearly Gavin hadn't either. 'What?'

'Or is there always going to be something else, something . . . sexual, between them?'

Gavin said gently, 'Debs, you know that I like you. I respect you. But as for anything else—'

'Oh shut up.'

Couldn't he be serious, just for once?

'I suppose it depends,' Gavin said, trying his best to look deep. 'I mean, I couldn't be friends with Tanya or any of those. At some point I'd probably let myself down and try to ride them,' he added apologetically. 'And as for Alex . . .'

He needn't say any more. Debs didn't even want to look at his trouser region.

'I probably wouldn't be able to be friends with her either,' he said with admirable restraint. 'But, you know, it's worked for you and me, hasn't it? I've never done anything to you, even after a skinful of beer.'

He winked to let her know that he was only joking.

As if Debs would entertain him anyhow. There had come a point in their relationship, round about the time she had discovered him cleaning out his ear with the tip of his pen, that any fledgeling attraction had been killed stone dead.

Still, she was glad she had spoken to him. It put her mind at ease about Bob. Naturally they were just friends. How silly she had been, getting so upset about him mentioning his wife! There had been no need at all to avoid him the whole week, and even less to change sandwich shops. Theirs was an innocent, enjoyable, even pure, friendship, and she had been hasty in terminating it.

Now that she had given herself licence to see him again, she was in great good humour. She went to the pub after all with the lads and got scuttered, and had a great laugh, and then on Saturday she got the bus over to Fiona and little Stevo's for dinner even though she had been avoiding them, and their cosy domestic set-up, like the plague.

'Lovely pasta,' she complimented little Stevo.

'Have you met someone?' Fiona asked, suspicious at the general lack of misery.

'Me? No.' Which was perfectly true. She hadn't. Not in that sense anyway. But wasn't it great that she had found a new friend who understood her like almost nobody else?

She was so convinced of this that she was even able to admit to herself how much she had missed him over the week. She lay on the couch in her flat replaying snippets of their conversations, remembering in delicious detail the little dimple in his chin, and the way his eyes crinkled up at the sides when he laughed.

He made her feel good about herself. And that had to be worth a lot, didn't it? When she was with him it was like all the negativity in her life was airbrushed out.

Friendship like that was to be treasured. Protected. She had been foolish to throw it away because he had innocently mentioned his wife.

Perhaps one day Debs might even meet her. They might have a laugh over how Debs and Bob, the closest of friends, had been a bit worried in the beginning about the fact that he was married.

'Imagine fretting about a little thing like that!' Geri would laugh heartily. Debs had no idea why she attributed heartiness to Geri. Maybe it was her name. It suggested a certain robustness. She imagined a no-nonsense kind of woman who slapped big dinners on the table and who liked quiz shows.

Finally Monday morning came. Debs woke up bursting to get to work, which was a first. She dressed carefully in her most slimming pair of black trousers, and carefully applied some make-up. She was in work fifteen minutes early, which had Marty running to see whether his clock was wrong.

At one o'clock on the dot she left the office. She turned her back rudely on Krusty's and set off on the familiar path to the sandwich shop.

The lads, of course, were in a huff. 'Don't feel you have to come here,' Dodek said stiffly.

'I don't,' Debs said back, in great good humour. 'And I'd like a bit more ham than that, please, or I might never come back again.'

Bob wasn't there yet. But in her eagerness to see him she was a few minutes early. She took her sandwich and hung around at the condiments for a bit, waiting. There was still no sign of him after five minutes, and then Mr Bean muscled in, forcing her to abandon her patch at the napkin dispenser, and leave. She would wait for Bob in the park instead.

He didn't come that day. Debs ate her sandwich anyway, and talked to the ducks, and enjoyed the sun. There was any number of reasons he wasn't there: he could be sick, or working away from his desk for the day, or didn't get time for lunch. She would see him tomorrow, she breezily told herself.

Tuesday lunchtime came and went without him either.

On Wednesday it began to drizzle and she ended up shouting at the ducks. Then she walked the whole way around the park in case he had somehow got their seat mixed up, and was waiting for her somewhere else.

On Friday it was clear to her that he wasn't going to come to the sandwich shop again. Debs plodded to the park all the same, with her sandwich and two bags of crisps – sod it, she might as well – and tried to tell herself that it didn't matter. She had hardly known him. She would make a new friend, just as good as he was. If fact, she already *had* plenty of friends. What did she need him for anyway, when she had Fiona and little Stevo, and Liam and Gavin? All lovely, trendy people – some of them, anyway. Even Alex was thawing a bit these days. Well, until Debs had annoyed her. But *that* was how popular Debs was.

So she didn't need to hang around park benches like some saddo, waiting to spend her lunch break with a middle-aged computer software salesman. It was his loss, not hers.

It was just as well, because there was somebody else sitting on 'their' bench: a couple, to add insult to injury, who were all loved-up and feeding each other bits of sandwich.

It was enough to sicken Debs. She stood and glared at them for a bit, but they didn't take the hint and in the end she was forced to go and sit on the grass. Which was damp, only she didn't realise it until she got up and had to peel her trousers away from her bum.

She wanted to cry. She walked quickly towards the park exit, her head bent. She felt stupid and emotional for letting herself get so wound up about someone who clearly hadn't read half as much into things as she had. Good friends, indeed. He probably hadn't given her a thought since he'd last seen her.

The couple were still on the bench. They looked really pissed off because someone had plonked themselves on the end of the bench, clearly uninvited, and was munching away on a sandwich.

It was Bob.

For a moment Debs didn't know what to do. Her instinct was to walk by, say 'Hiya!' and keep right on going. That would be the sensible course of action. That's what she should do were they just casual friends.

But they weren't. Everything she'd been telling herself since she'd last seen him was a big, fat lie. The way her heart had jumped upon the sight of him told her that. Her mouth was dry and her skin tingling. None of her other friends had that effect on her.

And then he looked up and saw her. His whole face transformed into a smile of relief. He got quickly to his feet, abandoned his sandwich, and came to meet her.

They stood by the duck pond. Debs suddenly felt shy and awkward.

'You didn't come last week,' he said.

'No,' she said. 'I . . . work was mad.' There was no sense in getting into the whole business of his wife. Not that she could be ignored or anything. But right now it was just Debs and Bob.

'*You* didn't come *this* week,' she said now.

She shouldn't have, of course. She should have played it cool. Let on that she hadn't noticed his absence at all.

But somehow things had gone a bit further than game-playing.

'I've been stuck in the southside office all week,' he said apologetically.

The explanation was as simple as that. Debs felt so buoyed up inside that there was a real danger of her taking off at any moment.

'They took our seat,' Bob complained, flicking a thumb at the courting couple.

'Damn them,' Debs said, smiling so hard her cheeks hurt.

The air between them was suddenly thick with anticipation; a sense of inevitability. There was a tiny crumb of sandwich stuck to his lower lip and Debs was suddenly gripped by an insane urge to gently brush it away. And it was at that moment that she knew she had fallen for him.

'Do you want to go somewhere else?' Bob said at last. 'Just for a coffee,' he added hurriedly, lest Debs have a vision of a seedy hotel room somewhere.

Which of course she immediately did. And sex. Naked, forbidden, dirty sex. Dear God. She felt her face go beetroot red.

Bob was obviously having the same problem, because he looked like he wanted to bite his tongue out.

It didn't help, of course, that the pair on the bench were snogging the faces off each other, and wet kissing noises filled the air.

Bob stared hard at his shoes for a minute, and when his colour was a bit more under control, he said, 'But if you have to get back to the office . . .'

'No,' said Debs. She was surprised by her boldness. Her mother would have a heart attack. 'Let's go for a coffee.'

And Bob threw the remainder of his sandwich at the ducks, hitting one of them squarely on the head, and they set off together out of the park.

Chapter Six

Looking back afterwards, Geri would have said there was a slight distance in Bob. Sometimes she had to repeat herself a couple of times when enquiring what channel he wanted to watch. But that was it, really. He certainly didn't go around lashing out at anybody – that was Susan's job – or being overly critical of Geri, apart from that unexpected gripe about Pizza Hut. There were no tortured looks, or big moody sighs or the occasional irrational outburst in the kitchen about not being 'understood'. They'd all have gathered round in amazement to watch and laugh.

Instead he just went a bit quieter. And because he was normally fairly quiet, nobody noticed a thing. In fact there was a period of about three days when he said absolutely nothing at all, until Susan had poked him at the dinner table one evening just to see if he was alive.

'Can I have some cash?' she demanded, when she had

ascertained satisfactorily that he was, indeed, still with them.

'No,' he said energetically, having had a glass of wine with dinner. 'I gave you fifty euro at the weekend.'

'But I've spent that,' she said, looking incredulous that he should think fifty euro would last all the way from Saturday until Tuesday evening. Also, hadn't he noticed her new denim jacket, which had sequins sewn across the back and which had cost forty-nine ninety-nine?

Clearly he hadn't. 'I'm not giving you any more.'

Geri nodded approvingly. She was always at him to toughen up when it came to Susan. It appeared that he had actually been listening to her all those times when his eyes were glazed over.

'Please, Dad.'

Now she was starting to flirt with him, batting her eyelashes helplessly. When she had first started doing this a year ago it had been so long since anybody had flirted with Bob that he had informed Geri briskly that Susan needed a trip to the opticians.

He was putty in Susan's hands, only he didn't realise it. Geri watched now as Susan smiled her sweetest smile, cleverly calculated to remind him of his lovely, sweet, soft daughter – the one who had been eaten by the sullen, made-up monster in black biker boots who had come to live in their house uninvited.

Bob looked like he was wavering. Geri gave him a sharp kick under the table.

'No!' he said to Susan, back on the straight and narrow. Then, in an unusually clever twist for him, he said triumphantly, 'If you want more money, you can earn it.'

Susan was flabbergasted.

Geri was thrilled with him. Now Susan would know who was boss! (Geri, of course.) Geri gave him an encouraging smile across the table. He managed only a half-hearted response, but he was probably wrecked. He'd had another late night at the office last night. He hadn't even complained, even though he would usually give out yards. It was fecking this and fecking that when he would ring up Geri to ask if she could keep dinner for him.

Last night he had grabbed something on the way home, saving her the bother altogether.

She had been delighted. She was late home from work herself. One of the trainees had taken five attempts to set up an IV line in a patient's arm and they had both been screaming by the time Geri intervened. She'd only had time to cobble together a shepherd's pie that had turned out both runny and stodgy, which was quite an achievement. Also, she was already keeping dinner for Davey, who was over at his friend Ben's, and Susan, who was out in places unknown – with the elusive Karen? Or Rebecca? (Who hadn't given up hockey at all, according to her mum. Geri smelled a rat.)

When she finally got home the hamsters had to be fed. They were Susan's, in theory, bought for her eleventh birthday, and they were called Ernie and Bert. Bob and Geri had only given in at all because the man in the shop had assured them that the hamsters had a life expectancy of a meagre four years, max.

Liar. Five years later, and they were still there, although Susan had long since abandoned them to Geri's care. Geri also discovered early on that Bert was in fact female, which explained some of Ernie's over familiar behaviour, and the pair of them began to reproduce with gusto every time she turned round.

'Mum! There's four more,' Davey would shout up the stairs what seemed like every Sunday.

It was a constant struggle to find new homes for them all. Bob offloaded one on George and seemed to think that that was his bit done. Geri was the one left to hang around the school gates like a drug dealer, clutching several hamsters in a bag, and waylaying innocent mums.

'He's lovely, honestly, and he hardly bites at all. Look, he'd even fit into your handbag.'

Thankfully the hamsters' reproductive years had now passed. Ernie could barely get up on the hamster wheel with his bad hip, never mind anything else. And Bert had lost all interest in her appearance, to the point of shedding hair liberally from her nether regions.

Even though she was fed up of them, and often threatened to drown them, especially when they made a mess on the carpet, Geri sometimes got a bit teary when she cleaned out the hutch now, knowing that the end was near for them. She had grown quite attached to them over the years. Out of her whole family, they were the only ones who were always reliably delighted to see her at the end of the day.

Across the table Bob had somehow allowed himself to get drawn into bartering with Susan.

'Forty euro, then,' she was saying.

'No!'

'Thirty and we'll call it quits. I'll even let you throw in a lift down the town later on.'

Bob was looking a bit unsure as to whether this might not be a good deal after all. '*I* would give *you* a lift?'

'Well *I* can hardly give *you* one. I'm only sixteen.'

Geri intervened quickly. 'Dad's right. You can earn the money.'

Susan chewed her lower lip for ages. 'As in . . . *work*?' she said at last.

'As in, get a part-time job in McDonald's, you lazy lump,' Davey chimed in shortly. So far he had ignored the conversation, concentrating on shovelling forkfuls of pasta into his mouth as though he were on the brink of starvation, and studying the label on his bottle of Coke.

His interjection had a predictable effect on Susan.

'Shut the fuck up, you stupid nerdy fucking eejit.'

Still, she had only managed two fucks in one sentence, which wasn't too bad, Geri thought guiltily, before bellowing, also predictably, 'Susan!'

'What?' said Susan. 'He *is* a nerd. Look at his hair. There could be things *living* in there.'

Davey only looked entertained by this. Besides, it was true. Personal grooming wasn't high on his list of priorities. His hair had grown into an unplanned bob that hadn't seen a brush or comb in a number of years. 'At least I don't let myself get driven around in that dick Leo Ryan's souped-up car,' he said.

There was a deafening silence.

Susan tried to pretend that Davey hadn't said it at all, and went on calmly twirling her pasta.

Geri looked at Bob fearfully. She didn't know too much about Leo Ryan, but she was well acquainted with his car. The whole neighbourhood was. It was low slung and white, with an enormous contraption built onto the back that looked like a fin. It had shiny, dangerous-looking wheels, and logos painted on the side, and so many head-lights and fog lights that it could safely guide a plane in.

But the worst thing was its exhaust. The noise of it shook the neighbours out of their cosy armchairs during *Emmerdale* as it roared out of the estate. Then it shook them out of their peaceful beds four hours later when it roared back in. Sometimes its windows would be down, and wild, anarchic music would spill out, terrifying them all with its menacing *boom-boom-boom* undertones.

'Did you hear him last night?' people would whisper to each other over their hedges at the weekend, eyes sunken from lack of sleep.

Nobody had actually seen Leo Ryan in recent years, because every window on his car was blacked out. You could peer in all you liked, but you wouldn't see a damn thing, except maybe the pits of hell. Apparently Mrs Phelan up the road had spotted him getting out of it one day, but he was wearing one of those hoodie tops, and sunglasses, and looked like he was on his way to rob a bank.

There were other sightings too; him sitting on the wall outside his house, moodily pulling on a cigarette and violently flicking back his long, dark hair; or striding down the street in a leather jacket with a six-pack of beer under his arm (but it could equally have been a loaf of bread). James Dean wasn't in it.

Everything immediately fell into place: Susan wasn't on drugs at all. She was in lurve.

Bob must have put two and two together as well; he

looked back at Geri, his eyes full of resignation, and his thoughts clearly saying, 'Beam me up, Scotty.'

Geri glared at him: maybe now he'd get out that toolbox and dig up Susan's diary from under the floorboards. The only question left was, had Leo Ryan got at her virtue? Judging by the order she had recently put in for French underwear, it was likely that he had.

'Is this true, Susan?' he asked thunderously.

Geri sighed. As though Susan was going to say yes.

'He was just giving me a lift,' Susan explained. Oh, but she was good. Geri would admire her sang-froid if she wasn't so flipping raging.

'She's been seeing him for about two months,' Davey said, eyes now glued to the ketchup bottle.

'I have not!' Susan yelled.

'Six weeks then,' Davey corrected politely. 'Beats me. Guy is an arsehole.'

'Takes one to know one,' Susan jeered.

It was time for someone to come the heavy. A quick glance at Bob confirmed that he was looking about for a napkin — anything — to retreat behind.

It was Geri who cleared her throat in an ominous fashion. 'Susan, what's going on? Are you dating Leo Ryan?'

Susan gave a little snigger. 'Nobody *dates* any more.'

That brought Bob out of hiding. He didn't like it when the kids were disrespectful to Geri. They could get drunk, high, fail their exams, or join an on-line nudist club but give their mother *lip*? No way, José! She had given *birth* to them. He knew. He had been *there*. Well, in spirit, anyway. At one point he'd had to be carried outside.

'Answer your mother,' he said with ominous quiet.

Susan, foolish girl, didn't heed the warning. 'Relax, Dad, would you? You're like the Gestapo.'

It was a mistake to have told Bob to relax (the Gestapo bit wouldn't have bothered him). His was a classic passive/aggressive personality, Geri reckoned: he could putter along for weeks or even months without so much as raising his voice, but inside he would start building like a pressure cooker and it just took one thing – the order to relax in this case – to make him see red.

In a very impressive display, he stood up so fast that the chair went crashing backwards onto the ground.

'Bob,' Geri murmured cautiously, even though when Bob blew they were all secretly excited, so long as his anger wasn't directed at them.

He ignored her, and swung around to point to the stairs, finger shaking with rage, and a string of spaghetti swinging wildly from his lower lip.

'Get upstairs.'

'But, Dad—'

'Now. And if I hear of you in that little shit's car again, I'll drag you out by the hair of your head, do you hear me?'

'All right!' she shouted, but not too loudly.

She sighed dramatically, threw her fork down, and left.

'I hope you die in your sleep,' she said softly to Davey as she passed.

They all waited as her big black boots stomped upstairs, then across the landing. Finally her bedroom door closed with a slam that sent the lightshade swinging.

'Pass the bread,' said Bob, looking rather sheepish. His

rage always passed as quickly as it had blown up. He picked up his chair and removed the string of spaghetti from his mouth.

'Sorry about that, Mum,' Davey said.

'No, no. I'm glad you told us.'

'Although why you couldn't have enlightened us a tad earlier . . .' Bob muttered.

Bob and Davey didn't really see eye to eye. At fifteen Davey was bigger than his father, for starters, which Bob was beginning to find upsetting.

'He could take me down, do you realise that?' he often said to Geri.

The misunderstandings had started much earlier. Bob assumed he was getting a miniature version of himself. Davey had been a colicky baby, though, and rather sensitive, and had been quite unable to handle the way that Bob would grab him when he came home from work and toss him roughly in the air, whilst shouting, 'Who's your daddy!', and would promptly puke. Then Bob would have to hand him back to Geri, one sobbing and traumatised, and the other just as bad.

'He's not like other boys,' Bob had whispered to Geri worriedly once, as the machine gun he'd got for Davey's birthday lay ignored.

He was always trying to bond with Davey through toy imitation artillery. He would doggedly get him tanks and rifles and light sabres, but young Davey would only look puzzled as Bob would launch himself off the sofa with a blood-curling 'Aaaghh!', whilst wielding a plastic sword.

'He's laughing at me. He thinks I'm mad,' Bob would say, embarrassed.

'He doesn't,' Geri would soothe, even though Bob was right.

Later on Bob tried to get Davey into sports. Well, it was a father/son thing to do, wasn't it? To head off in the lashing rain on a Saturday morning to cheer on a crowd of mucky men on a pitch somewhere in a Dublin suburb. But Davey had no interest in sports, not even on the television, even though he would dutifully sit on the couch beside Bob, and let him excitedly reminisce about World Cup Italia '90.

'You weren't even born,' he would tell Davey mistily. 'But Ireland got to the quarter-finals, son. I can still remember exactly where I was when Packie Bonner saved that penalty.' He always got a bit choked up at that bit. 'Which was, um, here.'

Davey would escape as soon as he could and get out his stash of graphic novels and spread them across the table.

'Is he not a bit old for comic books?' Bob still grunted every now and again.

'They're not comic books. You should read one sometime. They're quite clever.'

Recently he and his friend Ben had got into computers. It was all double Dutch to Geri, but they were designing some program, or game, that seemed to take up most weekends and evenings over at Ben's house.

'It's probably a cover. He's probably out drinking,' Bob said, sounding excited.

But he wasn't. Geri phoned up Ben's mother and they were exactly where they said they would be: in Ben's bedroom, in front of the computer, laughing at things that only they understood.

Bob wasn't happy about all the time he was spending with Ben. One day, he said to Davey at breakfast casually, 'How's Ben?'

Davey had given a little sigh. 'I'm not gay, Dad.'

'What? As if I—'

'I know you're wondering.'

'Well! I . . . ! Honestly . . . ! I can't believe you actually think I . . . !'

'And neither is Ben.' And he went back to eating his cornflakes and memorising the back of the cereal box.

Geri had glared at Bob across the table. He gave her a look back that said, 'What? I know you were wondering too.'

'If you want him to spend less time with Ben, why don't *you* do some work with him on his program?' she said to him later.

Bob went scuttling off in the opposite direction. 'I only sell software. You hardly think I know anything about it, do you?'

Geri worried about them. Imagine if she died – of something not too painful, with luck – and they were left to cope by themselves. Once they had dispensed with her remains, probably down by the compost heap at the bottom of the garden, they wouldn't have a thing left to talk about. Geri had unsettling visions of them passing each other awkwardly every now and then on the stairs, and having short, embarrassing conversations.

'Nice weather today!'

'Yes! Anyway, um, see you later.'

Sometimes she was so upset by these sick fantasies that

she would put on a tracksuit and gallop around the park a few times in a bid to ward off serious disease and death. Without her facilitating skills, her family were sunk.

'I . . . suppose I should go around there and let the air out of Leo Ryan's tyres,' Bob said with a sigh after dinner.

He was saved by the phone.

Davey went to answer it. When he came back in his face was full of doom.

'It's Auntie Nicola,' he said. 'She's coming round.'

You never saw a house clear faster. Jackets were grabbed, and wallets, and mobile phones, and there was a general stampede towards the door as though the plague were coming to town.

'Quick, we'd better go out the back way or else we might run into her out the front,' Davey said to Bob.

'Good thinking,' he replied.

They were the best of friends now, of course, holding doors open for each other as they planned their escape. Even Susan was released from exile on the strict condition that she went to Rebecca's house. And Geri would be ringing up to check.

'Would you not stay even for a bit?' Geri pleaded to Davey, even though she knew it was useless.

'No. Sorry, but she's just too bloody miserable.'

Well, yes, but there wasn't much they could do about that, bar drive over to Glasnevin Cemetery and dig up poor Fintan (may he rest in peace). Fintan was Nicola's deceased husband. Hence her misery.

'Susan?' Geri called, hopefully. She was in so much trouble that surely she would try to garner favour?

But she just said, 'Text me when she's gone,' and ran out the door.

'Bob,' Geri called sharply, just as he was about to weasel out after her.

And he used to be great, too. Well, at least he used to stay in the same room as Nicola, and make vaguely comforting 'hmm' noises while she cried at the table.

'Oh, look, she's more comfortable with just you,' he said.

That was his standard get-out clause. Leave the women to it. They wouldn't be able to talk about things properly with a big, thick lump of a man sitting there, spoiling it all.

Really, he was just fed up with Nicola. He never said anything – well, apart from things like, 'Sweet Jesus, not her again' – but in typical male fashion he thought it was high time the whinging stopped and she got on with things.

'Oh, I'll just tell her that the next time she comes then,' Geri would say to him sarcastically.

'Which should be any time in the next bloody hour,' Bob would grumble.

He wanted Geri to pretend they weren't in sometimes when she dropped by. How childish was that! Did he think they were all going to crouch under the kitchen table in the dark while she fruitlessly rang the doorbell outside?

'You know, it wouldn't hurt to tell her every now and again that we're busy,' he said now.

What a heartless man he was. A man made of stone.

'But we're not busy.'

'We are. It's Friday night and we usually watch a film. The kids like it.'

Was he delusional? The kids had just stampeded out the door, no doubt delighted to get out of the tedious weekly ritual of watching a 'family film' with their parents.

'At least *they* have a mother and a father,' she retaliated. 'Look at Derek!'

Derek was Nicola and Fintan's son. He was a plump little fellow with an obsession with light switches, but that was probably because his dad had died so young. He and Nicola were very close. He often climbed up on her lap even though he was ten now, and heavier than her. He slept in her bed too. 'He keeps me company,' Nicola would confide. Geri hadn't plucked up the courage yet to suggest that, at some stage in the very near future, this was going to be highly inappropriate.

'Derek would be fine if everybody would stop fussing over him and giving him chocolate bars to help him get over the trauma,' Bob said grimly.

That was aimed at Geri, of course. She kept a special stash of Penguin bars just for him. She felt guilty now as she imagined his little arteries hardening with all that fat. Penguin fat, too.

'You don't recover from something like that overnight!' she said defensively.

'Geri, the man has been dead nearly eighteen months.'

Geri couldn't believe him. He was a monster!

'He and Nicola were childhood sweethearts,' she said rigidly.

Bob looked at her. 'They didn't meet until they were twenty-two. Why are you trying to make it out to be more dramatic than it actually was?'

Probably because poor Fintan's death had been so mundane. Cancer was tragic. A heart attack was shocking. But Fintan had driven into the back of a tractor pulling a trailer of hay whilst scrabbling to get his ringing mobile phone out of his arse pocket. The emergency services had to find him amongst all the bales when they'd arrived at the scene.

'Cut down in his prime,' the priest had intoned dramatically at the funeral, even though poor Fintan had only been going at thirty miles an hour.

He was always poor Fintan. Overnight he had acquired a certain tragedy, a mysteriousness that he had never quite captured in real life.

Geri felt terribly protective of him now that he was dead and couldn't fend off vicious assaults on his character from the likes of Bob. And as for Nicola . . . she was her sister, and it broke her heart to witness her despair. What kind of person would Geri be if she were to tell her that she was sorry, but that it was Friday night and she couldn't spare fifteen minutes out of her cosy little life for someone with a broken heart?

Not that it was ever fifteen minutes, mind. Nicola tended to stay for two-hour blocks, unless it was a weekend, when this could stretch to three or, once, four – at which point Bob had started to make dinner around them, banging pots and pans noisily in a most unwelcoming fashion. Geri had been furious with him.

He sighed now. 'I just don't think it would do any harm for her to visit Emma once in a while, or your mother.'

Oh, so really it was *Geri* he was concerned about.

It wasn't anything to do with his own evening being disrupted, or his silly male fear of emotion.

She was fed up with him. Other husbands supported their wives. They didn't cook up plans for them to hide under kitchen tables and get out of commitments.

And anyway, he knew very well that Emma could hardly cope with her own life. She had three children under the age of four, and thus was usually unavailable for crying sessions and long philosophical arguments around the question of 'Why me?'.

Nicola wouldn't go to Mam any more. Mam had apparently made some appalling remark along the lines of, 'Plenty of other fish in the sea.'

'I was only trying to cheer her up,' she had said to Geri, bemused.

Besides, Geri was a nurse. Everybody seemed to think that this made her more qualified than they were to deal with grief, and if all else failed, she would slip Nicola 'a little something'.

'Valium, or one of those,' Mam had said enthusiastically. 'It'd do her the world of good.'

Mam was always hitting on Geri for free stuff. 'Go on, it's just a chest infection, you could give me an antibiotic, save me going to the doctor.'

'But, Mam, supposing it's *not* a chest infection?'

'An antibiotic won't do me any harm either way.' She loved antibiotics. She thought they were like vitamin pills: the more she took the better she would feel. When Geri had warned her that antibiotics killed all the good bacteria along with the bad ones, she had been delighted about that too. 'Kill them all, I say.'

Nicola arrived ten minutes later, into a starkly empty house. She looked around and said sadly, 'People are great for the first three months, I find. After that, you'd nearly start to think they were avoiding you.'

She always brought a little rush of cold air in with her, no matter how warm the day outside might be. Davey said it was spooky. And it didn't help that she had long, straight dark hair, a very pale face, and a tendency to dress entirely in black. Tonight she had more than a passing resemblance to Morticia Addams.

Geri tried to compensate for her bad thoughts by doing a great deal of cheerful bustling about – 'Give me your coat, there' – and making the usual massive pot of tea, and getting out the Penguin bars for Derek.

'Take two,' she urged, then guiltily noticed his little double chin. 'Or maybe just one.'

Nicola watched closely as he scoffed down the bar in case she was required to spring forward and perform the Heimlich manoeuvre. She regularly checked him for moles too. When he had eaten the bar, and survived unscathed, Geri let him out the back to play with the hamsters, which was probably safe enough.

'You can feed them if you want,' she encouraged him.

Nicola sank down at the kitchen table with a sigh. 'You're great, Geri.' She was always extremely grateful for Geri's support. She might come round and whinge and cry for hours on end, but at least she was always very thankful to Geri afterwards. Which made it all the more difficult to hide under the kitchen table and pretend there was no one in.

'So!' said Geri, putting on her work voice – firm yet compassionate – and asking, 'How did work go today?'

Nicola had only just started back to teaching for the first time since Fintan died. She had tried to go back six months ago, but had kept breaking down in front of the children. The principal had finally taken her aside when she'd been discovered under the desk, crying, and with all the children gathered round, murmuring, 'There, there.'

'I got through it,' Nicola said cautiously, as though she had been to a war zone and back.

'Good for you,' Geri said strongly. Getting back to work might be just the thing Nicola needed.

'Although I don't think anybody knows what to say to me. They all go a bit quiet in the staff room when I walk in.'

This was a common complaint amongst young widowed people, apparently. It was the lack of empathy. Nobody else really understood what it was like to be died upon at the tender age of thirty-five. While everybody else was having babies and juggling careers and making plans for the future, bereaved young people were burying their own plans in a box. A box, Nicola usually repeated for emphasis.

Nicola suddenly blurted, 'I'm after getting another letter today.'

Oh, no. Geri had thought they'd stopped.

'I can't take any more of it, I just can't,' Nicola said, her face crumpling.

'It's just a mix-up, that's all.'

'I've told them and told them, but they just won't leave me alone.'

Fintan used to be a member of Fit & Slim Gym. His membership had lapsed for obvious reasons, but in the hopes of tempting him to rejoin, the gym kept sending out seductive offers to him in the post. At least once a fortnight Nicola would open a letter addressed to him informing him that his life expectancy could be extended by up to ten years if he spent only fifteen minutes on the StairMaster every day.

The latest letter, produced from Nicola's handbag, warned him breathlessly that he was missing out on the new hydrotherapy pool that promised to relax him like nothing else. Except perhaps death, of course.

'He only joined that bloody gym at all for the children's pool,' Nicola sobbed lustily.

'This is disgraceful!' Geri thundered. 'I can't believe they're so incompetent that they can't take his name off the computer database, like you asked!'

Nicola dabbed her eyes and said, 'Well, I'm not quite sure if I specifically asked them to remove his name.'

'But you rang them up, didn't you? Dozens of times! Honestly!'

'Once or twice anyway,' Nicola said.

Geri stopped pouring tea mid-cup. 'Did you ring them up at all, Nicola?'

Nicola flung her tissue aside rather crossly. 'Just because I'm not as efficient as you! Do you know how many things I've had to do since Fintan died? On my own? It's hard enough to drag myself out of bed in the mornings without posting off blooming copies of his death certificate to every jackass who sends a letter through the post to him!'

She had a big gulp of her tea. 'Could you help me?'

'With what?'

'Letters. I've had the insurance people on, and I can't deal with it.'

The stuff she was talking about should have been dealt with ages ago, by the sounds of it.

'OK,' said Geri, after a moment's hesitation.

She wouldn't tell Bob. He hadn't been impressed at all when she had sorted out Nicola's gas bill for her last month, and that problem with the solicitors about the will.

Nicola looked up hopefully. 'Really?'

'And leave that letter with me. I'll ring the gym.'

Nicola got all teary again, but this time it was from pure gratitude. 'Thanks, Geri. Honestly – I don't know what I'd do without you. I really don't.'

She just needed time, that was all, Geri was sure. Time and a bit of support, and not the kick up the arse that Bob regularly advocated.

As she filled the kettle at the sink to make a fresh pot of tea, she could see Bob through the kitchen window. He was up by the hut, walking back and forth, talking into his mobile phone with unusual animation. Must be on to Argos or one of those.

She gave him a little wave from the kitchen window: *truce*.

He didn't see her and eventually she let her hand fall.

Chapter Seven

Debs was officially a mistress. She couldn't quite get her head around it: she, a *femme fatale*? There was more chance of her crashing through the glass ceiling in Fitz Communications. Anyway, weren't mistresses supposed to be tall and willowy and wear red dresses slashed to the thigh like Kristin from *Dallas*? Debs still remembered them all sitting around the telly at home on a Saturday night, and when Kristin would appear on screen, as bold as brass, they would all suck in their breaths and hiss viciously, 'Boo!'

Debs definitely challenged traditional notions of adulteresses. Her bum went against her, for starters. And her wardrobe. On those first tentative dates with Bob – coffees at lunchtime, and then progressing to an early dinner or two, strictly platonic, of course, or so they had fooled themselves into thinking at the time – she had rifled frantically through every drawer in the flat in search of something vaguely siren-ish, and the best she could come up with was a red top that had been through one wash too many.

Also, she didn't know how to behave. Well, what did mistresses *say*? It seemed to her that the usual rules of dating didn't apply: all that awkward small talk with a new boyfriend about family, and life goals, all that careful sounding each other out. She and Bob didn't talk about family, for obvious reasons, although she filled him in about her mother and father and her proper grown-up sister, Edel (who would, no doubt, have a collective heart attack had they known they were being discussed with a married man). Plans for the future, thoughts on children – all that was pretty much redundant too. Their relationship was in the moment. No past, probably no future, they were just there, on a park bench every day.

It was great. Bob wasn't some twenty-seven-year-old gobshite trying to impress Debs with the number of pints he had drunk, and then puked up, the night before.

He was mature. Sophisticated. He knew big words like 'homogenous' and wasn't afraid to use them. He didn't bore Debs with minor matters, like when he next thought he might change his car, or when Aston Villa might possibly win the cup.

Instead, sitting chastely together on the park bench at lunchtime, he told her about how the moon's surface expanded when the sun rose over it.

'Really?' She was uncertain whether he was pulling her leg.

'Really,' he said, delighting in the look on her face.

He liked all that stuff about the universe; proper, scientific stuff, and not horoscopes or anything like that, which was a slight disappointment. Debs had wondered about him at first: despite his outwardly conventional appearance, could he actually be a bit odd? But he wasn't. He just liked it. And she liked listening to him talking about it: the way he told it, the universe was a wonderfully mysterious and romantic place. The day he informed her that new galaxies were being discovered practically on a daily basis, in his rich, deep and rather dreamy tones, she had nearly swooned.

'We're so . . . insignificant,' she had said. Which sounded awful the minute it was out of her mouth, of course, and she desperately wished she could snatch it back.

But he just said, shyly, 'Yes.'

And they had looked into each other's eyes for a long moment, and Debs had known that she was falling for him in a big way.

(Had Fiona been there she would have laughed her head off. Debs and galaxies? Galaxy bars, maybe.)

Debs lived for their conversations. They talked about deep things: the meaning of life; and sometimes, after a strong cappuccino, the existence of God; you must be joking, said Bob, whereas Debs liked to think there was a benign old fellow up there with her best interests at heart. If only he would get a move on. Still, he had sent her Bob, hadn't he?

And in between all the talk, and the office gossip, the sexual thing was growing day by day. They were acting almost like boyfriend and girlfriend now, even though nothing had actually happened yet. Bob would touch her on the small of her back when they rose from their park bench, for instance, and she would feel her whole stomach tightening with nerves or pleasure, or both. She would give him a quick, half-embarrassed peck on the cheek when they parted at the park gates, like she would a very good friend, although he wasn't her friend and they both knew it, even if neither of them was going to say it out loud.

'So!' she would say, mortified yet thrilled at the same time. 'Same time, same place tomorrow?'

'Or we could push the boat out and meet in a *different* park,' he suggested.

'Do you want to?'

'No, I'm just worried that you'll think I'm a boring old fart who freaks if there's a break in his routine.' He suddenly looked worried.

'I would *never* think of you as an old fart,' she assured him.

He often made little jokes about the age difference betwen them; he, too, was thinking along the lines of a relationship even though neither of them dared mention it out loud.

Underneath it all was the knowledge that, at some point in the near future, they were going to end up in bed together.

And at the thoughts of it, Debs felt completely out of her depth. She hadn't a clue how to be a mistress. She would probably make a balls of it. Should she start flirting incessantly with him, or leaving naughty messages on his voicemail? Otherwise he might feel cheated. If she was going to be a mistress, then there must be some guidelines that she should be following, that involved heaps of red lipstick and a certain type of underwear.

'What are you looking at those for?' Fiona asked suspiciously on one of their shopping trips as Debs fingered a huge, lacy, plum-coloured bra with enormous padded cups and matching siren-type bloomers. They were awful. But the important question was, were they appropriate?

'Just wondering who wears this kind of stuff,' Debs said back with a convincing derisory cackle. Maybe Fiona would say, 'Sexy mistresses,' thus giving Debs a clue.

But Fiona sniggered too. 'Fat old tarts.'

Maybe that summed up Debs too. But she left the underwear behind amid fresh worries that she wasn't fast enough for the job.

Then again Bob wasn't your typical philandering husband either.

Debs knew from her habitual reading of women's magazines in the hairdresser's that men generally had affairs because their wives apparently didn't understand them. She had been prepared for a seduction that involved all sorts of whinging such as, 'We haven't had sex since October two years ago,' and, 'Nothing I ever do is *right*.' No doubt some night he would get drunk and tearfully declare that he had been living a sham all these years but hadn't realised it until he'd met Debs. And that he would leave his wife. Soon. Soonish, anyway.

But he didn't. He scarcely mentioned his wife at all, and then only under extreme duress. (Not that Debs wanted to talk about her either. She was consorting with the woman's husband, after all.) Far from taking her to cheap hotels and leaping on her with a dirty laugh, Bob could actually be classed as reluctant.

So much so that things got a bit stuck around the hand-holding and back-touching. Debs, brazenly, would now arch towards him a bit at the park gates when she gave him her goodbye peck on the cheek, sure that any day now he would grab her and kiss her. It was bound to happen. The tension between them was becoming unbearable. Any day now he would make a move on her.

But he didn't; not even when she took him to a very dark café for their lunchtime coffee, where smoochy samba music was playing in the background. It would melt a stone.

It didn't do a thing for Bob. He thanked her politely and sincerely at the end of every lunchtime, and went on his way.

She began to be a bit insulted. Didn't he *want* things to progress?

Then she got paranoid. She was probably too fat. He might be trying to work himself up to it; build up his courage, so to speak. He might be thinking, she's a lovely girl, but God, that *backside* . . .

Doubts began to ambush her. He might just be in it for the laugh: chat up the fat bird at the sandwich bar and see if he can make her fall for him. Shouldn't be too hard; it was bound to be a fair while since anyone had made a play for her. He might even have a bet on with his mates back at the office. Dear God, they might be listening in on the daily lunchtime conversations in the park via some remote listening device – Debs wasn't too clear on that bit but she was sure it was possible – and rolling around the place laughing as he wound her up about the moon expanding. Worse again, she might end up on some piss-take site on the bloody Net.

And then one night it happened.

They spent the night together.

It was when she was least expecting it. In fact, she had been quite cool to him all week. She was a bit hurt. She had thought they had been pretty straight with each other so far. She knew damn well he was married. He had never made any attempt to hide that fact. But now it seemed that he was growing cold on her. Possibly he had merely been amusing himself and was now bored. He had even phoned her up to cancel their regular lunchtime slot that day.

'I've got a meeting. Boring as hell, but I have to go.'

Yeah, right. It was Friday too, not even tomorrow's lunchtime to look forward to.

'No, I do not want to go to the pub!' she said in a strop that evening to Gavin. These things always happened at the weekend, of course. Now she had two days to obsess and brood and eat junk food. And she had been doing so well too. Since meeting Bob she had been on a rigorous diet: no crisps, no wine, no carbs. Any time she felt herself weakening she thought about Bob's thick dark hair, and the way he threw his head back when he laughed. He had lovely teeth. One had a little yellow mark on it that she assumed was the result of a childhood antibiotic or something, and the thought made her feel very tender.

If ever they did manage to end up in bed, which was looking increasingly unlikely, she wanted to be thin for him, not a porker. She had done so well these past weeks that she had managed to lose one of the four pounds she had regained after losing six that time she was ill. In other words she was three pounds lighter than she had started out all those weeks ago.

Actually, put that way it was a bit depressing. It was *pathetic*.

Every sensible diet plan advised to lose weight slowly, but that was ridiculous.

To hell with it, she'd have a pizza tonight. She was sick of everything. Mostly she was sick of herself for being so stupid as to get involved with a man who was married to someone else.

'Nobody asked you to come to the pub,' Gavin piped up now, adding insult to injury.

She was sick of him too.

'Oh. Well . . . good!' she blustered.

And now here came Alex, all perky and pink-cheeked, to further blacken her mood. She had just come back from a dirty mid-week break with her boyfriend. Everybody knew because she'd been overheard talking in very low voice to a fancy hotel, where she had booked a double room.

'She checked whether the bed was king-size, I swear,' said Tanya, even though everybody knew she was exaggerating for effect. It made for a great topic at the water cooler, though. Janice maintained that when Alex arrived back in the office that morning she could barely walk. Who gave a damn, Debs had thought irritably. Honestly, were they all so in thrall to Alex that she dominated the conversation even when she wasn't there?

'I haven't booked the DJ yet, OK?' Debs said rather testily, before Alex could ask.

She had been left to carry the can regarding the Christmas party while Alex was off getting shagged. Marty had got a hot tip from one of his clients for a guy called Sledge. Imagine ringing him up on the phone: 'Hello, can I speak to Mr Sledge, please?'

'Gay as a lark,' Marty had confided, as though tipping them off.

Debs was unsure what to do with this information so she merely offered him a sickly smile. Alex just sat there, stony-faced. But she could get away with that kind of non-response. Anybody else would get fired. Just like she had taken three days off mid-week, and Marty had let her. Janice, of course, had licked up to him sickeningly in Alex's absence in the hopes of currying favour.

'I'll ring him in the morning,' Debs added rather defiantly. She wasn't going to jump just because Alex said so.

But Alex didn't mention the DJ. 'Bob is downstairs for you.'

Debs froze. 'What?'

Her mind was a jumble of questions: what was he doing there? How had he even remembered where she'd worked?

She slowly became aware that everybody else in the office was looking over too. Janice cast a doubtful glance at Tanya: Debs? And a man? It was bound to be a mistake. Probably a courier who had lost his way.

'He's waiting for you in reception,' Alex clarified.

If she too was surprised she didn't show it. Still, Debs couldn't help thinking, take that, Miss Perfect. Debs had a male caller. A real, live man waiting for her in reception, hopefully in a nice suit and with his expensive-looking brief-case. All right, so he mightn't be as gorgeous as Alex's man, but at least he was real. Not like Tanya's made-up boyfriends, whom she boasted about but whom nobody believed in.

'Thank you,' Debs told Alex with astonishing calm.

It was the best feeling in the world to stand up and turn off her computer, and then sail out past them all – Mia, Janice, Marty, Gavin, Liam and Alex, especially Alex – with her head high and her handbag swinging. She only paused briefly at the door to call out jauntily, 'Have a good weekend!'

'Sorry about lunchtime.'
  'That's OK.'
  'I tried to get out of the meeting but I couldn't.'
  'Really. It's fine.'
Her heart was singing and she was smiling all over her face, even though she shouldn't be. A part of her knew that she was far too eager when it came to Bob. Needy, even. But sometimes he seemed a little needy too.
  'Anyway,' said Bob. He cast a glance at Jennifer, who was watching them closely. He kept it officious. 'I was just wondering whether you wanted a lift home.'
  Debs saw then that his BMW was parked outside the door. Please God let Jennifer have noticed it. Hopefully she would go and tell the rest of them immediately.
  'OK.'
He had never offered to drive her home before. He lived in the opposite direction, for starters, in a rather salubrious Southside suburb, while she was firmly on the Northside in a very much less salubrious neighbourhood.
  The minute she sat in on the soft leather upholstery of his BMW, she began to have second thoughts. Not only was the area run down, but her apartment block was ancient. Perhaps she could pretend to live in the block next door, which was modern and had lots of expensive cars parked outside.

'All set?' he said, giving her a very warm smile.

'Absolutely,' she said back, even as she was thinking, shit, would he expect to be invited in for coffee? What would he think of her tiny flat, with its worn furniture and the couch that sagged in the middle? And the smell. Not hers, she hastened to add. But there was a problem with the drains recently and the stench could be downright nasty.

'You'll have to give me directions,' he said.

'Sure,' she said, her voice very thin now. She was thinking grimy sinks, and grubby mirrors, and the bin in the kitchen that really should have been emptied two days ago. The problem with living by yourself is that there was no pressure to do the recycling, or pick up the trail of dirty clothes littering the floor. Since Fiona had moved out the flat had begun to look uncared for.

Her cheeks began to burn now as she thought of the scales, still sitting in the middle of the bathroom floor since her ritual hop up on it that morning. And the slice of half-eaten toast that she had abandoned on the little telephone table on the way out, late for her bus again. Her flat wasn't fit for visitors. It wasn't really fit for human habitation, if you wanted to get down to it.

'You're very quiet,' Bob remarked.

'Am I?' Of course she was. She was desperately trying to come up with some excuse to avoid inviting him in. Maybe she could give him the wrong directions. She would have to pretend utter surprise when they ended up in, say, Clontarf.

'Is everything all right?'

'Fine. Never better.'

Then she began to get cross. He'd scarcely uttered a word so far himself, except to ask the blooming way. She didn't know why he'd bothered to pick her up at all, if he couldn't be bothered to make a little conversation with her.

'Just great,' she said, even louder.

She was always the one who did the talking in this relationship. Which was bloody hard work sometimes. It was much easier to sit back and be amused by somebody else's account of their disastrous day than to make the effort to actually say something about your own day. About *yourself*, instead of the fecking universe.

'Debs?' He was looking at her worriedly now.

And so well he might! He had revealed nothing of himself in this relationship, whereas she had blurted out every tiny, most boring, most *embarrassing* detail of her entire life to him on that park bench, seduced by the warmth of his gaze. She, on the other hand, knew next to nothing about him. She didn't even know his home address, or telephone number. She didn't know who he worked with. She didn't know the date of his birthday. She didn't know his *children's names*.

She was OK to dish out a few scientific facts to, it seemed, and to have a bit of a chat about office politics. But the juicy stuff, the information about his other life, with his wife and children, his *real* life, that was off limits, it seemed. Not to be shared with someone he merely ate lunch with every day.

'You can let me out here,' she said tersely.

'What?'

'I can walk home from here.'

'Debs, we're at least two miles from the address you've given me.'

She didn't care. She just wanted to get away from him. She felt cheated by him. He was, she thought, a cheat on many fronts.

'Anyway, there's nowhere to pull in.' He was confused now. Let him be. 'Look, what's wrong?'

'There's nothing wrong with *me*.' She sat as far from him as she could, pressed up against the passenger door rigidly, and wishing she'd never met him. He, in turn, turned his face away from her, hurt, and drove on in silence.

The traffic was mental, of course, and by the time they finally reached her flat, a chainsaw wouldn't have cut the atmosphere.

He turned to her in the car. 'I said I was sorry about lunch.'

She stared at him. 'You think that's what this is about? You missing lunch? Not that I know what meeting you were actually *at*, or even who you were with!'

He was still looking baffled. 'You want to talk about *George*?'

'No, I . . .' She tried to sound calm. 'I've just realised that we're virtual strangers.'

'What?'

'We don't really know each other at all.'

'Well, what do you want to know?' he said, looking eager to sort this out. 'You just have to ask.'

Oh, so now she was supposed to get the information out of him question by question. It would be like pulling teeth.

'It doesn't matter,' she said curtly. 'Thanks for the lift.'

And she got out of the car and slammed the door on his bewildered face – men were so thick – and she didn't look back.

She had reached the top of the front steps when he finally caught up with her, huffing and puffing. 'Debs, wait.'

She didn't turn around. 'I don't want to talk, OK?' she said, stabbing her key in the door.

'I got these for you. You might as well have them even if you never want to see me again.'

He was holding out a bunch of flowers – a gorgeous bouquet of lilies and daisies, her favourite. He must have had them in the boot.

But she couldn't just *take* them. Not after all that.

'Give them to your wife,' she said coldly.

He gave her a reproachful look, which had the effect of making her feel rather small and cheap. 'If you don't want them you can throw them in the bin.'

And he plonked them into her hand and turned to go, jaw stiff with hurt.

Now she didn't want him to go. Not like this, anyway.

'Why did you give me a lift home anyway?' she asked, still rather petulant.

He waited, his hands dug deep into his trousers pockets. 'Because it just so happens that I have a free evening.' That was a first. Debs grew still. 'I thought we might have dinner or something. Spend some proper time together.' His raised an eyebrow at her. 'I could fill you in on all those important bits of personal information that you don't know, such as my shoe size and the fact that I'm allergic to nuts and if I even see one I swell up like a puffer fish. Bet you didn't really want to know that.'

Debs gave a reluctant smile.

'Look, we mightn't know every little detail about each other, but we know the things that are important.' He looked a bit embarrassed. 'At least I think so anyway.'

He was breaking her down. Again. She couldn't even sustain a tantrum in the face of his, well, loveliness.

'I suppose,' she said.

'Will you have dinner with me? That is, unless you've got other plans?'

The smart thing to do was probably to lie, and tell him that she *did* have other plans. She could let on that she was going out to dinner with a mysterious person. A proper, accomplished mistress would do that. Keep them hanging.

Instead she smiled happily, and said, far too enthusiastically, 'I don't.'

'Well, then,' he said.

'How much time have you got?' she asked.

He shrugged. 'The kids are both on sleepovers and Geri's on a night shift.'

There was a little silence.

It wasn't hard to do the calculations. He didn't have to go home that evening. He had all night.

'Oh! Right!' said Debs, her voice coming out in a horribly unsophisticated squeak.

She must have looked terribly naïve or something, or else completely petrified, because Bob said, soothingly, 'I have a couple of hours anyway.'

'Sure. OK.'

He looked around the rather dingy neighbourhood. 'So! Where would be good to eat around here?' He kindly tried not to sound incredulous.

'There's a pizza place around the corner . . . Or else I could rustle up something?'

'Are you sure?'

'Absolutely,' she said, trying desperately to sound like a sophisticate who entertained married men at her home the whole time. Inwardly she prayed that she had a bag of pasta in the press.

Bob pretended not to notice the state of her flat.

'Nice view,' he commented charitably from the living room.

Debs, meanwhile, cobbled together a spaghetti bolognese in the tiny kitchen, completely forgetting that it was one dish you should never consume on a first date. And it felt like a first date. Now that the sex thing may finally have come to pass, she was petrified. Her hands were shaking and she was throwing back white wine for courage.

'Lovely,' said Bob, complimenting her pasta.

He seemed to mean it too, because he was actually eating it.

Debs couldn't eat a thing, another first. Her stomach was churning sourly. She wondered whether it was possible to sneak off to the bathroom and brush her teeth silently. She just wasn't ready for this. She thought she was, but now that it was here, hanging between them, she'd rather have jumped off the end of a pier.

And there was Bob, watching her with those lovely

brown eyes, and she was even more nervous. He probably thought he was in for a whale of a night. A girl like
Debs, who had invited a married man into her flat, and
cooked for him, was bound to be a right little goer. Little
did he know that she wanted to vomit.

'Dessert?' she blurted.

Immediately she blanched. Did he think she was
offering sex? Was he going to say, 'Yes, please!' and stand
up and whip his clothes off?

But he just said, 'That would be nice,' and remained
fully dressed.

She stumbled into the kitchen, only to realise that there
was no dessert. She thought she'd had a tub of ice cream
in the freezer, but obviously she had been struck by the
munchies some night previously because there was
nothing in the tiny freezer box except a couple of dodgy
fish fingers.

She rifled through the presses and found two Snickers
bars. They would just have to do.

She leaned against the sink, cooling her palms on the
stainless steel, trying to buy time. Because once the meal
was over, then surely it would be time to get down to
the dirty deed.

He was married. She'd tried to play it down, but now
that the moment had come, she couldn't get past it. She
had somebody else's husband in her flat, and she had secretly
changed the sheets on her bed while he had nipped out
to the corner shop for the bottle of white wine.

I am evil, she thought miserably. This whole thing was
wrong.

'Everything all right?'

Bob was standing in the doorway.

'I have no dessert,' she admitted, trying to cover up. 'Except for Snickers bars.'

And he laughed. And it was such a lovely sound that she laughed too, and the funny tension finally broke, and they were Bob and Debs again, and she felt fine.

'I love Snickers bars,' he said, and the way he looked at her said that he wasn't talking about Snickers bars at all, and Debs could hear a funny humming in her ears.

'So do I,' she said, although that was probably obvious.

And then Bob took her in his arms and kissed her, and it felt so natural and right that Debs didn't care any more about him being married, because something this good couldn't be wrong, could it?

It was perfect. He was perfect. She had only one moment of pure self-doubt, and that was about her bottom when he was about to ease her trousers off in the bedroom. Would he be shocked when confronted with all that cellulite and the little handlebars of fat sitting on her hips?

'I'll just pull the curtains,' she whispered. They were the thick, dense blackout kind, hand-sewn by her mother to keep out those awful, harsh city lights, and dampen down the sound of the sirens that she was sure pulsated through Dublin city the whole night long, wrecking your sleep.

They would come in handy now to camouflage Debs's naked body.

'We don't want the neighbours seeing,' she explained to Bob, who seemed to buy it, even though the place was now so dark that visibility was reduced to zero.

Debs took off her own trousers and groped her way

to the bed, while Bob did likewise, only bumping into the locker once.

'Damn.'

'Are you OK?

'Fine, it's just my toe . . .'

They lay down on the bed. Debs always felt skinnier lying down. Her stomach flattened out nicely, although the downside was that her boobs did too. She arranged her thighs to their best possible advantage – no easy task – and then, when there was nothing else she could do to make herself smaller, gave herself up to their lovemaking.

Bob's experience showed. There was no panicked grappling with her bra fastening, or nasty premature ending, followed by a sheepish, 'Sorry'. Somebody else had broken him in, all right, even if Debs felt a bit guilty about reaping the benefits. Out of ten she'd have given him nine. (She and Fiona used to rate men. Anything over five was a find. Seven was in the gifted department. Fiona had boasted she'd had an eight once, although Debs had her doubts.)

But it was about so much more than technique. Bob held eye contact with her through the whole thing, even in the pitch-darkness, which she found amazingly erotic, having been used to fellows who mostly engaged with her breasts. He did things like stroke her hair, and say her name, and she was completely sure that, to him, it was about much more than just riding her.

Please God, anyway.

Because it was for her.

'You're lovely,' he said, with gratifying sincerity and feeling, and she began to relax.

And after a bit it didn't matter about her bum. It didn't

even matter about her little single bed – installed by the landlord in a misguided attempt to force abstinence upon his tenants – although Bob clearly was used to something king-sized as there were one or two mishaps. And when it was over they fell asleep in each other's arms and he was still there when she awoke briefly at four a.m., even if he had one foot on the floor to balance himself.

'I'll ring you later,' he whispered as he left at seven. She knew his wife's night shift ended at eight. After he had gone she lay there thinking of him letting himself into his house, which she had never seen, and putting on the kettle for a cup of tea for his wife when she arrived in, tired and blissfully ignorant, and the magic of the previous night fell away and Debs felt a little bit flat.

But then Bob texted ten minutes later, from his car, to tell her how wonderful the night had been and how he couldn't wait to see her again.

And so Debs officially became a mistress.

In the mornings now, after weighing herself – still no significant downshift, dammit, even with energetic sex twice a week – she examined herself in the mirror for a long time, turning her head this way and that.

She thought she would look different somehow. Mysterious. She was hoping that maybe she had a secret Mona Lisa smile in a certain light.

But she was still the same old Debs, although she made more of an effort with her make-up now, and she had gone out at the earliest opportunity and bought one of those scary bras when she wasn't with Fiona.

Her and Bob still met at lunchtimes every day. They would sit as close together as they dared, and hold hands surreptitiously under their sandwich bags. Bob would sometimes bring her a little bunch of flowers, or a bag of cheese and onion Walkers, (she was far too embarrassed to tell him she was on a diet, and always behaved as though she was just 'big-boned'), and they would bend their heads together, laughing and whispering silly things to each other.

He would come back to her flat twice a week, usually Tuesdays and Fridays. He didn't come into the office to collect her again. Instead she would hurry out at five minutes to six and wait for him on the corner. He would draw up in his car, having already phoned home to say that he would be working late.

She would cook for him in the flat: pasta, stir fries, omelettes – things that could be whipped up easily and eaten before they hurriedly retired to the bedroom. He would have to go soon afterwards, kissing her and promising to text her on the way home.

He always did: 'See you at one tomorrow for a ham and cheese sandwich xx.'

It was a pretty big trip for a fat girl from County Leitrim. Every night she would press her head into the pillow, able to smell him even though he wasn't there. And she would lie there and replay their last conversation, or picture the little scar on his forehead that he'd said was from a fall off his bike when he was nine. She would sleep for as long as she could, trying to pass the hours until he was back in the flat, in her arms, and she would feel complete again.

Chapter Eight

Bob and Geri met when they were both students working part time in an American-style burger joint off Grafton Street in Dublin. Ireland was in deepest recession and any kind of a job was a great bonus, and to be hung on to at all costs. Geri came on shift one Saturday morning to find that a new, short-order cook had started upstairs. She went up, adjusting her uniform of deeply unflattering white frilly apron and boat hat, to find Bob filling one of the big deep-fat fryers with clean oil. He wore a boat hat too, and had longish hair tucked neatly into a net, and a boyish face. He was very industriously emptying a large container of vegetable oil into the fryer. Clearly he had got in nice and early and was already ahead with the day's tasks.

Geri approved of punctuality and hard work. (Was she a pain in the arse even back then?)

'Hi,' she said.

'Oh. Hello.' He seemed shy, but friendly. 'How many of these does this thing take?'

'Just the one,' she said, confused.

His face froze. 'What?'

And they both looked down at the same time to see a massive oil slick spreading around their feet like a malevolent shadow.

The source of the slick was the back of the deep fat fryer.

'Fuck,' Bob said, paling. 'I forgot to put the plug back in.'

Geri, with two years of nursing training already under her belt, wasn't scared of a mess. She took a catering-sized roll of kitchen paper, efficiently tore off a wad, and said, 'Here. Start mopping.'

It took them an hour to clean up the oil, and then the floor had to be washed three times with soapy water. They worked on their hands and knees side by side, only rising to get some more kitchen roll when they ran out. By the time the supervisor arrived in, blessedly late, there was no sign at all that, half an hour previously, the place had been like an ice rink.

Bob was pathetically grateful. 'I'd kiss your feet only they're a bit oily.'

'You're welcome,' Geri said. She had quite enjoyed her little rescue mission. Her cheeks were rosy red from the exertion, and Bob's admiring eyes on her back were gratifying.

He was now trying to fit the plug back into the fryer, which he should have done in the first place. The way he scratched his head and said 'Hmm' in a puzzled voice made her suspicious.

'You've done this before, right?'

Waitresses they hired off the street, so long as they were half competent and didn't have too much of a drink problem. But the cooks were always at least semi-qualified. Nobody wanted to risk poisoning half of Dublin with undercooked chicken burgers.

'No,' he admitted.

Geri looked over at the supervisor. 'But how did you . . . ?'

'I lied.' And the way he said it was so open, so lacking in cunning, and yet so deliberate, that she laughed.

'You couldn't show me the ropes, could you?' he begged.

She should have told him to get lost. She was already way behind in her own work. But she did anyway, pointing out where the cold room was, showing him how to clean down the grill, and even how to flip a burger.

'And now you're on your own,' she told him sternly at the end of the improvised session.

'You're magnificent,' he told her with humble gratitude.

That evening she saw him at a bus stop in the pouring rain, stoically waiting for his bus home. She was hurrying by under a brightly coloured umbrella and wearing a slick of her new Cherry Bloom lipstick.

'I don't suppose you'd like to go for a drink?' he asked. 'Just to say thanks.'

'There's no need,' she said.

He hadn't needed her help for the rest of the day. Any time she'd looked over at him he was diligently firing out bowls of fries, and managing to fool the supervisor that he'd been doing it all his life.

'I'd like to,' he said, looking at her in that shy, yet steady way that she found rather appealing.

'I can't,' she said. 'I'm . . . meeting someone.'

A boyfriend. She didn't need to say it.

'Ah,' said Bob. 'No problem.'

She thought he would be a bit embarrassed in work next day. But not a bit of it. He just went on flipping burgers and making fries as usual, and waved at her cheerily as though they were the best of friends.

He asked her out again a month later.

She laughed. 'I'm still going out with my boyfriend.'

'OK,' he said, smiling too. 'I'll wait.'

It was all hugely flattering, even though she brushed it off as a running joke amongst the other staff. Everybody knew that Bob, the rather dreamy-looking new guy, had fallen for Geri, the waitress with the loud laugh who didn't take any crap from the customers.

The day after she broke up with her boyfriend – she couldn't even remember his name now – Bob came up to her again.

'You've no excuse now,' he said.

He took her to a big, dark, run-down pub on Baggot Street with a handful of grungy-looking customers. A band was setting up on a tiny stage near the front. Bob got her a drink and settled her at a table.

'See you in a little bit,' he said, and then, to Geri's utter surprise, he stepped up on stage and joined the rather motley-looking band. He sat down behind the drum kit. She watched, fascinated, as he picked up his drumsticks and began to warm up. He didn't look at her again. There was the shyness of an artist about Bob, the introspection.

The band was called The Balbriggan Rats (out of respect

for The Boomtown Rats), and it was their third gig ever. They were brutal. The lead singer was so nervous that his voice kept breaking hysterically, like he was fourteen again, and the guitarist had to turn his back because he maintained he couldn't play with everybody looking at him. Bob valiantly kept things going in the background, belting away at the drums as hard as he could with his thin, sinewy arms.

Geri found herself clapping furiously at the end to try to make them feel better.

'You've very kind,' said Bob when he rejoined her. He knew they'd been crap too.

'You never said you were in a band.' Most other guys would have broadcast it in the hopes of pulling girls if nothing else.

'It's what I'm going to do full time,' he told her steadily.

She smiled. 'And what about your computer course?'

He thought she was making fun of him. 'That's just to keep my parents happy,' he said dismissively. 'I probably won't even finish it.'

'Sure,' she said quickly.

'We're getting a new singer. We're going to rehearse three times a week. We'll cut a demo next summer, take it around the studios in London, see if we can get a deal.'

He sounded utterly convinced. She believed him.

'We need some groupies,' he told her seriously.

Geri found herself laughing.

'But we're very choosy.' And he gave her a look that warmed her to the soles of her feet.

His perseverance was infectious. She felt hugely desirable, even though every now and again over the years she would wonder whether she hadn't so much been won over as worn down.

For years now Bob had complained bitterly about the dwindling sex. Well, bitterly for him, which meant going around with a face like a slapped arse, or giving a rather mournful sigh in bed when she promptly turned her back on him and snapped the light off.

'I'm tired, Bob.'

It was the truth. She was knackered. Most nights she was too tired even to do the whole cleanse, tone and moisturise routine, and instead used one of those all-in-one facial wipes, even through Andrea warned her sternly that it would take her skin the whole night to overcome the abuse. Honestly, was there anything left in the world that you didn't have to feel guilty about?

'I'm tired too,' Bob would return bravely. 'But I'm prepared to make the effort.'

Well, yes, but what effort was involved on his part really when it came down to it? All Geri had to do was put on what had been known for years now as her Sex Nightie – as opposed to her lovely comfy flannel pyjamas – and he was all excited and raring to go. They were such simple, basic creatures, men.

Whereas for *Geri* to get in the mood was a complete production. Years ago all it took was two glasses of red wine. But now the evening had to start much earlier for her, beginning with a nice, non-confrontational family dinner, where nobody stormed off or announced their intention to get their tongue pierced. This had to be followed by a quiet evening on the sofa snuggled up to

Bob where hopefully he wouldn't say anything too stupid to antagonise her, such as, 'Oh, who wants to watch Colin Firth – *Match of the Day* is on over on Five.'

This cosiness was accompanied by the prerequisite glass of wine, although one glass was enough nowadays to get her a bit piddly-eyed, and she would lay her head on his shoulder, and enjoy an earnest heart-to-heart with him, which usually involved confiding her fears about Susan, and her determination to book their annual holiday on time that year. She presumed he was listening, because he would murmur every now and again, 'Yes, yes, I know exactly what you mean.'

At bedtime she would have a quick swipe of a facial wipe and then whip on the Sex Nightie, which Bob would whip off just as quickly. It would be getting late at that point, no time to hang about, and they would assume the missionary position post-haste and the whole deed would be over and done within ten minutes, thank God, and they would be asleep by midnight.

But to do all that *twice a week*?

Every so often there would be some disturbing poll in the Sunday newspapers – although not usually the 'quality' papers, it should be pointed out – that concluded that married people on average had sex twice a week. Twice a week? The first time Geri had read this she had gone around for a whole week feeling terribly inadequate, and viewing all her married neighbours and friends suspiciously, sure that they must all be having rakes more sex than she and Bob. Then, after a couple of years and dozens more polls, Geri realised the truth: the poll respondents were only saying they had loads of sex because they were too embarrassed to look the pollster in the eye and tell him or her the truth: that they had it once a fortnight like every other tired, overburdened married couple, if they were lucky, and that it was the usual fumble under the sheets, the same tired words spoken, the same ritual, and they could virtually do it in their sleep. Which, actually, would be very handy: the older you got, the more sleep became an issue, especially in the days around a cake sale or a junior sporting event, and most married couples would probably have a lot more sex if they *could* do it in their sleep.

Twice a week, her eye. Hogwash! She wasn't inadequate at all; she was just one of the few honest people left in the world.

But then Bob would say, 'Pass me the Sunday paper,' and the trouble would start.

Poor Bob: the problem was that he wasn't as discerning as Geri, and didn't cop that most of the respondents had lied through their teeth. He would get his hopes up pathetically, and would leave the newspaper open on the relevant page in a very prominent position on the coffee table, on the off-chance that she hadn't seen it. If she ignored it, which she always did, he would move it to the kitchen and place it strategically on the worktop. She would eventually briskly use it to line that damp patch under the washing machine.

Cue a week of resentful, deprived looks on his part, to the point where she would lose her rag and throw on her Sex Nightie on a Tuesday or a Wednesday night and shout, 'Come on then, for feck's sake, if you think everybody else is having so much more than you! Get it out then!'

In recent years they had come to an unspoken compromise. They had sex once a week, but only at the weekends where nobody had to get up for work in the morning, or make school lunches.

This arrangement didn't hold when Geri was on a night shift, obviously, or when Bob had to go into work on Saturdays (this had happened once or twice recently), or when one of the kids was sick, or missing, or playing loud music in his or her room until two a.m. All of which happened more often than one might think.

Tonight was Saturday night.

Sex night.

Geri wasn't on a night shift. Bob wasn't required to be in work. The only impediment to the act was Nicola, who was sitting at the table on her third cup of tea.

The tragic look on her little face would extinguish the rampaging lust of a seventeen year old let loose in Temple Bar and with thirteen pints of lager under his belt.

'I just can't choose between the Sunset Red and the Starlight Pink – what do you think, Geri?'

These were not colours of a flashy new dress, unfortunately, or a new shade of paint for the house. They were the colour of memorial stones for Fintan's grave.

At least she was getting around to it. Up to now she had found it too painful, and so poor Fintan had gone without a headstone for nearly twenty months now. After those fierce rains in March it had been touch and go whether they'd ever be able to locate him again.

'The red is quite eye-catching,' Geri said. 'It kind of suits Fintan's personality, don't you think?'

Privately, she thought that the Cloudy Grey would probably be more appropriate in that case, but she was trying to keep things upbeat.

'I just can't make up my mind.' Nicola chewed her lip worriedly. 'I mean, this is something I'll have to look at for the rest of my life.'

Geri looked at her sideways. 'Exactly how much time *do* you spend in the cemetery?'

This was meant as a little joke. But Nicola considered it for a bit, and then counted up on her fingers. 'Well, we go on a Sunday after Mass, and then on a Wednesday night so that Derek can tell him the results of the football. And we usually pop in on Monday on our way home from swimming.'

Was she for real?

'You go *three times a week*?'

'It's for Derek's sake more than anything else,' Nicola insisted.

In the name of God, would somebody not take that girl out and get her blind drunk instead of letting her hang around cemeteries like a ghoul in those awful black clothes and dragging that fat little child after her, Mam was always exhorting Geri and Emma. She'd take her herself only she was hopeless to hold her drink and was usually asleep after two sherries.

Emma wasn't any better. 'The pub? *Me? Tonight?!*' She always sounded hysterical on the phone these days.

Excuses, Bob muttered, but only when he thought Geri couldn't hear him. As if Emma had had three kids in three years just to spite everybody.

'Let's just choose one, will we?' Geri said to Nicola

rather impatiently. They had been on page one of the brochure now for over an hour and there were five more pages to go. And that wasn't including the separate brochure on fibreglass statues and plastic floral arrangements 'for that everlasting touch'.

But Nicola had lost interest in the brochure. 'Derek was asking whether we're going on a summer holiday this year.'

They hadn't last year. Nicola hadn't felt up to it. Instead they had joined Geri and Bob and the kids in West Cork on their holiday, for a long weekend. Which had turned into six days. It was just while it was all so fresh, Geri had explained to everybody.

'You should. Go to the sun. You'll have a great time.'

'Oh, I don't know,' said Nicola. 'The two of us rattling around Majorca for two weeks? What would we *do*?'

'Swim. Go to the beach – what everybody else does.'

Nicola just looked more disconsolate. 'What did you say you were doing this year?'

She knew well what they were doing. They were planning to go to the West for two weeks, to a cottage, maybe at the end of August. Geri had meant to book it last week. The kids had already started a campaign to get out of it.

'Just the usual,' she said.

'I'm just thinking. It'd be great if we all went together again, wouldn't it?'

'I think those cottages are quite small . . . and Bob's keen to do a lot of day trips, just the four of us . . .' She was blushing now with all the lies.

'Sorry. He probably doesn't want me muscling in,' Nicola said quickly.

'No! No, not at all,' Geri cried, doing her over-compensating bit, as usual. 'It's just . . . well . . . I'll talk to him.'

Coward. She was raging with herself. What was wrong with her that she couldn't explain in simple, mature tones that they needed their space? That *she* needed her space? Now she had ended blaming it on Bob. Which, actually, was quite handy, and got her off the hook nicely, even if she didn't feel brilliant about herself.

'Where *is* he anyway?' Nicola enquired, looking around warily. Usually his return put an end to the tea drinking fairly rapidly.

Good question. He had left at about three o'clock to go to one of those monster DIY stores for a vital supply of nuts. Any excuse to get out of the house before Nicola came, although he knew damn well that they were going to be discussing the brochure, and that Father Nugent had hinted to Mam last week that it was past time that they got Fintan sorted on the everlasting memorial front.

Geri began to get a bit steamed up. Bob hadn't been asked to do a single thing all week, except this. He knew she didn't know one lump of stone from the other. Couldn't he have put in an appearance for once in his life?

'He's been gone *three hours*?' Nicola said, when Geri explained. 'I hope he didn't have an accident.'

More like an allergic reaction to human grief. But Nicola always imagined the worst. You couldn't go to the shops for ten minutes without her thinking you had met a sudden death.

'I doubt it,' said Geri callously.

'All the same, you'd better ring him.'

And so Geri did, just to keep up appearances. To her embarrassment, he didn't answer. 'He's probably driving.'

Davey and Susan emerged from their bedrooms, attracted by the smell of dinner in the oven, and got caught up in all the excitement.

'Your father's gone missing,' Nicola told them very worriedly.

'Fantastic,' said Susan.

She wasn't speaking to Bob since he'd grounded her – on Geri's instructions, naturally. She wasn't going to set foot outside the front door without giving an assurance that things were over with Leo Ryan.

'I don't believe this!'

'This hurts us more than it hurts you,' Bob had assured her.

'You just want to stop me being happy!'

Bob had lifted a corner of his mouth in a manner that had infuriated her further. 'With *Leo Ryan?*'

'What's your problem with him anyway?'

'Oh, let me see. He has no job. He wears hoodies. He drives a car that isn't, in my opinion, roadworthy. Those front tyres look bald to me. And I'm pretty sure that his modified exhaust isn't legal.' He had been doing great until he'd gone off on a tangent.

'You're only sixteen, Susan,' Geri had said, sounding just like her mother, something she had sworn never to do. 'You have exams next year. You're too young to be involved with someone so . . .' So thick-looking. '. . . so much older.'

'He's only twenty.'

'That's a four-year age gap.'

Susan gave her a look that clearly said, 'You're so past it that I can't even think of a word for you.'

And maybe Geri was. Certainly, she couldn't remember what it was like to be sixteen, and madly, crazily, in love with a boy that your parents disapproved of.

'She's only doing what she's hot-wired to do,' she'd said to Bob later.

'Exactly. And we have to put our foot down, like *we're* hot-wired to do,' Bob had explained excitedly. 'Give her something to rebel against.'

'I suppose.' She'd thought for a bit. 'And *then* are we going to let her date him?'

Bob had crossed his arms across his chest grimly. 'Like hell we are.'

And here he came through the front door now, a box of new DIY supplies under his arm – a rather small box, given the length of his absence – and a chilled bottle of white wine in the other.

He looked perfectly normal, and unflustered. 'Sorry I'm late,' he said, looking easily around at everybody. 'Here, your favourite.'

He handed Geri the wine, which actually *was* her favourite, looking quite pleased with himself.

'Thank you,' she said, surprised and a little pleased.

'Can we just *eat*?' Susan threw at them, before stomping off into the dining room.

That night in bed, Bob thanked her for cooking dinner.

'What's with all the compliments?' she said.

'It's just one compliment.' He sounded in a bit of a huff. 'But if you don't like them . . .'

'I do, I do. And thank *you* for helping Nicola with Fintan's headstone.'

Bob had poured wine for them all, and been very civil to Nicola, and they had spent nearly two hours discussing Fintan's final resting place. Nicola had gone home very late and half sozzled, but looking quite peaceful.

Geri had been touched by the time and effort Bob had volunteered.

'Hey, it was nothing,' he said, butchly.

And then he kissed her, and she turned the light out, and it was only when she heard his deep, even breathing that she realised that, although it was a Saturday night, and she was wearing her Sex Nightie, Bob had not wanted sex.

Chapter Nine

Bob was coming to Debs's Christmas party with her. She had begged and pleaded and basically worn him down.

'We never go out in public much,' she had whinged. Which was a bit unfair. They could hardly paint the town red, what with him having a wife and two kids stashed at home.

Bob had that white, pinched look about his mouth. Debs called it his Big Fat Liar look – as in, he hated being a big fat liar, and hated even more when he was forced to confront the fact that he *was* a big fat liar.

The pet. He really wasn't cut out for this affair lark at all. It was taking a terrible toll on him. Sometimes Debs wished he was more like the adulterers in the magazines in the hairdresser's – cheating toads called Andy and Ian (not their real names) who rampaged through women's bedrooms without a care in the world before cheerfully going home to the missus for their tea.

Instead Bob was always breaking into a sweat about things. He would fuss endlessly about his mobile, for instance, and would check it ten times during their dates to be sure that his wife hadn't phoned. Usually it was just to say that she'd keep him some shepherd's pie, or to remind him to get a pint of milk on his way home. Domestic things. Debs felt a bit superior that she and Bob never wasted time talking about milk.

He also wasn't that hot on the whole email or text thing.

'It's not that I don't like getting texts from you, it's just that I'm afraid I'll forget to delete them,' he said to her apologetically. 'I've a memory like a sieve.'

Which was slightly worrying. How were they supposed to conduct a secret affair if he couldn't remember half the time what he'd said to whom, and when?

'I think I told her I was at a meeting. Shit. I can't remember.' And he would agonise and turn himself inside out, and then carry on a guarded telephone conversation with his wife until she reminded him that he'd said he was playing golf. 'Ah, yes! No, I'm just, um, teeing off now.'

And he would hang up, wringing his hands guiltily, red to the tips of his ears from all the lies, and mutter to Debs, 'I hate all this.'

Well, yes. That much was obvious. As philandering husbands went, she was rapidly coming to the conclusion that he was a bit hopeless in the deception stakes. Not for him the thrill of sneaking around, or enjoying the illicitness of a double life. He always had one eye on the clock, and had nearly done himself a terrible injury that time they'd been in bed and the doorbell had rung. It had just been the girl from next door delivering some misdirected post but Bob had had to lie down for half an hour afterwards with the blinds drawn to get over the fright.

Debs had been half amused and half annoyed; who had he thought it would be? His wife?

But she supposed in one way it proved that he was an honest person. And it was clear he hadn't done this kind of thing before. No, Bob was essentially *good*, she would muse fondly at night. Just because he was shagging her behind his wife's back didn't really change that, did it?

Debs, on the other hand, quite enjoyed the mystery and intrigue surrounding her new relationship. This probably made her a very bad person. The worst. As bad as Kristin in *Dallas*, the poster girl for low-down dirty mistresses everywhere.

But Debs couldn't help it. Whenever she would skip surreptitiously to the loo in the office to apply a fresh layer of lipstick before slipping off to meet Bob, she would be filled with the delicious sensation of suspense and tension. There was no denying it; seeing a married man was so much more exciting than a chap called Keith from, say, the billing department.

'I can't believe you're putting yourself in danger for me,' she breathed one night after a couple of glasses of wine.

Bob had looked over his shoulder warily. 'Am I?'

'I mean you're risking stuff for me.' Like his job, his family, his house. He had a whole life built up over twenty years, and he was putting it all on the line for Debs.

But Bob didn't seem as thrilled by the thought as she was, and went off home early. Shit. She should have kept her mouth shut.

Mostly, though, it was great. They were like teenagers, always waiting for the next date, the next phone call. When they were together their time was full of laughter and excitement and sex.

'I'd love to just stay here all day,' Bob said one Saturday afternoon while they were in bed together. He hardly ever got away at weekends. He always had to invent some excuse about visiting his mother or going to the hardware shop.

'Me too,' Debs said, tracing a little pattern with her fingers on his chest. It was hairy, but not too hairy. It wasn't a *rug*. She liked the way it tickled her cheek when she rested her head against him.

'I know,' she said. 'Let's run away.'

She meant it only as a silly joke.

Bob played along. 'Where would we go? Cork?'

'Cork? Jesus Christ, have you no imagination at all?'

He laughed. 'The Caribbean then.'

'Too touristy.'

'I didn't realise you were so fussy.'

'Well, I am. I'd like to go somewhere unspoiled. Like, say, South America.'

She must have sounded like a seasoned traveller because Bob said, 'Which part have you been to?'

'Oh. None, yet.' She didn't want to tell him that the furthest she'd got was a sun holiday in Majorca. Travelling was another thing on her To Do list. She just hadn't got around to it.

'OK, OK, you've twisted my arm,' said Bob. 'Let's do it.'

Debs laughed. 'I'll book the flights today.'

'Make it business class. We might as well go in style.'

All right, so it was a fantasy. But some days, like when his wife got a stomach bug and she hadn't seen him for a whole week, Debs pretended that they really were going to escape to Peru, just the two of them.

In the meantime they spent all their time in her flat. Her bedroom became like a boudoir. She did a massive spring-clean and even bought new, sexy sheets for the bed, seeing as that was where most of their 'dating' took place. Then, after a while, she began to enjoy the before-sex bit just as much; there was a cosy domesticity about cooking for him in her little kitchen, and she sometimes even secretly pretended that they were married as she tenderly fed him omelette in the kitchen (if he was getting fed up of them he never complained).

He loved the attention. Anybody could see that. Well, who wouldn't? But there was a slight air of neglect about Bob. Just one of her welcoming smiles could make his whole face light up. He thrived on her fussing, scoffed down her omelettes, and then swept her off to bed, and to hell with the washing-up.

'You're very masterful tonight,' she would tease.

'I know,' he said, looking surprised at himself.

Clearly his home situation didn't make him feel that way, a little voice in Debs's head said. Again she felt just the teensiest bit superior. Certainly, what she was doing was wrong, there was no denying that; but at the same time, Bob couldn't be all that happy at home if he was with Debs in her flat two evenings a week, could he?

Tuesdays and Fridays. They had become 'their' days. He would park his BMW around the back of the block and they would shut the flat door on the world.

'Will we go out?' Debs said one night.

Bob looked up. 'Out?'

'Yes. To a pub, maybe. Or a restaurant.'

'But I've only just arrived.'

'I know. But to be honest, if I have to make one more omelette . . .'

'I'll cook.'

'Why not let somebody else cook? Like the guy in the restaurant around the corner.'

Bob looked unenthusiastic.

'All right, so he'll never win a Michelin star, but his cannelloni is fairly edible, and I've never found a hair in my food, not even once.'

'Why don't we just order in?'

Debs began to smell a rat.

'Well, if nobody wants to cook . . .' he said with a shrug.

'It's not about cooking. It's about going out together, like normal people.'

The truth was, she was dying to show him off. Having Bob on her arm was as good as shouting, 'Look at me! I have a man! Even though I have a large-ish arse.'

She was desperate for people to know, even strangers in Mario's restaurant, that she was part of a couple, that barometer of success. She had, finally, successfully ticked off one of the goals on her list.

'Nobody's going to spot you all the way out here,' she told him.

'It's not about that!' He thought about it for a minute. 'All right, it *is* about that.'

'And even if somebody did, it's just a bowl of pasta.'

He sighed. 'And what innocent explanation could there be for me sitting in a dark corner eating pasta with a young woman miles from my home?'

'We won't sit in a dark corner. We'll sit in the window. Under a bright light. Please.'

He didn't want to. That much was plain. Debs told herself it didn't matter. The important thing was that they were together, right?

Bollocks to that, she thought grimly, as she flung pots and pans around in the kitchen, and deliberately overdid his omelette.

A week later he arrived on her doorstep. She knew from his face that he was holding something in.

'What?' she said, feeling the familiar thud of alarm. Had his wife found out?

'What are you doing at the weekend?'

Nothing. Sitting around the flat trying not to eat too much, and maybe shopping for a new, scary bra to augment her collection.

'Why?'

He took out an airline ticket pouch rather dramatically. 'Will you come to Paris with me?'

'*Paris?*' After that she was speechless.

He had to go over for a sales conference. They could have a whole weekend together, in the world's most romantic city, without him having to scuttle off at seven in the morning to get home before his wife came back from a night shift.

'I'll have to work during the day,' he warned.

Debs didn't care. She would, she decided bravely, explore the city on her own while he was doing his thing They would meet up for dinner like lovers did in the movies, and stroll through darkened streets hand in hand, and it would be dead romantic.

'Fantastic!' she yelled, throwing her arms around his neck.

'Better than Mario's, eh?' he said modestly.

They were going to have a dirty weekend away. Debs had never had one before. It would be marvellous.

The only slight problem was Bob, and his nerve. The closer the date got, the more anxious he was.

'I'll have to stay in a different hotel from everybody else, and George will want to know why, and what if Geri rings up looking for me and discovers that I'm not where I said I was?'

'Tell George to mind his own business. And if your wife wants to contact you, won't she just ring your mobile?'

'It's not that simple.' He was tense and belligerent. You would think all this had been her suggestion, not his.

Debs was already learning that confrontation didn't work with Bob. She had to support, and coax, and let him come to his own conclusions. 'If it's all too much, then maybe we should leave it.'

Her doubt was enough to send him running in the opposite direction. 'But then that's not fair on you. We never do anything that a normal couple does. We'll go.'

★   ★   ★

They went. It was a disaster. Debs was on the same flight, but sitting on her own down the back because Bob was with George. His conference ran over on both nights, and they missed dinner entirely one night. Debs was sure that the French woman who ran their little *pension* knew exactly what they were up to – a married man and his bit on the side – and was convinced that she was giving Debs the evil eye over breakfast in the mornings. Bob said she was imagining things, but he looked tired from the strain of it all too.

Then, on the Saturday night, just as they were about to have romantic, French-inspired sex, Bob said, 'Why do you never let me see you?'

Debs gave a little laugh. 'You're seeing me now.'

'You know what I mean. Naked.'

She froze. She thought he hadn't noticed the blackout blinds, and the way she always dived into bed while he was in the bathroom.

'I'm a convent girl,' she joked him. 'You wouldn't believe the hang-ups I have about sex.'

She certainly wasn't going to admit that she was too mortified to parade her bum and thighs around the room, inviting ridicule.

'You don't seem to have too many hangs-ups to me,' he said, in a way that made Debs blush wildly.

It was true. Once under cover of darkness and duvet, her shyness disappeared. In fact she could only be described as enthusiastic.

'Don't disappear into the bathroom,' he cajoled, as she tried to make her escape. The curtains in the *pension* weren't made of the same stuff as her mother's. The street lights clearly shone in. Very shoddy workmanship altogether.

'I'll be back in a minute,' she promised.

But he held on to her hand. With the other he began to unzip her dress at the back.

'Bob . . .'

'Just making you more comfortable.' He gave her a cheesy wink.

Her voice rang out. 'Just stop, would you?'

His hand dropped away immediately. 'Sorry.'

Debs could have bitten her tongue out. 'No, *I'm* sorry. I'm just . . . I just need a bit of time, Bob. That's all.'

'Sure,' he said easily. 'No problem.'

But it kind of spoiled the night, even though she did her best to make it up to him by snuggling into him in bed, and remaining in his arms the whole night long.

It was all her fault. If she wasn't so out of control in the food department, then she would be lovely and thin and he could strip her off all he liked.

She *must* make more of an effort. And it wasn't like she hadn't the motivation now – a gorgeous man who was mad about her. The only thing ruining it all was her and her jelly bum.

She went to bed that night with a steely determination to lose some weight once and for all. Only this time, she was going to keep it off.

They were glad to get back to Dublin. By mutual consent they hadn't been out since they'd got back, except to Mario's, finally, for her birthday. She was thirty-three. Bob bought her a beautiful gold pendant embedded with a diamond.

'Thank you,' she said, her eyes shining. Nobody had ever given her anything so expensive.

'You're worth it,' he said.

She flapped him away, embarrassed.

'I mean it,' he insisted. Then, a little shyly, 'I love you, Debs.'

They'd had lots of wine at dinner. It was probably just the drink talking. But it was still thrilling to hear. Nobody had mentioned the love word yet. Certainly not her: she knew from bitter experience that it was the one thing guaranteed to send most men running for the nearest hill.

'Thank you,' she whispered, and they held hands over the table for the rest of the night.

Everything was rosy until the Christmas party reared its head.

'Just because Paris was a disaster doesn't mean we should never leave the flat again,' she argued.

'It's too public,' Bob insisted. 'I could run into anybody in that hotel.'

'Yes, but what are the chances of that? Really?'

'It just takes one person and the whole thing is over. Have you thought of that?'

In other circumstances she might have backed down. But the temptation to show him off in front of her colleagues was too great. She couldn't face another staff do on her own; left to guzzle wine in the corner with Gavin and Liam whilst Alex paraded around with Marty sniffing after her.

Bob gave in eventually. How could he hold out in the face of sustained pressure and even a little blackmail?

'I probably won't even go if I have to go on my own,' she had said rather sulkily.

'One hour,' he declared threateningly. 'Then I'll have to leave.'

An hour was all she needed to redeem herself in the eyes of her colleagues.

'Done,' she said.

Fiona didn't approve of Bob. Debs was bitterly regretting telling her about the new relationship in the first place. But it had been in a moment of weakness, when Fiona had called over to the flat and asked, rather pityingly Debs thought, 'Have you found somebody to share with yet?'

For once Debs hadn't felt like a victim of her own failure. High on her own pulling power she opened her mouth and blabbed about Bob. She boasted about his lovely eyes, his great sense of humour, Paris. She'd had to ham that bit up and make it sound much more romantic than it had been.

'Oh, Debs. I'm thrilled for you,' Fiona shrieked. Of course she was. Now she could stop feeling guilty about having abandoned Debs to lonely flatland.

'Now I just have to persuade him to leave his wife,' Debs joked.

She hoped that if she normalised it, then Fiona would too. Because it wasn't such a big deal, was it? They were modern women, after all. Sophisticated. People had affairs all the time; there was no shock/horror factor any more.

But Fiona's reaction was very disappointing. Quite backward, actually. She gasped, and looked appalled, and really, in Debs's opinion it was all a bit over the top.

'Debs, are you sure about this?' she asked, as though Debs were going to jump off a cliff.

'Look, it's not ideal. But he's great. And I know exactly what I'm doing.'

Honestly! Wouldn't you think she could be just the teeniest bit happy for Debs? After all those years of assuring Debs that she would eventually – with a bit of luck, and the help of the gods, and maybe a good weight-loss programme – meet someone worthwhile, and now that Debs *had*, she wasn't a bit happy!

She then promptly went home and told little Stevo.

The two of them obviously had a big serious chat about it, because they called round the very next evening, and more or less attacked her in her own kitchen.

'Who is this guy anyway?' Stevo demanded.

You would think he was going to lie in wait and beat him up or something.

'He's an unemployed layabout with a gold medallion and several women on the go, and probably a couple of illegitimate kids that he refuses to pay maintenance for.'

Stevo wasn't amused. 'I hope he hasn't fed you any lines.'

Oh, what did Stevo know anyway? Engaged to her best friend, and planning a wedding that was already spiralling fabulously out of control. He, who had stolen Fiona away from her, and left her to moulder away in the flat by herself. And then having the gall to corner her in the kitchen and give her a lecture about being able to 'do better for herself', and not letting herself 'get taken advantage of'!

They had already made up their minds about Bob. And they hadn't even met him.

'We just don't want to see you getting hurt,' Fiona had said.

Fine. Debs could see her concern. On some level she appreciated it, even if she was certain that Bob would never intentionally hurt her.

'I can look after myself.'

'We know that,' Fiona had said hurriedly, even though the look she shared with Stevo said, oh there goes Debs, fecking things up again.

Things were a bit stiff and awkward between her and Fiona after that. It was a shame. It would have been nice to have had someone to confide in about Bob. They had always talked about men. Little Stevo had been discussed thoroughly at the beginning of his relationship with Fiona, although he didn't know it.

'I just wonder about the height thing,' Fiona had fretted. 'I'm actually taller than him by two inches.'

In normal circumstances, one of them landing a new man would have propelled them to the nearest off-licence. Two bottles of white wine and crisps would have been purchased, and then they would have settled in for a night of gory detail. Nothing would have been left out, from that very first glance to what he was like in the sack.

'Does he have nice loins?' they would each demand of the other. Fiona had once brought home a stack of old Mills & Boons from the charity shop she managed and they had spent a whole winter reading them and cackling aloud.

Once the poor, innocent man's looks and personality had been thoroughly dissected and rated on the scale of one to ten, they would move on to his prospects. This, naturally, was far more important. If he could even hold down a job, he automatically entered the running for the position of The One. Add in a car and a pension plan and his ratings went stratospheric.

'He owns his own *house*,' Debs had marvelled about Stevo. Neither of them had ever been out with some-body so together. Fiona's previous boyfriend hadn't even owned his own teeth, having lost them in a brawl somewhere.

All this discussion would take them till about two in the morning, and then usually one of them would try to make a pizza out of Brennan's bread and a jar of Dolmio, and then they would stagger off to bed, satiated with alcohol, food and shite talk.

There were no such cosy gossiping sessions over Bob. Whenever his name was mentioned Fiona's mouth went all puckered up. Debs couldn't believe it: Fiona, who had done things in the past that Debs wouldn't even remind her about now – but think Spanish sailors on an overnighter in Dublin – had come over all prudish and moralistic just because Debs was going out with a married man. Unbelievable!

She was desperately sorry now that she'd asked her to come shopping with her. They were in the evening-wear section of a department store, trying to get something for the Christmas party. Debs was half-naked in the dressing room and trying to stuff herself into a dress that was clearly made for a woman with smaller boobs than hers. She was just tucking them under her armpits when Fiona said through the curtain, 'Look, have you thought about his wife?'

Debs froze. Oooh. That was low.

'Of course I have,' she stammered.

And that was a lie. Half the time Debs tried to pretend the woman didn't exist at all, even when Bob would furtively leave the room to take a phone call from her. She couldn't even bring herself to use her name – Geri. In those rare instances when she referred to her at all it was as 'your wife'. It was easier that way. Less personal.

But there was an unspoken code out there, Debs knew. Women who stole other women's husbands were snitches; cheats; betrayers of the sisterhood. And she had broken that code.

Her face flamed with guilt, but also a kind of defensive anger. You would think she had walked up to Bob on the street and carted him off protesting and fighting her every step of the way. What about his wife? Had she no part to play in all of this? A woman who only ever rang Bob to remind him to pick up milk on the way home, and who hadn't noticed that Bob had left his golf clubs in the hall at home that day he'd said he was playing golf? (Bob had nearly had a heart attack upon the discovery. So had Debs.)

Debs wasn't going to take it. All right, so having a relationship with Bob was wrong. But he was the one who was married, not her. Bloody hell! What about a little support here? A little comradeship?

She whipped the curtain back furiously. The motion unleashed her boobs from under her armpits.

Fiona took a step back. 'I'm not sure about that dress.'

'You don't even know her,' Debs said accusingly. 'His wife.'

'I'm just saying. There are other people involved here. Children.'

167

'His children are teenagers. They're not in nappies.' She looked at Fiona hard. 'You're just saying all this now because you're getting married and you're worried someone might steal Stevo in the future.'

'I am not,' Fiona scoffed.

'You are. You said earlier that you were sick of all this wedding stuff, and that you'd go mad if you ended up divorced after all this effort.'

'Well, yes,' conceded Fiona. 'But I don't think anybody would try and steal him,' she said, with a little sigh.

'You never know,' Debs told her.

That perked Fiona up a bit, and the tension between them subsided. 'Look, you're right – I don't know his wife. But I *do* know you. And to see you pinning your hopes on a married man—'

'What "hopes"?' Debs enquired.

'So this is just a bit of fun for you?'

'It might be.'

She tried to sound casual. But they were on dangerous ground now. Debs hadn't even gone there in her own head. Anytime her thoughts wandered towards the future she hauled them back brutally.

It was too soon, she told herself. Besides, they were enjoying themselves too much. There was no need to go spoiling it all with loads of angst.

But Fiona was going to have a jolly good try. 'I thought you wanted to get married and have kids? What was all that whinging in the flat over white wine for otherwise?'

Debs said patiently, 'Well, of course I do. But that's all in the future, Fiona.'

'The future? You're thirty-three.'

Debs was starting to feel a bit depressed. This was supposed to be a happy outing, looking for a sexy frock for her Christmas party where she would parade a thoroughly respectable man for once in her life.

And now here was Fiona ruining it all by bringing up Debs's age. Not to mention implying that Debs was a guileless fool if she was counting on any kind of a future with Bob.

She was off again now, arms folded sternly across her chest, her engagement ring glittering smugly on her fourth finger, or so it seemed to Debs. 'You don't want to waste years of your life with him, Debs. And end up at thirty-nine on your own.'

She had to pick the year before forty, of course. Forty, when you were all washed up, and your ovaries shrivelled up like a pair of prunes, and no man in his right mind would give you a whirl. It was enough to strike fear into the heart of thirty-nine-year-old women everywhere.

'I mean, has he said anything about leaving his wife?'

Oh, for heaven's sake! They were only together a wet weekend! She didn't even know what his shirt size was, or whether he liked marmalade with or without the peel. But they were supposed to have had in-depth discussions about him ditching his wife for a more permanent relationship with Debs?

Fiona went on relentlessly, 'If they don't mention it in the first three months, then they're probably not going to do it.'

It was low of Fiona, to frighten her like this. Bob would be furious if he heard his character being slated in such a fashion.

Even if he hadn't actually said anything about leaving his wife.

But that didn't mean he didn't intend to. And their three months was barely up. Given that they had only two proper dates a week, it was completely ridiculous to think that they were ready for a conversation like that. Fiona was cracked. Imagine if he had announced on their second date that he had already packed his suitcase and would be moving in with her! She'd have run a mile.

She was feeling better and better now. Fiona was just scaremongering. Engagement to Stevo had turned her into a very judgemental type of person, Debs concluded. Not every relationship had to end in marriage within the year. There were different types of relationships; some took a little longer than others to grow into something more solid, due to circumstances. But that didn't mean they didn't *have* a future.

'And how do you know all these things?' she enquired loftily of Fiona. 'From all the affairs you've had yourself?' She was quite pleased with that.

'I just think you have to be careful. If it's a bit of fun, fine. Just so long as you both know exactly where you stand, that's all.'

Debs wasn't going to take the 'bit of fun' thing lying down. It cheapened her. It cheapened Bob.

She rose to her full height, clasped the shiny dress to her bosom, and announced, 'He's told me he loves me.'

Fiona looked a bit surprised. Good. No doubt she thought Bob was just in it for the sex.

'And do you love him?'

'Yes,' said Debs. And because she said it without

thinking, she figured it must be true. She *did* love Bob. Somewhere along the way the lust and excitement of the affair had given way to feelings she hadn't experienced before: a nervous jump in her stomach when she thought of him and a pain in her heart when he was at home with his wife.

It was then she realised that there was no point any more in trying to push away thoughts of the future. They had gone beyond the beginning stages, the time when they could have called a halt to it without anybody getting too badly hurt. Well, except for maybe a dented pride.

But now it was different. She had invested herself in him. And now that Fiona had brought up her age, and marriage, and babies . . .

When she counted properly, she realised they had been seeing each other four months. A whole month past the apparent cut-off date of when he should be mentioning leaving his wife. And Bob hadn't so much as made a murmur.

It looked like it would be up to her.

Chapter Ten

Once the niggling doubt was there it was hard to push it away: the feeling that there was something wrong, something that Geri couldn't put her finger on.

Then she would think that she was just being daft. What on earth could be wrong? And with Bob, of all people? He went to work and came home as usual. He fixed things in the back at weekends, like he had always done. And every morning he hummed, 'You're Never Fully Dressed Without a Smile' in the bathroom while he shaved, and even though it occasionally almost drove her to violence, there was something comforting and completely normal about it.

Silly cow, she would berate herself fondly. Talk about being paranoid! And now here was the poor man spending his whole Sunday up in the attic, clearing out stuff in preparation for the attic conversion Geri had been threatening to get done for the past ten years, but was only getting around to organising now.

Susan was going to study up there. But that was before she'd been banned from seeing Leo Ryan. Now she was never studying again, apparently. Or talking to her parents.

'I haven't had this much peace in years,' Bob said happily.

'Sssh,' Geri warned, as Susan emerged from her bedroom.

She gave her parents a dark look. An evil look, Bob later maintained. 'It's all right,' she said. 'I know you're talking about me.'

'Actually, we *have* been talking,' Geri said cheerily. 'And we were wondering whether you'd like to go out and see a film with us tonight, and then maybe have a pizza?'

This was the first Bob had heard about it, but he nodded vigorously anyway.

Susan looked at the two of them as though they needed intervention.

'You think I can be bought off with a *pizza*?'

'No—'

'I'm not five any more, you know.'

'She's not,' Bob agreed. Turncoat.

Geri could see that this was back-firing badly. She had just wanted to do something nice with Susan, as a family.

'Look, I asked around about Leo Ryan, Susan.'

'You've been snooping behind my back?'

'I was just trying to find out more, that's all.'

'You could have asked *me*. Or does my opinion not count around here any more?'

'I'm just not sure you know him as well as you think you do,' Geri said in a placatory way.

Davey squeezed past now, on his way into his room, and carrying a mound of sausage sandwiches on a plate.

'He's got three speeding convictions,' he remarked conversationally.

What? Geri had discovered that he had left school at sixteen without any qualifications, and had thought that was bad enough.

'Right! That's it!' Bob shouted excitedly. 'You're never seeing him again!'

'I was never seeing him again anyway,' Susan pointed out.

'This time you're *really* not seeing him. I don't want to be called out by the guards in the middle of the night to identify your body that they've scraped off a dual carriageway somewhere.'

'Stop,' said Geri weakly.

'Anyway, see you later,' said Davey, and disappeared off into his bedroom, uncaring of the fact that he had kicked off the whole thing in the first place.

'He might know more,' Bob told Geri. 'Leo Ryan might have other convictions that we don't know about!'

This was too much for Susan. 'You're pathetic, the two of you!'

And she stormed out.

'I don't think she meant *pathetic*,' Bob consoled them. 'More misguided. And she needn't have shouted.'

He shook his head in a the-youth-of-today fashion, before climbing up the ladder again into the attic like everything was normal.

And it was, pretty much. Except that he wasn't having sex with her.

Usually that would be fine in Geri's book. A relief, actually. But at the same time she knew that husbands didn't suddenly stop wanting sex for no reason. She was going to say something about it, just casually, such as, 'What's up with the old pecker then?' Make a joke of it.

But somehow she didn't. And then the builder had phoned three days previously and said he had a window in his schedule for next March or something, ages away anyway, but Bob got prematurely excited about it.

'We'd better get the attic cleared out at the weekend,' he dictated, voice aquiver.

This was his chance to get involved, along with his toolbox, in a proper, bona fide DIY project, run by professionals. He could hardly wait for Sunday to arrive. He got up early that morning, and straight into his torn jeans, the pair that he saved specially for DIY jobs and that he thought made him look cool, and barely stopped for a bowl of cornflakes in his haste to climb up into the attic.

'I might just tidy up these wires for them as well,' he called down to Geri authoritatively.

It was taking the whole day to sort through everything. Most of the stuff was Bob's, things that he fantasised about fixing and selling on eBay one day. 'Laugh all you want, but that Hoover could be worth a fortune some day.'

There were other things too. 'Would you look at this,' he would say every so often, handing down one of the kids' cuddly toys from when they'd been babies, or the tent they'd gone camping in one summer years ago, only to come home that very same night, frozen and petrified after a cow had tried to join them.

'Bloody thing was *huge*.'

They laughed merrily at the memory now. It was all very cosy and intimate, and Geri went off to bung the tent into the recycling pile and make him a cup of tea, wondering what in the blazes had got into her, to think for even a second that there might be something wrong between them.

No, they were in this together, she thought stoically in the kitchen. Their marriage was a solid thing, with foundations built on trust, respect (sometimes), shared history and a few other things, if only she could remember. Certainly not sex, at least not at the moment. There was a slight oasis there, but nothing to worry about.

Still, she went to the calendar on the kitchen wall, and counted back. It was a bit of a shock to discover that they hadn't had sex for six weeks, not since the night they got the takeaway Chinese and watched a 'documentary' on the making of pornography on Channel 4. 'Disgusting,' they had agreed rather animatedly to each other.

But she realised now that they had hit a new low (the six weeks, not the porn).

She would pick an opportune moment, she decided. She would delicately suggest that he haul himself off to their doctor, who was male, thankfully, and drop his pants. There may well be something physical accounting for his lack of libido. She couldn't think of exactly what, off the top of her head, but there might be a twisted tube down there, or some mineral deficiency that caused symptoms of droopiness.

As for herself, she would go out tomorrow and buy herself a new Sex Nightie. She'd had her old one *years*. It had seen in the new millennium, for God's sake. Poor Bob. He might need a new challenge, such as buttons to undo, or a bow to untie – she had learned how to make a sailor's knot in the Girl Guides years ago, which she could do for added titillation. And it probably wouldn't hurt to get a wax every now and again. Andrea knew a good waxer. Geri might nip over after work some day for a tidy-up and surprise Bob some Saturday night.

She felt better now. She had a plan of action. There was no need to panic. Plenty of people in middle age experienced some slow-down in the bedroom department.

'Twice a *week*?' her sister Emma had screeched when Geri had run the Sunday papers poll past her during the week. Just casually. 'Twice a bloody *week*?' No further words were necessary.

'What are you smiling about?' Bob said when he came in looking for his tea.

Now was her chance. They'd always been able to talk about anything. She would simply point out, without any recrimination, that he'd been copping out of his conjugal duties. 'Six weeks? Are you serious?' he would no doubt say, clapping his hand to his forehead in amazement. 'Do you know, Geri, I think I might be a bit low on iron.'

And then he might say, to hell with the attic, and cart her off to the bedroom for a mid-afternoon session, and everything would be fine again.

'Nothing,' she said.

What was stopping her? Surely she wasn't *afraid*. She really was losing it.

As the week wore on she found herself caught in this odd seesaw between thinking she needed her head examined, and a growing sense of unease.

Then one night she awoke suddenly at three a.m. and

thought, He never wears that lemon shirt any more. The one that made him look jaundiced.

A stupid thing. It was an awful shirt, anyway, and she was glad he'd finally had the sense to throw it out. And what did it have to do with the lack of sex anyway? Nothing.

But she lay there for hours, unable to sleep, listening to Bob's even breathing. Trying to find comfort.

The following morning Geri did an awful thing: she went on his home computer. It had occurred to her during the night – and this really was sick – that he might be addicted to porn. She had read somewhere that a lot of men were so obsessed with the stuff that they no longer bothered having sex with their wives. That Channel 4 programme could have been the start of it. And there was Bob in the computer industry and everything – he could be looking at all sorts of filth and she wouldn't have a clue.

'Sorry, Bob,' she murmured guiltily as she keyed in his password – they knew each other's passwords; that was how trusting they were – and prepared herself for shocking images of women in improbable positions. She would blame herself, of course. He hadn't known a thing about computer porn until she herself had shown him, that time she was putting all kinds of blocks on various sites to protect the kids. Davey, of course, had cracked them all in two and a half minutes.

But now maybe Bob had a taste for it. He might be spending hours at work hunched over his computer, salivating, or worse. Real women mightn't be enough for him any more. He might get excited only by cyber chicks, with their enormous fake breasts and hairless bodies. Geri in her tired pink Nightie, reeking of red wine, might be a total turn-off for him now.

Counselling, she resolved fiercely. They'd wean him off gradually. Teach him what was normal again. Geri, she hoped. The kids would be told nothing.

There wasn't a thing on his computer. The last sites he'd visited were Argos and B&Q, at the weekend. He was squeaky clean.

The clouds lifted from Geri's eyes and she was shocked at herself once again. Imagine suspecting Bob of being a dirty raincoat! She felt so guilty about her actions that she went and made a green chicken curry for dinner mid-week, Bob's very favourite meal, which took her four hours to make.

'What's this in aid of?' he enquired.

'Nothing. Can I not spoil you any more?' As though she'd ever spoiled him to begin with, but there was no need to mention that.

'Oh.' He might look a bit more pleased.

'You know, we should go out on Saturday night,' she said gaily. She had no idea where that came from. But it was a good idea. She'd take him out for another curry, and they'd have a few beers, and a laugh.

Also, she didn't want to stay at home. Normally it would be a sex night. She was afraid, she realised, about how it would end.

'I can't,' he said, apologetically. 'I have that sales dinner. I'm going with George, remember I told you?'

She didn't.

'I won't be late,' he assured her.

Another door opened in Geri's mind, one that she would find hard to close again.

The following day at work the ward was excellently staffed at about ten a.m. Everywhere you looked there were nurses, sometimes in groups of twos and threes.

'I see Dr Foley is due to make his rounds,' Andrea observed.

Geri seized upon the opportunity to take her mind off things. 'I think he likes you.'

'He's petrified of me,' Andrea said with great satisfaction.

'I don't know why you have to be so nasty to him.'

'Because I fancy him, of course,' she said with a sigh.

Geri looked at her. 'So, what, you're going to behave like you're twelve and pretend that you hate him?'

'Have you got a better plan?'

'Yes. Go out with him.'

'He hasn't asked me.'

'Not the way you're treating him,' Geri agreed.

'Oh, look, I can't.'

'If this is more of your paranoia about the whole place talking about you—'

'It's not paranoia. Alison over in Oncology was up in Dundalk last Tuesday evening in a little dark chemist down a side street buying a pregnancy test, and within forty-eight hours Sharon in *Texas* knows! This place is fucking incestuous.' A man shuffling past in pyjamas stopped uncertainly. 'Sorry, Mr O'Reilly.'

Geri had no idea where her optimism was coming from but she said, 'I think you should take a chance on him.'

'Why?'

'Because he's nice. He's *lovely*. He goes to visit his mother every weekend, and he mows her lawn.'

'How do you know? Actually, don't bother answering that. And anyway, if I *were* to go out with him, even for a coffee, the whole place would find out in ten minutes flat and I just couldn't bear it, even if I do desperately want to ride him.'

A throat was cleared politely. They looked up to see Dr Foley standing there.

Andrea went so pale that Geri thought she was going to be sick.

But Dr Foley was awfully nice about it and pretended not to have heard. 'Lovely morning,' he said politely.

'Yes,' Andrea stuttered.

As he picked up his files in preparation for his rounds, Andrea frantically motioned at Geri: *Go With Him Because I am Too Morto*.

Geri turned to Dr Foley and said, nicely, 'Would it be OK if Andrea went with you today? I have a bit of a headache.'

'Of course,' said Dr Foley. 'I hope you're all right,' he added with concern.

Behind him, several nurses exchanged glances: wouldn't you run *away* with him?

Off he went with Andrea trailing behind him, making violent gestures at Geri with a thermometer.

Geri wasn't even lying; she did have a headache. It was getting so bad that she was tempted to cry off work, sick.

But what was there for her at home? All that time on her hands to sit and brood and think about things that she didn't want to think about.

181

She wished she could rewind until that morning. Why had she bloody well said anything at all about going out on Saturday? Then he wouldn't have mentioned about the sales dinner, and her day could have proceeded in its usual hectic fashion, and she would be laughing now at Andrea trying to regain her composure at the bottom of Mr O'Reilly's bed.

Instead she was staring blankly at case notes and all she could think of was that Bob never left his mobile phone on the hall table any more like he used to.

She didn't realise she had noticed that. But she must have. Filed away in her brain under things that she didn't want to think about.

Reason kicked in again now. So he kept his phone in his pocket. Big deal. Susan had probably been using it to ring friends in Turkmenistan or someplace, and he'd had to remove it from plain view.

See? Taken one by one, everything was perfectly innocent. Just because he wasn't having sex with Geri, and hid his mobile phone, and didn't wear unflattering clothes any more, and got haircuts without being nagged, and was supposedly going out to dinner with George on Saturday night without the wives, were not reasons to suspect anything at all.

Oh Jesus, she thought.

What firm held a dinner on a Saturday night?

Especially a firm as mean as his?

Why hadn't he mentioned it until now? Because he hadn't. She was sure of that.

And why had he refused to meet her eyes?

Impulsively she picked up the desk phone and rang Bob.

He answered promptly on the second ring. (See? she told herself. There were advantages to keeping your mobile with you at all times. Bob was clearly one step ahead.)

'What's happened?' he said immediately.

'Nothing. Everything's fine.'

She never phoned him at work, only when there was a crisis.

'The kids are OK?'

'Fine, yes.' Then, 'Where are you?'

'At my desk. Working.'

Oh. She was starting to feel very foolish. Of course he was sitting at his desk. Where else would he be at eleven o'clock in the morning?

'I just wanted to say that I'm nipping into the shops after work, and wondered did you want anything?'

There was a puzzled pause at the other end of the phone.

'Like what?' he enquired.

'I don't know.' She was stumped herself. She never asked him if he wanted anything from the shops. 'Deodorant?' she tried.

'Do I smell?' he enquired.

'No, no. I was just wondering, that's all.'

There was another pause. 'Is there anything else?' he asked. 'Because I'm actually with a client at the moment.'

Geri felt herself go red. 'Sorry. Go ahead. I'll see you later.' She hung up quickly before she caused herself any more embarrassment. She could just imagine his face at the other end of the phone.

'Everything all right?' Hannah, who had just come on shift, enquired.

'Yes. No. I mean, everything's fine.' She couldn't tell

183

Hannah. Or even Andrea. Andrea would, probably sensibly, tell her she was being daft. She would ask Geri what evidence she had – real evidence: lipstick on collars and the whiff of cheap perfume, that kind of thing.

She would probably advise that she go home and ask Bob about it.

Geri felt sick at the thought of that. Supposing he said yes?

Besides, if she said it to anybody then it would somehow make it more real. Right now it only existed as a wild theory in Geri's head, which could be happily blamed on the sheer amount of stress, overwork and aggravation in her life. Anyone who baked as many buns as she did for cake sales was bound to be prone to delusions. If she said nothing, and just carried on, then there was a very good chance that all this would blow over, and everything would be normal again.

And so she tried it. All day long she pretended that everything was fine. She trotted busily up and down the ward in her Scholls, dishing out pills and urine-sample containers, and giving the patients a bit of lively jip every now and again:

'Now, Mr Keane, I want to see all of that beef stew polished off! There won't be anything else later; the girls in the kitchen told me to tell you that.'

She even asked the girls if anyone knew a good waxer.

'What are you planning on having done?' they asked, looking concerned.

'Just the usual.' Honestly. Just because she was forty-two didn't mean she had to roll over and let nature reclaim what had been hers in the first place. No, this might be a bit of a wake-up call for her to brush up on things a bit. It might be something positive.

Why then did she end up in her car in the car park after work, crying her eyes out? It came over her, just like that. She felt foolish and stupid sitting there blubbing like a baby, but she couldn't stop herself. It wasn't the dinner on Saturday, or the stupid lemon shirt. It was the gut feeling in her stomach that something was seriously wrong, and no matter how hard she tried, she couldn't pretend any more that it wasn't.

She didn't know how long she sat there, hunched over the steering wheel and bawling, but it must have been a few minutes anyway.

Long enough for someone to spot her.

There was a gentle rap on the window. Her head snapped up. It was Dr Foley. Sweet Jesus.

He had his coat on and his bag in his hand. Clearly, he had been walking past on his way to his car and seen her distress. He looked like he was in a hurry, yet felt duty-bound to stop.

She would just have to brazen it out. After a wild swipe at her face she rolled down the window. 'Hi there!' she said in her cheery Nurse Murphy voice, hoping he wouldn't notice that her eyes were puffy and red and her nose streaming.

'I don't mean to pry. I was just wondering if you were OK, that's all.'

'Me? Oh, never better. Tip top!' Tip top? No wonder he was looking at her warily.

'OK. Well, if you're sure . . .'

He cast a glance across to his own car. Clearly she was keeping the poor man from his dinner.

'Absolutely,' she said. 'Thanks again. See you tomorrow,' she jabbered as he gave her a bit of a wave and walked on.

Geri let her head flop back against the headrest. The day really could not get any worse. All she wanted to do, she realised, was to go home to her family, and cook dinner like normal, and flop down in front of the telly with them all just like she had done yesterday.

But she couldn't. Her mind was racing with suspicions and doubts. And there would be no normality until she got to the bottom of it.

Her hands were shaking when she took out her mobile phone. She had what seemed like several thousand numbers stored on it – all the parents she knew from school, the women down at hockey (even though Susan had given up), neighbours, friends, relations. The builder who was coming next March. She even had the number of the local pizza delivery outfit. Davey needed it at least once a week.

She had no fewer than four Lisas. She scrolled down until she came to the one she wanted: Lisa, George's wife.

Before she lost her nerve altogether she dialled.

Lisa picked up on what seemed like the twentieth ring. But it was ten past eight, and she had children much younger than Geri's. 'Hello?'

She didn't sound that welcoming. But then again they usually only rang each other when there was the threat of a social occasion involving the firm, which, granted, wasn't that often, and they would have a moan over what they were required to cook.

'Hi, Lisa!' Geri kept her voice light and cheery.

Then she didn't know what to say next. Damn. She should have thought out the conversation a little bit more before she jumped right in there.

'How are you?' she prattled, buying time.

'Busy, actually,' Lisa admitted. There was a violent crash in the background underlining this.

'Right, well, I won't keep you. I was just, um, wondering whether we could meet up on Saturday night for a few drinks?' She just blurted it out. Well, she could hardly ask whether Bob was lying through his teeth about the sales dinner.

She could tell by Lisa's silence that she was stumped by this invitation. No doubt the last thing she wanted was to be dragged out on a Saturday night into some noisy pub with the wife of one of her husband's work colleagues. They hardly knew each other, for heaven's sake.

'We could . . .' she said, very reluctantly.

There was nothing for it but to plough on. 'I just thought you'd be at a loose end, what with the boys going to that dinner thing.'

There. It was out.

Her hands were slippery on the phone. She could hardly believe she was having this conversation at all. She wanted to hang up before Lisa answered. She wanted to throw up.

Please God, let it be OK, she found herself praying.

But of course it wasn't. She had known that somewhere inside all along.

The words, when they came, were shocking all the same.

'What dinner thing?' Lisa said.

Geri was proud of herself afterwards. 'I'm probably getting my dates mixed up,' she said without skipping a beat, as Dr Foley's car drove past. The top of Andrea's glossy head was just visible in the front passenger seat.

'Oh. Well, we could meet up anyway,' Lisa said valiantly.

'Listen, I'll let you get back to the kids,' Geri cut in. 'Why don't we do it another time?'

And she said goodbye and hung up on Lisa, and then she bowed her head over the steering wheel and cried again.

Chapter Eleven

'When are you coming home?' Debs's mother asked plaintively on the phone. 'We haven't seen you in months.'

'Soon,' said Debs, the stock answer.

But her mother wasn't giving up that easily. 'There's something going on up there. I know there is.'

Debs laughed merrily. 'Don't be ridiculous.'

Her mother pounced. 'Normally you'd agree. You'd say you were sleeping with seven different fellas and stuffing loads of drugs up your nose. The very fact that you're denying it means there *must* be something going on!'

She was delighted with her reverse logic.

'I'm worried about you up there in that flat on your own,' she went on now, concern clouding her voice. 'Did you get any responses to the ad in the paper?'

Debs felt bad. Now that she was seeing Bob, naturally she didn't want anybody to move in to replace Fiona. What, some stranger sitting at the kitchen table while she made Bob his omelette, and casting judgement when they nipped to the bedroom ten minutes later? No thanks. But her mother had kept on and on, and in the end Debs had rashly promised her that she would put an ad in the *Evening Herald* looking for someone to share.

Of course she didn't do anything of the sort. And so she still had the little flat all to herself, even if it was costing her an arm and a leg. She didn't say this to Bob, mind. He might feel that he had to contribute or something. And that gave Debs an icky feeling.

'Not yet,' she told her mother. 'I don't think the ad's been in yet.'

'What do you mean? I thought you said you'd put one in.'

'I mean it didn't go in until this week,' Debs hastily amended. 'I'll probably get a few enquiries over the next couple of days.'

'Maybe I should come up for a visit,' her mother suggested. 'We could spring-clean the flat together, make it attractive to potential tenants. We could even give it a lick of paint.' She got quite jovial now. 'And then you could take me to that nice pub down the road from you and we could have a little drink.'

The last time Debs's mum had been up for a few days she'd had such a good time that it had been a bit of a job to get her to go home again.

'I'm too busy in work at the moment, Mum.' Another lie. She had been coasting for weeks. She was in love, for heaven's sake – how could anybody expect her to apply herself to her job? But Marty was a bit of a spoilsport in that he kept giving her things to do. Ever since the

Tom Brunt episode she had come onto his radar. Up until then she'd had a relatively peaceful, if stupefyingly boring, existence under the stairs, but now whenever there was a job to be done Marty seemed to pick Debs. Debs wondered whether it was a coincidence that the tasks often involved physical exertion, such as fetching and carrying up and down the stairs, or making the 5.30 p.m. post box at the end of the street. He seemed to get some perverse pleasure out of watching Debs's bottom wobble indignantly as she huffed out of the room to do his bidding.

Sometimes she caught Alex's eye during one of these errands. Alex looked reasonably sympathetic, but didn't intervene. Debs couldn't blame her. There was little anybody could do when you got on the wrong side of Marty. When Tanya had thought that Gotham City was a real place he hadn't let her forget it for weeks.

Debs told herself that she didn't care about Marty. So what if her job was going from bad to worse? She had a wonderful, caring, sexy, funny man in her life, who had told her that he loved her.

And she would be showing him off at the Christmas party. The whole office was waiting to get a look at him. She had eventually broken the news of his existence when Janice had done a final head count for the party. She had wrangled the job after suggesting to Marty that the organisation committee wasn't doing its homework properly.

'Well, we had so many freeloaders last year,' she said back tartly when Alex questioned her. And it was true. Some people, who couldn't be named but who knew who they were, had turned up with friends, neighbours, ex-lovers and grannies in tow, all looking for a free feed.

Janice moved around the desks, questioning people in the most unsubtle manner possible. She started with poor Tanya. 'Are you still plus one?' she asked sceptically.

'Of course,' Tanya said indignantly, even though Debs suspected the guy she was bringing was actually her brother. But anything was better than turning up at the Christmas party on your tod. You'd hire someone if you had to.

Janice continued with her grilling. Most of the rest of the office were plus-ones too, even the more ordinary-looking playmates, and the lanky guy with glasses who came in three times a week to do the accounts.

Then she came to the pathetic few who were not plus-ones. Those who were minus-ones. The sad group of losers and loners who would be condemned to a corner of the room, where they would have a table to themselves, the leper table, and hopefully they wouldn't bother anybody.

'Liam?' Janice asked softly, voice dripping with sympathy. 'Any change?'

'No,' Liam whispered, red to the tips of his ears with this public shaming.

She patted his shoulder with faux compassion, and moved on. 'Gavin?'

Gavin had almost pulled a woman in the pub the previous Friday evening. But then he'd confided to Debs that his heart wasn't really in it.

'This is not like me at all,' he'd said worriedly to Debs. 'To turn down a bird who's mad into me.'

She hadn't looked all that mad into him as far as Debs could see. She looked like she might have been only passing the time.

'Do you think you need to see a doctor?' Debs had asked compassionately.

He'd looked cross. 'Isn't it obvious what's wrong? I'm in love with Alex.'

'You've always been in love with Alex.'

'Yeah, but before it was just kind of a hobby. Now I find that I'm waking up in the middle of the night thinking of her.'

Debs hadn't wanted to go there, not in any detail, anyhow.

'She has a boyfriend, Gavin. An investment banker who's gorgeous and apparently fantastic in bed.' She'd enjoyed torturing him. Besides, Bob wasn't free that night, as usual, and she'd wanted to take it out on someone.

Gavin had had six pints at that stage and was moving into macho mode. 'I'm fantastic in bed too. Ask anybody. Well, obviously not you. Ask Janice. Actually, don't ask Janice. I think I might have been very drunk that night.'

'You slept with Janice?'

'Well, yeah. Hasn't everybody?'

Janice was obviously remembering that particular night now as she stood over him like some avenging angel. Loudly enough for the firms on the floors above and below to hear, she pressed him for an answer: 'You'll be on your tod then? Couldn't persuade anybody to come with you, no?'

'No,' Gavin was forced to admit, his face averted from Alex, the better to hide his shame.

'I wonder why,' Janice said under her breath. Then, 'I guess it's you and Liam and Debs at the table down the back as usual then.'

It was a stunning indictment. Debs's face burned. Then, with dizzying relief, she realised that she didn't belong there any more. Because she *had* a boyfriend now. Thank Christ. A real, live boyfriend who was going to accompany her to the Christmas party and spare her an evening of horror.

She opened her mouth to announce this triumphantly, when Alex took the wind from her sails by announcing casually, 'I'm a minus-one too.'

Well. Talk about dropping a bombshell. Janice nearly broke her neck looking from Alex to Tanya to Mia. Alex was coming minus the mysterious Greg? Had she dumped him? Better again, had *she* been dumped? This was the best gossip all year.

It took a moment of confusion before it dawned on Gavin: Alex would be sharing their table at the Christmas party, thus transforming it into the most desirable seat in the house. A huge, broad grin split his face. Debs could see him already planning his assault, God help Alex.

And right now every eye in the place was on her expectantly. But Alex, spoilsport that she was, wasn't going to shed any further light on the matter. She merely turned back to her computer as though the entire conversation bored her, and Janice was left standing there like a plonker, her petty list in her hand.

'Actually, I'm bringing someone,' Debs piped up.

But it was too late. Nobody gave a toss any more. Alex had ruined her moment: suddenly it was cool to *not* bring somebody.

Bloody hell, thought Debs viciously. Alex had done it again.

When Marty heard the news you could nearly see the little cogs turning in his head: now that she was single again, he might actually get to hump her, if only he could get rid of his wife for the night. He spent the rest of the day sniffing around her and slavishly offering her the plum jobs, which she accepted with her customary coolness.

Janice was furious at the way it had turned out.

'She does it on purpose,' she raged at the water cooler.

Meanwhile Gavin was frolicking around the place deliriously, annoying everybody with his Alex love-fest, especially Janice.

'As if she'd ever give the likes of you a whirl,' she said viciously.

'You never know unless you ask,' Gavin said back. 'By the way, when you were standing over me there I noticed that your moustache needs bleaching again,' he added helpfully.

Janice gave him a killer look. Deciding to pick on someone weaker, she turned to Debs.

'*You're* bringing someone?' She managed to sound flabbergasted.

'Yes.'

'Who?'

Debs had never mentioned anything about Bob to her colleagues, not even under the influence in the pub on a Friday night.

'My partner,' she returned loftily. Partner sounded so much more mature than 'boyfriend'. It suggested a long-term, grown-up relationship with a man who read broadsheet newspapers and owned an umbrella.

Janice and Tanya and Mia were mildly impressed. 'What's his name, Debs?'

'Bob,' Debs said, wishing, not for the first time, that he was called something a little more dashing, like Myles or James.

'Is he the one who came to collect you here one evening? Oh, he was quite cute, wasn't he?'

And for the first time ever in the office, Debs felt like she fitted in.

Bob wasn't a bit happy when he'd found out that she'd gone public. 'We didn't talk about this.'

'About what? You coming to my apartment and having sex with me twice a week?' She was angry at his denial. Did he want to keep them a secret for ever?

He looked angry too. 'This party on Saturday – am I to turn up with or without my wedding ring? Or have you thought that far?'

Actually, she hadn't. She had just wanted people to know that they were an item. That she had sufficient pulling power to attract a decent-looking member of the opposite sex. She hadn't intended on getting into explanations about him being married, and still living with his wife and children, and consequently her being a brazen hussy with the morals of an alley cat, or any of that.

'Without, then,' he said sarcastically, seeing her face. 'Another lie.'

Listen to him, all high and mighty – and he himself lying his socks off every day of the week to his wife!

'At least I'm trying to be more open about things!'

she flung back at him. 'I'm not going to creep around behind closed doors for years just because it suits you.'

'You think this *suits* me?' He looked appalled.

'If it didn't, you wouldn't be here!'

It was their first proper row. She was shocked at the things she was saying to him.

But it had been building in her since that day in the changing rooms with Fiona: the lack of a plan, the lack of any kind of statement on his part of where he saw them in the future. He seemed content to come to her apartment twice a week for the rest of his life without ever moving this thing on.

As for her . . . well, her mind had been weaving worryingly realistic fantasies about him leaving his wife and moving into her little flat. She had the details down pat: he would have the wardrobe in Fiona's old room for his suits, for instance, and she would move all her rusty razors and curled-up tubes of make-up so that he could have the middle shelf to himself in the bathroom cabinet. They would chuck out her little single bed and invest in a massive new one instead. With silk sheets. Quickly they would establish a cosy little routine, whereby she would get home first in the evenings, and prepare a light repast for them in the kitchen, her heart lifting when she heard him use his own key in the door, and then greet her with the cheery cry of, 'Honey! I'm home!'

It didn't stop there. Although it should have. But the problem was that there was nobody to call a halt to her madness and so the fantasies went on. They even involved marriage and babies, although not necessarily in that order. (Apparently it took years and years to get

CLARE DOWLING

a divorce in Ireland – disgraceful.) After her conversation with Fiona, Debs had acknowledged, grudgingly, that she did indeed want babies, if not right this very moment. In her grand plan, the finer details of which had to be worked out yet, she had thought they might have two children – one of each, with a bit of luck. And it wouldn't matter that she and Bob weren't hitched yet. They would be cool, alternative, non-married parents until his divorce papers came through. Then they would plan a great big wedding, and invite all their friends, and everybody would say that it had all been worth it in the end.

(After all this planning usually she would have to go have a lie-down for a while.)

Bob, of course, knew nothing about his future commitments. Bob, who was iffy about even coming to her Christmas party with her.

'Do you even *want* to be with me?' she asked him now in a voice that came out horribly whinging.

A clever mistress wouldn't go on like that. She would never reveal her hand emotionally. Instead she would grow aloof, and become busy and unavailable for sex sessions. He would grow keener, and start to believe that he couldn't live without her, and give his wife her marching orders before the month was out.

But Debs wasn't clever like that. Right now she was hurt. And a bit confused.

'Debs,' he said in a reproachful voice. As if she even had to ask, the implication was.

But he hadn't actually said that he *did* want to be with her.

'Well, do you?' This could backfire badly on her. But she had to know.

He ran a hand through his hair, leaving it in spikes. 'You know how complicated it is.'

'Meaning we should leave things the way they are?'

He looked under pressure now. 'We're having problems at home with my daughter at the moment, did you know that?'

How could she know when he'd never told her? Always acting like his family would be contaminated by the mere mention of them in Debs's presence.

'And what about me? Don't I count in this at all?' She was very close to tears. And that would be a disaster.

'Oh, Debs.' He put his arms around her and hugged her tight, planting little apologetic kisses all over her forehead. She tried to resist; nothing had been resolved, after all, but she felt herself weaken and lean in to him. Pacified once again.

'I don't know what to do,' he said, mouth pressed into her hair. 'I'm sorry.'

And he sounded so worried and sad and confused that Debs felt the last of her anger melt away. He wasn't playing games. He was just caught between a rock and a hard place.

'I just need a bit more time. That's all.'

What else could she do except nod and say yes? She couldn't demand that he choose between her and his wife; right now she knew exactly who he would choose.

She would have to go slowly, she saw. Work on him a bit. Coax him along. He couldn't be forced into any decision or else she'd be blamed if things didn't work out.

Being a mistress wasn't half as glamorous as she had initially thought. Darn tricky at times.

'Will you come to my office party with me?' she asked.

'Yes,' he said. 'I'll be wearing a wig, and a big long black coat, and a fake moustache in case anybody recognises me. And I'll have to leave by the back door.'

Then she had made him an omelette and they had gone to bed and had brilliant make-up sex, and as they lay there afterwards she tried not to wonder whether they would be having the same row in five years' time.

Nothing resolved still.

Her mother rang her up early Saturday afternoon, the day of the party.

'I've just got a copy of the *Evening Herald* in town, and there's no sign at all of your ad in the Accommodation section.'

'Are you sure you looked properly? They can be tricky to find.'

'I have my glasses on and everything. And your dad is after having a look too. The only thing we can see in your area at all is a house share with three men, and I presume that's not you.'

It was tempting to waffle on about the paper probably having made a mistake. But it was time to tell her. And Debs was an adult after all, wasn't she? Free to make her own choices. It was ridiculous to be afraid of her mother's opinion at the age of thirty-three.

Of course there would be some disapproval. A married man wasn't exactly what every mother dreamed of for her daughter. But at the same time it wasn't like he was a murderer, or a member of the Peel family, up the street from them at home, who were all, according to local lore, 'a bit queer'. Queer meant odd back home, not anything more exciting.

They might even be glad. They never said it, but nothing would make them happier than to see Debs meet someone nice. They wouldn't have to worry about her any more, all the way up in that evil metropolis of a Dublin, if she had a nice, solid man to look after her. Even if he happened to be married.

OK, now she was just time wasting. Putting off the moment.

'I just want to let you know,' she told her mother in a very brisk and confident voice. 'I'm seeing someone.' And before the champagne could be broken open, and the streamers set off, and her father called from his comfy chair to join the celebrations and possibly plan the wedding, she said quickly, 'He's married.'

There was a silence at the other end; a hideous, deafening silence. The kind of silence that Debs hadn't encountered since she'd been eight, and had taken scissors to Mum's best dress in the enthusiastic belief that that would improve it.

Debs had, she realised, read her mother wrong. Possibly she had overestimated her liberalness. It was becoming increasingly clear that her mother was not ready for the idea of her daughter with a married man.

Seconds went by. Then what seemed like minutes. If this carried on for much longer Debs would have to go and get ready for the party.

Hold firm, she urged herself. Ride it out. Don't give in to her. She would break eventually.

She didn't. In the end it was Debs who buckled under the strain.

'But he's separated,' she lied.

Ah.

The silence at the other end softened slightly. This wasn't so bad. Highly irregular and deeply undesirable, of course, but marginally better than what it had been at first. Obviously, the situation would have to be put to her father in a very delicate way. Her mother might have to mention divorce proceedings, and assets, that kind of thing, and God forbid that the neighbours should find out. But all in all it wasn't the worst thing that Debs could have done. No, the worst thing would be taking up with a married man and breaking up a loving home.

'I see,' said her mother, in a very chilly voice. But she was talking at least. That was practically the seal of approval.

Debs was raging with herself. So much for coming clean. Now she was left with a big, fat half-lie. Wait till Bob found out that, in Deb's version, he was heading straight towards the Family Law Courts without stopping at Go. He'd go mental altogether.

On cue, her mother said stiffly, 'When are we going to meet him?'

Never, at this rate.

'He's out of the country at the moment,' Debs said. She was becoming worryingly good at lying. But then again, weren't all mistresses? She thought of all the mean little deceits she and Bob had engaged in over the past few months in order to keep their affair a secret.

'I suppose he has a wife,' her mother said sarcastically. Well, yes. Naturally.

'She's, um, a nurse.' What relevance that had to anything, Debs didn't know. But she didn't know a single thing else about her, she realised. Just that, and her name, and that she occasionally rang up Bob to remind him to pick up milk.

Imagine. There was Debs, sleeping with this woman's husband, and yet she knew practically nothing about her. Not a thing! And didn't *want* to know, if the truth be told. Bob's protective silence regarding his wife suited her down to the ground, really. It made it far easier to imagine some cartoon character with a hearty laugh whose reaction to the discovery of her husband's affair would be to dash after him with a rolling pin whilst *Tom and Jerry* music played in the background. Someone who couldn't really be hurt.

Geri. A nurse. Bob's wife. Mother of his two children. The woman who rang Bob's mobile every now and again but otherwise didn't impinge unduly upon Debs's secret affair.

Debs found herself wondering guiltily now what she was really like. What colour hair did she have? What age was she? Older than Debs, anyway, if she had two teenage children. Was she plump or thin? Did she have a quick temper or a good sense of humour? Did she plonk her tired feet up on the coffee table at night in front of the telly, like Debs did?

Oh shit. Debs had a sudden urge for a Snickers bar. Two of them. Anything to give her a bit of comfort in the face of this new wave of guilt.

Anyway, she told herself defiantly as she got rid of her mother and ransacked the kitchen presses, Bob clearly wasn't happy at home. That wasn't *Debs's* fault, was it? No! If any fingers were to be pointed in that department then surely they should be at his wife? Debs couldn't be held accountable for Geri's mistakes. In some ways, she only had herself to blame if Bob sought satisfaction elsewhere.

The Snickers bar didn't taste too good. She had another one, sitting at the kitchen table, stuffing it into her face. Great – and she after starving herself and everything for the past five days in the hope of getting into her party dress tonight, or at least without a corset.

And the Snickers bar didn't even do its job; Debs still couldn't stop thinking about Geri. She was cross with herself when she should have been excitedly getting ready for tonight. And what was with the sudden burst of guilt anyway, seeing as Debs hadn't really spared her a thought so far?

It was her mother, Debs thought darkly. After talking to her, Debs was always more aware of her conscience. It must have been all that enforced Mass-going when she was a child.

And now there was Bob's wife, Geri, invading Debs's thoughts, making her feel bad. Making her feel *terrible*. And she was a nurse too, which somehow made it worse. All the time Debs had been dropping her knickers in the flat, Geri had probably been out saving lives. Why couldn't she have been a traffic warden instead?

Debs might as well face it: it just wasn't right, what she and Bob were doing. She had known it in theory all along, of course, but now she knew it someplace worse: her conscience. Damn her mother anyway.

I really am a bad person, she sighed gloomily to herself. No doubt when her time came she would be judged before a panel of duped wives, all of them livid and pointing fingers at her righteously and shouting, 'Immoral bitch! Home wrecker! Burn her at the stake!'

No, there was only one honourable thing to do here when it came down to it: give up Bob altogether.

And obviously she wasn't going to do that – she loved the man, she *adored* him.

So that left the other option: give up Bob altogether until he actually split with his wife.

It might be honourable, but it was also a horrible option. It sucked. It wasn't realistic either, because it would be akin to handing Bob an ultimatum. After their argument over the Christmas party, and her agreeing to give him time, how could she now turn around and tell him that she didn't want to see him until he had left his wife? He would think she had gone crazy.

Maybe she could suggest that they simply cool things instead.

But what would that achieve? They would still be seeing each other behind his wife's back, just not as frequently. No Brownie points there in the conscience stakes.

The sequins on her new black party dress twinkled at her, mocking her. It was hanging up in the corner of the living room, in plastic. And she had just consumed five hundred and sixty calories worth of sugar.

She felt the familiar self-loathing creep over her, adding

to her guilt over Bob's wife. This was on top of the stress over the party tonight. The blooming DJ had already phoned to ask vaguely what hotel it was in. What *hotel*? She had only told him fifty million times and faxed the address to him on Thursday. She'd be lucky if he showed up at all.

Alex would blame her, of course. The DJ had been Debs's job.

It all became too much. She barely made it to the bathroom before she vomited.

Sledge turned out to be a very cool-looking guy with a goatee and earrings in both ears. He looked completely bored at the prospect of doing someone's office Christmas party, especially in September, although he was still agreeing to do it, Debs noted.

'I did Ibiza last month,' he informed her, just so she knew how important he really was.

Marty had already tried to high-five him in the foyer, just to impress everybody, but had missed and ended up slapping Janice instead. Everybody said it was too good for her.

Here came Alex now, looking predictably gorgeous in a plain black dress and with no make-up. No make-up! Everybody else was plastered with the stuff, especially Sledge the DJ, but Alex still looked better than anybody else. It was depressing.

And Bob was late. He usually phoned when that happened but there had been no word from him. Debs hadn't spoken to him all day. But that wasn't out of the ordinary, not for a Saturday, which was always a busy family day for him. They went a lot of weekends without talking, but usually managed to text. There had been no text from him either. She tried not to read anything into it. He was probably trying to find parking and would be there in a minute.

Alex looked over at the free bar, where gangs had already congregated with a mild sense of panic, and where a blustering Marty was surrounded by Janice and the playmates, and she gave a little sigh. 'At least the food looks good.'

'Yes,' Debs agreed in great disinterest. She hoped that her stomach didn't rumble. She was starving. It had been a long time since those Snickers bars had left her stomach. But at least all those calories were down the toilet now instead of settling themselves on her hips. The thought made her feel curiously light and free.

Alex was still loitering. Debs wished she would shove off. There was nothing like standing next to the most beautiful girl in the room to make you feel like one of the Ugly Sisters. Knowing her luck Bob would walk in at that moment, and wonder if he could have done better for himself.

'It's been nice working together on the organisation committee,' Alex commented a little awkwardly.

Had it? Debs tried to remember all those zany meetings filled with laughter and comradeship, but couldn't quite.

'I suppose,' she said, wondering what was with all the small talk. Alex was probably just trying to kill time before she had to go take her place at the losers' table. *Not* her style at all.

But then Alex confessed, 'Look, I'm sorry if I bit your head off when you asked about who I was bringing tonight.'

Imagine remembering that after all these weeks. Debs had long ago put it out of her mind. 'No problem,' she said, not quite sure what to say. 'And, eh, sorry to hear about you and . . .' she risked, 'Greg.'

But Alex only looked puzzled. Damn. It must have been Jack, then. Or Jed.

Debs decided to come clean. 'Look, I'm not being nosy, OK?' Of course she was. 'But we all know there's been someone.'

Alex looked at her for a long moment. 'Yes,' she said eventually. Reluctantly. Like it was a state secret or something. 'Actually,' she admitted, 'we're still together.'

Well. This was juicy news indeed. There had been no big bust-up at all – more office gossip with no basis in reality.

So why wasn't he here tonight? Unless, of course, he was a blooming rock star or something, or a famous actor, and couldn't just show up at these events like normal people, or at least not without a platoon of bodyguards. She wouldn't put it past Alex.

But Alex didn't look like she was dating a rock star. She looked like she had a headache. 'It's a bit difficult to explain,' she admitted.

Debs hoped her eyes weren't like saucers. Imagine Alex being in a relationship that had its challenges! And to think that Debs thought they'd had nothing in common. Heck, they were practically soul mates.

'I know exactly what you mean,' Debs confided

impulsively (she'd had two glasses of wine already). 'I'm going out with a married man myself.'

'Really?' said Alex, all ears.

Debs shrugged as though to say, 'I'm mad, me.'

Alex jerked a head towards Janice and company. They were stampeding past in a puff of party frocks and aggressive high heels, shrieking with laughter. 'And do they know?'

'You must be joking.'

'Well, exactly! That's what I feel.'

Debs was beginning to work out that Alex's boyfriend had some, well elements that Alex clearly didn't want everybody to know about. And, seeing as he wasn't married – she'd have said, surely – it must be something else.

'You just don't know how people are going to react,' Alex whispered.

Debs had brief, wild visions of facial tics or uncontrollable body hair growth. A married man was beginning to look tame in comparison.

'No,' she concurred.

Alex hesitated. She looked at Debs for a long moment as though pondering the kind of stuff she might be made of.

Obviously something about Debs must have inspired some kind of confidence, because she said, 'Will we get another drink?'

Yes! Debs wanted to shout. She felt like the chosen one. Of all the trendy people in the room, Alex had picked her in whom to confide about Greg's dark criminal past. Or whatever.

'Of course,' she murmured maturely.

But then the whole moment was ruined by a bellow of 'Alex!'

Here came Marty now, glass in hand, and in worrying good humour. He always loved the Christmas party. He got to drink too much, and be centre stage, and go around all his employees like some kind of generous benefactor, knowing that they had to humour him because he paid their wages every Friday. It was like a massive birthday party just for him, and usually he didn't go home until the hotel staff chucked him out at about five a.m.

'Two lovely ladies with no dates!' he boomed in mock horror.

And he patted their bottoms. Alex locked eyes with Debs and they both shared the same thought: dickhead.

'Sorry?' said Marty.

Debs realised that she may have spoken aloud. She tried to cover by saying, quickly, 'I said that actually I have a date.'

Marty remained deeply suspicious. He snatched his hand from her bottom as though it were contaminated.

'His name is Bob,' Debs prattled now.

It would have been great had Bob walked through the door at that second. It would have been perfect. But Debs's life never seemed to have those kinds of moments and the only person to walk in was Gavin, fresh from the jacks, where he had obviously applied more Joop! aftershave because they could smell him from there.

Debs had a nasty premonition that he and Liam would be her lot for the night; the three of them sitting at the back and going around at the end of the night holding up wine bottles to the light in the hope that there was something left in them.

But she was being silly. That was the old Debs, the one before Bob. He was just late, that was all. Any number of things could have delayed him. And he wasn't even very late, just half an hour or so. He had probably left a message on her phone.

She checked surreptitiously. He hadn't.

Still. There was plenty of time.

Here came Gavin now. Along with the aftershave, he was wearing his Best Clothes – a white shirt so sheer that you could see his nipples through it (ugh), teamed with a salmon-coloured silk tie and a pair of tight, tight trousers. There was enough gel in his hair to hold up a seven-storey building.

'Hey,' he said to them with a bit of a swagger. Debs cringed.

'Oh. Hello,' said Marty, merely looking annoying. He fancied himself as an alpha male and didn't appreciate smaller, punier ones muscling in on the action.

Gavin turned to Alex. He tried to keep his eyes on her face, but they kept sliding down to her breasts and he had to haul them back up again.

'I'm keeping a seat warm for you at our table,' he said, his voice shaking with barely suppressed excitement.

Alex looked like she would go, too. Anything to get away from Marty and his roving hand.

But this was a step too far for Marty. Especially when he had only just got hold of her. He brushed Debs aside rather rudely, the better to protect his star employee from the lascivious attacks of a little upstart. There was so much testosterone in the air that Debs had an urge to crack open a window.

'Go get me a drink,' he growled at Gavin. 'And take off that pink tie. Between you and Sledge, it's like a party for the fucking Village People in here.'

There was a horrible silence.

Gavin opened and closed his mouth. He was mortified.

Tell him to stuff it, Debs pleaded with him silently. But of course he couldn't. Because they all valued their jobs. Well, they didn't, but they *needed* them, which was much more important. And Marty could say what he liked and they would have to swallow it.

Gavin turned and walked away quickly in the direction of the bar, red to the back of his neck.

Debs caught Alex's eye. She looked furious too, and there was something else in her eyes as well – hatred, Debs saw, for Marty.

But then her gaze slid away, because she was thinking the same thing as Debs: that they were both cowards when it came to him.

'Excuse me,' Debs said, unable to bear any more. She crossed the room, avoiding everybody, and slipped downstairs. In the foyer she found a quiet corner, and took out her phone and dialled Bob's number. He would no doubt tell her that he couldn't talk, that he was in the car and he would be at the hotel in five minutes.

He didn't tell her that.

His phone was switched off.

Debs hung up with the awful knowledge that she had been stood up.

Chapter Twelve

Geri waited until Saturday evening. She didn't know why. Maybe she was giving him a chance to exclaim, 'Do you know something? I've completely mucked up my dates. The sales dinner is not on until *next* Saturday. What an eejit.'

But he didn't. He went upstairs at half-past six and she could hear him in the shower.

'Are there any long bits of rope around?' Susan enquired, slouching dejectedly into the kitchen. 'Or spare bottles of sleeping pills?'

Her enforced separation from Leo Ryan was taking a dreadful toll. Or so she said, anyway. She maintained that her teeth were mere nubs from all the grinding of them that she did during the night, dreaming of him.

'You have no idea what it's like to be in love,' she said darkly to Geri. '*Really* in love. Not just putting up with each other, like you and Dad and other elderly people do.'

'We don't just put up with each other.'

Susan gave her a look as though to say, you're fooling yourself, old woman. And maybe she was right.

'Why don't you go out with Davey to a movie and get a burger?' Geri felt guilty. She just wanted them out of the way. There was no sense in having them stand by while she beat Bob to death with his own lump hammer.

'You'll probably put a tracking device on me.'

'No, I won't. It'll do you good to get out.'

'Watching a movie isn't going to make me forget about him, you know. My feelings for him run a little deeper than that.'

Maybe, but really, how deep *could* they be, Geri wondered a little callously. Susan was only sixteen. Geri had had a crush on a different guy every week at that age. But maybe that just made her lightweight.

And who was to say that what Susan had with Leo Ryan wouldn't last the test of time? That Leo would be faithful forever after and Susan would never end up standing in her own kitchen, sick with suspicions?

'I'll pay,' she said tersely. She just wanted it over with now.

Susan sighed. 'The movie, maybe. Not the burger.'

While she had been dating Leo she hadn't been able to eat. Now that she wasn't dating him, she couldn't stop. It was, according to her, totally rank.

'If she gives me the slip, I'm not running after her,' Davey warned Geri.

Susan punched him, he kicked her back, they called each other lard arses and noobs, and then the two of them went off out the door quite happily.

Geri was left on her own to prepare for battle.

She didn't, she realised, know what she was going to do. Cry? Scream? Rant? Call him a hateful, cheating toerag?

She could see it now, unfolding itself in the kitchen (where she had chicken bones simmering on the cooker to make stock for a soup; practical even in the face of a life-shattering crisis). It was all so horribly predictable, like something out of a soap: he would stand there in his finery, looking like a miserable chump, and she would flail about screeching and cursing, and with her nose all swollen from crying. He would plead to be forgiven; she would threaten to go round to his mistress's house and set her on fire.

Or maybe he wouldn't plead. Maybe he would say, 'Well, if you want to know, she's much younger and more attractive than you, and doesn't bake at all, so cheerio, I'm off.'

The thought sent daggers of fear through her heart altogether.

At least it can't get any worse than this, she thought.

Except, of course, that she had still to confront him.

She wasn't great at confrontation. She was much better at nagging, and the odd nasty jibe, rather than outright hostility. He was hopeless at it too, which was why they'd stopping having rows years ago, and resigned themselves to bitter looks.

So she didn't confront him. Instead she hung about downstairs in a rather cowardly fashion, stirring the chicken bones and trying to bite down the urge to vomit. Well, she didn't want to have it out with him upstairs while he was in his underwear. It would tip an already unreal situation into the farcical.

Finally she heard him briskly descend the stairs. The stench of nice aftershave wafted in from the hall. He scarcely bothered to put on deodorant for Geri these days. Nor her for him, in fairness, even though she didn't give a shite about fairness at that point.

'Have you seen my car keys?' he called.

'No.'

They were in her handbag. She didn't know why she had done that. Maybe she was afraid that he would storm out before she'd had her say. And she felt cheated enough as it was.

He was in the kitchen now, hunting about on the worktops and under Davey's graphic novels. 'I'm going to be late.'

Her hands were shaking so much that she had to clasp them tightly together behind her back, like a policeman. Which was, perhaps, appropriate in the circumstances.

Don't attack, she had read on an internet website for cuckolded wives. Lead into it slowly, and preferably without recrimination (as if). It was, apparently, better to present the facts in such a way that it became impossible for him to deny the affair, and he would admit the whole thing, thus saving her an awful lot of anguish, and giving her the moral upper ground to boot. As if she didn't have it already. It's not as though *she* was off riding one of her colleagues while he was at work.

She had it all planned out. She would do things by the book. But somehow it all went out of her head as she watched him hunting about and cursing under his breath, and she blurted out, 'Bob, are you meeting a woman tonight?'

The atmosphere suddenly emptied, like all the air had been sucked out of it.

He stood there, looking at her in a stunned fashion. His mouth opened and closed again.

She had made a balls of it. Now he would deny the whole thing, and she would be forced to lay out all her pathetic little bits of evidence – the lemon shirt, the hidden mobile phone, the mortifying phone call with Lisa – like they were in a bad episode of *Inspector Morse*, and it would all be dreadful and even more upsetting than it already was.

'Yes,' he said.

'Yes?' she repeated stupidly.

She must have heard wrong. Her Bob, admitting to having an affair? Just like that?

She didn't know what to say next. The website hadn't covered an immediate admission. Instead it had prepared her for all manner of cowardly squirming and defiance on his part, along the lines of, 'I can't *believe* you're actually accusing me of something so . . . !', and, 'What do you take me for?!' and she had mentally rehearsed her replies up to the point of, 'Oh, just admit it, for God's sake! Don't put us both through this!'

Clearly, he wasn't going to. He had fessed up. Just like that.

'Yes,' he said again.

He looked miserable. Guilty. Anguished, etc.

He also looked relieved.

Inside Geri felt something breaking. She thought it

might have been her heart, but no, it just kept on beating dully, like the chicken bones on the cooker kept on hissing gently. The smell of them didn't help the situation.

His face was white and pinched. 'I'm so sorry, Geri.'

Well, that was all right then. No problem. Just don't do it again. Or at least don't get caught.

But she didn't say any of that. She didn't think she'd ever be able to speak again, the shock was so tremendous. But I already knew, she kept telling herself, as though that would somehow make things better.

'Geri,' he said.

He wanted her to speak. To say something. Anything. To chuck a plate at him, even. Not this awful, un-Geri-like silence. She'd talk to anyone about anything, for heaven's sake, as her mobile phone bill every month attested to.

And Geri would have obliged him, had she known what to say. But what *do* you say when you discover, unequivocally, that your husband of seventeen years has utterly betrayed you? And then looked for Brownie points for being decent enough to admit it?

'I know that nothing is going to make this better.' He was clutching the back of a kitchen chair so hard that his knuckles shone white.

He was right about that much.

At least he didn't come out with any of that crap about how he had never meant to hurt Geri; that he hadn't set out to have an affair, that it had just happened.

'For feck's sake, do they expect us to believe that they were sitting there in their office chair minding their own business one day when a naked woman just happened to land in their lap at just the right angle that they somehow ended up having full-blown sex?' Andrea always said in disgust about these 'it just happened' explanations.

At least Bob didn't say that. At least he didn't insult her intelligence.

She didn't know why she was excusing him. But it was either that or physically attack him, and she didn't want to sink that low. Not yet, anyway.

She supposed she had better ask. 'Who is she?'

She knew that other women would be desperate to know. But she had been oddly uncurious in the two days since she'd learned of Bob's probable affair. She hadn't lain awake at night constructing a Barbie doll type in her head, and sticking needles into it. It was Bob she'd been sticking the needles into.

'You don't know her,' he said.

'Who is she?' Her voice was a bit louder now.

'Her name is Debra. She's . . . I work near her.'

How dare he sound protective of her. Sparing with his details. Geri felt the first ice-cold shafts of pure rage shoot through her.

Debra. It sounded odd. American or something. Geri had a mental image of a pompom and a tanned, toned thigh.

'How long has it been going on?' She supposed she had better ask that too.

'Geri . . .'

'Please don't keep making me repeat myself.'

'A few months. Three, four.'

'I see.' And she nodded clinically, thinking, at least it wasn't years.

It was a bit weird the way she kept trying to see the good in the situation. But it was probably because a part of her still couldn't believe it; that Bob, who was standing before her now in a shirt that she had bought for him, Bob with his lovely, kind brown eyes, could have done this to her. It was so awful, so incomprehensibly dreadful, that she had to water it down so that she could actually deal with it.

If she didn't, she knew she would sink to the floor in a foetal ball and rock back and forth and wail, and probably beg for a bottle of hard liquor. And she wouldn't do that in front of him. She wouldn't let herself.

'Geri.' He made a movement as though he were going to touch her.

She recoiled violently.

They stood there for ages, the kitchen table between them like an unbreakable barrier.

'I don't know what to do, Geri,' he said at last. His voice sounded tight and high. 'I don't know what to say.'

You knew what to do and say when you seduced that bitch months ago, Geri wanted to bawl viciously at him. No flies on you *there*.

But she kept up the robotic, silent front. She could see it was unsettling him even more. In a minute she would go and make a tray of cupcakes and frighten the life out of him altogether.

'Do you love her?' She didn't know why she'd asked that. No good could come of it. If he said, 'Yes,' well, that would be terrible, but if he said, 'No, can't stand her, I'm just in it for the sex,' then that would make *him* terrible. Even more terrible than he already was, that is.

'Please don't do this,' he said. He wasn't going to answer, probably knowing too that no good could come of it.

'Sorry, am I making you uncomfortable?' She was getting a bit bitchy now. And, frankly, she felt entitled.

'Geri.' He looked anguished. It was awful looking at him, even though she shouldn't care. He had brought it upon himself; upon both of them. And all she had ever done was cook his bloody dinners and iron his bloody shirts, and tell his mother when she rang that he wasn't in, even though he was avoiding her down in the shed. The list went on.

'I'm not even going to ask if you still love me,' she said. She had meant for it to be sarcastic, yet it came out sounding horribly pleading and slightly hysterical. In a minute she would be on the floor and hanging on to his trouser leg. She tried to redeem herself by adding, 'You shit.'

He winced at that (and she did too). 'Look, Geri, we need to talk.'

Oh, so now he got to be the mature one. The one who put on the big voice and did the whole 'We should really sit down and discuss things in a mature fashion' routine.

She was even more furious.

'About what? You shagging your head off behind my back?'

Dear, oh dear. She was really starting to let herself down. But, she thought, why not? Why bother to stick to civilities? Why not go hammer and tongs for it, sling a few plates, roar a few obscenities? To hell with the website and its advice. Losing it might make her feel better. It might make him hurt, and right now hurting him was the one thing she wanted most in all the world.

'You're pathetic,' she said to him venomously. 'If you'd wanted to "talk" – presumably about how unhappy you are – then you should have done it before you decided to cheat, not afterwards.'

He just stood there like a lamb, head bowed, accepting the insults. He wasn't even going to defend himself. It made her angrier still.

'That would have been the courageous thing to do. The decent thing to do.' She looked at the top of his head, and a stupid rush of emotion made her say, 'We've been married for seventeen years, Bob. *Seventeen years*.'

And suddenly she was crying – awful, wounded sobs, deep, like an animal's, and she couldn't stop. She had sworn that the one thing she would not do was cry in front of him. And there she was, letting herself down again.

'I'm sorry.' He was crying now too. She didn't think she'd ever seen him cry before; at least not like this. 'I'm so sorry, Geri. I wish I hadn't.'

'But you did.'

'Geri . . .'

'Get away from me. Don't you touch me.'

It was like somebody had died, the way they stood there, distraught, but unable to offer any comfort to the other at all.

Everything has changed, Geri thought through the upset. It'll never be the same again.

At last she got control of herself. Across the table Bob was wiping his face roughly with the sleeve of his shirt.

There was a funny silence, like all the emotion had gone from the situation. Which was probably a good thing.

'Will we sit down?' he said at last. 'I'll make you some tea. Or get you a drink or something.'

It was tempting. She felt rubbed raw. Part of her wanted to sit down beside him, stay up all night with him, drinking and shouting and talking and asking him questions. Who was this woman? What was the first thing he had noticed about her? Was it just the simple fact that she wasn't Geri?

But she resisted. Drinking and shouting wasn't going to solve anything.

'I'm going for a walk,' she said quietly.

She couldn't bear to look at him for another second.

'OK,' he said. 'Maybe when you come back we can . . . I don't know. I'll wait here for you.'

'I'll be out for about an hour,' she flung over her shoulder. 'When I come back I want you gone.'

He took a small bag of things. Some clothes for work. Toothbrush, shaver, that kind of thing. She rifled through his drawers upstairs and knew exactly what was missing, even down to how many pairs of socks.

She couldn't believe it. He had actually gone. The fool had taken her at her word and gone. Didn't he know that she hadn't really *meant* it? Well, she had at the time, but that was because she had been feeling dramatic and hysterical and incredibly hurt. He had cheated on her – what was she supposed to say? 'Sorry, mate, but it's the spare room for you tonight'?

Of *course* he had to be kicked out. That's the way these

things went, wasn't it? No self-respecting victim – that would be her – did anything less. Whether they wanted to or not, they declared they couldn't bear to share the same roof with their cheating toad of a husband for a single night more, and promptly threw him out, with the vicious threat to produce a shotgun if he ever showed his dirty mug around the place again.

She remembered something else from the website now: no matter what happens, no matter how heated things become, even if they were reduced to name-calling or hair-pulling or worse, Do Not Throw Him Out. It was, allegedly, the very worst thing she could have done, because now he had swanned off into the night and she was completely alone, with no clue where he was or what he felt, or indeed what they were supposed to do now.

Fool, she berated herself.

She walked around for a bit in a daze. She didn't even know how he'd made his escape, seeing as she had his car keys in her handbag.

A thought struck her: had he phoned *her*? This Debra woman? Had she swooped by in her sports car – Geri somehow imagined she had one, a tarty red one with one of those roofs that folded back – and borne Bob away into the sunset, their hair blowing merrily in the breeze?

I've driven him into her arms, Geri thought, horrified.

But she saw that it had started to lash rain outside. So, no windswept hair, at least.

She noticed now that his car was in fact gone. She'd been so upset coming in that it hadn't registered. A quick check of the kitchen drawer beside the sink confirmed that the spare set of keys was missing.

That's not to say that he wasn't with her right now. Debra. He might have driven straight over there, for all she knew.

It was becoming her party trick, she realised. Not knowing. Being kept in the dark. Poor old Geri, not a clue, God love her, and her husband merrily riding his secretary, or whoever she was.

He hadn't left a note. She felt stupid for even looking. But surely he wasn't going to leave things like this: this . . . nothingness. Surely, if he was truly concerned about her at all, and their marriage, then he would have written on the pad that she always kept by the cooker, the neon orange one that held shopping lists, and other lists of Things To Do, and the number of Nicola's childminder in case of emergencies, and Davey's neck measurement for a new school shirt (she really must get around to that). She had just bought a new pen that attached to the worktop via a wire device — well, every other pen went missing — and it was positioned handily beside the pad. Bob could easily have picked it up and written something like, 'I'm sorry. I know you're desperately upset now, but I'll phone you later and we can talk. Oh, and dinky little pen.'

It didn't have to be flipping Shakespeare. Just something to show that he actually cared.

But if he cared he would have stayed. Risked her wrath. He would have been waiting inside the door when she had arrived back from her walk — an hour spent bawling in the toilets of a fast-food restaurant down the town — and he would have begged her to let him stay. He would have sworn to do whatever it took, if only she would not throw him out.

She thought again of the relief on his face. He had been glad it was out in the open. Maybe he had been glad to leave too.

It was nearly worse than the discovery of the affair: this sense of abandonment. Here she was, in her own house, in *their* house, and her husband was gone.

She stood there in the middle of the room, frozen like a statue. What was she supposed to do now? She didn't know. So she just kept standing there, waiting. For what, she had no idea.

When the phone rang ten minutes later, she nearly broke her neck in her rush to pick it up.

'Bob?'

'Geri?' It was Nicola.

Geri's heart sank. If Nicola was going to go on about headstones, Geri might just have some kind of a break-down, right now, this minute. She might even ask Nicola to order one for her while she was at it.

'Oh. Hi, Nicola.'

'Are you OK? You sound a bit funny.' Nicola was always attuned to possible distress and misery.

Something stopped Geri blurting out the whole mess. Shock, maybe. A part of her still didn't believe it was happening.

'I'm fine,' she said, trying to cover up, even while she was thinking, *why* hadn't Bob phoned? Even just to see whether she was all right?

'Well, if you're sure . . .' said Nicola. She sounded excited.

Well, excited was probably pushing it a bit. Animated was more like it. Minimally. 'You'll never guess what's after happening.'

'What?' said Geri, amazed that she sounded so normal.

'Andy asked me out.'

'The bin man?' He was ancient, with a scraggly grey beard. Geri didn't even know how she recalled that detail. Not when her whole world had just collapsed all around her.

'No, *Andy*. From school. He started last September.'

Geri remembered now. He had walked into the staff room on his first day to discover that he was the only male on a staff of twenty-five. Even the janitor was female. But he had fitted in nicely, being careful never to snaffle anybody else's Special K or non-fat yoghurt, and to offer up use of the men's toilet whenever there was a log-jam outside the ladies' at breaktime.

But Nicola sounded horrified. 'He knows I'm widowed.'

'He'd hardly have asked you out if you weren't.'

'It's only been twenty months. It's too soon. He should know that.'

Not unless he hung around bereaved people the whole time, or skimmed *Coming to Terms with Loss* as bedtime reading.

'Do you like him?'

'Well, *yes*.'

Geri wondered how long Nicola would stay on the phone. Every word was becoming an effort.

'Then you should be flattered.'

But Nicola was in a right flap. 'I must have sent out vibes.

He wouldn't have asked me out otherwise. Maybe I was subconsciously giving him the come-on.'

What, in those awful black clothes, and with stringy hair falling into her eyes? Unlikely.

'Nicola, I'm sorry, but I'm busy right now.'

'Oh,' said Nicola. 'Sorry.' She was always so quick to take offence.

For once Geri didn't pacify her. She simply did not have the energy. It was all she could do to remain upright.

'I'll ring you tomorrow, OK?'

Whether it was or not, she didn't wait to find out. She hung up on Nicola and then she turned out the lights and went upstairs. The kids had keys; they could find their own way in.

In the bedroom she threw Bob's pillow and pyjamas from the bed and onto the floor: take that, you bollocks. Then she stripped off and got into her own pyjamas. She left her clothes where she dropped them, and she didn't brush her teeth or take off her make-up. Then she got under the sheets, with a vow never to get up again.

Chapter Thirteen

Bob stayed in a hotel for a week after his wife kicked him out. It was one of those budget places near the M50, with a mean, hard bed and the constant sound of traffic outside.

He didn't come to see Debs. He didn't really do anything at all that week, except stew in his own upset and guilt. He didn't even go to work. He told Debs that he couldn't, that he had ruined everything for everybody, and that he couldn't just carry on like things were normal.

Debs knew that his wife was refusing to talk to him on the phone. And he couldn't talk to his kids either; Geri had dictated that they be told nothing yet, except that Bob had gone, last-minute, to some sales conference. Now that Geri knew, he was desperate to come clean with the kids too, yet at the same time he was sick at the thought of them finding out.

'What are they going to think of me?' he worried to Debs on the phone.

And she couldn't even comfort him – predictably; she was the protagonist in all of this.

He was resentful of her too. It was there in the way he'd phoned her up on Monday evening and told her not to call by, that he wanted some time to himself. They hadn't slept together since his wife had found out.

It was all going horribly wrong.

'What did you expect?' Stevo said. 'A round of applause?'

Debs glared. She had only gone round to cry on Fiona's shoulder, not to partake of Stevo's scarily fundamentalist attitude to life. If Fiona wasn't careful, he'd start growing one of those funny beards, and make Fiona dress in long white aprons, and ride around in a horse-drawn buggy with him.

'Bob's obviously got a lot on his mind,' Fiona said diplomatically. 'He'll come round.'

But Debs thought that Fiona had a slight 'serves you right' attitude about her too. And she had shaken her head very sorrowfully at the mention of Bob's wife, and clicked her tongue sympathetically.

You would think that Debs was enjoying all this. That she got great satisfaction out of ripping people's lives apart. When Bob had finally phoned her up the night of the party – it must have been nearly midnight, and Debs had been morosely pissed with Gavin and Liam at the rejects' table down the back – and told her that his wife had found out, Debs had gone to the toilets to take the call, and had then been physically sick. And it wasn't just the seven glasses of white wine and all that food she'd finally succumbed to at the buffet earlier.

'How was the weekend?' Fiona asked gently.

Bloody awful, that's how.

'I survived,' Debs said. Stevo was still in the vicinity and she didn't want to come across as too self-pitying.

But it *had* been awful. All day Sunday she had spent with a vicious hangover and waiting for Bob to ring. He hadn't. Then she started to worry that his *wife* would phone. Or, worse, come round to confront her. She might have throttled Bob until he'd revealed Debs's address and phone number. She could be on her way over at any moment in a rage, and ready to punch Debs's lights out, and who could blame her? Debs had huddled in bed with a cup of tea, jumping every time the front door of the apartment block slammed. She wouldn't answer if the doorbell rang, she decided. But that was just *too* cowardly, wasn't it?

His wife didn't come round. Nobody did. Debs began to feel alone and abandoned as night drew in with no word or appearance from Bob. She wondered what kind of scene was going on at his house. Had he promised his wife that he would never, ever contact Debs again? Had she been dumped only she didn't know it? In the end she plucked up the courage and phoned his mobile, only to find that he was in a hotel room, and had been since the previous night.

He hadn't come to her.

'You understand why I can't,' he had said, apologetically.

'Yes, yes,' she had rabbited back, even though she didn't.

But she understood this much: his wife still came first, like she always had. And even though she obviously didn't want him any more, she was still number one on Bob's list of concerns. Debs was a poor runner-up.

'He wants to get back with her,' she said grimly to Fiona when Stevo eventually went off into the living room to watch the telly. Good riddance.

'Has he said that?'

'He doesn't need to say it. He's over there in a crummy hotel room and I'm here.'

She was still slightly shocked by it: that he had spent a whole day in a hotel room without even letting her know.

'Look, maybe he's waiting for the dust to settle. Imagine how it would look if he went straight from the family home to your flat. It wouldn't be fair on his wife.'

Right now Debs was getting pretty fed up of everyone's concern for his wife. It wasn't that she was trying to downplay the woman's probable shock and distress, but what about Debs? People didn't think mistresses had feelings too. They thought they waited in the wings like vampires, ready to swoop in and snatch other women's men. And if they were hurt and upset too, then it bloody well served them right – they should have kept their paws to themselves in the first place.

But most of all Debs was hurt by Bob's coolness. This was a guy who had said he loved her; a man who had traced little patterns on her skin with his thumb, and who said that she always smelled of buttercups (which she hoped was flattering, and not a reflection of how much Dairy Maid she spread on her toast every morning). Wouldn't you think he would be even the tiniest bit happy that they now might have a future together?

Nobody was expecting him to be jumping around the garden, but if he couldn't see anything positive in the situation at all, as in an open relationship with Debs, then what was the point of it?

'I don't know where I stand, Fiona. And I'm afraid to ask him.' She felt close to tears. How had she ever let herself get into this mess?

Fiona considered this. You could see she was trying to put a good face on things but thought it was pretty hopeless too.

'If you want my advice, don't put pressure on him. Let him think things through. That way you'll stand a better chance of him coming down on your side.'

It all sounded like a lot of game-playing to Debs. And, being a relatively unsophisticated country girl with confidence issues and a weight problem, she wasn't cut out for all that lark.

She'd rather put up a fight for him. But every time she thought of her opponent she shrivelled up in shame: Geri, a nurse, a mother of two children, a woman whom Bob had promised to love and honour. A woman who probably loathed Debs with every fibre of her being.

And right now Debs felt she deserved every bit of it. It was hard to meet her own eyes in the bathroom mirror these mornings when she stepped off the scales.

'All right,' she told Fiona with a sigh. 'I'll give it a shot. I'll give him some space and see if it works.'

What else could she do? Clearly Bob was in no frame of mind for a big chat about their future. Debs had the suspicion that if she brought up 'them' at all he would simply break the whole thing off there and then.

And so all week she tried to ignore him. This was harder than she'd thought it would be, given that when she arrived in the office on Wednesday having spent Monday and Tuesday slogging around the bookshops with a cookery writer who looked like a domestic goddess but smelled of BO, she discovered that the entire office knew that Bob was a married man.

'How could you!' she hissed furiously at Gavin. He and Liam had been at the table when she'd cried bitter tears after Bob's phone call, but Liam had been asleep in a bowl of trifle.

'Me?' he said, wounded. 'I didn't say a word.'

For some reason she believed him.

So that left only one person: Alex.

Debs gave her filthy looks all day, and mentally beamed the word 'bitch' at her. And she had been so chummy that night too! Seeking Debs out to confide in her about her boyfriend's petty little problems, whatever they were. Well, Debs might just start a few rumours of her own. She might let it slip at the water cooler that Greg suffered from serious erectile dysfunction problems, which was no mean feat when you were going out with someone as sexy as Alex. See how she would like *that*.

She seemed to have no clue at all as to her gaffe. Over she came straight away on Wednesday morning, a big sympathetic expression on her face, and cornered Debs.

'Listen, I was really sorry to hear what happened with Bob,' she said in a low voice.

Bloody hell – now she knew that the affair had been discovered too. She must have been eavesdropping under the table on all fours.

Debs looked at her very coldly. 'Thanks,' she said. 'But you can save it.'

Alex looked confused. And hurt. Let her. For someone who was so protective of her own privacy, she didn't seem too careful with anybody else's.

It quickly became apparent that the entire office was in on the gossip. Debs felt like an animal in the zoo as she walked through the office and took her place under the stairs.

Nobody seemed to know what to say to her. Most of the younger playmates were completely unable to hide their surprise that Debs had the necessary pulling power to attract a normal man, never mind a married one (who clearly already had access to regular sex, and so didn't need to go looking for it). They looked her up and down in a rather baffled way, and she could almost hear them decide in their heads, 'She must be great in bed, or something.'

Even Marty knew. Debs was horrified. But he seemed to think it was a big joke, Debs having it off with a married man, and gave her lots of dirty winks and told a really bad joke at coffee break about how many mistresses it took to screw a light bulb in. Debs left the kitchenette before the punch line.

'Sorry,' Gavin said sourly afterwards. 'I had to laugh. Otherwise I'd probably have lost my job.'

Alex hadn't laughed, Debs noted. But no doubt she was worrying about what jokes Marty would pull once Greg's little idiosyncrasies finally came out. As they would. You couldn't keep that kind of thing under wraps for ever. Sooner or later everybody would find out.

'Look, do you want to go out for lunch?' Gavin enquired.

At least he was being nice about it. Everybody else seemed to think that Bob was some lecherous creep in a shiny suit who took off his wedding ring the minute he left the house. And Debs had fallen for it, God love her; poor, plump Debs – but who was still a bit of a tart for putting out for him.

That was the crux of it, really: Debs wasn't thin enough to be a proper mistress, the seductive, alluring type that men with children and wives and dozens of commitments simply couldn't keep their hands off. And because she wasn't the alluring type, she must be desperate, to the point of letting herself get picked up by shabby, married men for their sexual gratification.

'No, thanks,' she whimpered to Gavin. Could they possibly be right?

She had a great urge to crawl to the loo and cry. But they would all know she had been crying, and she wouldn't give it to them. She hated them, every single one of them. She had even spent an hour that morning on jobs sites on the internet; there was bound to be something better out there. But she would have to update her CV, and probably do a course to brush up on her interview technique, and lose a few pounds to get into a suit, and honestly, she just didn't have the energy right now. Not when she felt so down. Not when Bob clearly didn't even notice that she was ignoring him. Or, if he did, he was glad.

Marty suddenly exited his office. 'Can anybody tell me how to work this fucking thing?' he roared, waving around the new BlackBerry that his wife had finally made him get and that was giving him piles.

Gavin gave him a vicious look and burst out viciously, 'God, I hate this place!'

'Leave, then,' said Debs, in a spineless fashion.

'But I'd have to update my CV, and brush up on my interview technique, and honestly, I just don't have the energy right now,' Gavin moaned. He cast a tiny look in Alex's direction. He hadn't been able to make eye contact with her since his public humiliation at Marty's hands. It had been a serious setback to his hopes of conquering her, if it hadn't sunk them altogether. 'Anyway,' he said wistfully, 'could I leave her? Even if she thinks I'm just Marty's whipping boy?'

'Give up, Gavin. Have some respect for yourself, man,' Debs commanded. Mind you, there was more than a little irony in that.

'You're right. I'll update my CV immediately.'

'So will I,' Debs resolved, in a rare burst of initiative. Why should she sit around waiting for Bob when there might be a fantastic new job out there for her?

'Actually, would you mind if we waited until after lunch?' Gavin said. 'I'm starving.'

'Me too.'

Wednesday limped into Thursday, and then Friday. No work was done on the CVs, unsurprisingly. More importantly, there wasn't a dickybird from Bob.

'It's over,' Debs told Fiona fearfully.

'It doesn't look good, all right,' Fiona said, little Miss Sunshine.

'This stupid plan was all your idea!'

'What?'

'All this business of giving him space. I've given him so much space that he's decided to shaft me.'

'You don't know that.' Now she was trying to be positive, even though any eejit could see that he was hardly making a big play for Debs.

'I'm going over there.'

'I wouldn't,' Fiona cautioned.

'Why not?'

'It's never a good idea to do all the running.'

Debs wanted to remind her of the way she had thrown herself full force at Stevo once it had become apparent that he was The One. It had not been a thing of beauty.

'I can't just sit here. I'm going mad.'

Fiona looked around at the kitchen. The worktop was strewn with empty frozen pizza boxes and crisps bags and litre bottles of Coke and Wagon Wheel wrappers. 'You haven't eaten all that, have you?'

'Me? No,' Debs blurted. Given that she lived alone, it quickly became apparent to both of them that this was a lie.

'I might have had a few blow-outs during the week,' she admitted. Normally she would have disposed of the evidence pronto, mostly because she couldn't stand the sight of it herself. 'Pig! Pig!' she would mutter in a rage as she flung it all in the bin. But she had been too upset that week to bother tidying up.

Fiona looked concerned. Debs wondered how much of her overeating she had noticed when she had still lived at the flat. But Debs had always been so careful to keep her binges under wraps. She would wait until Fiona had gone out with Stevo, or else she'd take a stash of food into her bedroom and tuck in with a trashy magazine ('Lose Ten Pounds in Five Days!').

'Maybe you should take up some exercise,' Fiona suggested. 'Just to relieve the stress of everything.'

She was going to get on Debs's case. She had that look in her eye. Next thing she would suggest that they go power-walking together after work.

'Look, it was just a bit of comfort eating,' Debs insisted. 'It's not like I do it all the time. And I haven't put on any weight.'

Her scales were blessedly the same as always when she had stepped up on them that morning, even after everything she'd eaten that week (it was too embarrassing to list them out all).

'Just so long as you're looking after yourself,' Fiona lectured. 'Your health is the most important thing.'

'Yes, yes,' said Debs, who knew damn well that the most important thing was to be as thin as possible using any means at your disposal. And Fiona had thought so too before she had landed Stevo and started to let herself go.

In the end Debs persuaded Fiona to drive her over to Bob's hotel.

'Will I wait for you?' She was full of concern.

'No,' said Debs in a cavalier fashion. 'I'll probably be ages.'

Or else she could be less than five minutes, depending on how things went. But even if it was a disaster she'd rather have her cry at the bus stop, in peace.

She knew Bob was there because his car was parked in the car park. It didn't appear to have moved position in a week, judging by the leaves that had gathered on the roof.

At least he hasn't gone back to his wife, she told herself as she went upstairs in the lift. She didn't ring through first to let him know she was here. He might tell her to go home.

Standing outside his door, she could hear the television playing. Some documentary on seals. God, he must be really depressed.

She was starting to wonder now whether coming here mightn't be a seriously bad idea. What if he really *didn't* want to see her? What if his lack of communication during the week had meant, it was all over?

Her knees felt a bit weak. She stood there until it became embarrassing, with people giving her curious looks as they passed. In another minute someone would alert reception that there was a prowler on the third floor.

Finally she knocked. 'Room service!' she called. It was just a little joke to steady her nerves. But the minute it was out she was sorry.

Bob appeared unamused too when he opened the door. He was a bit scraggly-looking, as though he had lost interest in his appearance. And his eyes were puffy and his face looked unslept in.

'Hi,' he said. Rather unenthusiastically.

Debs was suddenly cross. She had come all the way over here on a Friday night, taking two buses – well, she would have had to except for Fiona – after a whole week of silence, and he couldn't be bothered to look grateful.

'Can I come in? Or is that out of bounds?'

'No. Sorry.' He stepped aside.

The room was a mess. A tray of congealing food sat on the floor. The air was stuffy and a bit smelly.

Debs looked around slowly. 'You're really feeling sorry for yourself, aren't you?'

He looked startled. 'You don't know what's been going on this past week.'

'Why don't you tell me then?'

He shook his head tiredly.

'Oh,' said Debs snappishly. 'I'm being kept out again, I see. Don't tell Debs anything.' She barrelled on before she could stop herself. 'You know, I don't know what you ever wanted with me. Unless it was just sex.'

'Debs. For God's sake.'

He looked like he had a headache coming on. Clearly he hadn't expected her to come here and attack him. He had probably thought she would do the usual submissive just-glad-to-be-together routine, and accept his silences and his secrets and his distance.

'People in normal relationships talk to each other,' she told him, rather dramatically. 'They confide things. They share. We just eat omelettes and talk about the shagging moon.'

She hadn't meant to curse. No doubt the people in the room next door were rolling their eyes and going, 'Oh God, not another domestic.'

He was looking at her now in a way that wasn't nice. 'You said you liked our conversations. You said you loved them; that most guys talked rubbish and that I was a refreshing change. So what are you saying now – you were just pretending?'

'No . . .'

'What then? What is it you want, Debs?'

It was like she was just another thing tugging out of him, another problem to be solved.

Well, to hell with that. She wasn't going to slink off, head hanging, just because he was in the wars with his wife.

'More,' she told him coldly. 'You're not exactly a great prize, you know. You think I *like* the fact that you're married? You think I'm enjoying being the other woman in this mess? I could have gone for someone much simpler than you, you know.' Chance would have been a fine thing, but there was no need to mention that. 'But I didn't. I gave up the idea of a normal relationship to be with you. And what have you given up for me? Nothing!'

Bob gave a short laugh. 'Oh, yeah? Here I am in a shitty hotel room, with my family miles away, because of you.'

Ah yes, here it came now: the resentment. The blame.

'You're only here because they found out,' she bit out. 'It wasn't because you told them.'

'I hadn't things worked out yet, I wasn't sure—'

'Oh, shut up.'

'It wasn't time, Debs.' He was impatient now.

'For you, maybe.'

He gave a bit of a snort and threw his arms wide. 'What, are you saying that after three short months we were ready to jack everything else in and make some big commitment to each other?'

'Yes,' said Debs simply.

She shouldn't have said it. But everything else was out in the open, so why not?

Bob was stopped in his tracks. He stared at her as though

he were only truly seeing her properly for the first time since she'd arrived in his hotel room. He seemed very surprised, as though somebody couldn't possibly want him that much; that he wasn't worth such a definite and early commitment. He looked like he was resisting the urge to look over his shoulder to see whether somebody more attractive than he had just entered the room unexpectedly: the real room service, maybe.

Debs's heart rose protectively. She wanted to wrap her arms around him, to press him to her breast tenderly. She wanted to take him back to the flat and look after him, and cook for him, and fatten him up. She wanted to make a home with this gentle, rather confused, moon-loving man, and make him forget all about his wife and kids. Well, not completely, but surely in time he would reach an amiable relationship with them, and there would be phone calls once a week on a Sunday evening, or whatever, and everything would be fine. Otherwise he and Debs would be left alone to pursue a blissfully happy existence as a bona fide couple.

Oh, why couldn't he just play along?

'I can't,' he began hesitantly. 'Not at the moment.' He looked so torn that Debs would have felt sorry for him if she wasn't so cross.

'Why?' she demanded. 'What's keeping you here? The food?'

That earned her a look. 'I have to think of Geri.'

'Who won't talk to you. Or has anything changed?'

It was clear from his face that it hadn't.

'What do you think that tells you, Bob?' He didn't want to hear it, but it was time somebody spelled things out for him. 'What's your big plan – hang around here for the next however long, running up a massive hotel bill and wallowing in your own misery? Hoping against hope that one day you'll be allowed to crawl home, tail between your legs, to spend the next twenty years saying you're sorry and trying to make it up to her and the kids?'

There was no need to elaborate further. Bob sunk down onto the bed, his head buried in his hands, no doubt contemplating his outlook. Which wasn't great, as the Irish weather forecasters would say.

'Or you could come home with me,' Debs said quietly.

Afterwards she wondered at the choice she had offered him. It wasn't really a choice at all.

After a moment he got up from the bed and began to pack his things.

Chapter Fourteen

Staying in bed on a permanent basis wasn't as easy as it sounded. There was all that daytime television for starters – Australian soaps and make-over programmes and people sitting on studio couches whinging about how their badass husbands were spending the household budget on sex chatlines. As if Geri wasn't disturbed enough already.

And the food was dire. She had somehow imagined that delicious meals would magically be delivered to her room by some kindly person, perhaps wearing a uniform, who would pat her sympathetically on the shoulder with the words, 'I'm sorry for your troubles,' before whipping off a dome cover to reveal an aromatic chicken tikka masala.

She wanted a chicken tikka masala. She *deserved* a chicken tikka masala.

But there was nobody to bring Geri food. The kids had gone for the week: Davey to Ben's house and Susan to Rebecca's. Geri had lied to all concerned that she had the flu. Really, she just hadn't felt capable of looking after anybody, including herself.

'Can't Dad come home from his sales conference?' Susan and Davey had looked worried. Geri *did* look pretty awful.

'No,' she'd choked out. 'Look, I just need to stay in bed. I'll be fine by Friday.'

She didn't know how she was going to tell them. All she knew right now was that they had to be protected from the truth – at least until everything settled down.

She sent Bob a curt text to that effect. When she was sure it had gone through, she smartly turned her phone off: communication over.

And so she was stuck in her bedroom, heartbroken and ravenous, with nothing to do except watch *Jeremy Kyle*:

'Did you *know* that your wife was pregnant before you ran off with her sister? Did you *care*?'

'No, Jeremy, I didn't, I swear. I mean, I didn't know.'

'You lousy sod!' the wife would chip in. 'You bought me the pregnancy test.'

Tears all round. Geri would join in. She could go for hours once she got up a good head of steam.

Actually, she didn't mind the crying bit so much. It was probably the first time in seventeen years that she was able to have a cry in peace. Someone would always stumble upon her just as her nose reached hideous proportions, or else one of the kids would take fright and think she was dying, and she would end up having to forget her own upset and cuddle them on her knee and assure them she had nothing terminal.

So it felt good to cry. It was cathartic. She would sit up in the puddle of sheets and let rip. She would turn her face to the ceiling and howl like a crazy woman. Boxes of tissues were used. Her ribcage began to grow sore and her eyes were two narrow, swollen slits, and still she cried.

Mostly her tears were of disbelief. 'How could he?' she would sob quietly to herself. 'How could he, the shit?' Actually, *how*? Bob, conduct an affair? Behind her back? It beggared belief. The logistics of it alone were mind-boggling. How the blazes had he pulled it off? The man was harmless. How had he managed to sleep with an entire other woman under her very nose for months on end? He was the kind who broke into a cold sweat whenever he had to ring in sick to work, even when he *was* sick.

'Think about it,' Nicola urged her on the phone. 'It'll all start to make sense.' (Geri had told her that morning. And to give her her due, she had phoned every half-hour since to offer support, because she 'had been there.')

And of course it did. Geri thought of those furtive phone calls down by the garden shed. The long trips to DIY stores with nothing to show for it except a single light bulb. The late nights at the office once a week. Or it might have been more. It was possible, she told Nicola, that he might have been late some other nights and she hadn't noticed.

'You didn't *notice*?' Nicola said.

'I was busy, OK? I hold down a full-time job, with shifts, in case you don't know, as well as running a house, and rearing two kids, and baking bloody chocolate-chip muffins. And making tea for you.' She might as well get it in.

Nicola sounded like she was trying to decide whether to be in a huff, or to get worried about Geri's mental state. 'Nobody's blaming you, Geri,' she said at last.

'I should bloody well hope not.'

She might be guilty of being a fool, but she would not sit there − well, lie there in her bed − and assume the blame for poor Bob having to go and have an affair. No way.

'You think you know somebody,' she said to Nicola a bit viciously now, 'but you don't at all.'

Nicola was in agreement. 'No offence to him, but, I mean, *Bob*.'

Indeed. Overnight he seemed to have transformed from a cuddly, dependable man who was handy around the house into a devious cad with the ability to scheme and lie at every turn. And without Geri suspecting a thing! Well, hardly a thing, anyway. He was, she decided, the moral equivalent of the Incredible Hulk, turning green and ugly the minute he stepped out the front door.

'I wonder,' Nicola pondered, 'if she's the first?'

'What?'

There was a little pause. 'Did I just say that out loud?'

'Yes.'

'Don't mind me.' She was trying to backtrack now. 'However much of a louse he is, I'm sure he'd never . . . it's not like they're lining up . . . I have to go now.'

Geri was left to think about the monstrous: that this Debra woman might merely be the latest in a string of conquests. Bob might have been at this kind of thing for *years*. All right, it seemed unlikely, but meeker men than he had been revealed to have led exotic double lives for decades, with women up and down the country.

After all, how was Geri to know? She'd barely copped this time around, even when the evidence was glaringly obvious. He might just be slipping up, having been a dab hand at deception for years.

Right now she didn't feel she knew Bob at all.

And that was nearly the biggest shock. Seventeen years of shared history were suddenly cast into doubt. Was it all an illusion? Had they ever been truly happy at all, or had there always been another woman in the background? And if not, had Bob been discontented for years, putting on the face of a happy family man, but in truth merely hiding his unhappiness?

That was the one and only time she phoned him. It was the Monday morning after he had left, when she had sat up nearly all night.

'Geri?' He sounded hugely relieved. She listened hard to see if she could make out where he was from background noise – crossing her fingers that she didn't hear a woman's voice – but there was only silence.

'Were there others?' she asked. It was amazing how calm she sounded again. Not once had she gone to pieces in front of him. 'Other women,' she said, just in case it needed clarification.

'No.' He said it quietly but forcefully. She believed him. She felt a small weight lift from her heart.

'That's all I wanted to know,' she said.

'Geri, wait.'

She didn't want to wait. She was afraid. Her calmness was only skin deep.

'What?' she said.

'We need to talk,' he told her.

His assertiveness, his ability to plan in the midst of this awful time annoyed her. He had already decided that they needed to talk, whereas Geri couldn't even figure out whether she needed to go to the bathroom or not. Didn't he realise that her mental state right now was the equivalent of being hit by a bus? A double-decker bus?

'We have nothing left to say,' she bit back at him coldly, sounding like something from a bad movie.

The problem was she *did* want to talk. She was dying for a rant. She had spent most of the night composing vitriolic monologues that she was desperate to unleash upon him. Even through her shock and horror she had managed to think of upwards of a hundred dreadful insults, such as his poor performance in bed (not that her own was anything to write home about), and the way his children automatically bypassed him whenever a decision had to be made about even the smallest thing.

She wanted to tell him that he was the lowest form of life: a cheat, a betrayer, a mean little man who snuck around behind his family's back to conduct his shoddy affair. She wanted to let him know how much she despised and hated him.

Why then did the sound of his voice, so familiar and steady on the phone, make her want to burst into tears and beg him for comfort?

'Can I come over?' he said. Not 'home'.

Geri clutched the receiver to her ear, torn. Surely any

kind of conversation would be giving in to him. Letting him think that what he had done to Geri was somehow OK, because at least they were *talking*.

He was appealing to her reason. Good old Geri, the sensible, practical one, would surely be open to an appeal by him, or least a jolly good explanation for his behaviour. She was a coper; she'd take this one on the chin too.

But that morning Geri didn't want to cope. She didn't want to be reasonable. Her heart had just been broken by her husband and she would talk to him when she felt like it.

'No,' she said.

'We need to talk about the kids, at least.'

'Shame you didn't think about them when you were in bed with your girlfriend.' It came out with terrific bitterness.

There was a defeated little silence, and then he persisted, 'We're going to have to tell them, Geri.'

The cheek of him. *He* was trying to dictate to *her* about the kids?

'We'll tell the kids when I'm good and ready,' she told him coldly, and hung up on him.

It felt good. Now he would know just how hurt she was without her having to say a word.

The following day her position became more entrenched. Her need to convey to him the depths of his depravity had become her priority.

'Geri—' he only got out before she hung up on him again. It was great. Now he *really* knew what he had done.

By Wednesday he had obviously got the message

because he didn't phone at all. Geri sat there in the bed telling herself that she was glad.

Then, as evening drew in, she grew bitter. Oh, so he wasn't even going to persist. Three lousy phone calls and that was it! He wasn't going to bother any more. Now he'd be able to tell all his friends and family, martyred, 'Well, I *tried* . . .'

Wouldn't you think that at the very least he'd be concerned for her wellbeing? He must know that she was distraught. He might have phoned just to hear her voice and assure himself that at least she hadn't taken an overdose of Vitamin C, which were the only tablets in the house.

But he didn't phone. He wasn't too concerned about her at all. He had probably moved on already. Geri had seen on daytime TV that people who committed affairs were already emotionally detached from their spouses and that when it all hit the fan, they were far better positioned to deal with it than their poor, betrayed other halves. 'Oh, why do you have to keep banging on about it?' one man had said crossly to his wife on *Jeremy Kyle* – a whole forty-eight hours after he'd confessed to riding their son's music teacher.

When Bob eventually rang late that evening Geri was so full of bottled-up rage and hurt that she just lost her cool completely and he'd barely had a chance to say 'Hello,' before she shrieked down the line, 'Oh, just leave me alone! Go to her, because I don't want you any more, OK?'

He didn't say anything. There was a long, empty pause on the phone and then he hung up quietly.

Geri wept bitter tears that night. And for once she wasn't hungry. All the adrenalin of the past few days seemed to have deserted her and she felt flat and heart-broken. After a bit she stopped crying over Bob and began crying over other things, just for a change. The gradual loss of her youth, for instance, brought on by the discovery of a fresh batch of grey hairs in the bathroom mirror when she went to the loo.

'I'm shagging *ancient*,' she bawled inconsolably.

It was one thing to have your husband cheat on you before disappearing off into the sunset, or wherever he had gone, but quite another to have him do it to you once you were past the age of thirty-five. What chance had she now of getting back at him with a new man of her own? Bugger all, at her age. If he'd had any consider-ation at all, he'd have done this years ago, and at least left her with a few options.

She flopped back into bed, consumed by fresh tears and rage, and a burning urge to do him serious harm. If he were standing in the room right now she would be quite capable of murder.

Then the tears eventually stopped and the silence of the house hit her. Her own aloneness was almost as bad as his infidelity. After seventeen years of marriage, she felt like only half a person now that he had gone.

Word spread and people began to phone and leave messages.

'Geri? It's Mum here. Nicola told me what happened. Oh dear . . . Would you ever give me a ring when you get up?'

'Hi, Geri, it's Emma. Look, I know you're very upset,

and probably don't want to talk to anybody right now, but maybe you'd call me or Mum just to let us know that you're all right.'

'Geri, it's Nicola, just checking in with you. Again. If you don't ring back in the next hour or two I'm going to start worrying about you, and I might have to ring the guards and get them to go around and check on you. So please ring. Talk soon.'

Geri didn't. She lay in bed and wondered whether Bob really loved Debra. She tried to remember his face when he had mentioned her name. Had his expression been all soft and gooey? Was he with her now, both of them glad that it was finally in the open and they could be together?

That set her off howling again, even as she told herself that they were welcome to each other. Let them be together, if that's what they wanted! They could set up a den of iniquity, with lots of plump red cushions scattered about the place and sex toys in the bedside cabinets. They could bonk morning, noon and night, for all Geri cared! The romance would soon wear off. She, of all people, knew that. She'd give it six months before they started moaning at each other about socks on the floor and whose turn it was to put out the bins.

'We're home!' There was a shout from downstairs. The kids. Damn – was it Friday afternoon already? All she had done since they'd left was cry and think venomous thoughts.

But now it was time to come clean. She couldn't pretend forever. Plus, they ought to know what their father was *really* like.

And so she patted down her wild hair and brushed a

few stray cream cracker crumbs from the front of her pyjamas. It wouldn't do to look too slobbish or she might lose their sympathy altogether.

'Children!' she called. There was a feeble, tragic note to her voice that was rather pleasing. She arranged herself tragically on the bed while she waited for them to rush upstairs, full of concern.

'I had the remote control first, you fat pig!' came a shriek from below.

She was forced to abandon her pose and bellow crossly, 'Susan! Davey!'

Here they came, huffing and puffing as though she were putting them out. She tried not to take offence as Susan lingered just inside the door, sniffing the air rather suspiciously. Well, it had been a while since a window had been opened.

Geri patted the bed gently like she had seen them do in *The Waltons*.

Davey and Susan exchanged glances before reluctantly coming to perch on the very edge of the duvet.

'You're not contagious any more, are you?' Susan enquired.

Geri ignored that.

'You know the way your father is away at that sales conference?' she began. 'Well, that's not actually where he is.'

'Where is he so?' Susan asked.

It was too embarrassing to admit that she actually hadn't a clue and so she said, 'Look, there's been a bit of a development.'

She had already decided that she was going to be

mature about this. There would be no cursing or violent hand gestures. She would simply give them the plain, unadorned facts. They would easily come to their own conclusions that their father was a lying, cheating scumbag who should be castrated forthwith, preferably without an anaesthetic.

But they wouldn't hear it from *her*. By God no. She was entirely blameless in this whole shoddy mess and would retain the high moral ground even if it killed her.

So she looked at them with great compassion and said, 'He's having an affair.'

They would be shocked, naturally. They might even cry. She readied her arms to administer comforting hugs.

'An affair!' Susan said, breaking into a volley of disbelieving snorts. 'That'll be the day.'

Davey was smiling too, although he looked slightly disapproving that Geri should spring such a tasteless joke upon them.

'No, really, he is,' she insisted.

She hadn't expected that they would refuse to believe her.

'With an actual *woman*?' Susan screeched, looking highly entertained.

'Yes.' Geri was getting cross now. 'Her name is Debra, and she works near him.' Was that all she knew? It didn't sound very convincing. 'And she's American.' Well, she might be. And it sounded rather more mistress-like than some plump one from Crumlin.

Davey looked concerned. 'Are you sure about this, Mum?'

And they both looked at her as though she were slightly batty.

'You think I'm making it up?' What did she have to do – produce a pair of red lacy knickers?

'Sorry,' Davey said hurriedly. 'It's just, well, *Dad.*'

Yes. Bob, who tinkered about in the shed, and who had a can of lukewarm Heineken when Arsenal were playing on the telly. Two, if they won. She could see why they might be having problems.

'It's a shock to me too.' Perhaps now they might look at her with sympathy.

But no. They were still staring wide-eyed at each other across the bed, no doubt entertaining lurid fantasies of their father, who used to carry them around on his back when they were small whilst making giddy-up noises, astride some young one called Debra, shouting, 'Yes! Yes!'

She could barely think of it herself without the urge to throw up. She felt sorry for them. What a thing to learn about your father.

'To be honest,' Susan said at last, 'we thought there was something up.'

'Well, yes,' Geri confessed relief. 'I hated lying to you about having a bug. But what could I do? I didn't want to upset you.'

'No, I meant in the last couple of months.'

Geri had her second nasty shock in a week.

'We didn't suspect an affair, obviously,' Davey hurriedly assured her. 'But, you know, all that odd atmosphere.'

Geri nodded even while she thought wildly, What odd atmosphere? What were they talking about? Everything had been fine, surely? The telly might have been on a bit more than usual, and her and Bob might have grunted at each other slightly less than was customary, but that was *normal.*

Odd meant shouting and screaming and chucking saucepans across the kitchen.

And anyway, her kids were so self-obsessed it was doubtful they noticed that the sun rose and set once a day, never mind anything else.

But it seemed that they had.

'And Dad out all the time,' Susan intoned gloomily, as though the whole house had been falling apart all around her. 'And you . . . well, doing your thing like you always do.'

Making muffins, she meant. Apple and cinnamon muffins. And those ones with icing and little sprinkles on the top (which took absolutely *ages*, for anybody's information). And driving people places. Driving *her* places.

Geri didn't nod now. She wanted to slap Susan. Both of them. Hard, across the backsides. How dare they sit there and smugly list out all the warning signs they had earmarked? *They* hadn't been making muffins. Or picking up their dirty underwear off the bathroom floor, or putting it into the wash. Or doing fucking anything around the house! Except criticising Geri every now and again, of course. No wonder they had the time to act as anthropologists! Maybe Geri might have cottoned on to Bob's affair if she had nothing better to do than sit around pining after Leo Ryan or sitting in front of a computer game.

'Poor you,' Davey said.

But she didn't want their sympathy now. She was sick of them. She was sick of herself.

'Go and ring him,' she said.

'What?' They were confused now.

'Your father. Obviously you'll want to hear his side of the story too.' She said this rather viciously. But if they were determined to be so mature about things, then they could blooming well suffer through Bob's stuttering explanation of how he ended up shagging some silly girl with a name like a cheerleader. She only wished she could listen in.

'Well, obviously we don't want to take sides . . .' Susan said, with another look at Davey.

'No,' he concurred very philosophically.

It was at that point that Geri resolved that she would never bake a muffin again.

'We'll try and be there for both of you,' they promised her.

'That would be lovely,' Geri assured them. 'Oh, and in the meantime, I'm staying in bed, so you'll have to manage by yourselves for a while.'

She enjoyed the startled look on their faces.

'"Manage?"' Susan clarified.

'Make your own lunches, and put on a few washes. That sort of thing,' Geri said brightly. 'I don't feel up to it at the moment, I'm sure you understand.'

'Yes,' Susan said, rather more reluctantly.

'And who will make dinner?' Davey enquired naïvely.

'I have no idea,' Geri confessed. 'You can get stuff out of the freezer. Or maybe Bob will. I'm sure he'll want to see you regularly, wherever he ends up.'

'You mean he's not coming back?' Susan said.

'No. Not right now.'

OK, this was a different thing altogether. While it was quite exciting to discover that your parents could still rock the boat despite being ancient and boring, nobody wanted any permanent inconvenience.

'But you'll still go to work, right?' Susan said, looking distinctly worried now. No doubt she was wondering who would fund her mobile phone bills. Being in love wasn't cheap, especially when you were barred from face-to-face contact with your adored one and were reduced to sending hundreds of texts every day – oh, yes, Geri knew about those – not to mention the whispered nightly hour-long conversations. 'Tell me what you're wearing,' Susan's end of such a conversation had begun last night. 'Just so I can picture you.'

'No,' Geri announced now, startling everybody. 'I won't be going back to work at the moment. I'm taking some time off.'

They did some kind of compassionate leave, didn't they? It was for bereavements, but she was sure that mental stress would fit the bill too.

The girls would cover. There were plenty of capable people out there besides Geri. Right now she didn't want to be capable any more.

'I suppose there'll be some kind of vicious custody fight over us,' Susan said, looking a bit excited.

'I doubt it,' said Geri cheerfully, snuggling back down into bed and reaching for the remote control.

Chapter Fifteen

Bob didn't like Alpen. He liked Weetabix, though. He was good at fixing things but not good at tidying up after himself, and he didn't seem to know how to work the washing machine, and had little curiosity in finding out.

Not that Debs minded. She was embarrassingly happy to do things for him. She bustled around the little flat like a newlywed, straightening cushions and ironing and expanding her dinner repertoire to include grilled pork chops and, very adventurously, lasagne. It was tricky stopping the sheets sticking together, and she had several disasters before she had to ring up her mother and ask her advice.

'Harrumph,' her mother said. She didn't approve of Bob living with Debs. Not only were they not married, but he was already married to someone else. It confounded her small-town sensibilities, and there was no more loose talk of coming up on the bus to meet him.

261

But Debs soldiered on. They would accept the situation eventually. In years to come they would all look back on this and laugh. Well, maybe not laugh – there had been too much upset all round for that – but she hoped people would come to appreciate what they had gone through to be together.

In the meantime Debs had never been happier. Of course, it had taken time for them both to adjust. The first night had been tricky. Bob had stood inside the front door with his sports bag at his feet, looking not so much like a lover about to move in as a puppy who had mislaid its owner. Debs had had the awful feeling that she was a thief. But she wanted him too much to give him back. And why shouldn't she have a chance at happiness too? And so she brushed aside all those feelings of wrongness, and had gathered him into her arms and held him so tightly that eventually he had relaxed and buried his face in her neck as if seeking comfort.

'Got room for another?' he had said, half joking.

'Just so long as you don't throw your stuff about,' she had said, mock grouchy.

There was a lot to learn in the coming days and weeks. There was all the practical stuff for starters: the breakfast cereal thing, for instance, and the intricacies of sharing a bathroom with someone who wasn't Fiona. Keys had to be cut, and bills changed into both their names. The landlord had to be alerted to the fact that Debs had a new flatmate.

'Why is he looking at us in that knowing, sleazy kind of way?' Debs had whispered to Bob.

'He's not. You're just being paranoid.'

'I should warn you now, I'm slightly given to paranoia.'

'Are you? In that case, it's only fair that you should know that I suffer from nocturnal upper respiratory tract obstruction.'

'What's that?' She had worrisome visions of trying to resuscitate him some night at four a.m.

'I snore.'

There was so much to learn about each other. Sitting on park benches talking philosophy could only deliver so much hard information. Debs had had no idea that Bob was left-handed, for instance, or that his birthday was on 18 March. He always had to have music playing in the background, and had a mother who did some kind of geriatric modelling work and had notions above her station because of it.

Debs hoarded away each little new discovery like it was gold dust. Obviously not all of it was fascinating; his tendency to nod off on the couch, and treat her to some nocturnal upper respiratory tract obstruction while he was at it, was less than endearing, but she was in love and so she didn't care.

'Tell me about your other life,' she would nag him.

'You mean my one as a secret FBI agent?'

'Your life before me.'

And she would try to get as much information out of him as she could. Illogically she couldn't bear to think that he'd had more than forty years of experiences prior to even meeting her. And Bob did his best to satisfy her desire for knowledge. He came a cropper on tales from his childhood, though, as often, he admitted, he just couldn't blooming remember.

'I'm getting old.'

'You're a spring chicken.'

'I'm older than you, though.'

It was the first time they had addressed the age gap.

'Only by ten years or so. That's nothing,' she scoffed.

'It's enough.' He considered her for a moment. 'I've been there and done that, and you're only starting.'

He meant marriage and kids.

'I have plenty of time for all that,' Debs said, wondering why she brushed it off. For the first time they were talking about all the things that she had been afraid to bring up before.

But somehow she sensed that Bob wasn't bringing them up in a good way; not in an I'll-make-a-decent-woman-of-you-yet way. Instead he looked a bit worried on her behalf.

Not the atmosphere she wanted, and they were only just after moving in together.

'Let's talk about something else,' she said.

And it was the best feeling in the world to sit there chatting and snuggling with him in the evenings before an open fire. Or rather her little gas heater, but the effect was nearly the same. It was enough to make her forget the odd little blips that seemed to crop up out of nowhere.

'I've a better idea,' he said. He seemed as anxious as her to play along. 'Let's go to bed.'

Debs never needed asking twice.

It was the time of the day that she loved the best, going to bed with Bob. And at a normal time, too, and not ten past seven with indigestion from wolfing down dinner. There was a lot of lovemaking, which was marvellous, even if it necessitated many furtive dives under the sheets whilst Bob was in the bathroom or putting the bins out. (Imagine! She now had a man to put the bins out for her. Truly, she had arrived.) She would lie there, artfully arranged under the sheets and wearing a white lacy nightie that she often managed to keep on during sex, and that was very handy for concealing wobbly bottoms when it came time to get out of bed and go to the loo.

'You're lovely,' Bob would say afterwards, gathering her in his arms on the makeshift double bed that he'd constructed by hauling in Fiona's old single bed from the other room and nailing the two beds together. There was no room left to stand up, mind, and the door could no longer be fully opened or closed, but that didn't matter. The main thing was that Bob was still there in the mornings when she woke up, and had not vanished silently sometime during the night to go back to his real home.

'Bloody hell. I need coffee,' he would moan. Another discovery she had made was that he was not a morning person.

'Leave it to me,' she would soothe, and she would pull down the white nightie before getting up and walking across the bottom of the bed to squeeze out the door.

Things were so good that sometimes she doubted it was real. Sometimes she felt that she was only pretending to be grown up, that all this cosy domesticity was make-believe. But then Bob would arrive into the kitchen behind her, yawning and scratching and touching her shoulder in passing, and she would know that it was truly happening. Her and Bob were together at last, and everything was just fantastic.

Except for the small fact that he was completely and utterly miserable.

He did his best to hide it, of course. He came home in the evenings from work with a smile on his face just for her, and he oohed and aahed over her dinners in a satisfying way.

'Beef bourguignon!'

'I know. I'm really pushing the boat out. But watch out for the bouquet garni. I kind of lost it in there somewhere.'

He didn't complain about anything, not even the smallness of the flat or the fact that there weren't enough parking spaces and he often had to leave his BMW out on the road. He even brought home a basil plant one night and put it on the windowsill in the kitchen as though he truly belonged there and was trying to make a real home for the two of them.

So it wasn't the fact that he looked miserable, but rather that he was doing his level best *not* to look miserable. You never saw anybody try harder. It was as though he had made a pact with himself that she would never walk in unexpectedly to find him bawling inconsolably, or pleading with his phone to just ring, dammit. (It never did. Or at least it was never Geri.) It was as if he were afraid of letting her down, or maybe it was himself, if he betrayed even the smallest hint of his upset.

But it was all pretence. There was always something at the back of his eyes that he couldn't cover up no matter how hard he tried. And his smiles were too bright, and too tight at the corners. On Saturday mornings he slept too late, as though he didn't want to get up and face the day.

Debs tried not to be offended. He was newly separated.

He was going through emotions and hardships that she couldn't even imagine, nor did she want to. If his way of coping was to pretend that he was delighted with his new living arrangements, then that was fine with her. If they all pretended hard enough then maybe one day it might actually come true.

'You OK?' she would ask every now and again. Just to let him know that she was aware of what he was going through.

'Me? Fine.'

But they didn't talk about the break-up. It was a kind of an unspoken pact. It was sensible in a way. What, after all, could Debs contribute? She was too biased to be able to counsel him either way, and she would end up feeling miserable and guilty. And as for Bob, well, he had a hard, closed look about him whenever the conversation seemed to veer in that direction.

But because they didn't talk about it, an undercurrent of uncertainty pervaded the little flat, and Debs's happiness, on a permanent basis. Every time his phone rang she stiffened: was it some family member, offering to broker a deal? Or Geri herself, cool and in control, summoning him back for a 'talk'? Or one of his kids, whinging that their mother was high on wine and chocolate, and that he needed to come home, pronto?

Debs lived in dread of his phone. She tiptoed around it, throwing it baleful looks. Often she banished it to the table out in the hall, where it was chilly and dark, and shut the living room door on it. Which was silly, as he spent most of his day in work and was far more likely to talk to his family on the phone there.

She lay awake at night, listening to him breathing, wondering how long it was all going to last. He might have moved in, and fixed that squeaky press in the kitchen, but nothing had been settled yet. It could all change in the morning. Sometimes she suspected that he was awake too, thinking the same thing. On those nights, the little divide between her single bed and his, which she had tried to fix by covering it over with a blanket and then a sheet, seemed like the Grand Canyon.

But as each day went by, and there was no contact with home, at least as far as she knew, she grew a little more secure. Or at least a little less uncertain. It's been too long now for reconciliation, she whispered to herself, feeling like the Wicked Witch of the West. And did Bob look a little less miserable? Or, rather, a little less like he was trying *not* to look miserable? Yes, she deduced hopefully. They just needed time, that was all. Time and routine, and maybe even a little distraction.

And so she invited Fiona and little Stevo around for dinner one Saturday night.

'He's not as old as I thought he would be,' Fiona said in the kitchen.

'No,' Debs agreed, 'and he has all his own teeth, too.'

'Sorry. It's just that I don't really know what to say to him.'

'He's just a normal person, Fiona. Say what you'd usually say.'

Fiona looked doubtful. 'What, about Gillian in work getting so hammered that she snorted two lines of Sandra's

268

dry shampoo by mistake and then got sick into her new handbag?'

'Of course. He'd love all that,' Debs said airily. She hoped he wouldn't be shocked. Now that she thought about it, she hadn't told him about some of her wilder nights out with the girls. It wasn't that he would disapprove. Not at all. But at the same time she didn't want to spoil his vision of her as a cool, mature woman who would never horse down nine tequilas followed by a shish kebab. If indeed that *was* his vision of her. She was doing her damnedest to live up to it, in any case.

'He seems mad about you,' Fiona announced.

'Really?' said Debs giddily. Actually, she'd thought that Bob was being rather distant tonight. He was mortified, of course; he knew that Fiona and Stevo knew all about his marriage break-up. Debs had tried to assure him that they wouldn't judge him, but that fell flat when Stevo promptly glared at him upon arrival.

'I can tell by the way he looks at you,' Fiona said sagely.

This, of course, was music to Debs's ears. 'Do you think?' She hoped she didn't sound too pathetic.

'Oh, yes. Anyway, he's moved in with you, hasn't he? Isn't that what you wanted all along?'

'I suppose,' said Debs. There was no point in telling Fiona that sometimes it didn't seem like anything had changed. She didn't feel more secure, or confident that they had a proper future. If anything she felt even more jittery. She wondered what it would take to *really* pin him down. She wished there was a manual that would tell her the right thing to do or say to make him stay for ever.

She was glad now that she had gone to so much trouble with dinner. No omelettes or other student-type food *tonight*. She had bought a posh cookbook by one of those doyenne-of-Irish-cookery types, and had tackled a fiendishly tricky recipe for slow-roasted pork with crackling and various tarted-up vegetables. She had been cooking most of the day.

'This is lovely,' Fiona said, sounding very surprised. Well, Debs had been queen of the takeaways when they had lived together.

'Thank you,' Debs murmured modestly, thinking, thank Christ the pork came through for her.

She enjoyed the warm look Bob gave her. Hopefully he was thinking how mature and sophisticated she was. She had even climbed into a dress for tonight, eschewing her usual black trousers. It showed every bulge, mind you. She would be able to eat no dinner at all without looking like she had suddenly grown a pot belly. Still, there were ways of taking care of that; she would nip to the loo straight afterwards. It wouldn't do to look slobby and greedy, not now that she had a man to impress, a man whose wife could ring at any moment and send him running back.

It was hard work being a mistress, Debs was beginning to discover. And it didn't stop once you'd actually landed your man. If anything you had to work harder.

Sub-consciously she sucked in her stomach another couple of inches.

Stevo had said very little so far. He just forked in his food as though it were a trial to be there. Debs was cross with him. He was bringing everybody down.

But Bob, fair play to him, cleared his throat politely and said to him, hopefully, 'Did you see the match on Saturday?'

It was a good shot. Everybody liked football.

'No,' said Stevo, and Bob deflated.

A minute later he tried again. 'Debs tells me you and Fiona are getting married next year.'

It was a mistake to have brought marriage up. Stevo looked at him belligerently. 'Why, have you got a few tips?'

Fiona rushed in with, 'We're hoping you and Debs can come, of course. To the wedding. It'll be great to be able to write your name on the invitation rather than the usual "Debs plus one".'

This had started out as a compliment, Debs was sure; Fiona hadn't actually meant to make Debs sound like a loveless spinster on the receiving end of everybody's sympathy.

Fiona looked like she wanted to bite her tongue out.

Debs met Bob's eyes over the table and they were both thinking the same thing: *Please God let tonight be over and they would just go home.*

Then she saw that Stevo and Fiona were sharing the exact same look.

They didn't stay for coffee. Stevo had an early start in the morning, apparently. There were kisses on the doorstep and vague promises that they would do it again sometime.

'I don't think they liked me,' Bob said.

'Don't be ridiculous!' Debs was protesting too hard and they both knew it. 'Anyhow, it's their problem. Stevo is such a little prig. Honestly, they deserve each other. They really do.'

271

She resolved never to invite them around to dinner again. And she might think twice about going to their wedding too. She didn't know if she wanted to be with friends who treated her new partner like that. If you could even call them friends. Maybe the time had come to draw back from them. If they couldn't accept Bob, then they could do without her company too!

'It doesn't matter,' Bob said, drawing her close. 'I'm not going out with them, I'm going out with you.'

Debs had thought they were a bit past the 'going out' stage, but she let it go. There had been enough aggro for one night without starting another stilted discussion on them and where they were going. Which was to bed, by the looks of things. And who was she to argue?

'You've lost weight,' Bob said in the bedroom.

She wasn't sure whether to be pleased or offended; should his tone not be a bit more disapproving, as in she really didn't need to lose weight?

'Maybe a pound or two,' she said casually, like she had scarcely noticed. As if: she still stepped on those scales every morning like clockwork, only now she had to be more secretive about it. There was no more dragging them out noisily and plonking them down on the floor; they had to be eased out with the same gentleness as when she stood up on them. The whole rigmarole took about fifteen minutes, and Bob clearly wondered what she was up to in there every morning behind closed doors.

He never closed the door. But then he didn't have a weight issue that needed to be monitored carefully with daily weigh-ins and pep talks into the mirror.

So, yes, of course she knew she had lost weight: three pounds to be precise, or four if she leaned ever so slightly to the left on the scales. It was probably down to stress, most of it. You didn't make off with somebody else's husband without it affecting your appetite – to its detriment in Debs's case, for once, thank God. Plus, there was all that increased sex; terrific for burning off stubborn cellulite around the arse. Rushing around preparing delicious meals in the evening had probably taken its toll too.

And if all that failed there were other means of weight control. You didn't have to be a blimp all your life, Debs was discovering. In fact there were times when it was very important not to be a blimp, such as when you had just shacked up with a freshly separated man.

'Don't you think it suits me?' she demanded, mock crossly.

'You're perfect the way you are.'

Bloody hell. You go without breakfast for four days in a row and they barely notice, much less appreciate it.

Or maybe they did. He was cupping her bum now. 'I love you,' he said.

And that was all that mattered.

The following weekend Bob announced that he would be seeing his kids.

And just like that, the honeymoon was over. It had only lasted two weeks.

'Right,' she said, smiling like an idiot.

'Obviously I won't bring them back here,' he hastily assured her.

She didn't know whether this was out of consideration

for her, or whether he was embarrassed about the tiny flat and didn't want his kids to see him in such reduced circumstances.

'Whatever you want,' she said. Some inner warming system told her to play it cool, that it would completely backfire if she freaked and screamed, 'You'll see your kids over my dead body!'

Of course he was going to want to see his kids. It was a completely reasonable thing to want to do. But as far as Debs was concerned, his other life – she tried not to think of it as his 'real' life – had just come calling, rudely unannounced, and was here to stay.

Some of her confusion must have shown through, though, because he said, 'I have to explain to them, Debs. I have to tell them what happened.'

It seemed to Debs that it was perfectly obviously what had happened: he had left their mother and was now having extramarital sex with a thirty-three-year-old PR assistant.

'I probably won't be long,' he said. His mouth turned down at the corners. 'They didn't sound that keen to see me.'

'They just have to get used to things.' Was that really her? Consoling him like she really hoped there was forgiveness and hugs and kisses all around? Not that she bore his kids any ill will. She had taken their father from the family home, apparently without a concern in the world for them. They probably hated her guts, and who could blame them?

The fact was that she was terrified of them. Kids brought acres of guilt and emotional pressure with them. How could

Bob try to convince them, and himself, in some suburban McDonald's, that he was thrilled with the way everything had turned out? That it had all been for the best? There was no way he could look them in the eye and still find Debs and the little flat a good idea. They wouldn't even have to say anything dreadful to him. Just their very presence, abandoned and forlorn over their Big Macs, would have him wondering what the feck he was doing.

She could see it all now: before the visit was over a whole rota would be worked out. He would take them every second weekend, whether they liked it or not, and drive them to the cinema and art galleries and the Phoenix Park in an effort to assuage his guilt. When the winter drew in, which should be any day now, and it started to rain on their outings, there would be mutterings of bringing them back to the flat. Debs would be presented to them eventually ('But she's *fat*'). Bob might even suggest that they start having sleepovers. 'It'll be fun, the four of us.' She would nod and smile encouragingly, because what else could she do?

His family: she just wasn't going to get away from them. No matter how hard she wanted it or wished that it wasn't so, Bob had baggage, and it was hers now too.

'You don't mind?' he said. As though she had any choice in the matter.

'Well, of course you have to see them!' she cried. She might as well start as she meant to go on.

Bob shot her a grateful look: she was being so *understanding*. 'All right, then. I'll go give them a ring, finalise arrangements.'

He went off with his mobile. Apparently he wasn't

going to ring them in front of Debs. She tried not to be hurt as he closed the kitchen door after himself.

She was left to brood and finger a bar of Cadbury's chocolate with intent, and think uncharitable thoughts. Not about his kids: as if she had a leg to stand on there.

No, at the front of her mind now was Geri; Geri, who had apparently dropped off the face of the earth weeks ago and hadn't been heard from since.

Debs had been glad at first. She had a clear playing field, so to speak. There were no unseemly scenes on the doorstep or phone calls at three a.m. Geri had, to all intents and purposes, shut Bob completely out of her life. She hadn't even set up this meeting with the kids, Debs knew. Bob had made the arrangement with them directly.

But now Debs wondered whether Geri was in fact playing a very clever game. Nothing was guaranteed to make a man wonder if he'd left the right woman when she did absolutely nothing at all to get him back. It must be very unnerving when an ex couldn't be bothered to throw a tantrum, or even show up drunk one night to hurl a few things or inflict some damage on his car. Geri acted like she didn't care. Like she scarcely *noticed*.

It was unsettling. And because she refused to speak to Bob at all, there was no closure in it for any of them. Debs and Bob could pretend they had moved on all they liked, but they had only moved as far as Geri had let them.

And now Bob would be seeing her again. Wasn't that what exes did? Met each other on the doorstep for access visits? Coats and hats and kids were handed over with a few brusque words: 'Have them back by four,' eliciting a sharp retort of, 'I always do.'

But words had a habit of leading to sentences. Sentences had a sneaky way of leading to entire conversations.

And Debs knew well how easily things happened without you meaning them to.

She took the bar of chocolate, and two more, disappeared into the bedroom and shut the door.

Chapter Sixteen

'I just can't believe it. The fucker. The *fucker*.' Andrea sounded stunned on the phone. Like most people, she'd assumed there was about as much likelihood of Bob having an affair as going to the moon.

'I know,' said Geri miserably. It was hideous, telling people. It was like confessing to some mouldering, smelly thing that had lurked under her bed for years.

'Well,' said Andrea at last, 'at least you're not sick.'

Geri had had to upgrade from the flu to the Asian flu to explain her absence from work, and then, when she couldn't go any further up the ladder without needing hospitalisation, she'd confided her situation in her very sympathetic GP who had given her a sick note detailing some vague chest complaint.

'Sorry. But I just couldn't face people.'

She sounded so down that Andrea clucked and said, 'You've done nothing wrong here, Geri. I hope you know that.'

Everybody said that. It was very kind of them. After they were finished calling him a bollocks and a bastard, they always quickly assured her that absolutely none of it had been her fault, even if she hadn't washed for a year, or beat him around the head with a saucepan on a regular basis.

'He forgot to take his nasal spray with him,' she blubbered suddenly. It was the little things that unhinged her.

'Great,' said Andrea viciously. 'Let's hope he gets so blocked up that he suffocates.'

Nobody wanted to hear a good word about Bob. It came from a desire to protect Geri, of course, which was nice, but it was also unsettling. Within five minutes of learning about his affair some of her friends were confessing down the phone, 'I never said it before, but there was always something about him that I didn't like.'

That was news to Geri. *What* didn't they like about him? Why hadn't they mentioned it before, maybe when it might have been useful, as in *before* she'd married him? Had they been pretending madly all these years? Kissing his cheek and laughing at his jokes – when really they thought he was a bit thick, or that his eyebrows were too close together for comfort?

'He's a total and utter shit,' they would assure her vigorously down the phone. 'Let's pray he trips and falls under a car.'

Geri didn't tell them that her emotions were far less black and white than that. It would seem like she was letting herself down or something. And mostly *she* thought he was a shit too. But then she would miss the sound of his voice so badly that she would have to stop herself picking up the phone and ringing him and begging him to come back.

'I can't believe he's moved in with that tart,' Andrea said grimly now. 'He puts in a week in a hotel for the sake of appearances, and next thing he's shacked up with her.'

'Yes,' said Geri, her voice wobbling.

There had been a chance. Just the smallest chance. They might have talked eventually; found a way back from the madness.

But he had thrown it all away by moving in with his girlfriend after one short week.

Geri felt like he had thrown *her* away.

'Look, do you want me to come over?' Andrea offered.

'No.'

'I could bring alcohol, and a DVD. Something like *Wives Get Even and Kill Their Husbands*. And you can have a good old whinge and a cry.'

'You don't want to listen to me crying and whinging.'

'I will for a while,' Andrea promised. 'But only if we can talk about me afterwards.'

Andrea had had three dates so far with Dr Foley, each one better than the other. That first evening, after he had borne her off in his car, she had impressed upon him the importance of discretion. He had taken her to some discreet bar all the way up in Howth, where they had got to know each other over two glasses of good white wine, certain that they would never be spotted.

Naturally it was all over the hospital the following morning. Andrea had left no stone unturned in her attempts to find out who had squealed on them: 'All right, who was it? Brian? You have an aunt out in Howth, don't you? Did you set her on us?' Brian had protested indignantly that his aunt had been dead a number of years, but Andrea had kept him on her list of suspects anyway.

But as the week wore on and the gossip mill began to grind to a halt – well, how much mileage could be had out of a civilised drink in a bar? According to Brian's aunt (she wasn't dead at all) they hadn't even held hands – Andrea calmed down a bit.

'I haven't let myself down,' she said to Geri. 'And it's kind of a relief to be able to talk to him at work now instead of pretending to ignore him.'

All this was said in an off-hand way to disguise the fact that she was mad about him. Well, it was difficult not to be. Along with being absolutely *gawjus*, he was intelligent, devoted, spoke three languages, and did indeed go around to his mother every weekend and mowed her lawn.

Andrea had found all this out on her second date, when she decided that an art gallery was the perfect, secluded spot to meet.

'An *art* gallery?' They were disgusted in the hospital when they found this out, as was inevitable. It was all too squeaky clean for words, and certainly wasn't enough to fuel the engines of the gossip machine upon which the very hospital *functioned*. Couldn't she get plastered some night in O'Shea's, where they could all see, and ride him in the car park outside? If it was good enough for 'Hotlips' Horgan in Cardiology, it was good enough for Andrea.

But Andrea was keeping a tight rein on herself. 'I still

haven't let him kiss me,' she confided in Geri. 'I think it quite excites him, actually.'

'Just so long as you don't play too hard to get.'

'I don't want to give in too easily, either,' she said, and Geri knew then that she was deadly serious about Dr Foley.

'Are you sure I can't come over and talk some more about myself?' she begged again.

'No. Anyway, I was planning an early night.' Not to sleep, naturally. But to rake over the coals of her marriage and wonder at exactly what point Bob had decided that he just had to have sex with another woman. Was it that Geri's ageing body no longer appealed to him? Or the way she spoke so sharply to him when he got under her feet in the kitchen?

Or was it just seventeen long years of living together; of looking into the same face over breakfast every morning, having more or less the same conversations, only tweaked a little? The same sex on a Saturday night?

That was probably one of the worst parts of telling people. They immediately thought of the sex bit, even though nobody ever said it out loud. You might as well declare that you no longer had what it took to keep your husband happy in the sack. Or even *in* the sack. Geri was clearly so unsatisfying that Bob had had to find sustenance in someone *else's* sack.

It was like saying you were ugly. Or frigid in bed. Or that you only did the missionary position except when you got drunk, and then you got on top, but only for about fifteen seconds until your thighs started to tremble uncontrollably due to shock and lack of practice, and you'd have to get off and apply some Deep Heat.

It was mortifying, being the butt of speculation. It was even more mortifying that the speculation was more or less true – they *had* had a crap sex life.

It was the first fleeting admission on Geri's part that something might have been wrong with them.

The idea came to her one night. It wasn't a good idea – not many were at three a.m. – but once it was in her head it wouldn't go away.

She was going to see where Bob and Debra lived.

Just to have a look, that was all. She wasn't going to *do* anything.

She knew it was stupid. But somewhere across this city her husband was living with another woman. He was leading a whole parallel life with someone she had never even laid eyes on! Where was the justice in that?

Geri sat in the dirty sheets of her bed the following afternoon, fuming and boiling with rage. And hurt beyond belief. She might as well hang a sign around her neck saying, 'Traded in for a younger model.'

A younger model whom she hadn't even *seen* yet. Who was this woman, anyway? This woman who had stolen her husband and robbed her children of their father? The very next time there was a referendum on the hanging, drawing and quartering of such women, Geri would put a big fat tick in the 'yes' box. Which wasn't very feminist of her, but to hell with feminism.

They lived in Apartment 2B Mincing Place.

Geri had a vicious little snicker at that. Well, it wasn't exactly Wisteria Lane, was it? It hardly reeked of romance and intrigue.

She had found the address under a pile of socks in Susan's bedroom. Bob must have given it to her on one of their little 'outings'. In fairness Geri had only gone in there in search of the diary that she was still sure that Susan must be keeping. She might get a little light relief from Susan's descriptions of Leo Ryan's hair, or the way her heart went all aflutter when he screeched past in that ridiculous-looking car of his.

All right, she wasn't as frivolous as all *that*. She was worried that they might be having sex. Teenagers usually progressed to that once they had categorically been banned from seeing each other. And, if they *were* having sex, was Susan clued in enough to use contraception?

But there was no diary, unfortunately. Geri did find Bob's new address, though, written on a scrap of paper in his neat, square handwriting. There was a telephone number too, and for a crazed moment Geri had been tempted to ring it, and shout, 'Surprise!' down the phone at the pair of them before hanging up.

Very childish.

But she kept sneaking into Susan's bedroom to look at that piece of paper, smoothing it over and over in her hand.

She couldn't believe he had done it: moved in with Debra.

All right, so Geri herself had told him that she didn't want him any more, but she hadn't actually meant it. Just like she hadn't meant for him to leave the house that day and not come back.

Why were men so thick? Why couldn't they read between the lines? Did they always have to be so pedantic and unimaginative, and take things at face value?

Bob and Debra: shacked up together in a city pad, like he was young all over again.

It was a cruel psychological blow. And, frankly, how many blows could one person take before they went off the rails completely?

And she had been doing so well, too. Brilliantly, in fact. She had been delighted with her defiant taking to the bed, her refusal to work or cook or mollycoddle the children. Saint Geri of the Muffins had finally been put to rest – and right in front of *EastEnders* too, which was handy.

'When was the last time those children had a square meal?' her mother had briefly interrupted her reverie only the other day. She had taken them to Pizza Hut and apparently they had eaten half the menu between them.

'There's a freezer full of food. And they know how to use the microwave,' Geri said. 'It won't do them any harm to look after themselves for a bit, you know.'

But her mother was curiously unimpressed by Geri's standing up for herself.

'I think it's time you got out of bed,' she said darkly.

'I'm in the midst of dealing with a personal crisis,' Geri told her snootily. 'And I'll thank you to let me get on with it.'

That would show her mother. And she needn't think she could come crawling to Geri for free antibiotics any more either, or those surgical stockings that she liked to wear under skirts to Mass ('so cosy'). No, those days were gone. There was a new Geri in place now, or at least there would be any day now, once she got her act together.

At the moment she was in what she called her 'period of reflection'. That's what people did in the aftermath of an affair, wasn't it? Geri had read heart-warming accounts of women who, post betrayal, decided that they would jack in their dreary lives and retrain as, say, an air force pilot. That would show that lying, cheating bollocks, right? Although apparently the correct feeling was one of 'self-realisation'.

Or else they lost two stone and dyed their hair red and went off on regular adventure holidays with other middle-aged people with hairdos that were too young for them, and had a whale of a time.

Yeah! thought Geri.

Why shouldn't she do the same? Now that she had shucked off the baggage that was Bob, what was to stop her climbing to base camp on Mount Everest before writing a bestselling account of her 'journey' and getting interviewed on the *Late Late Show*?

But Bob and Debra kept interrupting her journey. Every time she set about transforming herself she would end up obsessing about them instead.

It wasn't healthy. She didn't care. She spent hours imagining them in Apartment 2B Mincing Place. For some reason she pictured an American-style picket fence and little flower boxes on the windowsills.

And as for the inside of 2B? She thought about that too. It was torture. Various disturbing images played in her head as though on an unstoppable giant video screen: Bob and Debra curled up on the couch together, just like he and Geri used to do, watching reality TV and eating chocolate. Bob and Debra in bed together, Bob's broad back a solid, comforting bulk against which she would nestle. Bob and Debra in cosy intimacy in the kitchen, drinking tea and letting the occasional grunt at each other.

But hang on – *grunting*? She'd better rewind that bit. Grunting was Bob and Geri after seventeen years of marriage. Reality TV, too. And nestling in bed instead of having mad sex.

With Debra it would be different. All shiny and new. It would be like Geri and Bob back in the beginning: all that sitting up till four a.m., drinking crap wine, and with Bob boasting about his drinking exploits (wishful thinking), and that time they had thought the mole on his back might be 'something serious'.

Geri found that she was sick even thinking about them. Her hands were shaking and her throat tight and closed with . . . what? Jealousy?

She wondered, did Bob think about her at all? He must. She was still his wife, and unless he was psychotic, it would be impossible to go from one relationship to another without at least noticing the difference. Especially for someone like Bob, who wasn't the most adaptable person in the world. She wondered whether he was constantly stuck in some bizarre compare and contrast, like in the special offers section at the supermarket: 'This one is better value,' he would fret worriedly to Geri, 'but the other one has fewer additives/more omega 3/a nicer picture on the front. Oh God, I just can't make up my mind!'

Geri found that she wasn't keen on being pitched against a thirty-three-year-old. There were only nine years of difference, but they were nine *crucial* years. Thirty-three was still considered young, desirable, mature, sophisticated

– all the good bits. At thirty-three everything was still nice and firm-ish, at least on the surface.

But as for forty-two? Don't get her started. Really, don't. Because she could go on for hours about her udders and floppy bits and the way her perineum had never been the same after the birth of Davey.

Age and experience didn't count, by the way. Or at least only if you were a man.

It wasn't fair. None of it was in the slightest bit fair. She had been left for a younger woman, like something out of a cheap TV series.

She just wanted to see her. And why shouldn't she? The bitch had her husband.

'What can you possibly hope to achieve?' she could just hear Andrea bellowing. 'Nothing! You'll only be letting yourself down.'

Letting Yourself Down was a big no-no in this game. Ask anybody. That, and Having Some Pride. Sneaking over to one's estranged husband's new gaff to spy on him and his young mistress was definitely contraindicated.

Geri knew this. She knew that the proper course of action was to continue to make plans regarding a new hairstyle and possibly signing up for salsa dancing classes.

But she couldn't. Not while her husband was living it up on the other side of town with some high-heeled floozie. (Geri had embellished Debra in her head over the past few weeks. Debra now had cheap-looking blond hair whether she liked it or not, and a penchant for over-powering perfume. Oh, and she was slightly thick too.)

Anyway, it might give Geri closure. She was delighted now that she had thought of this. It lent the whole ill-advised mission a certain legitimacy. Jeremy Kyle would thoroughly approve.

She leaped out of bed, filled with a strange kind of excitement. Sick, sick, sick, she knew. But who was to stop her? Davey was over at Ben's again and Susan was out 'with friends' in places unknown, but Geri had heard the scream of a car's tyres going down the road earlier at about fifty miles an hour. She refused to worry.

So the house was gloriously empty, with nothing in the world between her and the front door.

First stop was the shower. She hadn't had a good scrub in ages. She found a razor belonging to Bob and went to work on her legs. It took quite a while to clear the backlog. She loofahed and conditioned and powdered and sprayed, and emerged smelling like she was on her way for the night shift in a brothel.

Now, what to wear? Definitely nothing elasticated or pleated. Finally she settled on a smart black skirt that flattered her legs and a new top that she'd got for someone's fiftieth party, but that everybody had assured her made her look only about thirty.

And now for shoes. High heels were entirely useless when it came to driving cars, and possibly hiding in hedges to spy – she wasn't quite sure what she would do yet if they didn't have a hedge – but she couldn't go over there in *runners*. It would spoil the whole look. No, four-inch wedges were in order. Hell, make it *five*-inch wedges.

And so, tarted up to the nines, she took final stock of herself in the mirror. Her eyes glittered rather manically and her cheeks glowed like Christmas lights. Hmm, was she really sure she wanted to go through with this?

But common sense had no place in a woman scorned. She was on a mission of discovery (note: not vengeance). The thoughts of seeing Bob and his new bit in their shared abode was just too tempting to pass up.

Besides, he would never know.

That was the best thing about it. She would have one up on him, and he would be none the wiser. It was like giving him a boot in the backside while he wasn't looking. *Now you can have a taste of what it feels like to be kept in the dark, buster.*

She put the radio on loudly in the car, hoping for some distraction.

Bad idea. It was eighties night on every single station, it seemed: the decade that Geri and Bob had met and romanced, had married and settled in together. She was soon reduced to sniffles by such appalling hits as the *Top Gun* anthem, and various offerings by Duran Duran.

They had danced to Duran Duran, she and Bob. Had *kissed* to them. In fact she couldn't be at all sure that Davey wasn't conceived to the strains of 'Hungry Like the Wolf'. A bad, bad song, but their song none the less.

'This one is for all you new lovers out there,' the DJ said smarmily.

That made Geri think of Debra again. Debra, who had hardly been bloody *born* in the eighties.

She had nearly turned back then. No good could come of this. But some self-destructive impulsive kept her foot on the gas, and before she knew it she was crossing the river and heading to the north side of the city.

She got lost, of course. Mincing Place wasn't exactly

jumping off the map. The streets started to get slightly more run down as she drove into what she hoped was the right area, peering over the steering wheel in the dark like some kind of demented private investigator.

Debra didn't live in the most salubrious part of town, it seemed. This bolstered Geri somewhat. So far everything had seemed to be in the other woman's favour — youth, impossibly good looks (in Geri's head, anyway), a glittering career in PR. The ability to snaffle other women's husbands. Fabulously talented in bed. Well, most likely. And if not, then what the hell was Bob doing with her?

OK. She was only a road or two away now, according to her map. She started to get nervous. Supposing she drove past Bob in his car, on his way in or out? Imagine his surprise to bump into his wife, dolled up to the nines and with a mad glint in her eye, when he had only popped out for a pint of milk.

She smiled a grim smile.

All of a sudden she was there: in front of a squat block of flats. There wasn't a white picket fence in sight, never mind a nice six-foot hedge behind which to park and snoop. Shit. She felt horribly exposed, plonked conspicuously there in her car practically outside their front window. She might as well honk her horn to let them know she was there.

Then, out of the blue, there *was* a honk, and she nearly had a heart attack. For a moment she wondered whether her hand had slipped. God knows, it was sweaty enough.

But no: a wild look revealed an irate driver in her rear-view mirror, no doubt wondering what she had stopped in the middle of the road for without any warning, and staring viciously out the window as though she were about to lob a bomb.

'Keep your hair on,' she shouted at him, and drove on at a leisurely pace before pulling in, pretending that she had merely forgotten where she lived.

She took a few deep breaths and regrouped. Coming over here was all very well in theory, but what was she actually going to *do*? Sit outside and watch for a bit before driving off? March up to the front door and ring their bell before demanding entrance?

This was a bad idea. A very bad idea. Possibly the worst one she had ever had.

The best thing to do now, the *only* thing to do, would be to drive away, and fast, and thank her lucky stars that nobody had seen her.

But now that she was here, she might as well have a proper look. If she just *saw*, then she would be satisfied, and she could go home, no harm done, right?

If she waited long enough Debra might even come out, with Bob. She didn't know what she would do if they did. Probably have a mini seizure.

But she turned the car round in the dark in any case and crawled back up the road. Luckily the apartment block next door – a much nicer block, in her opinion – was conveniently walled and gated, and she drew up outside and parked as close to the kerb as possible before hunching quickly down in her seat. If she'd been wearing a hoodie she would have pulled that up too.

When she was sure that she was safe, she dared to look out over the steering wheel.

Debra and Bob lived in a four-storey building with

old-fashioned wide windows and a flat roof. There was nothing remarkable about it. It had stone steps to the front, and about twenty letter boxes by the front door. Lined up haphazardly near the road was a row of rubbish bins, each marked in white paint with an apartment number. It looked like any other anonymous, not particularly well-kept block in any street in Dublin.

Then she saw Bob's car. It was parked in front of the apartment block, squeezed in between an ageing Clio and a motorbike.

Her heart dropped like a stone. Seeing it was like some kind of awful proof. The car was there and so, therefore, Bob must be too. But some tiny part of her must have hoped all along that Mincing Place was just a bad dream, that Bob wouldn't really be there at all, but instead living in some monastery waiting for her to take pity on him and invite him home.

She looked up at the apartments, finally, her mouth dry. Logically, 2B must be on the second floor. She scanned the line of windows.

Was it the one with the bare light bulb shining from the centre of the ceiling? But there was an exercise bike planted in the middle of the room so it was unlikely Bob was anywhere in the vicinity.

The window next door had the curtains drawn cosily against the dark night. Bob and Debra could be behind those curtains right at that moment, having dinner. Or sex.

Geri's gorge rose. So did her blood pressure.

Before she knew what she was doing, she was out of her car and skipping through the complex entrance.

She was just about to Let Herself Down spectacularly, but she didn't care. It was like anger had ignited a fuse deep inside her and she was about to explode.

The rubbish bin marked 2B was nice and full. She checked that nobody was looking before she tried to hoist it into the air. But it was a wheelie bin, a big bugger of a thing, and, already unsteady on her high heels, she nearly staggered backwards into a bush before she managed to regain control.

She turned the bin on its side and then upended it. The contents disgorged themselves all across the cement drive of Mincing Place. The whiff was appalling and she took a quick step to the side to protect her shoes.

Good God, what were those two eating in 2B? Junk food wrappers and pizza leftovers littered the ground. Not a crust of home-made brown bread in sight. She was fiercely glad. All that fatty, cholesterol-laden food. He was a walking time bomb.

For good measure, she gave a rotting cabbage head a good kick. She was hot tonight: it bounced satisfyingly off Bob's car, shedding leaves along the way.

Lightly, giddily, she ran back to the car. She couldn't believe what she had just done. Of all the silly, immature things . . .

But it felt great. She started the car and, heart thumping wildly, she pulled out and left Mincing Lane far behind.

Chapter Seventeen

The row started over the smallest thing, the way these things do. 'What will we do for Christmas?' Debs said as they got ready for work.

She had only been making conversation. Well, kind of. Naturally she'd had a hidden agenda too. Her mother had phoned up at the weekend and wanted to know whether she should put in an order for a large organic turkey from Tommy Mulligan, or just a small one. It was practically a bona fide invitation.

Debs had a lovely, rosy image of her and Bob sitting at her mother's dinner table, sculling back ham and Brussels sprouts. The *rightness* of it nearly brought tears to her eyes.

'Christmas?' said Bob, as though it were some tribal festival on a remote island in the middle of the Pacific that he had never heard of before.

'It's only forty-two shopping days away,' she said, wagging a finger at him lightly.

She told herself that men just weren't planners. There was no need to take offence. No need at all to start thinking that Bob's vagueness about anything beyond next week was in some way personal.

Then he announced, 'I'll be meeting the kids at some point.'

There went her place at her mother's table. But she made sure her expression didn't change. 'OK,' she said. 'I guess we'll spend Christmas here then. Just the two of us.'

She would cook a traditional dinner, she resolved: a turkey with all the trimmings, even though it would probably take them three weeks to work their way through the carcass. She would do turkey casseroles and freeze them, and a turkey curry, the recipe for which she had come across on the internet last week whilst browsing ideas for mid-week meals.

'It'll be romantic,' she promised him. 'Fun.'

They could unwrap their Christmas presents by the gas fire afterwards, over a glass of mulled wine. Debs might even get Bob some rude underpants and insist that he try them on straight away.

But then he said apologetically, 'I'll have to check first whether Geri wants the kids for dinner or whether I'll have them.'

Debs had a vicious image of two teenagers served up on a platter with roasted apples stuffed in their mouths.

Careful, careful, she cautioned herself. Mustn't let her resentment show. Or, for that matter, her anger, insecurity, frustration and sheer, unbridled desire to give Bob a good shake followed by several sound slaps across the face like they did in the movies, whilst shouting 'Come to your senses, man! This is the real world!'

Not that she ever would. Debs had become very good at checking herself. She knew instinctively that there were certain areas that she could not go. She was too afraid to. There was something so fragile about their relationship that any extra pressure might just tip them over into . . . well, she didn't know.

Sometimes they reminded Debs of the flat itself: makeshift, and held together with bits of tape and a few nails here and then. She could paper over the cracks with all the omelettes that she liked, but there was a transient feel about her and Bob that was most unsettling.

There were still nights when Bob walking through the door took her completely by surprise. He came home every night, of course, but she still wasn't used to it. She wasn't ever one hundred per cent sure that he actually *would* walk through that door.

'That's a nice welcome,' he would say when she would fling her arms around him in relief and nearly squeeze the life out of him.

'Just don't get used to it,' she would growl playfully.

She couldn't tell him her fears. He would start thinking she was being possessive and paranoid, and so she kept on pretending that everything was fine and that she was quite happy living with a man who still jumped up a tad too enthusiastically whenever his mobile phone rang.

It was just because things were still so new, that was all. She kept telling herself this over and over. Bob had barely got his feet under the bed. And now his kids were back in his life. One of them was sneaking around with a boy she was banned from seeing. He didn't say much about it, but she knew he must be thinking that certain things wouldn't be happening if he hadn't moved out.

They were always there, his family. Some days she fancied they were just outside the flat door, ready to spring in the minute it was opened.

But she didn't say this. She didn't say much at all, for fear of saying the wrong thing entirely.

It was a huge effort, behaving herself. Most days she had a pain in her stomach from holding everything in, and a vile, burning sensation at the back of her throat. It had got so bad last week that she had been thinking of going to see the doctor. Possibly she had developed a hint of reflux or something.

'Well, maybe you could do that,' she said to him pleasantly now. 'Check with Geri about Christmas dinner. You know, so that we can make plans.'

So that she didn't hold them hostage the way she'd done since the day Bob had left, in other words.

That threw him into a conundrum. Watching him was like reading an open book. He could hide nothing from her, the eejit. Every single emotion was played out across his face. It was almost comical – almost – to see him weighing up ringing Geri as opposed to incurring Debs's wrath.

'But Christmas is weeks and weeks away,' he said.

Debs's wrath it was, then.

'It's just one lousy day, Bob. Could we not at least *try* to make plans for it?' Her voice was rising querulously, despite her best efforts to remain placid and undemanding. But it wasn't like she was asking him to sign away the rest of his life. God forbid.

He was getting that narky look about him. He looked that way a lot these days. He raked his hair back and she could see where it was thinning rapidly on top. She used to think it made him look distinguished. Recently she had started wondering whether he'd be offended if she bought him a bottle of Regaine.

'I don't know why you're making such a big deal out of it,' he said.

Debs stared at him. Clearly he had never spent a Christmas on his own. He had never been reduced to getting a CIE bus down to his mammy and daddy in his early thirties, or traipsing back to a cold, empty flat on New Year's Eve when the entire rest of the world seemed to be in love.

That would not happen to Debs this year. Over her dead body.

'It'll be our first Christmas together,' she pointed out.

'I'm aware of that.' Sometimes he spoke to her like that, as though he was intelligent and mature, and she was young and rather silly.

'Obviously it's not as important to you as it is to me.' Sometimes *she* spoke to *him* like that, as though she was emotionally superior and he was a feckless, adulterous cad.

'Don't be ridiculous.'

'I'd really appreciate if you didn't call me ridiculous.'

This was turning into one of those niggling, cyclical arguments that nobody was going to win.

'I just want us to be together,' she said, hating that needy tone that kept creeping into her voice.

Why couldn't he understand? More worryingly, how

come he didn't feel the same need to cement their relationship as she did?

Christmas, she resolved. Christmas would be great, even if she had to feed his kids, and play a mammoth game of Monopoly afterwards, and didn't have a moment alone with him the whole day. She would smile for all she was worth and get through it.

And once she got that under her belt then she might be able to start moving things on a bit in the New Year. Tie things down, so to speak. Lay foundations. Well, they couldn't go on like this, living in a run-down flat like a couple of students. Even the area was bad. Some jackass had tipped over their bin a while back, no doubt for a laugh after the pub.

Her next mission – and Bob wasn't aware of this yet – was to find a suitable place for them to live. A permanent place. This time, Debs had her sights set on becoming a mortgage holder and a homeowner.

She loved that word, homeowner. It slid over her tongue like treacle, conjuring up images of buttered toast and Labrador puppies. She and Bob would be so happy there, with no draughty breezes coming in around the window frames. There would be a little garden at the back where she would grow herbs: basil, maybe, and a bit of parsley for her shepherd's pies. She might even get in an Aga.

'An *Aga*?' Fiona said last week, when they met up in a café one lunchtime. Well, Debs had had to confide in someone.

'I'm quite good at cooking now,' Debs said in her defence.

Fiona was looking her up and down in a motherly fashion. 'I hope you're eating whatever you cook. You've lost weight.'

Well, yes, Debs bloody well hoped so. After all that effort. She was a bit offended that Fiona hadn't noticed earlier.

Still, it was necessary to pass it off as though it didn't matter.

'I cook low-fat things,' she told Fiona nonchalantly. 'Stir fries. Tofu. That kind of thing.'

As though Bob would touch a piece of tofu. Or Debs, for that matter. The previous night there had been no cooking done at all. They'd had curry chips from the chipper and two battered sausages each. Bliss. Getting thin didn't mean you couldn't have the occasional blow-out.

Sometimes these blow-outs were more than occasional in Debs's case – usually when Bob went off with his kids or phoned to say he would be staying late at the office. (Was he really working late? Or having clandestine reconciliation meetings with Geri?) But thank God she had found a way to deal with them now. Overeating no longer meant that she woke up in the mornings a size bigger than when she'd gone to bed.

But Fiona wasn't as complimentary as she should have been. 'You look a bit tired,' she stated baldly.

What was she talking about? Debs looked *great*. You could see her cheekbones, for starters. And she had worn a skirt into work yesterday for the first time ever. Janice and company had looked at her skew ways. All right, so Debs wasn't exactly a threat – Alex's position as office siren was still secure – but at least she was becoming a bit more playmate-like. Marty had even remembered her name yesterday, instead of just calling her, 'Hey, you.'

Fiona was just jealous, Debs decided. Clearly her own diet in preparation for the wedding wasn't going so well. Debs could see two little handles of fat popping out over the tops of her jeans. Tut, tut. Must be all those cosy nights in with Stevo.

'Thanks anyway, but I'm fine,' Debs informed her in a rather superior tone.

But Fiona still had her mumsy look on.

'What?' said Debs, sighing. Might as well get it over with.

'Look, I don't want to criticise you or anything,' Fiona began, biting her lip to demonstrate how difficult she was finding all this. Bloody shut up then, Debs wanted to tell her.

'Did Stevo put you up to this?' she enquired instead.

Stevo's nose was probably out of joint since Debs and Bob had passed over a return invitation for dinner. Well, nobody wanted to sit through that again, so what was the point? Plus, Debs suspected she had offended Fiona by not going round any more on a Friday evening to drink wine and moan. But she had her own life now, thank you very much, and couldn't be hanging around Fiona and Stevo the whole time like some kind of spare part.

'This is nothing to do with Stevo,' Fiona said huffily. 'Look, I'm worried about you, Debs. You don't seem yourself, or something.'

'And which "myself" do you mean?' Debs asked. 'Old, fat Debs with no boyfriend and a crap job? The one who used to make you feel better about yourself?'

Fiona's lips thinned. But she kept her concerned face on. 'You've changed since you met Bob.'

Oh, for heaven's sake. How predictable. How corny. Debs wasn't even surprised. It had only been a matter of time. It was remarkable, really, how she hadn't come out with it sooner.

'You know, I thought you'd be glad for me,' Debs said slowly. 'I thought you'd be delighted that I had finally met somebody.'

Fiona was sticking to her guns. 'You used to be happy. Now you're just miserable all the time.'

Debs's mouth literally dropped open. 'Happy?' Had she really shared a flat with this woman for years, and all the time she thought Debs was *happy*?

'Well, all right, you had your ups and downs,' Fiona conceded hastily.

'My life was shite,' Debs said loudly. 'My life was a total crock of crap. It couldn't have got any worse.' People at the next table were looking over. She didn't care. 'The one good thing that's happened to me is Bob.'

'He's not going to fix your problems, Debs.'

Oh, so now Debs had problems. A minute ago she was deliriously happy.

'I'm not asking him to.' She was so angry now that it was an effort to stay in her chair. How dare Fiona sit there like an amateur psychologist and dissect her? 'And what "problems" are you talking about anyway? The fact that I'm not hanging around you and Stevo any more and you can't feel sorry for me?'

Fiona just kept looking at her sorrowfully. 'Debs, we've just had lunch and you've had two packets of crisps, a chocolate brownie and two Cokes, on top of your double-decker sandwich.'

Oh! Debs thought she hadn't noticed. She had been quite stealthy about the crisps, she thought.

Her cheeks flamed as she got abruptly to her feet.

'You've just told me that I've lost weight,' she fired at Fiona.

'I know, I'm just saying that all this binge eating isn't normal—'

'You should try losing a few pounds yourself before you go criticising others.'

'Debs. Please sit down.'

But Debs had a great urge to get out of the place. Her stomach felt distended with food and shame. There was a café across the way with toilets in the basement. She would go over there and make herself feel better.

'Debs, I'm sorry. I didn't mean to upset you,' Fiona was saying. Wringing her hands, of course, although it was too late now.

Debs looked at her coldly, even though hot tears scalded her eyelids. 'Get stuffed,' she said, and she walked out.

That had been a week ago. Fiona had phoned several times since but Debs had refused to take her calls. When she started behaving like a true friend instead of some misguided do-gooder, then Debs might take up with her again.

And what had food got to do with anything anyhow? The size of Debs's lunch, or indeed her thighs, had nothing whatsoever to do with her relationship with Bob.

Which was in trouble at that very moment; the argument over Christmas Day was still going on.

Debs was cross with herself. Why had she ever brought it up? When would she learn to keep her trap shut and not go upsetting things by making demands upon him?

Bob was looking all hot and bothered. He was huffing a bit and looking at his watch like he had to go.

Well, so did Debs. She had the day from hell ahead of her: a hundred press releases to write, promoting stupid stuff like hand wash.

'Let's not fall out over this,' Bob said tersely.

'Who's falling out? We're just discussing it.'

Just leave it at that, some warning voice told her. But his tone had irritated her. It had exacerbated the gastric reflux that was stinging the back of her throat.

'I just think it'd be nice if for once *you* brought up these things,' she muttered.

He possibly had a touch of reflux that morning too, because she saw a fresh flash of irritation on his face. It struck her how often he looked that way these days.

'We can't both be dissecting this relationship every second of the day.'

'Meaning I am?'

'Can we not just be together without all this bloody angst?'

Well. She wasn't going to take *that*.

'You know, I don't know what you come back here for every evening,' she flung at him. 'Bed and board maybe. Because that's what it feels like!'

She was sorry she'd said it the minute it was out of her mouth.

He was standing by the door, briefcase in hand, as if transfixed.

'Is that what you really think?' he asked quietly.

She hung her head. But maybe it was better that it was out in the open. 'I just want us to be together properly, that's all.'

He walked over to the table and slowly put down the briefcase and his car keys. Her heart rose. Maybe now they could sit down and have a proper chat. There was no use going on with all this uncertainty festering away.

'Debs,' he said softly.

'Oh, look, I'm sorry,' she burst out, opening her arms gladly. 'I'm such a blabbermouth. I didn't mean to say that.'

'No, no. I'm glad you did.'

But he didn't come any closer. She let her arms drop. Perhaps it was just as well. There had been too much hugging and sex in this relationship, and not enough work gone into the things that mattered.

'This isn't very fair on you, is it?' he said at last.

'Well . . .' said Debs. She didn't want to come across as a martyr. But at the same time it *wasn't* fair.

'I'm sorry.' He looked very sad. Worryingly sad.

'It's OK. We can work things out,' she said, hoping to inject a note of optimism into the proceedings. After all, nobody had *died*.

But he just stood there, head hanging miserably. This wasn't exactly turning into the happy meeting of minds that Debs had envisaged.

'Let's sit down. Talk,' she said encouragingly. 'I'll make some coffee.'

Work could wait. This was too important.

But Bob said, 'No.'

He was starting to frighten her now, the way he was looking at her.

'Bob, we're just going through a bit of a rough patch, that's all. It's only to be expected. Everything is just . . . new.'

It was her mantra. Her excuse for everything.

'Debs,' he began. He swallowed as though something was stuck in his throat. 'Debs, I don't think this is working out.'

Her heart plunged sickeningly. This wasn't happening. It *couldn't* be happening. And all over the size of a bloody turkey. 'Let's leave Christmas. I'm sorry. I didn't mean to put pressure on you—'

'I shouldn't have moved in with you,' he said. 'I wasn't ready.'

Chilling words. They came out of his mouth like nails into a coffin.

Debs tried a little laugh then. She would jolly them both out of this madness. She *had* to. 'All right, so it hasn't been easy. I know I'm a bit messy around the place – that towel on the floor of the bathroom is mine, by the way – but, you know, I can change. And if it's my cooking that's upsetting you, then I promise to stop. Right now.'

He didn't even crack a smile.

Shit, thought Debs dully. This was serious.

'We rushed into things.' *He* rushed into things, he meant. He was including her in it so that it looked like this whole mess was theirs collectively, not just his. Hoping, no doubt, that she would understand.

Debs was sick of understanding him. She had devoted whole months of her life to tiptoeing around him and his problems and his estranged family. When had he ever made an effort to understand *her*?

But hang on. She was wrong. He was going to have a stab at it now.

'You deserve a lot better than this,' he told her.

Could he not come up with something a little less cheesy?

'Oh, fuck off,' she said baldly.

That shocked him. No doubt he wasn't expecting her to descend to nastiness. Well, she had always been so grateful up to now, hadn't she? Thankful that he had ever deigned to look her way.

'I knew exactly what I was getting into,' she told him coldly, even though she wasn't at all sure that she had. 'So don't patronise me.'

Bob looked stricken now, and she immediately felt rotten. What were they doing, tearing into each other like this? Last night they had been saying 'I love you' under the darkness of the duvet.

'This is crazy, Bob,' she burst out. 'Let's not do this.'

He looked utterly miserable. 'I can't stay, Debs.'

'Why not?'

'Because it's too easy.'

'Easy is good. I like easy.'

'No, you don't. Not in the long run.'

'I promise never, ever to bring up the future again,' she said pleadingly.

'You'd be stupid not to.'

She couldn't believe this was happening. 'You just need to draw a line under things, Bob, that's all. Come on, I can't do all this by myself.'

She knew she was being completely pathetic now, practically begging, but could he not see? This was all his fault. If he would consign his bloody marriage to the past, where it belonged, then they wouldn't even be having this conversation.

But he just said, 'I'm sorry, Debs.'

It struck her afterwards that even though he had moved in with her, and slept beside her every night for weeks on end, he had never unpacked his bag at the foot of the bed.

Chapter Eighteen

Geri got out of bed one Saturday morning. She hadn't planned it or anything. She just kind of spontaneously flung back the duvet and walked into the shower.

Shit, she thought, I must be getting better.

She wasn't really prepared for it. She had lain in bed for so many weeks now that it had become her norm. Getting up meant making decisions. Like, what was she going to wear? Eat for breakfast? And it was only ten o'clock in the morning – what the hell was she going to *do* all day?

Getting better sounded like too much hard work altogether. Much easier to hop back under the duvet and fantasise about Bob contracting some rare, flesh-eating disease that struck at his weenie and caused it to go black and fall off.

But it wouldn't be ignored: that little stubborn streak of survival that had crept up on her unawares in the dead of night, and was now booming sternly, 'OK, the show is over, folks, normal life resumes.'

So the shower it was.

She stood under it for ages, the water beating down on her face. Every drop seemed to sting in a way it hadn't last week. She felt wide awake for a change; it was like she had tentatively come out the other side of an awful trauma. She felt . . . *alive* again, if that didn't sound too dramatic.

And it wasn't just because Bob had broken up with Debra. Honestly, it wasn't.

She had learned this from Lisa a couple of days ago, when she'd phoned up to say, 'George has just rung me from the office to say that he's offered Bob a bed for the night. Well, I could murder him. George, I mean,' she added quickly. 'I'm really sorry about this, Geri.'

So it was over with Debra. It must be. Why else would Bob be begging a bed for the night? No, he had been turfed out on his ear.

Geri felt a savage jolt of satisfaction. It wasn't right, it wasn't big, but God, it felt good.

Lisa, meanwhile, was tying herself in knots on the phone. 'I hope you don't think we're taking sides or anything.'

As if. They had four kids under the age of eight, two with 'behavioural issues'. Bob would get a better night's sleep had he curled up in a ditch by a railway track.

'Keep him as long as you want,' she assured Lisa.

She didn't crow for long. Well, only for about two days. She spent hours mentally wagging fingers and going triumphantly, 'What goes around comes around' and, 'If you lie down with dogs . . .'

She meant Bob. Not Debra. Actually, both of them.

It was great. Forget tipping over rubbish bins; to have your husband's affair fail spectacularly was the ultimate revenge.

'Woo hoo!' Andrea was nearly worse when Geri rang her. 'I knew it wouldn't last. I *knew* it.'

'Well, I wish you'd told me. It'd have kept me going all this time.'

'I wonder what happened.'

'I suppose it doesn't really matter, does it? The fact is that it's over.'

'She probably woke up one morning and thought, God, do I really want to spend the rest of my life with this old fart? With his saggy bum and his boring job flogging computer software? And that bald patch on top?' There was a little pause before she said, humbly, 'Sorry. That's your husband I'm talking about, isn't it?'

'Yes, Andrea.' And he *didn't* have a saggy bum, at least not as far as she remembered.

'Listen, Geri, I know this will come across as really insensitive, but could you get off the phone?'

'Why?'

'I'm expecting a call.'

Hmm. 'Anyone I know?'

Andrea admitted, 'We finally slept together. Me and Dr Foley. Although he insisted last night that I start using his first name, which is Gerard, by the way. He said that going down on a woman who kept calling him by his professional title made him feel like a pervert. So Gerard and I slept together and I don't care who knows!' She paused. 'Well, of course I do, so we did it in a tent in the countryside. There wasn't even a sheep around, so I'm keeping my fingers crossed that they won't find out.'

'They'll find out.'

'I know,' she said gloomily. 'But I'm trying to keep it quiet for as long as I can. Just so we can enjoy each other a bit more first.'

'I'm really happy for you, Andrea.'

'There're no wedding bells yet,' Andrea said sternly. 'He's only got to base one as far as I'm concerned.'

'You're a hard woman.'

'I am,' she said proudly, then totally let herself down by saying frantically, 'That beeping noise, it's someone trying to get through, it's him, it's him, get off the phone!'

'See you next week,' Geri shouted.

'You're coming *back*?'

'I rang HR this morning.'

'God,' said Andrea, 'you must be getting better. Oh, and if Bob rings begging to be taken back, you know what to say, don't you? It begins with an F.'

'Goodbye, Andrea.'

Somehow that put a dampener on the celebrations. Geri didn't want to think about the future. What would she say if he *did* phone up looking for some kind of reconciliation? Apart from Andrea's suggestion, of course, which wasn't a bad one.

But there had been no word from Bob. No tearful phone calls at one a.m. And she couldn't find a single excuse to go ringing up Lisa in the hope of getting some second-hand information, such as he was now dating that freckled girl from accounts.

Right. That was *enough*. No more speculation as to what Bob might or might not want.

She needed to concentrate on herself. She had moved on too. He needn't think she was the same woman he'd left behind months ago.

And so, freshly showered and newly single, she made her way downstairs. It had been so long since she had properly set foot inside the kitchen that she had to take a moment to acclimatise and find her bearings.

Dear God, the *sink*. It was rancid. And what was that lurking under a piece of tinfoil on the worktop? It looked like it was moving. On the hob were the bony remains of a very small piece of meat. She crossed her fingers that it wasn't one of the hamsters. Still, at least the kids were cooking for themselves – a first.

Cleaning up this lot would take her *ages*. But she must be careful not to do too much at once, in case the excitement got the better of her. She would eke it out, like a junkie rationing heroin.

Still, first things first. She threw open the windows, put on an apron, and in no time at all was calling, 'Children! Breakfast!'

This was greeted by a deeply suspicious silence. *Breakfast?* Was this some kind of sick joke?

'Ma?' Davey shouted down from upstairs. 'Is that *you*?'

All right, so she had been missing in action for several weeks but there was no need to suggest that she had mutated into an entirely different person.

Well, maybe she had, a little bit. Grief and fury did strange things to people. And, not to be flippant, but she had discovered a wart in the shower. Not a big black thing sprouting coarse hairs or anything; just a small little growth near her armpit. If that was what grief and fury did to you, she'd better calm down a bit in case they started popping up all over the place.

'I'm making pancakes,' she shouted up to Davey, determinedly cheerful. 'So get down here pronto.'

There was no sound from Susan's room yet. That certainly wasn't unusual on a Saturday morning. That girl could sleep for Ireland. Also, they had been out with Bob last night, on one of their 'access' visits.

'So where did you go then?' she asked Davey casually over the pancakes. 'He', 'Bob' or 'your father' was never mentioned. It was like Davey and Susan were beamed up in a spaceship at the bottom of the road and returned three hours later.

Of course what she really wanted to know was whether Bob looked like a man who'd been recently shafted by his toy girl. Did his back stoop with guilt and regret? Had he dark circles under his eyes that would frighten young children?

Had he asked about *her*?

'Town,' Davey said, studying the back of the milk carton.

Useless. Town could mean anything from the theatre to a lap dancing club. But it was all part of the code that everybody used when talking about these visits.

'Well, did you *eat*?'

Because she certainly hadn't cooked for them before they'd left. As if that was anything new.

'Yeah.'

Usually, the conversation ended at that. Well, it was too awkward all around. *She* made it awkward. She was dying for them to say that the visit had been awful; that Dad had been his usual plonker-ish self, asking blundering questions about school, and wearing those tight jeans that he thought made him look cool. That they had all been lost without Geri in their midst, the heart and soul of the family, the one who kept them all together.

It probably *had* been like that. But Davey wasn't going to say it. He was trying his very best not to let Bob down, or Geri.

'You poor pet!' She was suddenly on her feet and collecting Davey up in a huge bear hug. Tears of guilt stung her eyes as she pressed his startled face hard into her bosoms.

'Mum!' He was fighting now for release, horrified and half-smothered. 'What was that all about?' he panted, when he had finally wrestled free.

'Just . . . nothing.' And she planted a huge kiss on his forehead – 'Mum!' – and released him again.

Susan. She must go up and hug Susan too. Her baby girl. The best girl in the whole world (all right, a bit of an exaggeration). She would withdraw three months' worth of the Children's Allowance from the Post Office and the two of them would go to the shops and blow the whole lot.

'Are you crying, Mum?' Davey looked worried again now. 'Is it because we left the kitchen in such a mess?'

She quickly swiped at her eyes and gave him a brilliant smile. Her wonderful, wonderful children. 'No. Now, more pancakes?'

Susan was gone. She hadn't slept in her bed the whole night long. The little conniving, deceitful, lying witch.

Geri forgot about her being the best girl in the whole world and tore the bedroom asunder looking for her. When she got hold of her, by God . . .

'When did you see her last?' she bellowed at Davey.

'I just told you!' he returned through gritted teeth. No hugs *now*. 'Last night! Dad dropped us off at the end of the road and she said she was going to the shops for something.'

If Bob hadn't been so guilt-ridden, and Geri not so ferociously hostile, then he would have dropped them in their own front yard instead of at the bottom of the road, and this would never have happened.

'Don't say it,' Geri growled at Davey. 'Don't even think it.'

A good bit of Susan's stuff was gone, Geri now saw. Or at least the important things, like her make-up bag and curling tongs. Her schoolbooks and sensible black shoes she had left behind.

She had, Geri realised, run away. While Geri had been languishing in bed. And while, of course, it was great that abduction and murder had been ruled out, how was she going to explain the bed bit to the guards?

Worse, how was she going to explain it to Bob?

'Right,' she said to Davey grimly. 'We have to find her fast.'

'You can count me out. I'm going over to Ben's.'

'Davey, your sister is missing. She could be anywhere. She could be sleeping rough!'

Davey laughed.

And, thinking about it, it was unlikely. Susan wasn't one to skimp on creature comforts, even whilst on the run.

She'd be more likely to have checked into a five-star hotel and given them Geri's credit card number.

'What'll I do?' Geri said frantically. She had no experience of this kind of thing. 'Should I ring Rebecca to see if she knows where she might be, or maybe Karen?' She looked at Davey. 'Does Karen actually *exist*?'

'Mum,' said Davey, with the supreme confidence and worldly wisdom of a fifteen year old, 'if I was you, and to be honest I'm glad I'm not, I'd start looking in the most obvious place first.'

Geri looked around the bedroom wildly. What did he mean? The closet?

'Leo Ryan, Mum.'

'Susan? It's your mum.'

'You don't always have to introduce yourself, Mum. Your number comes up on my caller display, you know.'

Keep your temper, Geri urged herself. 'I'm just ringing to say hello.'

'Hello,' said Susan.

Little brat. Still, at least she had tracked her down. At least she wasn't refusing to answer the phone. 'I was just wondering if you were with Leo Ryan?'

'Yes.'

'You are?'

'I am.' Pause. 'Is there anything else?'

'No. Yes! Where exactly are you? And . . . Leo?'

They might be camping out in his car, or driving from cheap hotel to cheaper hotel.

'In his house.'

'You mean − around the corner?'

'Yes. I can see our back garden right now from the window.'

It was both immensely reassuring and deeply infuriating. She was less than two hundred yards away, in other words.

'Is there even *room* for you?'

From all the other boy-racer-type cars that often followed Leo up and down the road, Geri deduced that there must be at least six other angry young men sharing the house.

'Don't fuss,' Susan said languidly.

'Fuss? I was worried sick about you!'

Susan sounded slightly defensive. 'Sorry. But I didn't think you'd notice.'

'That my *daughter* was missing?'

'Well, you've so much going on in your own life . . .'

'Don't you dare lay that trip on me. Now, you've made whatever silly point it is that you wanted to make, so I'll expect you home soon.'

'No. I've moved out.'

'What are you talking about? You're sixteen.'

'Which makes me an adult.'

'An *adult*?'

'Yes. I'm old enough to join the army, to drive – well, a moped anyway – and to have sex.'

Ooh. Geri winced, just as Susan had known she would. Nobody wanted to think of their little girl having sex, and certainly not with that appalling lout Leo Ryan.

She didn't mention it. It would only cause Susan to strip off there and then and fornicate just to spite her.

'What about school?' she said instead.

319

'Is that all you can think about?' Susan said at last in amazement. 'School?'

'Well, like you say, there's nothing much I can do about you moving in with Leo Ryan.' Total lies. She would ring the guards the minute she hung up on Susan. 'But I'd at least like to think that you were going to finish your education.'

'Of course I am,' Susan said crossly. 'I'm not stupid, you know.'

'Good. Because even though you might think you're madly in love right now, there'll be a time when you'll need qualifications.'

There was a little pause and then Susan said, sorrowfully, 'Were you ever any different?'

'Sorry?'

'I have to go.'

And she hung up.

Chapter Nineteen

Debs didn't know how she got through the following days and weeks. It was awful. She hid behind her computer screen most of the time, pretending she was working on reports and spreadsheets and press releases. But her head was wrecked and her eyes stinging with hot tears, which she spent most of every day choking back.

Bob was officially gone. He had walked into the bedroom that morning that they'd argued and packed his things, which were pathetically few, when it came down to it. He had the job done in less than ten minutes in any case. And she realised then that he hadn't really moved in at all, not in his head anyway. He had been like a lodger who had come to stay for a while but who had always been going to go back home eventually.

He left his keys on the phone table in the hall. The sound of those keys being laid down had nearly broken her heart.

The whole affair had been so short-lived and tenuous that after a couple of days it was as if the entire thing had been a figment of her imagination. She would wander around the flat in a bit of a daze: had Bob *really* been there at all? Maybe she had concocted the affair because she was deranged at the prospect of a weight-challenged spinsterhood stretching endlessly ahead of her.

Shit. She was going mad on top of it all.

But then she would see the nailed-together double bed, or all those empty egg boxes atop the kitchen unit from the endless omelettes, and that her sister, Edel, had asked her to save for the kids' arts and crafts classes in school, and she would miss him so much that she would sink down onto her knees and have a little rock back and forth.

Her nights were spent in restless sleep and crazy dreams. Bob was always in them, and she was always holding out her hand towards him but, predictably, he was just out of reach.

'Bob! Bob!' she would be wailing. 'It's only twenty-eight shopping days to Christmas!'

Christmas. It loomed like a detested aunt. And Debs would be spending it on her own again, unless you counted the turkey.

Worse, she would be spending it with her parents.

'Are you all right?' Fiona said when she finally tracked her down.

'Fine,' said Debs. If she started talking about it at all she would cry. And she was at work, with a client coming in five minutes, so it might be a tad inappropriate.

'I'm so sorry, Debs.'

'You're not. You're delighted. You thought he was never right for me anyway. I bet you knew all along that he was going to go back to his wife.'

Fiona sounded mildly shocked. 'The creep!'

'No, he *hasn't* . . . I mean, he might have – I don't know, OK?'

'You mean he hasn't *phoned* you?' Fiona said ferociously. 'Even just to see that you're all right and that you haven't Done Something Stupid? As if you would,' she added under her breath, like Bob wasn't worth the price of a packet of Bic razors.

'He may have,' Debs blustered. 'I'm working a lot. I'm not at home.'

Yeah, but he had her mobile number, didn't he?

'Will you come over tonight? Please? Stevo's going to cook, and we'll open a bottle of wine and have a chat.'

Debs couldn't bear it: Stevo's we-warned-you looks, and Fiona giving her a pep talk along the lines of plenty of other shits in the sea.

'You don't want to stay in that flat on your own,' Fiona pressed.

Even she was admitting what a kip it was, and she had lived there.

'Thanks, anyway,' Debs said. 'But I have a few things to do.'

It was true. She clocked off on the button of five-thirty, and caught the bus home. She got off at the stop near the local Spar, hoping to God there was different staff on from the previous night. Yes, great – two guys who looked like they were on drugs. She got a basket and began to browse the frozen food section. She wasn't alone; loads of other people in suits and skirts were picking up pizzas too, too lazy to cook after work. They tended to stop at one, though.

Armed with pizzas, frozen chips and a bag of potato croquettes – delicious with ketchup – she made her way over to the ice cream. Bloody stuff was expensive. She didn't even want to think about how much of her weekly budget she was spending on food now. She could probably move into a decent flat if she cut down a bit.

But she was so hungry these days. There was a huge emptiness inside her that she couldn't seem to fill.

Once home she would close and lock the door and put on the oven. While everything was cooking she would change into her elasticated track pants, then sit down and eat the lot. The comfort only lasted as long as the last bite, unfortunately. Bloated on junk, she would quickly descend into disgust. Unable to bear the sight of the mountain of boxes and wrappers she would roughly tidy away, all the time berating herself:

'Right, that's *it*. And this time I mean it. It's Rosemary Conley for me in the morning. And Jane Fonda. Weak, weak, weak.'

High on vows of transformation and self-change, she would go to the bathroom. But the following night would usually pan out the same. It was beyond depressing.

Then one night Bob rang, breaking the tedious pattern.

'I just wanted to see how you are,' he said immediately.

No chance of getting back together, then.

'Bit late off the blocks on *that* score, aren't you?' she said sarcastically. Clearly he wasn't up on break-up etiquette.

'Sorry?'

But then she had to remind herself that he was ancient, and had been out of the dating game for years and years, and that at least he was ringing.

And it was lovely to hear his voice, even though it made her want to cry again.

'Debs? Are you still there?' He sounded so worried, so concerned, that her heart rose. See, she told herself, he *did* really care about her still.

'I'm here,' she said. There was a little pause and she said, 'Where are you staying?'

'At George's.'

Oh, yes – some work colleague with a rake of young children.

'It's very noisy,' Bob admitted.

Debs smiled. Inside she was thinking, He hasn't gone back to his wife.

And she thought how unfair it was that two people who so clearly had feelings for each other couldn't be together because of all this . . . *shite*.

'Bob,' she blurted, 'why don't you come back? We've both had a bit of time to think. Maybe we could work something out.'

She hoped it didn't sound too pathetic. But it was worth a shot.

And he sounded tempted too, if you could read anything into a silence on the phone. But she told herself afterwards that he *had* wavered a bit.

'I can't,' he said at last.

'Right,' she said briskly. 'That's no problem.'

'Debs . . .'

She couldn't bear the 'But it was good while it lasted'

and 'I'm very fond of you' platitudes and so she cut him off.

'It's fine, Bob. These things happen.'

It wasn't that she was trying to make him feel better. She was trying to stop herself from bawling and making a holy show of herself on the phone. More than she already had, that was.

'I'm sorry about everything, Debs,' he said. He sounded utterly miserable.

But she was done empathising with him. She was hurt, and abandoned, and betrayed too in all of this. Not that anybody gave a damn about her.

She wanted to get back at him a bit. Just because.

'Bob, I have to go. I'll see you around sometime.'

She hung up on him.

'You look like rubbish,' Gavin said.

'Thank you. Much appreciated.'

He loitered around her desk a bit, irritating her. 'Are you all right?'

'I'm fine.'

'It's just you seem a bit off these days.'

'Gavin, I'm trying to do some work here. So if you wouldn't mind . . . ?'

'Come here, did you hear the news?' he said. He was obviously bursting to tell her.

'No,' said Debs, dully. She couldn't seem to muster the energy to care about anything these days. She was only there at all because of her pay packet at the end of the month, which might as well be paid straight into the tills of the Spar.

'Alex is getting a promotion.'

'That's it?' Debs scoffed. That nugget had been doing the rounds for months.

'No, this time it's really happening. It *has* happened. Marty called her in an hour ago when you were out and the pair of them were in there for ages.' He threw a malevolent look at Marty's door and a low, menacing growl rattled his throat. Never when Marty was around, obviously – then it was all 'Absolutely!' and, 'You betcha, Marty!' – but the Christmas party shame continued to fester with him. 'I think I'm suffering from post-traumatic stress disorder,' he admitted to Debs once.

'Anyway,' he went on, 'when they came out, Marty was smiling all over his fat face. He announced the news and said that we'd be having drinks in the office after work to celebrate.'

That explained the black look on Janice's face, then. And the way Tanya was scuttling after her in a placatory kind of way.

'I'm here longer,' she was hissing at the water cooler now.

'I know, it's just not fair,' Tanya was saying slavishly.

'I bet she slept with him.'

'Well, of course she did!'

'She'd never have got promoted otherwise.'

'She was having it off with him from the minute she arrived in this office.'

Janice gave her a withering look. 'How the hell do you know?'

'I don't. I'm just surmising,' Tanya jabbered nervously.

Janice still brooded. 'Unless, of course, she's not having it off with him,' she said at last.

'True,' said Tanya. 'Unless she's just . . . *better* than us.'

They fell silent, pondering this unpleasant possibility.

Debs avoided them and remained at her desk, wondering what the hell she was doing in this place, with people she loathed – bar Gavin and Liam – and having to go to a drinks party to celebrate the lovely Alex's fresh success in her charmed life.

She could feel the burning thing in her throat again.

'Debs, are you sure you're OK?' Gavin asked awkwardly. He looked a bit worried for her, bless him, and for a moment she almost blurted out the whole sorry mess to him.

But she didn't. She was worried she wouldn't be able to get the words out without having some kind of breakdown. She might just cry and cry without being able to stop, which had happened to her a few times recently, thankfully at home. It would scare the life out of him.

'I think I'm coming down with a cold,' she lied.

Actually, she might spread that around a bit. If people thought she was sick then she might get to miss the drinks party entirely by going home early.

To an empty flat.

The thought was more than she could bear. She knew she would make her nightly stop by the Spar on the way home, and eat everything she'd bought alone in the flat. Why not? Who was she trying to lose weight for *now*? Nobody. Nobody gave a damn if she was six stone or sixteen. But she still didn't stop her trips to the bathroom. She couldn't. There was a kind of relief afterwards, a sense of peace, that nothing else in her life delivered.

'I might go home early,' she said to Gavin, laying the groundwork.

'I wouldn't,' he advised her. 'Marty says he expects to see us all there. I'll probably go along.'

As if he would miss it. She'd already seen him with his Chapstick out earlier, surreptitiously applying it behind his computer screen. He would probably go and get a haircut at lunchtime, and would spend the drinks party trying to brush up 'accidentally' against Alex, like he did in the kitchenette at coffee break even though he thought nobody noticed.

'She hasn't broken up with Greg, you know,' she informed him gently. She hadn't had the nerve to tell him this yet, but really, someone ought to. 'She told me at the Christmas party.'

He took it very well, considering. 'I see,' he said, with a little sigh.

'It sounds like it's pretty serious with him.' Well, it must be, if she was prepared to put up with whatever eccentricity she was too embarrassed to tell the office about.

He crumpled slightly at that. 'For now it's enough just to be around her,' he said bravely.

'Is she bringing him tonight?' Debs wondered. Finally they might get a look at him.

'Oh, I don't think so. She hasn't mentioned him at all, just said that her parents might pop in,' Gavin said authoritatively. The idea of Alex on her own obviously gave him fresh hope because he said, 'I might nip to the barber's at lunchtime.'

Debs watched Alex's skinny bottom darkly that morning. What kind of a person accepted a promotion at work but refused to invite their other half? She was, Debs decided, a person of little conviction. Even if Greg was challenged in some way, she should at least be upfront about it, instead of hiding him away like she was mortified about him.

'Folks!' she should say, loudly and proudly. 'I'd like you all to meet my partner, Greg. Greg, as you can see, is very, very short, but that's never bothered either of us, and he more than makes up for it in other departments. I'd ask you all to give him a warm welcome – and please don't offer him a chair to stand on, as it causes offence. Thank you.'

She even had the nerve to come up to Debs at lunchtime.

'Did you hear the news?' she said, a bit shyly.

'Yes,' said Debs, very cool. 'I suppose congratulations are in order,' she added in a tone that suggested they were not.

'Eh, thanks.' She seemed unsure of the situation. 'Do you think you'll make it along for drinks tonight?'

'I really, really doubt it.'

'Oh.' She looked like she was about to walk away and then she turned back. 'Look, have I done something to you that I'm not aware of?'

'*Done* something?' Debs gave a mirthless laugh. 'Apart from tell the whole office that my boyfriend was married?'

Alex looked shocked. She was quite good at it too. 'I did not.'

'You were the only one who knew.'

'I never opened my mouth.'

'I don't believe you.'

Alex looked quite angry now. 'As if I'd tell anybody

about Bob. Especially after what we spoke about that night. How could you think I would do that?'

Debs was less sure now. But she couldn't back down. 'Tell you what – from now on you keep your private life to yourself, and I'll do the same.'

'Fine.' Alex turned on her heel and marched away.

'Cocktail sausage?' Janice enquired sourly at seven o'clock that evening. She had been put on catering duty by Marty, much to her chagrin. 'Do I *look* like a maid?' she was saying to people.

'No, thanks,' said Debs. 'Actually, yes.'

Janice thrust the platter in her direction and turned to look at Alex. 'I thought there was a rumour she was bringing Greg?'

There had *never* been a rumour; it was just Janice's plain old curiosity.

'Well, he's not here,' Debs said shortly.

Only Alex's parents had shown up. They were pinioned against the wall by Marty in full flow. 'Naturally, I'll do all I can to encourage her. I'm a very hands-on boss, I'm sure she's told you. I like to get them young and mould them, so to speak. Your daughter has the makings of a mini me, and frankly, that's the highest compliment I can give her.'

Her sister had shown up too, and was making spirited small talk with Jennifer, the receptionist, and gamely drinking the lukewarm white wine. She didn't look much like Alex – she seemed to go in for body piercings – and someone else said she was just a friend. She seemed to be genuinely pleased that Alex had the promotion, in any case, which was a welcome change from the downright bitter looks on the faces of most of the playmates.

Alex herself looked a bit tense and nervous. She stood apart from everyone, looking like she'd rather be anywhere else.

'She doesn't even appreciate it,' Janice said, even more offended.

It wasn't often that Debs agreed with Janice, but she had no loyalty to Alex, not any more, and so she said, 'I know.'

'And she's not even sleeping with him,' Janice said in pure disgust. 'Imagine what you could achieve if you *did*.'

'Sleep with Marty?'

'I didn't mean *you*, Debs.'

Debs tried not to be insulted by this.

Janice was looking across at Marty thoughtfully. 'Have another sausage,' she said to Debs absently. 'Oh. I see you already have. Honestly, I thought you'd have left some for everybody else, Debs.'

'Sorry,' Debs muttered. 'I didn't have any lunch.'

That's what she told Mia when she came around with the samosas, and Tanya who was bearing some drooping ham and cheese vol-au-vents.

'Help yourself. Nobody else likes them,' Tanya encouraged her.

The fuller Debs's belly became, the duller her pain. She knew from experience it wouldn't last, but if it got her through the evening, then fine. She stood behind Gavin, surreptitiously stuffing her face, while Marty gave a little speech: 'DELIGHTED to welcome Alex to the management team . . . we'll be working very closely together in the future . . .'

Debs caught Alex's eye at that and looked away quickly. She was welcome to Marty, and he to her.

By eight o'clock the party was winding down. Alex's parents made their escape. Tanya and Mia began to touch up their make-up and talk about going on somewhere else.

Five minutes later Gavin approached Debs and said, 'We're all going to the pub.'

That was the natural next step. Everybody had had far too much to drink to even consider going home. They might as well carry on and get completely, stupidly drunk. Marty was already slurring his words and grinning around oafishly.

'Are you coming?' Gavin asked.

'Maybe,' she said, fudging. 'I'll help with the tidy-up first.'

'Leave that,' Gavin urged her. 'Try and get Alex to come along, will you? She said she might.'

'Fine,' said Debs, having no intention of doing so. She wondered when Gavin's tedious infatuation would end.

Marty was looking for Alex too. He always got randy when he got drunk. But he was distracted by Janice, who bore him off to the pub with a string of flattering lies such as, 'It won't be the same without you,' and 'You're the life and soul, Marty.'

When they were all gone Debs got down to the tidy-up: she hoovered up a stray bowl of crisps and dip, and the rest of the samosas, even though they were stone cold. It was like she couldn't stop, even though she really wasn't feeling too well at that point. Then – and there had been low points before, but this really *was* the lowest – she plucked a half-eaten sausage roll from the bin in the kitchenette and scoffed that too. She was pretty sure it was Janice's. There was bright red lipstick on the end of it in any case.

If Bob could see her now . . . She stood there, the sausage roll lodged in her gullet, filled with a sudden and deep disgust. No wonder he had left her. She had no self-control whatsoever. Even in her darkest hour she couldn't stop hoofing food into her, able only to think of her belly.

She turned and fled the kitchenette, gripped by panic and revulsion. Practically everybody had gone to the pub now and her progress to the toilets was unimpeded. Inside, it was cool and bright and blessedly empty, and she locked herself into a cubicle before getting down on her hands and knees. She was crying now, big salty tears of despair, even as she made herself vomit up every last bit of food until her stomach was sore and empty. Then she leaned back against the partition, her hands clasped around her knees hard, and bawling like a baby.

How had her life come to this? She had thought that Bob was, well, her answer to everything. Her passport out of this mess. And she had gone and mucked everything up, just like usual.

She stopped mid-sob at the sound of the bathroom door opening. Damn.

'I think everyone must be gone across,' she heard a voice saying.

Alex. Of all the bloody people.

Debs sat very still, choking down her upset. She couldn't bear to be discovered with a nose like Rudolph's and flecks of puff pastry on her chops. She would wait until Alex went into a cubicle and then she would make her escape.

But Alex didn't. Instead she was joined by somebody else.

'We should go too.' Another woman. Debs didn't recognise the voice.

'No.'

'Just for one drink. We don't have to stay.' Who could it be?

'Look, you came tonight, didn't you?' Alex was beginning to sound tetchy.

'So that should be enough for me?' The tetchiness was catching. 'And it's not like you *wanted* me here.'

'Don't be stupid.'

'Oh? I didn't see you introducing me around to all your friends.'

'That was never the plan.'

'Ah, yes. The *plan*.'

OK, Debs wanted out now. She wasn't sure what was going on here, but she knew one thing: Alex would most definitely not want an audience right now.

She frantically rubbed at her eyes in the vain hope that it would somehow make them go down. But all it did was transfer great globs of wet mascara onto her palms. She pulled out a square of loo paper and scrubbed at the damage. Now, if she could just get to her feet, she could flush the toilet and warn them that she was there . . .

Too late.

'Let's do it slowly, you said.' The other woman again.

'OK, I said. And here we are, eighteen fucking months later.'

'Would you keep your voice down?'

'Is that your answer to everything?'

'Just because you work with a bunch of *vegetarians*,' Alex flung back.

Debs found herself rooting for Alex, even though she had nothing against vegetarians, as such. She pressed her back against the flimsy cubicle wall. She had stood up a bit too quickly; she felt a bit weak.

'Marty's a moron, Alex.' This was said with disgust. 'They all are.'

Debs began to feel slightly indignant. There were some morons, granted, but not her or Liam or Gavin, or the guy who came in to do the accounts. And Jennifer was all right most of the time.

But Alex didn't defend Debs, or any of them. 'My point exactly,' she said tightly. 'We're not talking the most liberal people in Ireland here.'

'So that's it? We're going to cower in the toilets when you should be over in the pub on your big night?'

'Oh, just stop pushing me, Gemma, would you?'

There was a long pause. Debs wanted to get some air now. She really wasn't feeling well. But how could she thunder out in the middle of all the drama?

'You know something?' Alex's girlfriend said at last. 'I think I will. Because now that you've got your promotion, you're never going to have the bottle to tell them, are you?'

'That's not fair—'

'I'll tell you what's not fair. You promised you'd stop hiding us, and you have no intention of it, have you?'

A moment later there was the sound of the main toilet door opening and closing, and then silence.

Thank God. Debs scrabbled at the cubicle door. She felt weak and clammy and in desperate need of a cool breeze or water or *something*.

Shit. Alex was still there, drooping over a hand-wash basin. Her head snapped up in shock as Debs noisily emerged.

'Debs!'

'Alex.'

They locked eyes, one more uncomfortable than the other.

'So!' Debs said, fixing a manic smile to her face. Maybe she could pretend that she normally went into some kind of trance on the can and so hadn't heard a thing.

'Listen, Debs . . .' Alex began.

Her voice seemed to come from far away. Debs tried to take a step towards the sinks, but her legs seemed to give way.

The last thing she saw was Alex rushing towards her as she hit the decks with a bang.

Chapter Twenty

D r Foley never rang Andrea that day. The phone call
that had come through while Geri had been on the
line had only been some telemarketers. He didn't ring
her the following day either. On the third day when there
was still no word from him, and he didn't turn in to
work, Andrea was sure that he had suffered some awful
accident or misfortune – the huge lawnmower he sat up
on to mow his mother's lawn threw up several grisly
possibilities – and so she rang him herself.

This was how the conversation went, as relayed to
Geri:

'Hi,' he answered, sounding perfectly normal.

'Hi yourself,' she cried in relief. He was alive! 'I was
getting worried about you.' Normally she would never
admit this to a man, especially one she hadn't been seeing
for long. But they had just spent the most marvellous
night together and so she risked it. 'Gerard,' she added
shyly.

He laughed. It was a lovely sound. 'Aren't you a silly-billy,' he said.

Nobody had called Andrea a silly-billy in a great number of years, not since she'd been in school, but she laughed too. 'So!' she said. 'Listen, I, um, really enjoyed the other night.'

'Me too,' he assured her. 'It was great.'

Her heart began to beat with pure dirty lust. 'I missed you at work.' To hell with playing it cool.

'I took a few days off,' he said easily. 'But I'm working tonight.'

'Oh.' Andrea was on day shifts. But her evil mind began to work. 'I have an idea,' she said seductively. 'Why don't you drop by in the morning on your way home?'

She would put on her most fetching négligé, of which she had many, and brew a nice pot of steaming coffee — which they would drink in the bedroom.

'Thanks anyway,' he said, 'but I'm always wrecked after a night shift.'

Too wrecked even for mad sex? Maybe he was worried that he wouldn't perform to the best of his abilities, and let her down. 'How about Saturday then?' she said. 'I know a good bar.'

'I can't do Saturday,' he said regretfully. 'I'm taking my mother out.'

It was at that point that Andrea began to be suspicious. Nobody could be *that* devoted to their mother.

'Is everything OK between us?' she asked lightly.

'Of course it is,' he said, with another of those cheery laughs. 'Look, it was good fun, Andrea. Let's not sweat it, yeah?'

'He blew me off. On the fucking *phone*,' Andrea said now. There were little livid patches visible on her face under her perfect make-up. 'Can you believe it? I haven't heard from him since.'

'But he's so *nice*.' Geri was rather stunned.

'It's all a front,' Andrea said flatly. 'He just does it to hook women in. The more you resist him the better he likes it.' She hung her head. 'I just feel like such an eejit.'

'You weren't to know.'

'If I'd stuck to my rules, it wouldn't have happened. Stupid cow. *Never* again.'

But she was only being so hard on herself because she had really liked Dr Foley. Geri could tell by the way she hadn't touched her breakfast and had taken the head off poor, wandering Mr O'Reilly.

'I'm not the first, either,' she said.

'What?'

'I got Julie to look up his file in HR. He used to work in Tralee General a few years ago – where Susie moved, remember? I rang her up. She says he was famous for it there – worked his way through a whole wing, apparently.'

Dr Foley was becoming more of a degenerate as the conversation went on. In a minute he would be revealed as a child hater.

'And God knows what he got up to in Saudi, but it seems that he may have been asked to leave the country.'

OK, Geri didn't believe that. But as gossip went, it was Grade A.

'He's conned us all,' Andrea finished up.

Hannah walked by at that moment. She gave Andrea a sympathetic look. 'Feeling better at all today?'

'No,' Andrea growled viciously, sending Hannah scurrying on. 'I'll never live this down, you know,' she told Geri. 'Never. It's the best thing they've heard in ages.'

Later that morning, when Dr Foley arrived in to do his rounds, Andrea stood firm at the desk. Geri was proud of her.

'Hello,' he said, smiling pleasantly as though he hadn't a care in the world.

'Dr Foley.' Andrea bit the words out like missiles.

Geri contented herself with a ferocious glare.

None of this bothered Dr Foley in the slightest. He picked up the files, pretended to stagger under their weight and joked, 'You girls are certainly keeping me busy this morning.'

When Andrea began to twitch and jerk beside her, Geri stepped purposefully forward. There was no way she was putting Andrea through the torture of accompanying him on his rounds.

'Will we get started?' she asked him coldly.

'It's all right, Geri,' he said easily. 'Hannah's going to come around with me this morning.'

He gave Hannah one of his most charming smiles and off they went.

'There must be laws,' Nicola said that evening. 'Can she move out just like that?'

Geri had already checked out the legal situation. 'Apparently you can, once you're sixteen, but you must have parental permission.'

Nicola smiled. 'What, like you have to get a *note* or something?'

Susan's reaction had been the same. Geri had phoned her up to tell her that technically, she was breaking the law, seeing as neither she nor Bob had given permission for her to move out.

'How do you know, anyway?' Susan demanded when she'd stopped laughing.

'I asked the Missing Persons helpline.'

That stopped her in her tracks. 'You rang up the Missing Persons *helpline*?'

'Yes.'

'But I'm not missing. I'm around the corner.' Another pause, worried this time. 'You're not going to go around putting up posters of me on telephone poles or anything, are you?'

'Not yet.'

Susan had rung off, not quite as feisty now.

'At least she's nearby,' Nicola said.

What consolation was that? It was only a temptation to storm around there, which Geri had done several times, only to stop herself just as she reached the corner. What good would it do, turning up at Leo Ryan's house, demanding to speak to her daughter? She'd probably only discover the pair of them naked and at it, if not smoking a joint at the same time. 'Get home this minute and do your homework,' would be unlikely to cut any ice in the situation.

No, years of experience had taught Geri that when it came to Susan, retreat was sometimes the best option. The more belligerent Susan was, the more space she should be given.

'But why do we have to get her home at all?' Davey

had complained bitterly at breakfast. 'It's much nicer around here now.'

Geri, meanwhile, felt that if she kept on losing family members at this rate, then pretty soon she would be living alone.

'What does Bob think of the situation?' Nicola enquired.

'Bob? Oh. I'm not sure.'

'You're not *sure*?'

'We haven't actually spoken yet.'

'Geri.' Nicola shook her head in appalled disappointment; Nicola, who had a little laminated photo of Fintan on her key ring.

'He knows she's in Leo Ryan's, OK? I made sure of that.' She'd left a message with Lisa. Surely that got her off the hook?

Nicola wasn't going to pursue it. Packing up her things, she announced, 'I'd better go.'

This was unprecedented. She had only been there two hours. And young Derek was only on his fifth biscuit in front of the television.

'Is everything OK?' Geri enquired.

'It's Fintan's birthday tomorrow,' Nicola said solemnly.

As always, his name brought a pall of gloom to the proceedings. Outside the sun rapidly retreated and dark clouds began to gather on the horizon. In a minute they would have to put all the lights on.

And it wasn't even his fault. The poor man had done nothing except die. Little did he know that he would keep on getting dug up.

'He would have been forty-five,' Nicola sighed wistfully. And, actually, she was looking particularly miserable that day in some long black dress and a pair of scary pointy widow's boots. She'd given the neighbourhood children an awful fright when she'd stepped out of the car earlier. 'In his prime. Imagine what he would have been like.'

And Geri tried. But surely he would have been more or the less the same as he was at forty-three – a balding, slightly portly insurance executive, with a cheerful smile and a great love of quiz shows on the telly.

'He always said he was going to get a motorbike for his forty-fifth birthday,' Nicola confided.

OK, a new image now: Fintan astride a huge Harley-Davidson, the motor throbbing joyfully between his legs. It could have been a whole new chapter for him.

'I need to get home and bake a cake for him.'

'For . . . Fintan?'

'I did one last year too. A chocolate fudge one, his favourite, and we light the candles and sing a cheery happy birthday.'

Derek looked over from the television rather fearfully. His mother had finally gone cracked.

'Is that not a bit macabre?' Geri felt she had to say.

'Oh, it's not for *me*, Geri. I do it for Derek.'

But it turned out that Derek was most ungrateful for this thoughtfulness. 'I don't want to go home and bake a cake.'

Nicola was slightly cross. 'Don't be silly. Come on now.'

Derek's fat little face was bravely set. 'Dylan's father is bringing him to see *Spiderman* in the cinema. He said I could go too.'

Nicola was furious now, but trying to contain it in front

of Geri. 'Derek, pet, you can go to see *Spiderman* any time. But your father's birthday only comes around once a year, and we're going to make a nice cake for him.'

Derek's lip was quivering. 'Why?' he burst out. 'He's not going to eat it, is he? I wish I lived in Dylan's family!'

And he turned and raced out of the kitchen, and Geri could hear the back door slamming shut. He had gone out to the hamsters, she guessed.

'Honestly,' Nicola said with a sigh. 'We do everything we can for them, and they throw it all back in our faces!'

'"We"?' Geri enquired.

Nicola was lumping them together in terms of failure: abandoned by their husbands, engulfed in misery, and both with children who wanted to live in other people's houses. Worse still, Geri was actually wearing black that day too – a pair of Susan's leggings that she'd thought might be slimming but on reflection just made her legs look like sausages.

'Maybe it's something in our genes,' Nicola was saying gloomily. 'Mammy drank loads of Baileys Irish Cream when she was pregnant, did you know that? She thought that because it had dairy in it, it was all right.'

But I'm not like you, Geri wanted to whinge. And she wasn't. She just indulged her. Criminally, according to Bob. So, really, she only had herself to blame.

Hold on. Blame? *Herself?*

Finally, it had arrived. It had been coming for a while, but she had neatly dodged it up to now. It was probably all that practice in work of quickly side-stepping out-of-control trolleys and projectile vomit.

But now the moment of truth was here: it was time

345

to stop blaming everybody but herself for the state of her life, as Jeremy Kyle would say. Only probably much more eloquently. 'And you've got to start dressing more appropriately for your age,' he might add too, wagging a finger in the direction of her leggings.

(Although she wasn't going to blame herself *completely*, obviously. She wasn't a martyr. But she was prepared to take her share of the blame. Big difference.)

It was like a mini epiphany. She'd never had one before, except for maybe that time when she'd finally worked out how to send an email. It felt so significant that surely there should be some kind of lighting effects involved. Or maybe some background choir music to underline the moment.

But it was all disappointingly normal. She didn't even feel all light and free.

And now that she'd had the epiphany, she would have to put it into practice and tackle Nicola, which was a pain in the arse. She was starting to wish she'd never had the damn thing in the first place.

'Come in *this minute*,' Nicola was saying through the kitchen window at Derek.

'Nicola,' said Geri.

'What?'

What, indeed. Geri hadn't quite worked out what to say yet, which was always a handy thing to do *before* you actually got someone's attention.

What could she say? You've ruined my marriage by whinging at my kitchen table about your husband and stopping me spending time with *mine*? Or, you're never coming with us on a summer holiday again, or a weekend break, or even a day trip to the flipping seaside as long as we both shall live? Well, maybe a day trip to the seaside would be OK. How about, you're so miserable that your child is clearly overeating to compensate, and if you don't cheer up he'll end up having to be lifted out of an apartment some day by a crane?

Instead she blurted out, 'I think you should go out with that guy from school.'

'*What?*'

'That teacher. The one who asked you out.'

Nicola was looking at her like she'd lost her marbles. 'Geri, if this is your idea of a joke, the day before Fintan's birthday—'

'Fintan is dead. He's never going to have a birthday again, God love him.' She said it kindly. 'You have to move on.'

Nicola snorted bitterly. 'I was wondering how long it would take you.'

'What?'

'People get tired of you sooner or later. I thought maybe you were going to be different.'

'Nicola . . .'

Nicola was grabbing up her coat and her bag. 'Nobody wants a sob story, eh?'

'It's not about that.'

'I always thought it was Bob who didn't want me here. But maybe I was wrong. The minute he's gone, you don't want to listen any more.'

Geri told herself that Nicola was just hurt. That she didn't mean what she was saying.

'Would you go to counselling or something?'

'You mean *pay* someone to listen? Because my own family won't? Derek! Get in here this minute!'

'I could get you a recommendation.'

'I'm sure you could. Or maybe a good ride would sort me out, eh?'

Geri was sorry she'd mentioned the male teacher. Actually, she wasn't sorry. This was never going to be pleasant. 'You're only young, Nicola. You have your whole life ahead of you.'

'So just buck up and move on? You know, I'm amazed at you. You, of all people, know what it's like to lose your husband.'

'I haven't lost my husband.' Just temporarily mislaid him.

But Nicola was so upset that she wasn't even listening. 'Derek!'

'Do it for his sake, Nicola.'

'What?'

Geri could see that she was on dangerous ground now. But she had to plough on for everybody's sake. 'He's only a child. Let him be one.'

Derek trundled in now. Nicola grabbed him and stuffed him into his coat, and tried and failed to zip it up over his portly middle.

'Say goodbye to your Auntie Geri. We won't be coming around again for a while.'

'Why?'

'She's too busy.'

'Nicola,' Geri interjected uselessly.

'We can find our own way out, can't we, Derek?'

And she pushed him ahead of her out the kitchen door and they were gone.

Geri sat down at the table for a few minutes. She found she was a bit shaky. This epiphany business wasn't as easy as it looked. And now she had gone and upset Nicola the day before another emotional milestone for her. Supposing she wasn't able to cope? Supposing Geri had tipped her over the edge and she did something unthinkable when she got home and there was nobody there to stop her?

For a moment Geri almost sprinted out of the kitchen after them to try to persuade them back.

But she had spent nearly two years doing that and what good had it done? There was Nicola still going around in her widow's weeds and Derek being dragged to graveyards when he should be watching violent films at the cinema instead.

She had started this thing and now she would just have to let it play out. So no rushing around to Nicola's to make sure she hadn't OD'd on chocolate fudge cake.

And now to the second part of her epiphany. This was the really hard bit. Her stomach was in a knot even just thinking about it. It was very tempting to crawl back into bed and tell herself that at least she had made *some* changes for the better today. (Did kicking out your grieving sister count as a change for the better?)

But bed wasn't an option. Not any more.

She picked up the phone and she rang Bob.

Chapter Twenty-One

The whole thing was a ridiculous mix–up.

'I just didn't eat all day, that's all,' Debs protested in the Accident & Emergency room. It had been so embarrassing, being brought in by ambulance. It had arrived with shrieking sirens and a screech of brakes, and everybody in the waiting room had swung round, no doubt expecting a bloodstained car-crash victim to be ferried in on a trolley with people running alongside, shouting, 'She's gone into cardiac arrest!'

Instead, Debs had arrived, ensconced cosily in a padded wheelchair, and in rude health apart from a minor bump on the side of her head. Damn Alex anyway for dialling 999.

'Hello. Hi there,' she muttered, mortified, as she was pushed to the top of the long queue of actual sick people and was brought straight in to be assessed.

There, her blood pressure was taken and her chest listened to, and she was questioned closely: had she ever fainted before? How long was she unconscious for? Was she ever aware of an erratic pulse before?

'Only when I see a good-looking guy,' she quipped. See? She still had a sense of humour, which meant that it was unlikely she had any serious brain damage. The ambulance guys might even be able to give her a lift home. Right now she didn't feel up to getting the bus.

But the medical people, while they were very nice, told her that because she'd hit her head on the tiled floor when she'd fainted they'd like to keep her in a couple of hours for observation.

Terrific. If she'd known that she'd have brought along a book or something.

But at least it took her mind off Bob. She lay there on a trolley looking at other unfortunate souls who'd had heart attacks or were stoned out of their heads, and shouting at the long-suffering nurses to take their bleedin' hands off them.

Imagine if he knew where she was. He would be shocked. And her so hale and hearty the last time he'd seen her. Apart from having the stuffing knocked out of her, of course.

She was tempted to ring him now, to cry down the line – she was actually feeling quite shaky – and he would feel so awful that he would rush over and take her in his arms and beg her forgiveness for his cruel treatment of her.

Maybe she would text him. Play it cool. *Had a terrible accident. In hospital. But please don't worry about me.*

He would be over in a guilt-induced flash, possibly with a marriage proposal.

351

OK, that might be a bit extreme, but what was wrong with a little emotional blackmail, anyway? It might be just the kind of shock he needed. He would realise that, really, he loved her massively after all. This could be the best thing that had ever happened to them.

'You can't use phones in here,' a passing nurse informed her briskly.

Debs meekly put her mobile away. She had only been toying with the idea anyway. She didn't know if she had the courage to go through with it. What if he saw her number coming up and coldly cut her off? She didn't think she could bear that. He might decide that it was best for a clean break.

She could always leave a voice message. He would check that, wouldn't he? Yes. She wouldn't do it right now. She didn't want that nurse giving out to her again. But definitely before she got discharged. It would kind of spoil things if he rolled up outside frantic, and found her killing time in the hospital coffee shop over a big cream bun.

Here came a new doctor now, a girl who looked about twelve. She asked Debs about the vomit.

'Sorry?' said Debs.

'On your top.'

Debs looked down. She hadn't even noticed it. It smelled, she realised.

'Oh, that.' She smiled at her benignly. 'I've had a stomach bug. Actually, that might explain the fainting.'

The doctor was concerned about the vomit. A bump on the head and vomiting was apparently not a good combination at all. Now she was talking about scans and overnight stays and Debs began to get worried. What if she really *had* done something to her head? Her brain might be swelling up under her skull right now like a soufflé, and she didn't even know it.

Shit, she was getting worried now. Perhaps it might be better at this point to present the facts, in order to avoid any unnecessary surgery or anything. She really didn't think she could cope with her head being sawn open. Not after the day she'd had.

'The thing is, I vomited *before* I fainted, OK? So it's nothing to do with the bump on my head at all.'

But this only elicited another slew of questions. Did she vomit often? Did she regularly feel queasy? What had triggered the urge to vomit? How long had she had this stomach bug?

'A couple of months,' said Debs, just to be on the safe side.

Now the doctor looked *really* worried. A stomach bug should not last a couple of months, she said. It shouldn't even last a couple of weeks.

Debs felt she was talking them both into something fatal at this point.

'It's probably more like a couple of days,' she said, desperate now. 'And not all the time. Not continuously or anything. In fact, sometimes I hardly notice.'

'You hardly notice you're vomiting?'

Oh, Jesus.

'Well, yes, of course I do . . . What I meant was . . .'

It was no use. Her stomach was pressed. Her mouth was examined. A tube thing was pushed halfway down her throat, making her gag. Blood tests were ordered.

Many of them, judging by the amount of blood a nurse came to take from her arm. And did she have to look like she enjoyed it? Debs, queasier than ever, looked around at the junkies in desperation, hoping that they would start another fight and distract her.

But they were busy with girlfriends and significant others, who were grouped around their beds. The girl-friends were equally glassy-eyed and fractious, mind, but at least they were *there*.

Debs had no one. She lay on the trolley, with a possible brain injury and a vampire-like nurse sucking the last drop of blood from her veins, feeling that she had finally scraped the bottom of the barrel. Everything she had tried to build in the last few months had turned to dust. Again.

She wanted to go home.

But the flat was empty.

She wanted Bob.

But he was gone.

The nurse noticed her upset. 'It's all right, I'm done now,' she said with surprising kindness. She handed Debs a wad of tissue and went off.

Debs pressed her face hard into the tissue, crying as gently as possible to avoid bursting anything in her head.

At some point she was moved, still crying, from the A&E area into another holding area. She got a hut-like cubicle this time, with three walls and a curtain that pulled over. She was told to make herself comfortable.

Comfortable? Jesus Christ, how *long* were they intending to keep her? Apart from anything else, she was starving. The tears were wearing off and she felt so depressed that she needed food. There was a vending machine at the bottom of the corridor and she was tempted to nip down and get eight thousand calories' worth of junk.

But she was afraid that someone would give out to her – probably that stern nurse again – and so she sat down meekly on the edge of the trolley-bed thing. She didn't want to think about Bob any more and so she thought about Alex.

Actually, she was a bit cross with Alex. Wouldn't you think she'd have accompanied Debs to the hospital? But then again, maybe the situation had been too embarrassing. Maybe Debs had on some awful hick face that had betrayed her total uncoolness when it came to lesbian activity. Maybe Alex had taken one look at her and thought, Jaysus, this one's back in the ark – I was so *right* not to tell her.

And, of course, there was a part of Debs that was itching to stab out Gavin's number on her phone now and screech down the line, 'I have the best office gossip ever!' He would be heartbroken, of course, but it served him right for being such an eejit as to go fancying someone so totally out of his league in the first place, and Debs would thoroughly enjoy telling him so.

But of course, ringing up Gavin would be exactly the sort of gormless behaviour that Alex no doubt expected from her. It would be different if it was back in Leitrim, and it was discovered that, say, Bridie O'Neill, who worked in the butcher's, was having it off with Eileen Martin, the widowed postmistress. While it was certainly acceptable to be gay in modern small-town Ireland, it was still largely only possible if you were married with several children.

This, however, was Dublin. Which, these days, was practically a mini London or New York. Harvey Nichols had arrived, for heaven's sake and, more importantly, Lidl. Dubliners were walking around in Gucci, and with cheap German vegetables in their shopping bags. They watched *Sex and the City* and *Desperate Housewives*, and it didn't cost them a thought to drop into one of those dark basement shops in town to buy a little battery-operated something for themselves. Having a relationship with another woman was practically *de rigueur* in certain circles, and Debs was ashamed right now of her urge to go ringing up Gavin to snigger.

She might ring Fiona, though. Fiona had once snogged a girl at a party where she had got so off her head on tequila that, she maintained afterwards, she couldn't possibly be held responsible for her actions.

'So that was somebody else's hand stuffed down her bra?' Debs had enquired.

Fiona had then decided to be blasé about it. 'It was quite nice, actually. I might try it again sometime, you never know. And you needn't look at me like that. I didn't mean you.'

Then, when she met little Stevo, it had been, 'Don't ever EVER mention to him about me getting off with that girl, OK?'

'Don't tell me you're ashamed?'

'No,' she said grimly. 'I'm afraid he'll suggest a threesome.'

Actually, when it came down to it, Alex being a lesbian only added to her coolness, Debs thought glumly.

Trust her to turn her nose up at the useless, idiotic lumps who generally populated the office world (a.k.a. Gavin and Liam) and find herself someone who looked a bit, well, *dirty*.

From what she'd seen of her at the party, Gemma had a laugh that was loud and cackly, and a pair of rather lively eyes. Debs would bet that she was a regular in every late bar in town, and would drag Alex along even though she would be whinging about getting home because she had to work in the morning and Marty would go mad if she was late. 'He'll be fine if we give him a few photos,' Gemma might joke. Which of course would go down badly with Alex.

'I can't *believe* you just said that.'

'Oh, for fuck's sake, lighten up. And put away that pink handbag. It's embarrassing.'

If Debs wasn't careful, she would stop wanting to be Alex and start wanting to be Gemma instead. Gemma looked much more fun than Alex, who was so *serious* all the time. Far too earnest for her own good. And always so worried about what people thought of her. If it was Gemma, she'd have come out ages ago in the office, prob-ably whilst dressed head to toe in black PVC, and to hell with what anybody, including Marty, made of it.

But Alex wasn't Gemma. And the look on her face when Debs had barrelled out of the loo had been pretty much how Debs imagined *she* had looked that time Fiona had walked in unexpectedly and found her scoffing down an enormous chicken curry. At ten o'clock in the morning.

Alex, Debs decided rather piously, clearly had issues. What kind of a person went putting their career ahead of their partner? Who fudged and snuck around? Who basically lived a lie?

A person in denial.

Debs had always been very good at spotting when other people were in denial. She prided herself on it. It probably came from all those years of watching soaps and spotting, often before the scriptwriters themselves did, that Something Was Terribly Wrong With Gayle, if only she would wake up to that fact.

'There's something terribly wrong with Gayle,' she would shout out to Fiona.

Normally she wouldn't get a reply, because Fiona would be out with Stevo, or her friends from work, or else doing that silly course in creative writing that she had hankered after for years and had finally got around to doing. Fiona had, in other words, a life.

Never mind. Debs would reach for another family pack of crisps and settle in to help Gayle weather the crisis. The problem, of course, was that Gayle was in denial too. Debs would shake her head in despair, whilst cramming down crisps as fast as she could, without even tasting them. Why couldn't people just *see* it?

'Any more vomiting?' a nurse asked in passing.

'No, no,' Debs assured her sunnily. 'I'm feeling much better now.'

Surely they'd let her home any minute now.

They got to it in a roundabout, sneaky fashion. They started off with her potassium levels.

'They're very low,' the twelve-year-old doctor told her. There was another woman with her: middle-aged, dressed in civvies, except for an ID badge. In another life she looked like she might have cooked school dinners.

'Really?' said Debs, suppressing a yawn. It was getting very late now and she was wrecked; so wrecked that she had nodded off on the trolley a minute ago, her damp lump of tissue pressed to her face. She wanted to go home and cry. She wanted to go home and sniff Bob's shirt, the one that he'd put in the laundry and that she hadn't reminded him to pack that morning he was leaving, because she knew she would need something to hold on to later on. Frankly, she didn't give a shit about her potassium levels.

'Low potassium can disrupt heart rhythm. It can even lead to heart attacks, among other things.'

Debs was cross now. They didn't have to bring out the big stick just to get her attention.

'So what do I have to do? Eat more bananas or something?' As a relentless diet book and food label reader, Debs knew that potassium was found in bananas. So they needn't think they were dealing with some amateur here.

But instead of saying, 'At least three a day,' the doctor informed her that she also had swelling of the parotid gland.

'The what?' They were always flinging their knowledge around, these medics.

'The salivary gland. Just there. Plus, you've also complained of a red, sore throat.'

'I've had that for ages; it's really nothing to worry about.'

'We'll have to go down and have a proper look, but the indications are that your oesophagus is very inflamed.'

Debs was feeling a bit under attack now. She'd only come in about a blooming bump on her head, which had gone down now. And here was this doctor, casting aspersions. There was no other way of putting it.

'I have a touch of gastric reflux,' she announced with dignity. 'That's not a crime, is it? I'm sure a spoon of Milk of Magnesia will sort me out.'

The woman at the bottom of the trolley was smiling at Debs. *Smiling*. Gently, admittedly, but it was galling. It was like she knew something about Debs that Debs herself didn't.

'And on examination your stomach is slightly distended,' the doctor finished up.

Right. That was it. The final straw. She might as well have said, hey, plumpy, ever thought about shedding a bit of lard? It was incredible that you couldn't come into hospital with a bump on your head without your weight being commented upon. It was, Debs thundered in her head, unacceptable. She peered at the doctor's name badge: Moira Ryan. Right, well, Moira Ryan would find herself in the letters pages of the *Irish Times* the day after tomorrow. Under the heading, 'Hospitals Discriminate Against the Overweight'. The Slightly Overweight, perhaps. Debs had, after all, lost a good bit recently.

'Have you lost any weight recently?' the doctor asked.

Right, this was spooky.

It was also rather personal. Deeply personal, and Debs hadn't spent the best part of a decade slipping on and off a pair of scales silently without being able to handle such questions. It was child's play.

'I'm losing some right now,' she said with a vicious look

at the doctor and her sidekick. 'I've been stuck here since nine o'clock this evening, I've had no dinner, and I'd really like to get home now and eat something, if I could.'

'I'll ask them to bring you some tea and toast.' Then she repeated, 'Have you lost weight?'

But she wasn't sizing up Debs like those bitchy girls in clothes shops, or Janice, who would often cast a sideways look at Debs's nether regions in a judgemental kind of way.

She looked concerned. And concern was not something that Debs was able for right now. Too much concern and she just might cry.

'A bit, OK? There's nothing wrong with that. I know I'm overweight.'

The woman at the bottom of the bed did that smiling thing again. She was starting to remind Debs of Julie Andrews; she was clearly some kind of do-gooder whose job title Debs had yet to work out.

The doctor checked her notes. 'You're actually within your normal weight range for your height.'

At the upper end, though, she didn't mention. At the fat end of normal. Debs knew all about weight range and BMI and every other class of weight measurement known to mankind. She could sing it in her sleep. So she didn't need someone with a figure like a boy telling that she was 'within normal weight range.' Normal weight range didn't get you into size ten jeans, as every female on the planet knew.

'Debs, are you making yourself sick?'

The question was shocking. For a minute she wasn't sure she heard it right.

'Are you bringing up your food?'

She had certainly heard that right. But it was no less shocking, to hear such a secretive, shameful activity being spoken about out loud in otherwise polite-ish conversation.

Debs felt like things were crumbling around her. As if they hadn't crumbled enough already today. Here she was, practically being stripped naked by this . . . *child*, and she seemed powerless to stop it.

She also had a sneaking suspicion that the entire conversation was being listened to by the other occupants of the unit. She herself had overheard the complete, unabridged version of how the man across the way had a varicose vein running down his leg the size of a small python (his words, not the doctor's).

Could they all be listening to Debs's shame now? Thinking to themselves, With all that puking she's been doing, wouldn't you think that at least she'd be *thin*?

And there was that woman at the end of the bed, giving Debs that weird smile again. Debs felt that the woman could see right through her, through the layers of fat that still encased her, to the weak, pathetic individual inside.

Debs found that she was afraid of her.

'I want to go home,' she said in a curiously wobbly voice. She wanted Bob.

No. She didn't. She wanted her mother.

'I think it's best if we keep you in for a day or two.'

'I don't want to.'

'We need to run some tests.'

Debs was frightened now. 'What tests?'

'The potassium thing, for starters. Prolonged vomiting can cause an electrolyte imbalance. And we'll need to assess if there's damage to your oesophagus, or to your kidneys or heart.'

Her kidneys? Her heart? Surely to God they were over-reacting here. So she'd brought up her dinner a few times. Big swinging mickey. It wasn't like she was wolfing down ten Ecstasy tablets every Saturday night. Why were they going on like this was some great big medical condition, like cancer, or a blocked artery?

'I don't do it much,' she blurted in an effort at self-survival. 'I haven't been at it since I was seven or anything. Just . . . recently.'

And everything seemed to go so quiet that Debs could hear her heart beating (slightly erratically – the doctor was right).

The demented woman was smiling again, and the doctor just nodded sympathetically, but Debs knew what they must be thinking of her: how disgusting, that someone could eat masses of food, especially when half of Africa was starving, and then go and stick her fingers down her throat and bring it all back up? Tossing your cookies had got to be one of the least attractive things that a person could do. But to do it *wilfully*? All because of a piggish tendency to overeat and a refusal to control it, like normal people did?

Debs felt she should apologise or something.

Or slink off into the gutter.

'I'm just going to go and organise a bed for you,' the doctor said.

'Thank you,' Debs whispered. There she was, taking

up a bed because of her disgusting habit, probably ahead of other people with proper problems like varicose veins.

Even worse, the woman at the end of the trolley was making her approach. The way she slid forward, without making any sudden movements, and deposited herself beside Debs, close but not too close, alerted Debs immediately as to what she really was: a shrink.

'Debs,' she said. She even sounded like Julie Andrews. 'Would you like to talk?'

Chapter Twenty-Two

Bob came over after work on Friday evening, as arranged. He pulled into the drive rather hesitantly before parking in his usual place in front of the garage. He was wearing a suit that Geri had bought in a sale last year and it was hard to believe that he wouldn't take out his keys and let himself in as usual, calling out, 'I'm home!', to which Geri would reply, 'Shite, I forgot to ask you to get a loaf of bread.'

For a minute she felt like bursting into tears.

She managed not to. She had to bite down hard on the inside of her cheek until it hurt. Hopefully it wouldn't swell up like one of the hamsters'.

When the doorbell rang she counted to ten just so he would think she was very busy with other things, and not waiting right inside the door for him, which of course she was.

She felt a strange mix of nerves and sadness and anger as she opened the door and faced him.

CLARE DOWLING

He had lost weight, she immediately noticed. But she had too. And his hair seemed a little thinner. Although hopefully hers didn't.

They looked at each other for a long moment.

'Hi.'

'Hello.'

Curiously, there was a moment of connection; as though they were both survivors of what had happened.

Now that she was up close, she could see the dark circles under his eyes. Life at George and Lisa's was probably proving to be as sleepless as she had predicted. Although when she had run into Lisa at the supermarket last week she had let slip that he was looking for an apartment.

Geri shouldn't have been surprised. There had been no overtures from him for a reconciliation. There had been no contact from him at all.

Naturally she hadn't let on to Lisa. She had nodded coolly as though she had known about it already; that it was only to be expected that he would move into some kind of bachelor pad.

Once home the reality of it hit her: he wasn't planning on coming back then. Not that she was asking or anything.

It was all the more unsettling because the whole thing was so . . . unfinished. Married for seventeen years, yet there had been no formal goodbyes; no bitter wrangling over who would get the kids and the telly.

And him being there tonight, on her doorstep, the two of them being so *civil*, only confused things more.

'Can I come in?' he said at last. 'It's cold out here.'

366

'Sorry. Of course.'

Clumsily, she stood back to let him in.

The hallway seemed too small. He took off his coat and then didn't seem to know what to do with it. Obviously he thought it would seem a bit forward to put it on the coat stand, as though he still lived there. So instead he shifted it from hand to hand until Geri took it and put it on the coat stand for him.

'Where's Davey?' he asked.

A conversation filler if ever she heard one.

'Over at Ben's.'

She had packed him off just to get him out of the way, despite the fact that Ben's mother was getting a bit fed up with him being foisted upon her so regularly recently, and usually at mealtimes. Geri had been tempted to whip up a dozen of her banana muffins to placate her. Thankfully she had managed to resist the urge and had sent Davey over with a set of soaps instead. One of the elderly patients on the ward had given them to her as a thank-you present. The box was a sickly purple colour and the whiff of lavender could quickly overpower you if you weren't careful, but she couldn't find anything else.

Bob didn't ask if Susan was back yet. Well, there was no sound of a hairdryer screaming in the background, or the beep of a mobile phone receiving twelve messages in quick succession, so it was a pretty safe bet that she wasn't in the house.

'Come on through,' Geri said. Come on *through*? You'd think she lived in a mansion with several interconnecting reception rooms, instead of a semi-detached where the kitchen was just off the hallway. You didn't have to go 'through' any other room to get to it, as Bob well knew.

But she was nervous. Her palms were sweaty. And it was in her nature to talk, to gabble, and if she didn't play the role of gracious-hostess-of-a-thirty-room-mansion, then there was a great danger that she would mutate into Nurse Murphy, and that would send him galloping towards the nearest door, shouting, 'Not her again.'

'Tea?' she said in the kitchen. Well, it was hard to know what else to offer. A double gin and tonic was out of the question. And she'd be damned if she was going to cook him dinner.

'Please,' he said. He seemed to approve of the tea idea too.

She felt him watching her as she made it, trying her best not to bustle. Was he thinking how long her hair had grown? Had he noticed the grey in it? Was he thinking, she's let herself go?

But he just said, quietly, 'How have you been?'

Now she really *was* going to cry. Damn. She concentrated on pouring tea, biting back her upset again. She didn't want his concern.

'How do you think I've been?' she said back.

There. That would do him.

He duly bowed his head. 'Yes.'

But she left it at that. She hadn't invited him over tonight to have a go, even though she was perfectly entitled to. But it was almost too late for that now, in a way; she had given out so much in her head, and her bed, that she hadn't the appetite for it any more.

They sat down and faced each other across the table

for the first time in months, Geri and Bob, and it wasn't as bad as she'd thought it would be.

'Thanks for coming by,' she said.

'That's OK. I was glad you rang, actually.'

And he gave her a tiny, shy smile, and she knew without being told that he had changed his shirt before coming over tonight; that he had a whole 'sorry' speech worked out in his head; that maybe he even hoped that he wouldn't be going home to sleep on Lisa and George's wretched camper bed in the attic that night.

She saw from the way he looked at her that he still loved her, probably now more than ever.

Ah, irony. It was greatly overrated, in her opinion.

'Bob,' she said briskly, 'I asked you over because of the children.'

'I feel it's all my fault,' he said. 'I shouldn't have driven off that night until I'd made sure Susan was safely in the house.'

If he was disappointed that she hadn't wanted a big 'them' discussion then he was hiding it well.

'I should have made sure too,' Geri admitted. She didn't want to get into this too deeply in case she was forced to admit to her recent love of her bed, and so she said, 'I suppose the question is, what are we going to do?'

Bob stirred his tea. He still had his wedding ring on, she noticed. But then again so did she. Some habits were hard to break.

'Do you think it's because she's upset about, um, what's happened between us?' he ventured.

It felt a bit surreal, to be sitting there over mugs of tea

talking about his affair in this detached, second-hand way. Geri had a most inappropriate desire to laugh nervously.

'No,' she said. 'I think the problems started before that.'

They were talking about Susan, but when they caught each other's eye there was a great sense they were talking about other things too.

'Yes,' said Bob.

Well, he *would* agree, wouldn't he? It took the heat off him.

Damn. There was that anger again. Just when she thought it had gone away, it came roaring back again and took her by surprise.

He may have sensed this because he moved the teapot away from her slightly, and asked, 'And how's Davey doing in the middle of all this?'

'OK. Good, in fact. Even though he's still getting over that film you took him to see last week,' she said pointedly.

Bob looked embarrassed. 'So am I.'

Now that Susan was off breaking the law and thus unavailable for access visits, Bob was left to take Davey out on his own.

'He's taking me to some arty-farty subtitled thing in the Irish Film Centre,' Davey had complained energetically. 'It's going to be awful. They don't even have popcorn there.'

For his part, Bob had clearly chosen an outing that required no conversational skills whatsoever: just sit there and let the screen do the talking. And if in Italian, even better.

The film turned out to be called *Making Love to The Ladies*, when roughly translated by Geri later using a borrowed school dictionary, and involved a taxi driver doing just that. Several times. Mostly with his, and their, clothes off. The two boyos were sitting right up at the front with their box of toffees, petrified, with Bob blurting every sixty seconds, 'Close your eyes now, son.'

They had been so traumatised that they'd had to go for a burger and chips afterwards. Presumably they'd had to engage in some kind of conversation then. Davey hadn't elaborated, but they had got home quite late. And he had gone off with Bob on Tuesday again – this time kart racing, far safer – and hadn't done as much complaining as usual.

'It wasn't bad,' he said. 'Without Susan, I mean,' he added loftily, lest Geri think he and his father had suddenly become bosom buddies.

Speaking of which. 'Susan,' she began.

That was, after all, why Bob was there.

'Yes?' he said. And he looked at her expectantly, waiting for her to take the lead again, as she always had. Geri would know what to do, and Bob would be there to pick up the pieces.

But things were different now.

'I'm thinking you should go around there,' she said.

Bob swallowed hard and looked towards the front of the house as though expecting to hear an overexcited exhaust career down the road at any moment.

'To . . . Leo Ryan's house?'

If he could take his son to see a porn movie, then he could certainly handle Leo Ryan.

'Is that wise?' he asked at last.

'I don't know if it's wise. But we can't just leave her there.'

Bob wasn't happy. In a way she couldn't blame him – go around and confront his aggressive teenage daughter and her hooded boyfriend?

And he wouldn't even have Geri standing behind him, encouraging him on with such words as, 'Oh, for the love of God, just *do* it. I'm fed up of always having to do the dirty work around here.'

Suddenly he sat up a bit straighter at the table, took a manly slug of his tea, and announced, 'You're right. Leave it to me.'

Geri was surprised. She felt something like . . . well, something nice, anyway.

But then he said worriedly, 'I just hope I find the right thing to say.'

He could probably use a little help there. There was no sense sending him in totally unprepared. 'Just talk to her. See if you can . . . connect with her.' Because God knew, Geri didn't seem to be able to any more. 'Don't use the words, "young lady" or, "in my day".'

Bob deflated. There went his entire vocabulary. 'I never really realised before how good you are with them,' she thought she heard him mumble.

'Sorry?' she said.

He cleared his throat. 'I said, I never appreciated how much you actually *do*.'

It sounded like an apology. Clearly, the access visits had taken their toll. And his trips to the laundrette.

And it was good that he had come into this know-ledge. But at the same time, he was making her sound like some fecking demented hen, fussing and clucking around the place.

'I don't bake any more,' she told him suddenly.

'Oh,' he said, looking rather taken aback.

'Not a single bun. I've give it up.'

'Right, well, good for you.'

His lack of reaction was a bit disappointing. Couldn't he have managed a round of applause or something?

'I clean the toilet now,' he told her earnestly.

Oh, great. Now they were into some kind of bizarre confessional session, each trying to outdo the other in their domestic achievements, or lack thereof.

'Listen, that's great, Bob, and I really hope you enjoy it,' she said, hoping to bring things to a swift conclusion. 'But it's getting kind of late.'

They both looked at the clock. It was twenty minutes past seven.

He looked at her and said simply, 'I have nowhere else to go.'

She held her mug of tea tightly. 'That's not my problem.'

He looked embarrassed. 'No, I didn't mean I have *nowhere* to go . . . I don't know if Lisa was telling you but I just moved into an apartment.'

'She didn't,' she lied, not wanting to betray her avid interest in his movements. 'Is it nice? Is it close to work?'

He gave her a look that cut through her nervous chatter. 'It's an apartment, Geri.'

The tea was growing cold. And she hadn't even put out any biscuits. He looked like he could do with one. She found that she felt a bit sorry for him.

But he was looking at her as though he felt a bit sorry for her too, and she wondered whether she looked unloved as well. Probably.

'Can we talk about what happened?' he asked quietly.
She studied him. 'What is there to say?'

'That I'm sorry. That I wish to God I hadn't hurt you like that.'

Hurt her? He had torn her heart to pieces.

'And if there was anything at all that I could do to make it up to you—'

'Bob, stop.'

He did, looking hurt.

'You can't just say sorry, and make everything OK.'

'What can I do then? Just tell me. Please.'

'I don't even know that myself.'

'Well, let's talk about it. See what changes we can make. Maybe we can go to counselling or something.'

She held her hand up between them like a traffic warden. He ground to a halt.

'I can't do this right now, Bob.'

'Right. Sorry.' He looked at the table. 'I just want you to know. It's completely over. I haven't seen Debra since I moved out.'

Debra. For the rest of her life whenever Geri heard that name she would have a little jolt of shock.

She had a peculiar sense of finality about things. He hadn't said or done anything that had changed anything. An apology wasn't enough, no matter how many times he said sorry.

They sat there at the table, two people who still loved each other, or partly at least, and there was nothing right then that could be done to save them.

For Geri it was the worst moment of the entire affair.

After a moment Bob got up. He was surprisingly energetic, and he nodded briskly at Geri.

'I'll be in touch.'

Dr Foley had huge nipples.

'I don't even know why you're mentioning this,' Geri said.

Andrea shrugged. 'I was just thinking about all the ways that human beings are different, that's all. Some men are tall, some are short, some have dark hair, some blond. Some have enormous, gigantic nipples.'

'Look, is this something to do with Hannah?'

Dr Foley had taken Hannah out on Friday night – to the exact same bar in Howth. The guy was a walking cliché. But at the same time it wasn't going to do Andrea any good to be obsessing about it.

'If you mean am I madly jealous, then no,' Andrea said. 'I wouldn't spit on him if he was on fire. I'm just mentioning the fact that he has humongous nipples.'

'How humongous exactly?'

'You know those saucers in the canteen?'

'Andrea.'

'OK, they're not quite that big, but close enough. They kind of ooze across his chest, like a couple of fried eggs, and the nipple bit is all rubbery and pointy.' She shuddered. 'They're kind of freaky.'

'You didn't seem too freaked out at the time.'

'I was in a tent, in the dark,' she argued. 'I thought they *felt* rather strange, but it wasn't until first light that I saw how out of control they really were.'

'Do you have a problem with huge nipples?'

Andrea considered this.'Not normally. Not, for instance, if I was into the guy. Not if the guy was a nice, decent person who called me up after we'd spent the night together.'

'And if he wasn't?'

'Well, then I might have to warn other women about his nipples.'

'Andrea . . .'

Andrea was full of concern. 'It's only fair, Geri. I wouldn't want anybody else, say Hannah or one of the other girls, getting a horrible fright.'

Chapter Twenty-Three

Debs's family wasn't entirely convinced that she wasn't putting the whole thing on.

'Myra McGrath down the town had an eating disorder, she was six stone when they finally found all that food under her bed, but she was only seventeen,' her mother said on the phone, rather baffled.

The inference was that Debs, at thirty-three, was far too old to be springing something like this on them all, and worse, three weeks before Christmas. Only last week they had gone ahead and ordered the large-size organic turkey from Tommy Mulligan, and what were they going to do with fifteen pounds of turkey meat, now that Debs was staying put in Dublin and wasn't coming home at all? Although, if she *had* come home, fifteen pounds wouldn't have gone very far, by all accounts.

They were still trying to get their heads around this bulimia thing. It wasn't the same as anorexia, apparently, which they had at least heard about, after poor

Karen Carpenter. Instead Debs had some other, made-up-sounding disorder, that apparently involved (a) eating loads of lovely junk food, (b) drinking rakes of pints, and (c) still having an arse the size of Greater Dublin (not that anybody was tactless enough to say that to her face). What kind of an eating disorder was that at all? It sounded great. It sounded like a holiday. 'If that's bulimia, I think I suffer from it too,' said Debs's father.

But of course they were trying their best. It was all terribly worrying: first Debs takes up with a married man, then suddenly that's all off, and now she was refusing to keep good food down. Plus, there was all that counselling she was going to, sometimes three times a week. She often sounded very upset after those sessions, and would just cry and cry down the phone, but she said that was normal when you were coming to terms with something like this, and to just give her time.

'I wish you'd let me come up,' Debs's mother rang up to say. 'I don't like to think of you in that flat all on your own.'

'I'm not on my own. I told you, Fiona's moved back in temporarily.'

'HELLO, MRS MANNING!' Fiona bellowed from the sofa, just to prove it. 'SHE'S DOING GREAT. NO PUKING AT ALL.' Then she looked mortified. 'Sorry,' she said to Debs. 'I meant purging.'

There was a lot of jargon surrounding it, presumably to make everybody feel better. Nobody vomited, but they purged frequently. Family and friends became 'caregivers'. In a lot of the literature, which mostly seemed to be

American, Debs was a 'loved one'. At least she hadn't been so far gone that she'd been downing handfuls of laxatives every day, otherwise they'd have had to come up with a polite term for having the runs.

It really was like learning a whole new language. But then none of them had been down this road before. Eating disorders happened to spoiled middle-class girls, surely, who developed them as a way of passing time in their boarding schools.

Debs still wasn't able to think of herself as bulimic. Not that anybody was forcing her to stand up in a room full of other weight-obsessed people, and say, 'Howya, my name is Debs and I'm a bulimic.' For several counselling sessions she had argued quite convincingly that because she wasn't a serial puker, as in, she didn't do it religiously nine times a day and had never partaken of laxatives or diet pills (hmm, could you buy them off the internet?), she couldn't really be classed as a bulimic, now could she? But Cara, her counsellor, had given her That Look, the same one that the shrink in the hospital had given her, the one that said, 'Deny it all you like, love, but we *know*. And you will too, some day, probably nine thousand euro into therapy, which, thankfully, is being partially paid for by your health insurance seeing as you've taken unscheduled leave from your crap job.'

'How do you do that purging thing anyway?' Debs's mother asked suddenly.

'Why?' Debs was suspicious. Only yesterday her mother had been complaining about having to go to a Christmas do, and the skirt she'd bought was a tad too tight.

'I'm just trying to educate myself here.' She sounded

exasperated. 'We don't know anything about this, or why it happened, or how long it lasts.'

'Three weeks,' said Debs.

'Really?' her mother said in relief. 'That's great.'

'That was a little joke, Mum. It's a psychological disorder. Officially, I'm cracked and probably have been for years.'

In her sessions with Cara she had been encouraged to 'confront her past'. Which wasn't a pleasant thing for anybody to do, but especially not if you'd been surreptitiously weighing yourself several times a day for about twenty years. On banjaxed scales. Which never seemed to go down, only up.

She had thrown her scales out after her first session. It had been like an old friend dying. Actually, it had been more like murdering an old friend, and she'd had to have a little cry afterwards.

'Don't be so smart,' her mother said. 'I'm only asking. I don't know why you can't give me a straight answer about anything, ever.' Her voice cracked a bit.

'Mum? Are you upset?'

'Upset? And when would I have the time to be upset, what with you seeing therapists, and refusing to come home for Christmas, and getting entangled with married men?'

Debs suddenly felt horribly guilty. Look what she was putting her parents through. Although, of course, Cara would say that she was not responsible for other people's feelings, only her own.

But Cara wasn't there right now. 'I'm sorry, Mum,' she blubbered.

'No, *I'm* sorry,' her mother blubbered back, not to be outdone. 'Tell me straight now – was it something I did? Was it the way I wouldn't let anybody leave the table until they had finished their meal? Even when it was beef stew which, God knows, I couldn't even stand myself? But you always finished it, Debs.' There was another catch in her voice. 'And I always praised you and said you were a great girl.'

She really was laying it on with a trowel now. And, actually, Cara was right – Debs was not going to allow herself to get involved in this binge-fest of emotions. Or any binges, if she could help it.

'No, Mum,' she said briskly. 'You're entirely innocent in all this.'

'Oh,' said her mother, deflating.

Although there was a genetic component, apparently. If there was a history of addiction in the family at all then apparently you were more at risk. 'We can't blame your Uncle Ned for this,' her father had said worriedly.

Luckily there were other things to blame too: environmental factors, peer pressure, bloody *Cosmo* parading dozens of stick women on its fashion pages month after relentless month.

But Debs knew what she was doing once again. Transferring blame to other people for her own inability to deal with emotional issues. She hadn't made this up, by the way. Yes, that's right – Cara had said it. Cara was God. Debs was seeing her that afternoon. The very thought was making her knees go all weak, and not in a good way.

'SHE HAS TO GO NOW, MRS MANNING,' Fiona

yelled from the sofa. 'IT'S TIME FOR HER PILLS.' Fiona had put herself in change of dispensing the pills. The fact that one of them was an antidepressant made her a bit nervous. 'Supposing I get mixed up and give you two?' Debs assured her that it would simply mean that she would be extra happy for the day.

'I'll ring you later on,' Debs's mother promised. She would, too. It was as though by ringing every hour on the hour she would stop any urges to vomit in their tracks. Unless, of course, Debs managed to vomit whilst actually talking to her on the phone. Which wasn't outside the realms of possibility. Oh, Debs's mother was wise to the tricks that these bulimics pulled. She informed Fiona that she sometimes left a little unexpected pause midsentence, so that she might hear any puking noises in the background.

After the pills, Fiona made a 'light lunch' of vegetable soup and wholemeal toast. Everything she cooked for Debs these days seemed to be out of a *Good Housekeeping* cookbook, circa 1948. Then she sat down opposite her and serenely spooned up her own soup.

'Could you please stop watching me?' Debs enquired after a bit.

'I'm not.'

'I'm not going to hide the toast under my jumper, you know. That's anorexia. A bulimic will eat the lot, ask for more, and then make for the toilet.'

Fiona burst out, 'I just feel so *guilty*.'

She could join the queue.

'All that time we were living together . . . I knew there was something wrong, but I just thought you were . . .'

'Being a pig?'

'Yes,' Fiona admitted. 'And then when you started to lose all that weight when you met Bob – I should have done something.'

'Like what?'

'Well, I don't know,' Fiona said crossly. 'I just wanted to get it off my chest.' She pushed away her soup. It actually wasn't very nice. 'Did he notice? Bob?'

'Maybe. I don't know. He wasn't really here long enough to notice anything.'

Fiona was obviously struggling for the right thing to say. 'I know it all turned out crap, but I think he really had feelings for you, Debs.'

Debs didn't want to talk about it. She felt it would be going backwards or something. And the only way she could get through the days right now was to think that she was finally moving onwards.

She got up from the table and reached for her handbag and phone.

'Where are you going?' Fiona said, tensing. She began to look around uselessly, as though she had mislaid her Bulimic Panic Button that, when pressed, would unleash several large men in white coats who would burst forwards and save Debs from herself. 'I *knew* I shouldn't have brought up Bob,' she berated herself under her breath.

Debs sighed. 'Fiona, I know you mean well.'

'I do,' Fiona assured her earnestly. 'I know sometimes it doesn't come out right. But I'll get better.'

'You can't stay here for ever, watching me. Stevo's going to get pissed off, for starters.'

'Stevo can go hang.' Brave words from a woman who

had been separated from her fiancé for a whole week already, and who was clearly pining for him. 'You getting better is my main priority right now,' she said loyally.

It was very sweet of her. But she, like everybody else, seemed to think that Debs would recover in a week or two, like she was simply suffering from a bad bout of flu.

Indeed Debs herself had thought that, when she first went to see Cara. 'So!' she had said, half joking. 'How long is this going to take? One session? Two?'

And Cara had given her That Look, along with That Smile, and Debs had inexplicably started crying. Cara had that effect on people. It was scary.

'It's just until you get back on your feet,' Fiona assured her.

She didn't say, it'd be different if you had Bob; somebody who cared about you and was here to look after you. It'd be different if you had *somebody*.

'I've got an appointment with Cara,' she told Fiona, rather defensively.

Cara cared. Kind of. Even if she was paid to do so.

Fiona seemed greatly relieved. Now she could spend an hour on the phone to Stevo instead of shadowing Debs down the street like a cheap detective.

'I'll get your coat,' she said.

While she was out in the hall the doorbell rang, and she came back minus the coat. 'You have a visitor.'

Alex carried a massive bouquet of flowers.

'They're not from me,' she said. 'Well, they *are*,' she amended hastily. 'We did a whip-round in work.'

'Oh. Thank you.'

'Everybody's been asking for you, you know. And wondering when you're coming back.'

'Not for a few weeks yet,' Debs said vaguely.

It was all very awkward. They hadn't seen each other since that night in the office loo. Debs had been on sick leave from Fitz Communications since the fainting incident. Marty so far was absolutely fine about it. 'Take all the time you need,' he had said generously to her the week before last. 'Your job under the stairs will still be here for you when you get back.'

She deeply suspected his goodwill stemmed from a fear that she was going to sue him for a busted head, especially as Gavin had revealed that Marty had had some kind of a legal person in, and the two of them had huddled in the ladies' toilets for an hour, looking at the tiles.

At least she had managed to hide the whole eating disorder thing from the office. Her GP had put 'depression' on her sick note, so at least they only thought she was mental as opposed to a closet binger.

'I'll just go and find a vase,' Fiona said cheerily, clearly impressed that someone from work in a suit and driving a nifty car had come all the way out to visit Debs. And after all the giving out Debs did about that place, too.

'So!' said Alex, when she was gone. 'How are you feeling?'

'I'd tell you only I'm not sure you care.'

'What?'

'Listen, you needn't worry. I'm not going to tell anybody in work, OK? I presume that's why you're here.'

Alex opened her mouth to say something, abandoned it, and then sank down onto the couch. (Hopefully it wouldn't leave a mark on her nice cream skirt.)

'You know, I don't know what your fucking problem is,' she said.

Debs was mildly shocked. Alex wasn't one for foul language. Butter normally wouldn't have a hope of melting in her mouth.

'I go out of my way to be nice to you. To be friends with you. And, let's be honest here, it's not like they're queuing up, is it?'

Debs's face flamed. 'Nobody asked you to.'

'No,' Alex agreed. 'But I thought maybe we'd have something in common. I thought you were different from the rest of those idiots.'

'I am,' Debs insisted in a lick-arsey kind of way. 'Gavin is nice, too,' she felt she had to say. 'And Liam's not bad, if you can only stop him talking about cars and women.'

Alex waved this away and continued on, 'And all the thanks I get is some crap about me telling the office about your affair!'

'If you didn't, then who *did*?' Debs asked, trying not to sound like she was about three.

'Janice.'

'*Janice?*'

'Apparently she was in the toilets the night of the Christmas party when you made your drunken phone call to Bob. So. Mystery solved.'

And she sat back on the sofa and awaited the apology.

'Sorry,' Debs muttered. 'Terribly sorry.'

'Apology accepted,' Alex said maturely, leaving Debs feeling even more like a toddler beside her.

There was a long silence now. Neither of them seemed to know what to say.

'I have bulimia,' Debs blurted out.

Why, oh *why*? But she was probably trying to make it up to Alex; now they both knew something about the other that the world at large didn't.

'So what are you saying?' Alex enquired. 'Here we are, two freaks together?'

'No! No, no!' Debs was tying herself in knots here. In a desperate attempt to change the subject she asked, 'How are things with your girlfriend?'

But that was another dud.

'They aren't.'

'Oh.'

'Don't even bother to look surprised. You were there that night. You heard.'

'She did have a point,' Debs felt she had to say.

'Oh, so if you were me, you'd do it, would you? You'd march into the kitchenette some morning at coffee break and announce your sexuality to the whole place just as Marty finishes telling his latest light-bulb joke?'

'I can see where you're coming from—'

'But you still think I should have the bottle, don't you? You still think that it's better to be "true" to yourself than to be able to do a decent day's work without gobshites making your life miserable?'

'They make my life miserable too,' Debs argued.

Alex sat back for a while. 'Look, I'm sorry about the bulimia. Are you all right?'

'Not really. But I will be. I'm going to my counsellor now. Actually, I'm going to be late.'

Alex got up. 'Sorry . . .'

'No, listen, wait.' She felt that things were unfinished or something. 'You must want them to know.'

'And how did you work that out?'

'You were going to tell *me* that night at the Christmas party.'

Alex didn't deny it. 'You get sick of lying all the time.'

'Well, supposing I told Gavin?'

'But won't he tell Liam?'

'Probably.'

Alex thought about this. 'That's what Gemma – my ex – said. Just let the word filter out.'

'Look, it's up to you.'

Alex briefly closed her eyes in pain. 'Marty and Janice. Can you imagine?'

'They're just fuckheads.'

'I know, but I'm still scared of them.'

'Feel the fear and do it anyway,' advised Debs, veteran of a hundred self-help books. Although they had gone on the scrap heap along with her weighing scales. It had been carnage.

Alex stood and brushed down her skirt. And, oh dear, there *was* some kind of smudge on the back of it. 'Good luck with your bulimia.' Her forehead crinkled. 'That's binging and purging, right?'

Debs was dead impressed.

Debs wasn't sure she liked Cara. Sometimes she wasn't sure that Cara liked *her*. She never seemed to say much. She just opened the door three times a week and ushered Debs in, and Debs, for some inexplicable reason, would promptly break down crying. It was all very strange.

'I'm sorry,' she bawled. 'I don't know why I keep doing this. Maybe it's because I'm late.'

In the beginning she had put it down to the shock and shame of being landed in therapy. And she wasn't even living in LA. Or maybe it was because she was the sole focus of a highly qualified and busy counsellor's attention for a solid hour and a half, and she felt she should deliver.

But now she finally worked it out. It was nothing to do with therapy or pressure or Alex making her late. She was crying because finally, thankfully, somebody had stopped her. She didn't have to do the whole eating and then vomiting thing any more.

Cara was unperturbed by all this bawling. She simply eased a box of tissues closer to Debs and smiled in that intense way. Debs tried to do it back to her one day but it didn't seem to have any effect.

The hospital had referred Debs to her. She was, apparently, an expert in eating disorders. But she never seemed to want to talk about food. Debs had been quite prepared to come clean about exactly how many Penguin bars she could eat in one sitting (eight) and her feelings upon her first successful purging (great – light, free, thin. Ish). She had presumed that Cara would put her on some kind of monitored eating regime, and there would be a lot of encouragement and hand-holding.

But, disappointingly, Cara wasn't interested in any of this. Instead she would fix her rather pale blue eyes on Debs and ask her difficult, and often apparently useless, questions about Debs's need to control her environment (huh?) and her inability to accept herself for who she was.

CLARE DOWLING

'Correct,' said Debs with relief, glad to have got one question right.

'Sorry?' said Cara.

'I realise I have a lot to improve on,' Debs assured her diligently. 'But I'm working on it.'

That was the wrong answer. Self-improvement was not a target for recovering bulimics, apparently. In fact, Cara seemed to be hinting that, along with a lot of people with eating disorders, Debs was probably a closet perfectionist.

Debs had to suppress a wild snort. Whoever heard of a perfectionist with a crap job, no car, no apartment, no savings, no *life*?

Sometimes Cara talked a load of rubbish.

She also cost a fortune. Debs had swallowed hard when a copy of the first bill had come through from the heath insurance company. She could have had a gastric band fitted for the same price, and solved all her problems. Thank Christ she was on some all-singing, all-dancing healthcare plan, talked into by her father – who probably suspected that she would end up needing it someday.

God knew, she couldn't afford the bills herself, now that she was on sick leave for depression.

The depression thing wasn't a lie. She really *was* depressed. That's what they said, anyway, even though she felt no different from how she always did. Which was a bit miserable, now that she thought about it. Anyway, the upshot was that they had given her some antidepressants, which Fiona had nervously put herself in charge of. So far Debs didn't feel like jumping around the garden. But they said they would take about a month to work. A whole *month*?

Imagine if you actually *were* depressed, Debs had thought cynically, before inexplicably bursting into tears again.

Jesus. It was scary, all this crying.

While she waited for the pills to work she had Cara. But the alternative was checking into one of those rehab places especially for people with eating disorders. Imagine being locked up with a rake of other lunatics who were purging and binging and starving themselves to beat the band. She didn't think she could bear it.

'I'll give her a ring,' Debs had said at the hospital, half-heartedly taking Cara's card. She might, too.

'Do,' they encouraged her. Otherwise she risked fatally tearing her oesophagus or inducing a heart attack; it was up to her.

'We'll ring, we'll ring,' her mother had bleated, terrified. Silly woman. All of Debs's tests had come back clear. They were just being alarmist.

The only thing wrong with her really was all the crying, and the fact that she felt there was a black cloud following her around. One morning she had felt so down that she had just picked up the phone and rung.

Today, Cara waited patiently until Debs had finished that particular day's crying.

'Do you feel better now?'

'Terrific,' Debs growled back through a stuffed nose.

'Why are you so angry with yourself, Debs?' Cara enquired in that touchy-feely way that shrinks seemed to learn on their first day in college.

'I'm not.'

Cara wasn't happy with that answer but it would just have to do her.

'Today we need to confront your relationship with Bob,' she said.

Oh, for the love of God. She was always wanting Debs to confront things. What had Bob got to do with anything, anyway? Well, obviously he'd had plenty to do with Deb's romantic life, but shag all with her running to the toilet after every meal.

'He was married. He went back to his wife. End of story,' she said rather shortly, just to show her how irrelevant she thought this line of questioning was.

But Cara had a skin like a rhino because she didn't take a bit of notice of this. She just waited patiently while Debs burst into tears again.

'Shit,' Debs raged. Just as her nose was beginning to unblock itself too. How could a person cry so much? Now she'd be puffy-eyed for the rest of the afternoon, and Fiona would think she'd been at herself in the toilet again.

But this crying was different. It sounded alarmingly like keening. Dear God. The thing with Bob had been over *weeks* ago. Obviously she was still upset, but it wasn't like she hadn't seen the writing on the wall.

After a while she managed to quieten down to the odd hiccup and snort. She felt empty. That was nothing new. Before she used to fill up with food. Now that that option was gone, what was she was supposed to do? Go around with this big gaping hole inside her?

'Tell me about Bob,' Cara invited, just to compound her misery.

Sometimes Debs suspected she asked these things just so that she could sit back and Debs would have to do all the talking. Easy work if you could get it.

Well, this time Debs was ready for her. She read the problems pages of women's magazines. So she was pretty *au fait* with all this therapist speak.

'I probably picked him because he was married,' she announced knowledgeably. 'And thus unavailable. Obviously, I have a deep fear of commitment.'

'Have you?' said Cara, looking very surprised.

'Well, no. At least I don't think so.' Damn. She didn't want to add something else to her list of problems. It could only result in more sessions.

'So what was it about Bob that was so special?' Cara probed, and sat back again, all satisfied looking.

Debs began to sigh and huff and look at her watch in the hopes that the session was nearly over. Totally unrealistic, of course, given that it had only just started.

Cara, meanwhile, was waiting. Debs tried to dampen down her resentment and self-pity. Why should she have to sit here, being examined like this? Talking about Bob to strangers always made her feel defensive and in the wrong. And stupid, too, especially given that he had ended the whole thing to go back to his wife. As if he had ever been going to do anything else.

'Look, he liked me, OK?' she ended up saying rather lamely.

It made them sound like they were in nursery school.

Cara said nothing. Silence didn't knock a bother out of her. Whole minutes of it could pass and she wouldn't be a bit ruffled. Debs, meanwhile, would slowly go blue with mortification and would end up blurting out something completely irrelevant, such as, 'Did you see *The X Factor* on Saturday night?' just for something to say.

Cara did it on purpose, of course. It was a sneaky way of giving Debs enough rope to hang herself with.

Debs fell for it every time. Like now. 'I suppose we met at the right time in our lives.'

Cara crooked an eyebrow as though to say, 'Do you really think so?'

'Actually, maybe not,' Debs admitted. 'It was more like the wrong time in our lives.'

It was as though by saying it out loud she was able to see it for the first time: two drifting souls who happened to meet each other over a ham sandwich – Debs in her dead-end existence, and Bob in his frustrated one. But instead of setting off into the sunset, like in the movies, their relationship had pushed Debs into a fully fledged eating disorder and Bob into a life of lies.

What a pair. They were disastrous. It would have been far better had they not met at all.

But then Debs would never have confronted her problems, or at least not until more time had been wasted, and met Cara (would that have been such a bad thing?) and Bob . . . well, hopefully Bob had sorted himself out and made things up with Geri.

Debs was feeling quite philosophical now, and strangely benign. Joy to the world, and all that. Everything had been for a purpose. She felt strongly that, in a minute, something very symbolic would happen. The sun would shine in the window at just the right angle to bathe her in a revelatory light, or something like that.

Then she remembered that she'd drunk a Coke on the way over, on top of her antidepressant. Sometimes the combination tended to send her off her head.

But while she was still in that fuzzy place, she decided to say goodbye to Bob. Goodbye, she thought mistily. Then she couldn't think of anything else to say. And, um, good luck with things, she added hurriedly. Hopefully he would wish the same thing back at her, had he also been on Coke and strong antidepressants.

'I think we can leave things for today,' Cara said, rudely interrupting her little reverie. 'Unless you have anything else you'd like to talk about?'

'Not a single thing,' Debs assured her earnestly.

Cara must be worth all that dosh, because Debs felt better than she had in weeks when she walked out that door.

Chapter Twenty-Four

Bob's way of handling the crisis of their sixteen-year-old daughter living with a wretched bum was to invite him around for dinner.

'I can't believe you've done this!' Geri spluttered in the kitchen.

'I know you can't believe it. You've said it about ten times.' Bob was rummaging in a drawer to find the take-away menu for the Soon Fat Chinese takeaway service down the town. 'The fecking mess in here.'

Then, as if remembering that he didn't live there any more and so had absolutely no right whatsoever to criticise any part of it, he said, meekly, 'Ah. Here it is. Exactly where it should be.'

'At least you should have given me some *warning*.' Geri was in her gardening clothes. Not that she had been gardening or anything. But she'd hoped that the urge might come over her if she dressed the part. It had worked last week when she'd put on an old shirt she used to use

396

back when she'd dabbled in watercolour painting – long before the children had come along and wrecked her life, of course. But she had sat up at the kitchen table in her shirt, pottering away at a still life of the fruit bowl and feeling very arty and fulfilled.

It was all part of her mission to slow down. To take some time for herself. To prioritise.

'You've been listening to Jeremy Kyle again, haven't you?' Andrea had said with a sigh.

Geri didn't know now whether she was more upset to be discovered in stretch pants by Leo Ryan, or by Bob. He himself was dressed quite smartly. He had on jeans and a rather nice shirt that she hadn't seen before, and she self-consciously tugged down her own baggy granddad shirt.

'It was a spur-of-the-moment thing,' he assured her. 'I thought, well, one way to get her to come home is to invite them to dinner.'

It was rather cunning. She had to admire him.

'I would have cooked, you know,' she said.

'I thought you didn't cook any more,' he said evenly.

'I don't *bake*. I never said I didn't *cook*.'

'If I were you, I'd give that up as well.'

Oh! He was obviously remembering her shepherd's pies.

But he was smiling, and after a minute she smiled back. And she grudgingly accepted that it might be nice, for once, to have a family meal that she hadn't spent three hours putting together.

Even if it *was* with her separated husband.

And her estranged daughter.

CLARE DOWLING

And her estranged daughter's rather fierce-looking boyfriend who was, at that moment, brooding in the living room. He wore baggy jeans and the usual hoodie, but at least his head was exposed. He stood by the window restlessly, either looking for a means of escape or else checking that nobody was making off with his motor, which was parked audaciously between Bob's and Geri's in the middle of the drive.

'I'm just getting us some drinks,' Susan said, breezing in and opening the fridge.

'Put one of those back,' Bob said automatically without even looking up.

Susan looked mutinous for a moment, but then released one of the bottles of Heineken she'd taken from the fridge. She replaced it with a Coke for herself.

'It's really good to see you,' Geri said warmly.

Susan looked like she was wondering whether to remain aloof or not, but then she said, rather shyly, 'It's nice to be back. But not for good, obviously. Just for a visit,' she added quickly.

'Of course,' Geri murmured. 'How are you settling into Leo's place?'

'Great!' Susan said. Her smile dimmed slightly. 'Obviously, what with him sharing with all those others, it can get a bit cramped at times.'

'Still, I'm sure it must be great to have all that freedom?' Geri pressed. She was trying not to enjoy herself.

'Oh, it is,' Susan agreed, before turning back to see what she could scavenge from the fridge. She had been eating since she'd arrived. And Geri had seen a big bag of washing stashed in the utility room. Leo's gaff clearly

398

did not have a functioning washing machine, or a well-stocked larder.

In the living room Leo was peering in a puzzled fashion at an ornament of a rather demented-looking elephant that Bob's mother had brought back from a holiday in Kenya once.

'Is he . . . hungry, do you think?' Bob ventured cautiously.

He looked like he could eat a medium-sized cow.

'I suppose we'd better ask,' Geri said.

'Chicken chow mein or beef noodles!' Bob called out cheerily from a safe distance, waving the takeaway menu.

For some reason that was the wrong thing to say. Leo Ryan's head snapped up. His face, already sallow-skinned, seemed to grow darker. He strode over to the living room door and threw it open.

'Neither,' he ground out.

Bob and Geri shrank back. What could he possibly want – a dripping steak, fresh from the butcher's? Bob's head on a platter?

'Actually,' he said, smiling rather apologetically, 'I'm a vegan.'

He was having them on. He must be. This was his idea of a sick joke before he produced a penknife and carved them up.

'I know I don't look like one,' he confessed. 'But I haven't touched animal produce in nearly five years. It's not sustainable, you know,' he lectured them.

Beside her, Geri could feel Bob slowly let out his breath. Vegans were all right. Vegans were *harmless*.

'I'm one now too,' Susan announced.

'You?' said Bob, with a guffaw. 'She once ate seven hot dogs on the trot,' he told Leo.

Susan rolled her eyes: *parents*. 'That's all in the past. Me and Leo eat only tofu and lentils now.'

'Well, not just tofu and lentils,' Leo chided her gently. 'I don't want your parents thinking I'm some kind of hippy.' He adjusted himself inside his jeans – why did boys do that? – and gave Geri a crooked smile. 'We eat lots of veggie burgers and chips too. She's not going short, you know, Mrs M.'

Mrs *M*?

'Oh! Well . . . great . . .' Geri managed.

'Your front tyres are a bit bald,' he told her.

'What?'

'I was just looking out the window there. They're not dangerous yet, but you'd want to get them checked. I know a garage who'll change them for you cheap.'

This was all getting a bit too cosy, so Bob burst out, 'You drive too fast.'

Leo hung his head. 'I'm careful, though.'

'That doesn't matter. It just takes an icy patch on the road. Or an oil slick. Or for your brakes to let you down. Or . . . or . . .'

'For a child to step out from behind an ice-cream van?' Leo offered helpfully.

Bob glowered suspiciously. 'That's my daughter you're carrying around in your front seat.'

It was as close as he dared come to making a threat. Leo was, after all, an unknown quantity yet. He might be a vegan, but what if he was a black-belt vegan?

After a long moment Leo conceded, 'I'll slow down.'

Phew. Everyone could relax now.

But it was quickly time for the next test. 'I don't suppose you saw the match on Sunday?' Bob asked cautiously.

'I did,' Leo confirmed.

'Really?' said Bob. Leo was practically son-in-law material now. 'What did you think of the ref's decision? Absolute rubbish, wasn't it?'

But Leo's brow furrowed over again. 'Sorry, bud. I thought you meant the *hockey*.'

There was a little pause.

'No,' said Bob at last.

Geri was looking from Bob to Leo to Susan, as if trying to catch her balance. Leo's transformation from thug to vegan to obscure sports lover was too fast for comfort.

'That's where we met, me and Susan,' Leo informed them. 'Even though we'd been living around the corner all this time. I play hockey, you see. And so does she.' He looked over at Susan disapprovingly. 'Or she *did*.'

'Don't start,' Susan snapped.

'She had real talent,' he went on to Bob and Geri. Susan began sighing and crossing her arms. 'But I think she fell in with the wrong crowd. That Karen . . .'

'Leo!' Susan was furious now.

'What?' he said. 'I just hate to see you jacking it in to hang around that shopping centre, that's all.'

'I'm not hanging around. I'm shopping. That's what you *do* in shopping centres. But just because you hate shopping . . .'

'I just don't see the point of trying on stuff that you

have no intention of buying. Like that ball gown last Saturday. Where was the fun in *that*?'

At that point Geri and Bob began a slow retreat from the room. With any luck Susan and Leo would have broken up by the time dinner arrived.

'What are you thinking?' Bob asked, while they waited in the kitchen.

She was thinking that maybe Susan wasn't doing so badly for herself at all.

She was thinking how nice it was that Bob was there, and how lonely she had been. And how easy it would be to just brush the whole thing under the carpet and carry on like it had never happened at all.

Dangerous thoughts.

'Nothing much,' she said, moving away. 'I'd better go set the table.'

Bob called around a couple of days later.

'I noticed that the boiler is due for a service. I thought I'd better do it in case, well, you blew up in your sleep.'

He organised the boiler service and put in a new bulb in the yard light while he was at it, and then he drove off.

Another couple of days passed and Geri found him on her doorstep again.

'Bob,' she said, 'you can't keep doing this.'

'What? I have to fix that roof tile. Unless you're going to do it yourself.'

'Well, no. But I could ring someone.'

'Who?' he challenged.

'Someone who fixes roofs. A . . . roofer!'

He looked disappointed that she had got it right. He had the last word, though. 'Who would charge you a fortune and probably not do the job right.'

'Just the roof tile,' she warned him.

'Of course.'

He got the ladder out and climbed up on the roof and it was only after he had gone that she saw that the bins had been emptied, and that her car had been washed and hoovered inside.

She phoned him up. 'You didn't need to do that.'

'I know, but I wanted to. Oh, and Leo's going to organise those new tyres for you, OK?'

'Bob, I don't know how to say this—'

'Then don't,' he said. He seemed a little afraid. 'Just let me. Please.'

She didn't know if it was his way of saying sorry, or whether he was trying to get her back. Probably both.

'I just don't want us to drift back into anything, Bob.'

'Would it be such a bad thing if we did?'

'Yes,' she said.

'Why?'

Because then it would all have been for nothing. All that pain and heartache wasted, almost.

'Geri, I still love you.'

'I know you do.' And she loved him too. But what difference did that make?

He had obviously taken her words to heart because there was no sign at all of him for a week after that. Then one night she came home from work to find that the hedge looked suspiciously clipped, and the outside of the windows had been washed.

She rang him up again. 'Bob?'

'Sorry, Geri, I can't talk, I'm in a meeting.'

The following week there was a beautiful, blooming poinsettia left on the doorstep with a card from him simply saying 'Happy Christmas'.

'Look, do you want to come over for Christmas dinner?' she asked him. It was for the kids' sake, she told herself. But he politely refused, saying he had already made plans to go to his mother's. He dropped by Christmas morning, dispensed presents and then left.

He had bought her a cookbook. For feck's sake. After *everything* she had said . . . It was like the L'Eau D'Issey perfume. He had just kept on getting her more and more, like he was stuck in some kind of groove he could never climb out of.

It was a copy of *Can't Cook, Won't Cook*.

She burst out laughing.

There was a card tucked into the inside flap: 'I still cook. Will you join me for dinner some night?'

She slammed the book shut fast, her heart hammering.

He just wasn't going to stop. It was like all those years ago when they had first met, and he had kept trying and trying until eventually she had said yes.

She didn't reply to the invitation. And, in some knee-jerk act of defiance, she went out the first week of January and finally got the haircut she had been threatening for so long. She went to some trendy place in town, where she was at least twenty years older than the rest of the clientele. The stylist gave her a severe bob that she assured Geri rather too enthusiastically 'took years off her'.

'I *knew* I wouldn't be able to blow-dry the bloody thing at home myself,' she raged to Susan.

'Give me the hairdryer,' Susan said calmly, the pro. 'I can make a silk purse out of a sow's ear,' she assured Geri.

She had taken to spending the odd night at home now; three in the last week, actually. On those nights, Leo would come over for dinner or to watch telly. It was all very civilised. 'Where are you going, anyway?' she enquired.

'The pub,' Geri said sourly.

'The *pub*?'

It wasn't Geri's idea. Nicola had organised an outing with her new man. Yes, she was actually dating that teacher from school, Andy.

'But it's not because of *you*, Geri,' she was at pains to point out. 'I'd already made up my mind that I'd start seeing other people once Fintan was dead two years.'

'I didn't realise you were on some kind of count-down. I'd have saved my breath.'

Things were still tense between them. The tea-drinking sessions had been slow enough to start up again, even after the peace had been made.

'Why don't you come around?' Geri would urge.

And sometimes Nicola would, but was so wary of being accused of going on about Fintan that she went to the other extreme and refused to mention him at all.

'You remember that bloke I used to be married to?' she would say whenever the subject was completely unavoidable.

Things would settle down, Geri was sure. Nicola still had a way to go yet (hadn't they all).

In the meantime she had tentatively started dating Andy, the token male in school. But he came from a family of seven girls, and so he said he was used to it. With his longish hair and gentle hands, he was just perfect for Nicola.

'*And* he doesn't mind me talking about your man that I buried two years ago,' Nicola told Geri rather pointedly.

He did, however, draw the line at the cemetery visits. Nicola had tried to take him one evening 'just to introduce you two', and he had told her firmly (but gently) that he was a man who looked to the future, not the past.

That had a profound effect on Nicola, even though Geri had told her the exact same thing in the kitchen that evening. But maybe it sounded more authoritative coming from a teacher or something, because within a week Nicola was wearing red – *red* – and planning a night out for them all in the pub.

Geri would rather gouge out her own eyes.

'Please come along,' Nicola had begged. 'It's ages since we've been out together.'

There was a smile in her voice that Geri hadn't heard since . . . well, ever, actually.

'I'm sure you two don't want me hanging around.'

'Not at all. Anyway, you're recently separated.'

'So?'

'So you need to get out and about.'

Geri was suddenly suspicious. 'So it's just you, me and Andy?'

'Yes. Oh, and maybe a friend of his.'

'Nicola—'

'He's really nice, Geri. Plus, he's recently separated too.'

'I am *not* going on a blind date.'

'Relax. You might enjoy yourself.'

'I'm not sure about the graduation. Very passé, very Jennifer Aniston. If you want, I could fix it for you.'

Andy's friend Tomas was a forty-seven-year-old hairdresser, of all things.

'I'm not gay,' was one of the first things he said to her. 'Most people think that all male hairdressers are, but I can assure you that I'm one hundred per cent heterosexual.'

'Good for you,' Geri had told him nicely, checking out his footwear just the same. Not a cowboy boot in sight, although he did wear his hair in a ponytail. She suspected that it may be subtly highlighted as well.

He was now examining her bob. It wasn't good. He said this in a very nice way, though. He told her that with her lovely heart-shaped face that any style would look good. Except the bob that she had just shelled out over a hundred euros to get, obviously.

'Shorter might work,' he said suddenly.

She was afraid now. She had seen something glinting in his trousers pocket earlier and was worried that it was a scissors that he might whip out there and then in the pub and 'fix' her.

'He's lovely, isn't he?' Nicola whispered loudly, taking a brief break from having her hand held ever so gently by Andy. 'And he's a genius at what he does. A lot of the top models go to him.' Tomas was pretending he hadn't heard this, and stared off into the middle distance modestly. 'I know he's not exactly your type, Geri, but at least he's a change after seventeen years of Bob.'

The minute she said it those seventeen years flashed before Geri's eyes in a series of snapshots (for a minute she was worried she was dying). There was Bob, in an unfortunate pair of Hawaiian shorts on their honeymoon, tenderly spreading after-sun cream on her burned back. Then two years later, during Davey's birth at the hospital, Bob with slightly less hair promising her sincerely between contractions that he would now get the snip (he chickened out). Bob resigning from his band – they did weddings by then, and were quite in demand – because he didn't want to leave Geri alone on her own at nights with two young kids. And, more importantly, never ever mentioning it again. Bob, who had been solidly behind her at her father's funeral, and that awful time at work involving an internal enquiry, and who brought her a Terry's chocolate orange on his way home from work every Friday.

Bob, who had somehow got lost along the way and she hadn't seen it until it was too late.

'Nicola tells me you're separated,' the hairdresser said.

He had a name, she reminded herself. But it was hard to shake the feeling that she was at a hair appointment and they were making conversation over a wash basin. In a minute he would ask where she was going on holiday. 'Yes.'

'Me too.' He smiled at her. 'It's shit, isn't it?'

And Geri found herself warming to him. 'You could say that.'

'My wife went back to college and next thing she's pierced her eyebrows and dyed her hair pink. She said she was too mortified to be married to a hairdresser any more.' He drooped sadly over his drink. 'I got dumped by text.'

'That's awful!' Bloody hell, why was life so unfair? Why did bad things always happen to nice people?

And Tomas *was* nice, even though he looked like that man out of Status Quo. 'How about you?' he asked. 'Trying to move on too, eh?'

It probably looked like that; Geri, sitting up at the bar in a short black dress that Susan had talked her into, and with her new, younger hairstyle. She would only disappoint him if she told him that it was all a sham, and that really she wanted her marriage back if only she would work out a way to fix it.

'Yes,' she lied, smiling brilliantly. 'I've *so* moved on. Now let's have another drink, will we?'

She knew she shouldn't. In the cold light of day she would cross the road to avoid Tomas. While he was a decent man, they didn't have a thing in common except for broken hearts and wrecked marriages. Oh, and two bad hairstyles.

But for tonight that was enough, in fact it was *essential*, and they chatted and laughed and got drunk together. Tomas was very good at taking his wife off − 'I can't bring a bleedin' hairdresser to the Freshers' Ball!' − and Geri had tears of laughter rolling down her cheeks. Tomas was lovely. Tomas was *great*.

'I think you should slow down,' Nicola murmured at one point when Geri cackled raucously at a tale Tomas was spinning about an old lady who came into the salon demanding 'the new Beyoncé'.

'Sorry. I haven't had such a good times in years!'

Which was a load of rubbish, of course. She was drunk on white wine and a heartbeat away from bawling over her lousy cheating husband (all that teary-eyed snapshot stuff from earlier had passed).

Eventually Tomas got to his feet. 'I have a nine-thirty in the morning,' he slurred – God help them.

'I'd better go too,' she said.

She would have to sneak in by the back door. Leo was over watching a movie with Susan and she didn't want the pair of them to see her roaring drunk.

She waved away Nicola's offer to wait with her and Andy and they would drop her home, and she went outside with Tomas to get a taxi.

'You get the first one,' he insisted. In the harsh streetlights he looked even more like an ageing rocker – one that was already moving from foot to foot restlessly and obviously in mounting need of a toilet.

'You didn't deserve her,' Geri told him in a burst of affection.

'Too right I didn't,' he agreed wholeheartedly. 'And you didn't deserve . . .'

'Bob.'

Afterwards Geri tried to figure out whether she'd been motivated by spite, or revenge, or simply a desire to level the playing field between her and Bob. Maybe she just wanted to feel less of a victim in all this. Or maybe she needed Bob to know exactly what it felt like to be in her shoes: to taste the shock of being cheated upon; to know that the person who was everything to you had shared themselves with somebody else.

All she knew at that moment was she was grabbing Tomas and kissing him hard on the side of the street. His mouth felt strange and rubbery and didn't fit hers properly.

He was startled. He stood there like a frightened lamb, his arms rigid by his side, while she snogged him as hard as she could.

'Sorry about that,' she said, when she pulled away.

It had all been odd and wrong.

But she wasn't sorry. Not for one single moment.

'Um,' he said. 'That's OK.'

He seemed slightly confused and a bit worried that she would kiss him again. It was clear that a toilet rather than hot sex was uppermost in his mind.

'Listen, you go on,' she said kindly. 'I'll see you around, OK?'

'Yeah, sure. Thanks, Geri. Bye now.'

And he took off at a gallop down an alleyway by the side of the pub.

Geri phoned Bob from the back of the taxi home. He sounded groggy. But he had probably been asleep. It was, after all, nearly one a.m.

'Is everything all right?' He was immediately assuming that something unspeakable had happened.

'Fine,' she said. She didn't feel drunk any more. And she knew she would never tell him what she had just done. It was enough that she knew herself. 'I don't want to be worn down this time, Bob.'

'What?'

'Like when we first met. I want to be won over.'

He said, 'What do you think I've been trying to do?'

Chapter Twenty-Five

There was Massive News at work.

'It's all right, I already know,' Debs assured Jennifer, the receptionist, who was still sitting in the exact same position at the front desk as though she hadn't budged since Debs had seen her weeks ago.

Through the glass doors she could see the usual suspects: Tanya, Gavin, Liam, Mia and the guy who came in part time to do the accounts.

They all jumped up when she arrived in. Well, jumped was probably an exaggeration; rather, they looked up from their computers where they were all playing online poker or looking at porn.

'Debs!'

'Good to have you back.'

'You look *great*.'

People always said that, whether you did or not; it was just something to say.

Debs tried not to draw any inference from it either way.

412

This was a tad difficult, given that she was recovering from bulimia and every time someone remarked on her appearance she automatically thought about her arse.

It was a whole new way of life, trying to relearn some basic truths: that the size of said arse had no direct correlation with her mental happiness, for instance; that the only meaningful relationships human beings could have were with other people, not chocolate bars. Also – and this was a hard one to learn – sometimes life sucked and you couldn't puke your way out of it, no matter how hard you tried to fool yourself that you were, in fact, in control.

Debs was not in control. She *thought* she'd been. But drawing up elaborate wish lists of how fantastically brilliant her life was going to be once she'd shed a tonne/bought her own home/landed a hot new job did not constitute a viable plan.

'So I've got to be happy with what I've got?' she said narkily to Fiona. 'Which, let's face it, is pretty crap.'

'No, it's not,' said Fiona loyally.

'Yes, it is.'

'No, it's not.'

'Have you anything useful to say, or are we just going to pretend we're in a panto?'

'I think what Cara means is that you should be happy with who you are,' Fiona ventured.

'And who exactly might that be?' Debs said sarcastically. 'An ageing, plump, minor PR executive with an eating disorder who's just had her Snickers bars taken?'

That set Fiona back a bit. She began chewing her lip worriedly, and Debs could almost see her thinking, 'What the hell would Cara say?'

The problem was that there was no more Cara, or at least not as much. Debs's visits to her had tapered off. Well, she couldn't keep going three times a week for the rest of her life.

So she was being gently cut loose. It was a scary prospect. How was she going to cope on her own?

But Cara had looked at her confidently and said, 'Trust yourself.'

'But I don't.' Debs had felt a bit panicked. 'What if I can't cope . . . what if I fall off the wagon and go and buy up the Spar? Just one more session.' She was like a junkie now. 'Please.'

Cara had smiled in that otherworldly way of hers. 'Debs, you're ready.'

Yes, but for what?

It had all turned out to be a bit of an anticlimax. Debs had sat at home for a couple of days, waiting for something terrific to happen to her. Surely there must be some reward for all that soul-searching and therapy?

But there wasn't. Nothing happened. Her life didn't change one iota just because she had identified and tackled a difficult issue. It wasn't like on *Oprah*, where she would get a round of applause and a full make-over to fit in with her new persona.

Instead she just went on being Debs, only now she didn't have the crutch of food to prop her up. By day three the urge to weigh herself grew unbearable. Why the hell had she chucked her lovely scales out onto a tip? In desperation she'd even taken down the kitchen scales and wondered how much pressure they could take.

For a fleeting moment she even thought about ringing Bob. She had no idea why. But if she heard his voice maybe she wouldn't feel so alone.

By day four she wanted food. The image of a pizza lodged itself in her brain and she couldn't stop thinking about it. About *two* of them. And burgers and ice cream and Gummi Bears. She wanted to ram the whole down her throat until her belly hurt. She *needed* it. What was the use of all this trying to change herself business if nothing actually *changed*? She might as well go back to binging. At least there was ten minutes' satisfaction in that.

But she didn't. She practically had her coat on to go out to the Spar yet she stopped herself. Instead she sat down in a chair and did a few deep-breathing exercises – absolutely no use – and then, suddenly, she screamed. It was a blood-curdling scream of frustration and anger at the state of her life, and it gave them quite a fright upstairs. When she finished she felt that she had let out something that had been trapped inside her for years.

That night she drew up a list. It was a very short list. It didn't have massive weight-loss goals or lofty ambitions to own a yacht by the time she was forty.

In fact she wrote down only one thing. She would, she decided, change things one step at a time. That night she went to sleep with the list under her pillow, trying not to feel like she was in an AA programme.

And now here she was, in the office at nine thirty a.m., with a bowl of sensible cereal in her stomach jostling for space alongside some butterflies.

She hadn't actually eaten any butterflies, for the record. She was just a bit nervous.

415

'There's Massive News,' Tanya told her as she made her way to her desk.

'Yes, I know.'

Tanya looked confused. 'But you've been out of the office for so long . . .'

'I hear everything,' Debs assured her.

There was scarcely any need to wonder how the news had gone down. Tanya's face wasn't reassuring. She looked half thrilled and half scandalised – even after all these weeks.

And now here came Mia – the one who was a Janice in the making – and even though she had never spoken to Debs before, not even once, she confided immediately, 'Debs, you've missed *so* much.'

'I'm sure I haven't,' Debs said tightly, looking around. Where was Alex? Hopefully she was out at a meeting and not hiding in the toilets to escape the twitterings of the playmates.

'You should have seen Marty's face,' Tanya whispered.

Debs began to wonder now whether Alex hadn't been right all along; maybe it had been best to keep her private life to herself.

'He's still not himself,' Mia confirmed.

Debs ignored them and began to tackle her desk. It was covered with files and press releases and things marked 'Urgent', and 'Extremely Urgent'. Nice to see that her work had been divvied out while she'd been gone.

She scooped up an armload and took it over to Gavin's desk and dumped it down.

'Hey,' he protested. 'I'm busy.'

'Oh, really?' she said, craning to have a look at his computer screen.

He tried to shield it with his arm but not before she'd caught the heading of the email he'd been writing. It was addressed to minxy3049@yahoo.co.uk. God only knew what was in the body of the text. Debs didn't want to find out.

'Things going well, then?' she enquired.

Gavin tried to act cool. 'I suppose. We might be going for a weekend away.'

Debs gave a little whistle. 'Jesus, Gavin. You'd want to watch yourself.'

'What?'

'A weekend away. That's pretty serious.' And she began humming 'Here Comes the Bride' under her breath.

He was rattled now. 'Shut up. It's not like that. She's cool.'

But Debs could see the light of love in his little eyes. It was hilarious. But it was also sweet, she reminded herself sternly. Gavin deserved something nice to happen to him after the heartbreak of realising that Alex would never be his.

'She was never going to be yours anyway, so what's the difference?' Debs had argued, when she'd sat him down after Alex's visit to the flat that day to break the news.

He had looked off solemnly into the distance (this was after he had shouted 'Liar! Liar!' in an anguished kind of way). 'In a way it nearly makes her more attractive. Her total and utter lack of availability.' Then he had to go and spoil it all by saying, 'I don't suppose she mentioned whether she was bisexual?'

He had puffed up importantly when Debs had told

him that Alex had given him a little 'job': to pass the word on to Liam. 'In a mature way, Gavin, with no speculation about her private life, and no discussion about that porn movie you saw last summer.'

'God, what do you take me for?' Gavin had said in disgust.

At the same time his recovery from Alex had been remarkably speedy. Within a week of learning the news he was back in the pub with Liam, knocking back pints and trying to pick up women who should have known better, just like old times.

Then along came Minxy, real name Maryanne, who worked two streets away in an insurance company, and who called Gavin her little honey bunch. (Nobody was to know about this.) So far, so good.

'So listen,' Gavin said now in a low voice in case anybody overheard and mistook him for someone sensitive, 'how have you been?'

'Me? Great. Fine.' It was easier that way. And, actually, she *did* feel OK. The butterflies in her stomach had settled somewhat. The anticipation of something was often a lot worse than actually going through with it.

And anyway, if she could get through Christmas on her own, she could do this.

'It's nothing to be ashamed of, you know,' Gavin consoled her.

'Sorry?'

'Everybody gets a bit down every now and again. Even me,' he added manfully.

Alex hadn't gone racing back to the office then and announced excitedly, 'Depression, my nanny. She's barfing up all over the shop. Bulimia.'

And then she felt bad for even doubting Alex. But paranoia was part of this gig. When it came down to it, Gavin and Alex were the only two people she would miss from this place.

'Listen, Gavin – where's Alex today?'

Just then there was the sound of the front door closing with a terrific slam.

Everybody looked at each other in trepidation.

In thundered Marty. His face was black. 'Where's the Mother Hubbard file?' he snarled.

Mother Hubbard was a new brand of soup they had recently been trying to market. Well, times were lean.

Tanya was the unlucky finder. 'Here—'

'And why the FUCK wasn't it in my briefcase, seeing as I just had a fucking MEETING with that bitch –' More glances flew: Mother Hubbard herself? '– only I was left standing there like a TOOL because I didn't have the fucking FILE?'

His bloodshot eyes raked furiously across the office. Tanya cowered. Liam belched, but only out of pure nervousness. Finally, Marty's malevolent gaze came to rest on Debs.

'Oh. You're back.' There was a very tense moment, but then he managed a strangled smile. You could nearly see the words 'Potential Law Suit' flash across his brain. Better be nice to the bitch. 'How are you?' he asked, voice thick with concern.

'I'm just great, Marty.' She might as well enjoy this.

'Good, good.' The smile was stretched so tight across his plump cheeks that they looked like they would crack at any minute.

'I'm on pills, you know.'

'Um, great.' He was trying to inch away.

'They're great for the depression, but they haven't done much for the bump on the side of my head.'

His Adam's apple bobbed violently. 'Interestingly enough, I was reading a medical article only the other day that my solicitor . . . that I just happened to come across, and apparently most of us have bumps on our heads. They can be naturally occurring due to a number of factors—'

His phone rang, interrupting his gibberish. He looked at the caller display and scowled. 'Patricia,' he said grudgingly into the phone. He *never* took calls from his wife but today he turned away and muttered defensively, 'Yes, I'm in the office. Yes, I'll be home at half-past five. Yes, on the dot. Goodbye.'

He hung up, not meeting anybody's eyes.

He did manage a last, placatory grin at Debs though. 'You've got a new desk. A much nicer one, I might add.'

Debs didn't know what to say. For as long as anybody could remember, she had languished under the stairs.

'Thanks,' she said, taken by surprise.

'No problem,' said Marty. Then he turned to go into his office, screaming over his shoulder, 'Someone bring me a fucking coffee!'

Debs looked at Gavin, wide-eyed. 'Did I just get a *promotion*?'

She should bump her head more often.

But then her amusement died away, and that treacherous desire to belong rose unbidden: imagine if she finally *did* get ahead in this shitty company. A promotion would mean kudos. Acceptance. Invitations, even, to go down the town at lunchtime with the playmates . . .

'God, no,' Gavin scoffed, thankfully bringing her back to reality. 'It's because we're one staff member down now.' He looked at her meaningfully.

Debs gawked at him. Her heart plummeted. She looked around wildly, hoping that Alex would walk through the door at any moment, but of course she didn't.

'He can't do that,' she said roughly.

'Well, he did.'

'There are laws. She could sue him.'

'I don't think she's going to want to sue anybody.'

Debs felt terrible. She felt *culpable.* Those snide remarks she'd made to Alex, implying a lack of courage . . . and all the time Alex had been right. This was the wrong company, the wrong people, with whom to try to be yourself.

'She'll find another job easily enough,' Gavin said with surprising callousness.

Debs was starting to feel that the world was a place she would never quite understand.

'That's hardly the point.'

'Look, she brought it upon herself.'

'By what?' Debs said, voice shaking now. 'Being gay?'

Gavin blinked. 'Janice isn't gay. And I should know.'

'Janice?' Debs repeated.

Gavin looked at her as though she was being rather slow. 'I thought you said you heard the Massive News?'

'I told *you* the Massive News.'

'Oh, *that.* That's ancient history.' And he pooh-poohed it with a wave of his hand. 'Janice got fired yesterday.'

'Fired?' Debs felt as though she were doomed to parrot him for ever.

'His wife found out.'

'Oh, just tell me what bloody happened!'

Gavin pulled up his chair and leaned in like an old woman. 'Remember the night of Alex's promotion?'

'You mean the night I cracked my head open and ended up in hospital?' she said sarcastically. 'Vaguely.'

'Well, Janice rode Marty.'

'No!'

'They were all over each other in the pub. She was telling him that she wanted to be considered for promotion next. Marty said he'd definitely assess her assets. The rest of us were nearly sick. Then they went out to his car and did it.'

'*No.*'

'Wait, wait, you haven't heard the best bit yet.' He had a slug of his coffee just to draw out the suspense. 'Only didn't Marty forget to lock the keypad of his new BlackBerry – you know the way he can't really work it? – and it slipped under Janice's arse and she ended up dialling his missus.'

'Nasty,' Liam chipped in.

Debs was enjoying herself so much that she nearly took off her coat and sat down for a good gossip. But she remained standing.

'Go on,' she urged.

'Patricia, predictably, walks out. Threatens to take him to the cleaners. This is in the middle of him thinking he's going to be sued by you, by the way. And all the time Janice was going around the office saying she was in with a shot at being the next Mrs Fitzgerald. Hold on, my mouth is getting dry.' When he had refreshed himself again, he finished up, 'Anyway, yesterday Marty had had enough. He had Patricia in one ear, and Janice in the other. He was going *mental.*'

'It's been *awful* around Janice,' Tanya said with a shudder, as though it had ever been anything else.

'Anyway, yesterday Marty calls Janice in. Gives her her marching orders. We could hear the screaming out here, couldn't we? Then she came out and packed up and left.' He paused for breath. 'It was MASSIVE.'

Debs looked at Janice's desk. *Her* new desk now. It was as clean as a new pin.

'What about Alex?' she said.

Gavin looked a bit blank. 'What about her?'

'Well, did you spread the word? Does anybody actually *know*?'

'Course they do.' He looked wounded. 'I told every-body, even Marty. But to be honest, Debs, with everything else that's been going on, nobody really gave a shite.'

Debs was back at her old desk when Alex eventually returned from a meeting.

'Did you hear the Massive News?' Alex began.

'Yes. And apparently it isn't you.' She joked, 'Are you sure you didn't fiddle with Marty's BlackBerry just to create a smokescreen?'

'I'm surprised it functioned at all under the weight of Janice's arse.' Alex immediately clamped her mouth shut. Then: 'Sorry. I hope that wasn't, you know, insensitive of me.'

'Oh, shut up. Or else I'll feel I can't mention women's

breasts and things around *you*.' She thought about this for a minute. 'Not that I probably would anyway.'

Then she had to ask. 'How's Marty been about it?'

Alex grinned. 'He's terrified of me.'

'Really? No lesbian light-bulb jokes?'

'Not a single one. Every time I pass him in the hallway he presses himself against the wall in case it might be catching.'

'That makes two of us he's terrified of, then. Oh, and his wife makes three. It could be the making of him yet.'

'They've all been OK, actually, even Gavin and Liam. Janice was a bit nasty all right, but no more than usual. And Tanya was definitely worried for a while there about being left alone in the same room as me.' She snickered. She looked more relaxed than Debs had ever seen her.

Alex noticed then that she was packing up her stuff. 'I hear you're moving to Janice's desk.'

'Actually, no, I'm not.' She might as well tell her. 'I'm leaving.'

Alex laughed. 'Good one, Debs. We've all tried to leave but no one's ever managed it yet. Apart from Janice, of course.'

'I'm serious.'

Alex looked at her. 'All right, Debs, so you hate the place. I hate the place too. But things are getting better. Come on, you've even got a *promotion*.'

'It's not a promotion, it's just a new desk. Anyway, it doesn't matter, because I've decided. I'm going to do something else.'

'What?' Alex demanded.

This was where she should reveal her daring plan to

open her own glittering PR company, or her intention of taking two years out to soul search and save abandoned baby kangaroos in the Australian outback.

But she hadn't quite got that far in her list last night. Writing 'Change Career Now' had knocked so much out of her that she had lacked the energy to elaborate further.

'I'm um, not sure yet.'

'Debs, this is crazy. At least stay until you make up your mind.'

'Alex, don't. Please. Because if you keep talking I might just chicken out and that really would be the very worst thing for me. Trust me.'

Even Janice's desk was almost enough to tempt her. It was a fine big desk, with a lovely goose-necked lamp and easy access to the front door for that desperate escape each evening at half-past five.

That thought did it. Debs did not want to spend most of her waking hours wanting to escape from somewhere. She really would rather save baby kangaroos.

'Come with me,' she said giddily to Alex. 'And Gavin too. We'll even take Liam!'

They would have such fun in the outback, and to hell with Marty and Fitz Communications.

But Alex shook her head. 'Sorry, Debs. But I'm actually a deeply conservative person, in case you haven't noticed. But I'll come visit.' Her brow puckered. 'And where exactly would that be?'

'I'll let you know,' Debs promised her.

Debs walked through the park on her way to get the bus home. She had been there a hundred times before yet she still hesitated before stepping through the gates. It felt odd being there without a brown paper bag from the sandwich shop. Maybe she should have stopped by for old times' sake. But it wasn't quite lunchtime yet, and besides, she didn't want to risk a confrontation with a bag of Walkers cheese & onion so soon into her recovery. Also, it was cold and wet, so you couldn't sit on any of the park benches without getting pneumonia.

The ducks were there in the pond, swimming around as always. When they saw Debs they began to flap frantically towards the shore. They've missed me, Debs thought mistily, but then saw that they were only interested in her brown cardboard box. But they were out of luck, unless they fancied a diary or a Snoopy year planner.

Actually Debs didn't even want them. She went to the nearest bin to dispose of the box. It was quite a job as the box was big, and she had to use her foot in the end, even though the ducks looked at her as though she were cracked (or was that quacked?).

Without it she felt a bit naked. She was alone in the world now, floating along without any direction, or even *less* direction now, without even a Snoopy year planner, and she didn't know what to do.

She wished Cara was there. Or Fiona, or Alex. Even Gavin would do at a push; anybody at all who would reach out and make her feel better about herself.

She had been trying not to think about Bob – silly, when it was the thought of him that had drawn her to the park in the first place – and now he filled her mind. They'd sat on that bench over there, doing just that: making each other feel better about themselves.

She went over now and took out a tissue and wiped the wet from the seat. Then she sat down and immediately she was back there: those warm summer days when they had sat side by side, brown paper bags on their laps. Talking rubbish and smiling like lunatics and trading gossip and just so pleased to be there.

And she felt no anger today, no sense of shame at what she had done, or how foolish she had been. It was as if she and Bob had briefly collided, two stars in the galaxies that he was so interested in, and now they had gone their separate ways, like they were always going to.

She sat there for ages on the park bench, free of baggage and wrapped in the little comfort blank left by Bob. She sat there until the office workers started to straggle in, clutching their sandwiches and bottles of Coke and umbrellas to ward off the rain.

Then she got up and walked out of the park and into her life.

Chapter Twenty-Six

'Susan!' Geri bellowed. 'Have you seen my moisturiser?' There was a suspicious silence. 'No,' Susan called at last.

Liar. Geri stomped across the landing and into her room. She flung open the door to find Leo and Susan entangled on the bed. Thank God they were fully clothed, but only just.

'Mum!' said Susan, mortified.

'Sorry, Mrs M,' Leo said, struggling to his feet and covering his crotch with his hands in an embarrassed manner.

'There are some condoms in the bathroom cabinet,' she told him helpfully; leftovers from those occasional Saturday night sessions with Bob. They could well be out of date by now.

'*Mum*,' howled Susan.

'What? I don't want to be a granny at forty-three.'

That would cut short her new-found freedom fairly rapidly; she had only just managed to re-negotiate her hours in the hospital, downwards for a change, and didn't intend to spend them changing nappies.

No doubt plenty of people would think she was wrong to be letting her daughter have sex in the house. A year ago she herself would have been appalled. Three *months* ago she would had been appalled.

But that was before she had realised the true depths of Leo and Susan's relationship. No exaggeration, they put Heathcliff and that Cathy one to shame; when they were together the living room hopped with intense looks and hungry touches and anxious fidgetings if one of them left the room to go to the loo.

'He's got his hand up her *top*,' Davey would hiss, disgusted.

They really were in love. Not even living in a house where a marriage had recently and spectacularly imploded seemed to have any effect on them.

'It's been a learning curve,' Susan had confided. 'I'm not going to make the same mistakes as you and Dad.'

Geri wished Susan would enlighten her as to what she thought these mistakes were; even Geri herself wasn't fully sure at what exact point they had gone wrong.

Susan's optimism was, of course, sweet and naïve, and probably wouldn't last the year, but Geri didn't think of it like that. She found the sight of them together, Leo's big, leather-clad arm slung protectively around Susan's thin shoulders, to be touchingly optimistic.

It was a relief, in a way, to know that she hadn't gone all hard and cynical, after everything. That she still had hope.

'You were right, you know,' she'd told Susan. 'About Leo. We should have listened to you.'

'Well, halleluiah,' Susan had said. 'After sixteen years I'm finally right about something.'

'Hey. Don't push it.'

'Do you need a lift to the airport?' Leo offered now, when his trousers problem had subsided and he could look her in the face again.

'No, thanks. I've booked a taxi.'

She had grown very fond of Leo, but there was no way on this earth that she was going to get into his car again. He had given her a spin to the shops once and the vibrations alone had upset her stomach for the rest of the day. And the seats were so low-slung that she had felt midget-like and powerless, and had experienced a minor panic attack when they had drawn up alongside a towering Tesco truck.

And he still drove too fast. He always swore that he was keeping within the speed limit, and that the growl of the exhaust created an auditory illusion. 'In other words, it sounds like I'm going a lot faster than I actually am,' he'd explained, just in case she was thick.

'*There* it is.' She pounced on her moisturiser now, sitting incriminatingly on Susan's dressing table. 'It's nearly all gone, Susan.'

'You can always buy some more in the duty free,' Susan told her. 'Better still, you could buy *me* some,' she added brightly.

Some things never changed. Which was why Geri had drawn up a list of rules and regulations governing her absence from the house, and which she had pinned up on the fridge. She had also made multiple copies and scattered them around the house in case anybody needed reminding.

She called everybody downstairs in order to go through the list, just in case there was any misunderstanding or confusion while she was away.

Number one was no parties. 'A party is defined as a gathering of more than three people at any given time,' she explained helpfully.

'As if I would,' said Susan, sniffing as though she was above all that now that she was having sex with full parental permission.

Davey just looked at Geri and burst out, 'Don't make me stay here with those two.'

'Davey . . .'

'Watching them makes me want to vomit.'

'Don't watch then,' Susan suggested.

'Can I not come with you?' he begged Geri. 'I won't be any trouble, honest.'

He hadn't asked to tag along with Geri since he'd been about six.

'She won't want *you* around,' Susan said. 'Not when she's trying to patch things up with Dad.'

'I am not trying to patch things up with Dad,' Geri protested, even though her face flamed incriminatingly. 'We're simply going on a . . . short holiday together, that's all.'

Both Susan and Davey gave her one of their you're-fooling-yourself-old-woman looks. Only now it was more of an old-woman-who's-trying-desperately-to-look-like-a-younger-woman look. Her bob had yet to grow out to any discernible effect.

And she could see how things must look to them: Dad has ill-advised affair with younger woman – mid-life crisis and all that – Mum chucks him out, ill-advised affair inevitably ends, heralding period of reflection for both, then they start 'dating' again like they did twenty years ago, and now Dad is whisking her off for a romantic week away. It was textbook. In another six months they would be expected to renew their wedding vows in a cloying ceremony on some Bahamian beach, with their kids behind them throwing their eyes to heaven and making retching noises.

Holy cow. This was serious.

'It's called standing by your man,' Andrea said on the phone. She was practically back to her old self again, which was a mixed blessing. 'If it's good enough for Hillary Clinton, then it's good enough for you.'

'I am not standing by Bob.'

'You're going to take him back, aren't you?'

'I haven't decided yet.'

'What have those posh dinners out in restaurants been about then? And going for big long walks on windswept beaches? Don't tell me you broke all those veins on your cheeks for nothing.'

'We were just spending time together. Talking. Getting to know each other again.'

'Does Bob have hidden depths then?' Andrea enquired sceptically.

She was in her anti-man phase. And who could blame her? Not that Dr Foley had got the better of her in the end. The enormous nipple story went all around the hospital in a flash. By the time it came back to Andrea it had been embellished somewhat, and he now had nipples the size of dinner plates.

'Ugh,' Hannah said. 'I'm not even that fond of my *own* nipples.'

She was unavailable when Dr Foley invited her to an art gallery. She didn't mention the nipple thing to him, but she said afterwards that she wasn't able to tear her eyes away from his chest.

Dr Foley wasn't long in figuring things out.

'This is your doing, isn't it?' he said to Andrea. 'There's always one who's bitter.'

'Don't flatter yourself.'

'For the record, I'd like you to know that I suffer mildly from a medical condition called gynecomastia, which is breast growth. It's not something to be made fun of, you know.'

Now he had breasts too! Marvellous. Andrea dispensed this information as quickly as possible, and by the next morning he couldn't walk into the canteen without someone shouting, 'Go on, get them out for the lads.'

There was talk of him launching libel actions and lawsuits and all kinds of things, but in the end it looked like he was going to apply to Limerick Regional. No doubt he hoped the nipple thing wouldn't follow him down there, and he could start all over again. He didn't know yet that one of the porter's sisters worked in the catering division.

Andrea hadn't started dating again yet. She just didn't trust herself at the moment.

'You don't trust *men* at the moment,' Geri had pointed out.

But Andrea may have felt that she was raining on Geri's parade now, because she said, 'I don't mean to be all narky and negative. Go on holidays with Bob if you want. I just don't want to see you going through this again, that's all.'

As if any of them could see into the future. Even this holiday was a gamble. It was all very well spending a couple of hours together at a fancy restaurant with dim lighting and everybody on their best behaviour, but a whole week together would be different. They were trying to down-play the significance of it, but what if they drank too much one night and had a terrific row over Debra and ended up on the next flight home?

Even worse: what if, halfway through the week, they fell back into their bad old ways and ended up sprawled in front of the rented telly, with not a single thing to say except for, 'Pass me the remote control, love, would you?'

'I've been married seventeen years, Andrea.' Although sometimes it felt like a hundred and seventeen. 'I've got to give it another chance.'

'You don't *have* to do anything.'

'All right then. I want to.'

Andrea gave a little sigh, which Geri tried not to think of as disappointed, and said, 'Good luck then. Oh, and will you bring me back some moisturiser from duty free?'

When the kids were very young and they hadn't got a babysitter yet, mostly due to Geri's paranoia that any baby-sitter was bound to come with pyromaniac tendencies or a boyfriend who preyed upon small children, they used to pretend to have 'dates' at home. Bob's job would be to rent some class of romantic movie and procure a semi-decent bottle of wine. Geri would cook something nice and lay the table properly instead of just slinging down a couple of forks and a bottle of ketchup. They were both required to 'dress up', which was quite fun at first, until of course it became a pain in the bum, and once the kids were asleep they would sit down to their meal and let on they were in a restaurant, which meant no picking noses or reading the newspaper at the table.

'Tell me your deepest fears,' Geri would say.

'Confined spaces and Friday night drinks with George. Yours?'

'Getting cancer.'

He would give a little sigh. 'I thought we were trying to keep things light?'

'I know. But I can't help it. It's my deepest fear.' Since Davey had been born, and she now had two small people utterly dependent upon her for their very survival, Geri had become terrified of dying. Cancer was the biggie. She wasn't so much worried about car crashes or being violently murdered, for some reason.

'If I do die—'

'I know. Get the kids their vaccinations and don't let them have too much sugar.'

'Or chocolate.'

'I promise. Well, maybe on Sundays.'

'See? Already I can't trust you.'

But she did, really. She never worried about Bob dying, only her. Bob would never do anything as foolish or impulsive as *die*. He was always there, steady as a rock, so sure of himself when she seemed to spend her life flitting from worry to worry, and wondering whether she was more a mother than a nurse or else a grotesque combination of the two. And if she *did* die, she could take her last breath knowing that her children would be safe with Bob.

She could never have married a man that she didn't know that about. Or who didn't sometimes walk out into the back yard at night if the sky was clear, and spend ages looking up at the stars. Geri would sometimes come out and look up too, but she could never make out any of the shapes that she was supposed to – not even the plough, or the big dipper, or whatever it was called. She would try and try but the sky just looked like a big bunch of stars to her.

'Am I blind or thick or both?' she would ask Bob.

'Never mind,' he would console her. 'I can see them, so you know they're there.'

'Did you pack a map?'

'I thought you said you had the map.'

'I said I had the *passports*.'

It was tricky, packing separately. In the end Geri made Bob unzip his suitcase and stand there while she made doubly sure that he actually had the tickets, as he claimed, and that he had packed suitable shoes for walking around Paris.

She hoped to God it wasn't a mistake, choosing Paris. It had all that historical significance, of course, being the place that Bob had allegedly promised to take Geri but hadn't delivered.

Its other historical significance was as the place that Bob had gone with Debra to get his leg over.

He must be thinking this too, because he mentioned, rather randomly, 'It's twenty-five degrees in Spain today.'

The kids had already said goodbye and were gone out, and so it was just the two of them, waiting for the taxi. It seemed a little awkward between them today.

'So!' said Bob. Clearly he was feeling it too. 'I rang Ben's mother an hour ago.'

'Why?'

'She's going to let him stay there for the week. You know, because he doesn't want to be around Susan and Leo.' When she said nothing he looked at her with some trepidation. 'Is that OK?'

'Of course it is. He'll be glad.'

'He was delighted. I just rang him.'

'Great. Fantastic.'

Huh. For a man who couldn't get on with his son a year ago . . . Then she told herself to get a grip. If she wasn't bitching about Bob's non-involvement, it was because he was suddenly *too* involved.

Another silence.

'I hope the hotel is nice,' she said.

She knew it was. Bob had done all the research and booking, and she'd seen the hotel on the internet. The whole thing had been his idea and hard work. He was taking this business of winning her over very seriously.

The taxi pulled up outside. The driver, too lazy to get out and ring the doorbell, just beeped his horn before rolling down his window and lighting a fag.

'Here, let me,' said Bob, reaching for her suitcase.

'I can carry my own suitcase,' she said sharply.

He turned to face her squarely. 'Look, what's wrong, Geri?'

'Nothing.'

'You've been taking my head off since I arrived.'

'Don't be ridiculous.'

'I've said I'm sorry a million times—'

'So don't say it again. Please. I don't think I could bear it.'

Bob leaned back against the counter and folded his arms. 'What, then?'

Geri hesitated. She didn't want to admit to weakness. She'd just spent nearly a year recovering from an affair; she'd had to learn to cope on her own, to be single again, to protect herself. And here she was, about to throw herself into it again, without any guarantee that it would even work.

'I'm nervous,' she eventually admitted.

'I'm nervous too.'

'*You?* You've got a packet of sucky sweets in your pocket for the plane so that your ears don't pop.'

'So?'

'A person who packs sucky sweets clearly isn't nervous.' She was being irrational but she didn't care. 'You think it's all going to work out fine.'

'Yes,' he said. 'I do.'

'Supposing it doesn't?'

'Geri . . .'

'No, really. Supposing the whole thing goes arse up? Then we'll have to go through it all again.' Breaking up. She didn't need to say it out loud.

'We won't.' He sounded very confident, and it annoyed her.

'You're sure about that, are you? How do you know that the sight of me in my Scholls won't annoy the hell

438

out of you in a month's time? How do *I* know that I can put up with that noise you make brushing your teeth in the mornings?'

He looked wounded. 'What noise?'

'Maybe we're too old for this,' she said stubbornly. 'Too set in our ways. Too used to having crap sex on a Saturday night.'

'Yes,' he agreed. 'It *was* crap.'

That made her crosser. 'I'm not going to turn into—' She nearly said Debra. Jesus Christ. 'Into some Page Three girl, you know,' she stuttered.

'And I'm not going to turn into George Clooney.' He looked a bit disappointed at this. 'Look, we'll work things out.'

'But *will* we? Who's to say?'

'I do,' he said, magnificently. 'Because I want to. I want this marriage to work. And you do too.' He gave her a bit of a look and said, 'Presumably.'

'Well, yes,' she said.

'You could say it with a bit more passion.'

'Bob.'

'*I* sounded passionate.'

Dear God, he was starting to lose the run of himself.

'Are you going to meet me halfway here?' he demanded (passionately).

Outside the taxi beeped impatiently.

'Shag off!' Bob shouted at him through the kitchen window. 'I'm talking to my wife here!'

Geri began to laugh.

'What?' said Bob, deflating. 'I was on a bit of a roll there.'

'Sorry.' She laughed harder.

'Now you're insulting me,' he said, hands on his hips.

Geri finally managed to get control of herself. The laughter had done her good. Her whole body felt looser or something. Bob was smiling too.

'Thank you,' she said sincerely. 'For your passion.'

'I can try it again in Paris,' he suggested. 'The setting might be more appropriate.'

'I'd be delighted if you did,' she assured him.

'Really?'

'Really. I might even have a go myself.'

'Now that,' he said sceptically, 'would be worth seeing.'

He held out his hand to her. 'Will we go?'

She looked at him for a moment, then nodded and held out her own.